ONCE UPON AN
APOCALYPSE

Book I
The Journey Home

Original 2nd Person Narrative

JEFF MOTES

Note

This is a work of fiction. While some of the locations in the series describe actual locations, this is intended only to lend a sense of authenticity. Any resemblance to actual events or persons, living or dead, is purely coincidental.

This work is intended for entertainment and to promote "outside the box" thinking. This is not a "how-to" guide. Neither the author, publisher nor anyone else associated with this work assumes any responsibility or liability for the use or improper use of any information contained herein.

Credits
Editor – Richard E. Creel
Cover Design – Brandi Doane McCann
Cover Models – Kay Counselman and Dwain Roberts
Formatting – Polgarus Studio

ISBN - 978-0-9968691-0-2 (soft cover)
ISBN - 978-0-9968691-1-9 (hard cover)
ISBN – 978-0-9968691-2-6 (Kindle)
ISBN – 978-0-9968691-3-3 (ePub)
ISBN – 978-0-9968691-3-3 (audiobook)

Published by Pine City Press
R1.2

Acknowledgements

Many individuals have helped make this work possible; providing encouragement, advice, helpful tips and an ear to bend new ideas over. Some of you are truly the reason this work didn't stop months ago. I thank each of you: Brenda Dolbear Jones, Stephanie Andrews Atchison, Sheila Brandenburg Wright, Sam Meadows, Holly Meadows Bridwell, Glenda Allen, Sherri Plybon, Ron Steelman and J.R. Stewart. Lynn Chalkley White, you did it again, prompting me to do something without even knowing it. Without the help of my dear sweet sister, Lisa Lanier, this work would have never been more than a series of blog posts. A very special thanks to my wife, Donna, for her patience.

Jeff Motes—Author

Foreword

This story started out as a series of Facebook posts on "what if" type scenarios to engage my friends in thinking "outside the box" about cataclysmic events. To draw readers into thinking about preparedness for a deeply traumatic wide-scale event I decided to tell a story so as to place the reader inside the events portrayed. *Once Upon an Apocalypse* is the result of those efforts. The story is told from a 2nd person point of view from the chapter's main character. Keep that in mind and it should flow smoothly.

Acronyms have been used in various places. If you have difficulty understanding a term, please consult the Glossary in the back of the book.

I hope you enjoy the story as much as I have enjoyed writing it.

Jeff Motes—Author

Contents

Chapter 1 Jill - The Day - *The event…*

Wow. You're glad that meeting is over! You really didn't want to come to Birmingham anyway, especially with the short notice you had. Like a call last night asking you to be here today. The meeting started at 9:00 a.m. Your boss, Julia Sanders, called last night at 8:00. She had to cancel her plans to attend the last day of the meeting and wanted you to attend in her place. That was really aggravating. She should have called sooner, but she has always been nice, so you agreed to go. It did mean getting up at 4:00 this morning! The meeting, well, it was so boring, you kept dozing off. It was embarrassing.

At least it's over and you're on your way home. You and your daughter Lizzy are planning a trip to the Gulf this weekend. The room is already booked. It's just going to be you two girls. Your mom isn't going this time. She said she just wanted to stay home. You love your mom. She has always been good and kind to you and Lizzy. Especially considering the events surrounding Lizzy's birth. Since your dad died, she's been living with you. You didn't want her living alone and she didn't want to either. Even so, this weekend will be a good break.

You sip a little more of your McDonald's coffee. You bought a large this time, thinking you might need the extra caffeine to stay awake. McDonald's coffee is pretty good and less than half the price of Starbucks coffee. Picking up your phone, you decide to call your mom and let her know you're on your way. You hear her voice, "Hello Jill." "Hey, Mom, I'm on my way home. Let's see . . . it's right at 4:00, I should be home by 7:30 or so." "Okay, honey, drive carefully. I know you're tired." "Yes, I am a little. I have a large cup of coffee. I'll be fine. See you later, love you."

You turn the radio on to Sirius XM Love, channel 17, love songs, it's your favorite. You don't know why. You haven't been on a date in more than ten years. The dating scene wasn't what you were looking for. Ever since your

1

snafu with Clyde, the guys hitting on you really only wanted one thing. You weren't making that mistake again. You are waiting for Mr. Right this time, if there is such a thing. You've been waiting a long time, but love songs make you dream anyway.

Suddenly the music stops. The car slows down. The gas gauge goes to empty. The RPM needle drops to zero. The speedometer indicates zero, even though the car is still moving. Your car is a Nissan Murano, burnt orange in color. The inside is black, so on a hot summer day the seats get hot, really hot. You keep the oil changed every three thousand miles. You heard your dad fuss at your mother enough over running the gas tank down to near empty, that there is no way you would let the tank go below a quarter full. Well, except for that time . . . skip that thought. You've never had any trouble with this car. Why has it stopped? You start easing over onto the shoulder of I-459. Coming to a complete stop, you put the transmission in park and try to crank the car. Nothing. Nada. Even the radio won't come on. The battery must be dead or you've blown a main fuse or something. You're not a mechanic, but you do know how to check the battery connections. Popping the hood, you get out of the car, being careful to stay out of the traffic lanes. You lift the hood and inspect the battery. Looks like the connections are okay. The hood light is on. Good thing you joined AAA. One of the perks from the bank when you bought your house was a free one year membership in AAA. You've kept it ever since. You walk back and get in the car. Picking up your cell phone, you disconnect the charger. The phone is dead. It was low when you got in the car, but it's been charging for at least half an hour. You plug it back into the charger. Nothing happens. Even the little blue light on the charger is not working. This is not good. Not good at all. How are you going to call for help if your phone doesn't work? Maybe it just needs to build up a charge. You'll just sit here for a little while longer and give it a chance to build up enough charge to come on.

It's starting to warm up in the car. It's not really hot outside. The temperature is in the eighties, but this closed car with all the glass is like a green house. You try letting the windows down, nothing happens. You really don't want to leave the driver's side door open to the traffic, so you decide to move around to the passenger side, but first you try your cell phone one more time before getting out. It's dead. You leave it hooked to the charger and start to step out of the car, pause, then reach over to the glove compartment. Inside you retrieve your Glock 19 and its inside-the-waist-band holster. Your IWB holster is pink. Your dad rolled his eyes when he saw it. Well, you like pink. You also get the spare magazine. You tuck the Glock and its holster into your waistband and put the spare magazine in your left front pants pocket. Pulling the Glock from its holster, you check to see if it's loaded. It isn't. Racking the slide you load a 9mm round into the chamber. You holster the pistol and step out of the car.

You look around. Realization hits. Why didn't you notice before? No cars have passed by since you stopped. You look in both directions on both sides of the interstate. All cars are stopped, some on the side of the road, some in the road itself. This is getting scary. You remember your dad talking about something like this. In fact, he said one of the most convincing evidence of an electromagnetic pulse attack, or EMP event, was the mass stalling of cars. But if this is an EMP event, like what he described, stalled cars will be one of the least problems. If this is what he described, then practically all computers, electronics and those things depending upon them will cease to work. That includes the electrical grid, telephone systems, cell phones, internet and radios. In other words, you have no means of calling for help. Help is not coming. Not now, not later this evening, not in the morning, not at all.

You don't know what to do. You are at least 175 miles from home. This is scary. How are you going to get home? You can't panic. Your dad taught you how to control your fear. He said fear was the mind killer, and without your mind, you would perish. You must not fear and you must not panic, if you ever want to see Lizzy and your mom again.

You start assessing your situation. This is what you know. The car is dead. It's not out of gas. The electronics inside the car will not work. The phone is dead. You return to your car. From the rear seat you open your laptop bag and retrieve your laptop. It won't come on either. It had a one hundred percent charge when you left this morning and hasn't been used since. You are on the side of I-459 somewhere near Pelham. You're going to have to pull your road atlas and see if you can pinpoint your location better.

People are starting to mill about some walking, some just standing around. There are a few cars, not far away, stalled as well. Some to the north and some to the south. You see a young mother and her two small children, a construction crew stranded on their way home, and a police officer stalled with felons in his cruiser. His radio is not working either. That's a disturbing thought. No police services. There is also a man and his son walking. Each is wearing a back pack. The man has a pistol on his hip. It scares you a little, but they look okay, if okay has a look. As they come abreast of your car, you ask the man, "Excuse me sir. Do you know what has happened?" The man and his son stop. He looks at you with some pity in his eyes and says, "Not really, but I have an idea. Probably an EMP. You really need to get to where you're going within the next three to four days. We are heading up toward Fort Payne." You ask, "Three to four days? What does that mean?" He replys, "Things might get kind of tough around then, if it's an EMP like I think. We are in some serious trouble. Wish I could stay, but for me and my son to be home in three to four days, we have to leave now. Good luck to you." You have a foreboding thought that this guy is right. You just don't know.

Unbeknownst to you, this scene is being repeated all across America. The Chinese or the Iranians or the North Koreans or some other enemy, has managed to evade NSA probes and counter-terrorism efforts. They launched a nuclear missile from a large container ship off the eastern coast. The U.S. government had five minutes warning before the twenty mega-ton nuclear warhead exploded high in the atmosphere above Kansas. The explosion sent out a massive electro-magnetic pulse (EMP) that blanketed nearly all of the contiguous U.S. In an instant, nearly every electronic device in the U.S. has been fried. Cars don't work, the phones don't work. Nearly the entire electrical grid went down. No more lights, no more refrigeration, no more sewers, no more city water, no more 911, no more internet, no more mass movement of goods across the country. In other words, America has been sent back to the 1800s. An America unprepared for the 1800s. You shudder.

Despite the cars stalling and the progress of America coming to a halt, time has not. The day is moving right along and the sun is getting low. You decide to stay the night inside your car. It's probably not a good idea, but looking around, you really don't know what else to do. You don't want to be walking around in an unfamiliar area after dark.

Opening your purse, you get your small LED flashlight. It's a great little light. It uses a single AA battery, but puts out a lot of light. You test it, it works, and that's good. You also pull out your little can of MACE spray. Sitting in the passenger seat, you lock the doors. At least that works. As the sun sets, you lift the lever on the seat and let it recline. You start praying, "Dear God. I don't understand what has happened to us and why, but I trust you. Please guide me home to see my Lizzy and my mother. Please keep them safe and secure. Please help our country through this apocalyptic time. In Jesus' name, Amen."

Thoughts of Lizzy and your mother run through your mind. The EMP event, or whatever it was, happened after the school day. Lizzy should be home. Your mother should be home, too. Fear and worry invade your mind. You try pushing them out, but they hang on. The words of your father come back to mind, "Fear is the mind killer. Without your mind you will perish." You pray again, "Lord, please calm my spirit. I trust you. Amen." You slowly drift to sleep.

Chapter 2 Jack - The Day - *Uncertainty...*

Things are looking good. The promotion to Vice-President you received at Merchants Bank was a great milestone for your career in banking. The image of the new name plate on your office door makes you smile: 'Jack Chance – Vice-President'. There wasn't a large raise associated with the promotion, but perhaps with another year or so of experience, you'll be in a position to look for more advancement, either at your bank or one of the larger banks opening offices all over the place.

Your trip to Atlanta was great, your first as a bank vice-president. Phillip Smith, the bank president, sent you to the meeting. It was great rubbing shoulders with lots of bank executives, most with higher positions than your own. The conversations with these people is what has you considering possible advancement outside Merchants Bank. Rubbing shoulders with people from the Federal Reserve didn't hurt either.

You've been listening to Neil Cavuto's 'Your World' on Fox News. You love your Sirius XM, especially the news and financial networks. You like to stay informed about what's going on and you're usually switching between Fox News, Bloomberg and CNBC, unless, of course, your wife Melissa is with you. She can't stand the news channels. She prefers pop. A 'Breaking News' alert is on the radio. Seems to be a lot of these lately. Seldom, do they seem like breaking news. This one gets your attention. The host is saying, "This is a Fox News Alert – Fox News has just learned, the United Sates is under immediate threat of . . ." Then nothing. The radio goes dead, your car goes dead and starts slowing down. That's great. You're on the interstate somewhere between Atlanta and Montgomery and your car decides to die. Coasting to the side of the road, you stop the car and shift the transmission into park, then turning the key, you try to crank the car. Nothing happens. Not even a sound. The battery must be dead, because none of the dash indicator lights come on. Great, just great. You were hoping to be home before it got too late.

You pick up your cell phone to call for service, but it's dead. You plug it back into the charger. Maybe you won't have to wait too long. You use AAA service. It's pretty good. A few years ago you started providing a free one-year membership to each of your loan customers. It received such positive response that the bank decided to offer it to all of their new home loan customers. You even got a nice bonus for the idea. Personally, you've only had to use it twice in the past ten years, but it was worth it. Once for a flat tire on I-10, close to Biloxi and once, for the same reason, on your family vacation to Orlando. When your phone is charged, you'll make the call.

You're trying to recall where you actually are. Since you've been using the built-in GPS in your Infiniti, you haven't carried a road atlas, but you're pretty sure you are somewhere between Tuskegee and Montgomery. You were so involved in what Neil was saying on the radio, you weren't paying much attention to the road signs. You just can't remember.

There doesn't seem to be much traffic moving. Actually there isn't any traffic moving at all. That's really odd. Maybe odd is not the right word. Getting out of your car you look around. There are a few cars here and there stalled on the side of the road. You're just going to have to wait and see what happens. Somebody with emergency services should be coming by, checking on people on the interstate. Maybe they can explain what's going on. You sit back in the car and try to recline the seat. The electric controls won't work. You check your phone; it's still not working. You pull your laptop from its bag and turn it on. Might as well kill a little time playing Hay Day while waiting for emergency services to show up. This new laptop is state of the art hardware. A powerful i7 processor, large touch screen display, 4G wireless card and other useful features, including a seven-hour battery life. You push the power button, but nothing happens. That's another strange thing. This machine usually boots up in less than ten seconds. It's not coming on at all. Hmm . . . maybe this is something to be concerned about. Regardless, there is nothing you can do. You'll just wait.

Chapter 3 Jill - Day 1 - *Time to move...*

You awake early in the morning. It wasn't a good night. The car was hot. Now, the windows are covered with condensation from your breathing. The windows would not let down. You consider what you need to do. You're confident no help is coming. You pull the road atlas from the back seat. It doesn't give a lot of detail about the small roads, but it's a pretty good Rand McNally Road Atlas. You look it over. If you were driving, the thing to do would be to continue on to I-59 then turn south on AL5 near Woodstock, but you're walking. Distance is going to be critical, not how fast you can drive. Looking at the map you decide to take the exit at Hoover and work your way down to Montevallo, then to Brent, then back onto AL5 as if you were driving. Just guessing you figure there is about 175 miles to go before you get back home to Jackson. One hundred seventy-five miles! You pray, "Dear God! Help me along my way." Flashes of Lizzy flood your mind. You must do whatever it takes to get back to her. You have never been a quitter. You and Lizzy have pretty much been alone since before she was born. You carried the load of mother and father. Really, your dad was a great father figure for Lizzy. You are going to make it home. You must. You take your folding CRKT knife from your purse. It's the Drifter model, with a blade lock and pocket clip. It was a present from your dad for your birthday a few years ago. You had never carried a knife in your purse before then, but since you started, you don't know how you managed to do without it. You carefully cut out the two pages covering Alabama from the atlas. The rest of the atlas will be staying here. No need to carry it all the way home.

You look at your clothes. Business slacks, stockings, Docker shoes, and a lightweight white blouse. The shirt might work, but you have a complete change of clothes in the back. One of the things your father taught you at an early age was to keep contingency supplies in your car at all times. Ever since he gave you your first car, you've carried supplies. Right now is probably a good time to change clothes. With the windows covered in condensation, no one can see inside. You open the door and use the key to open the back latch. Retrieving your spare clothes, you return to the front of the car. With the door closed, you change clothes. Not wanting to get completely naked in the car, you keep the same undies and bra on. They'll be okay for today. You put on your Reebok walking shoes. You hope they hold up. The business shoes you had on are staying in the car. You'll bring the shirt and pants because you don't have another spare set, but neither was made for anything strenuous.

You go back through the glove compartment, looking for anything useful. You already got out the only useful items here, the map and your Glock. The other items, car registration and insurance information are staying with the car. In the center console, you pull out a notepad and pen, a nail clipper, and your emergency money. From the back, you get your laptop and try turning it on one more time. Nothing. It stays in the car. There is no way you're going to haul a dead laptop 175 miles.

Getting out of the car, you look around. Still nobody close. There are some small trees and brush close by. You really have to go. Better make it quick. When you finish, you clean your hands using the hand sanitizer from the door pocket. You open the back door and the hatch lid. You get the small box of supplies you always carry on out of town trips and the other useful items you found up front to the rear cargo area. Inside the box are some extra water and energy bars. These are added to your pre-packed get-home-bag. Some people refer them to as GHBs, or three day bags, or a number of other terms. Your pack has everything you're going to need for three days. It contains a sleeping bag, socks, undies, first aid kit, extra batteries, another knife, flashlights, a 32 oz. stainless steel water bottle filled with water, water treatment tabs, a small water filter, food, fire making materials, a small cook set, extra ammo for your Glock, a small tarp and a variety of other useful items, including toilet paper! Your dad helped you put this all together. In fact he insisted you keep it in your car at all times.

You're getting hungry, so you get the peanut butter crackers from the front of the car and the bottle of water. You eat the crackers while you finish packing the extra supplies into your pack. You remove the useful items from your purse and place them in the pack too.

You look at your watch. It's 8:30 a.m. Better get started, but first things first. You pray, "Dear God, I don't know how I am to make it home. I truly don't. My faith is in you. See me home safely and keep my family safe. In Jesus' name, Amen." You heft your bag to your shoulders. This bag is heavy! It must weigh about thirty pounds, but you're a fairly strong woman. You're 5'6" tall and weigh 135 lbs, depending on the time of month. Maybe you are carrying a little extra walking-around-weight, but you're probably going to need it for this journey home. You are used to toils and struggles. You've been a single mom ever since Lizzy was born, put yourself through college, and have been working ever since. You couldn't have made it without the help of your parents and God. God will be your help here too. As Psalms 23 says, "I will fear no evil, for you are with me." With a somewhat lifted spirit, you start on your journey.

It is hard to walk all that fast with this extra weight. You are a couple of miles north of Exit 19 and want to get off on Exit 13, then work your way through the roads and streets to Montevallo. Later, there will be time to pull out the map and study the route more closely after you get off the interstate. For now, there is no getting lost. Just follow the interstate to Exit 13, about ten miles away.

You see a few other people walking, but most aren't carrying back packs. They don't seem to have anything, even water. It makes you a little uncomfortable sticking out like you do with your pack. It seems most of the ones you encounter are either getting off at Exit 19 or walking further west. After about two hours, you spot a young woman and two small children sitting in the shade of a stalled car. Hearing the children crying, you slow down and look all around, making sure there is nobody else lurking around the stalled car. You approach with caution. As you come abreast of them, the woman asks, "Can you spare some water? At least for my children. They are so thirsty." You have compassion for this woman. The kids are clearly in distress. You say, "Sure, I think I can spare some water. How about a protein bar too? Maybe the kids could split one and you and I split one." The woman has tears in her eyes and says, "Yes, please."

You look around again; seeing nothing that might be a threat, you drop your pack. From within your pack you remove three bottles of water and hand them to the young mother. She opens one for each of the children, then opens one for herself. You can see their spirits lifted as they drink the water. You start removing the energy bars from your pack when you look up and see three guys rapidly approaching. You drop the bars back into your pack and stand quickly. The woman asks, "What's wrong?" You say, "Nothing, maybe. There are some guys coming here fast." The lead guy hollers, "Give us your water!" The second guy is laughing as he shouts, "Two sweet things! Oh, yes, two sweet things!" Your mind is racing. Adrenaline is flooding your bloodstream. You are under a severe threat. The training your father gave you as a teenager and young mother comes instantly to mind. The book he had you read, Principles of Personal Defense by Col. Jeff Cooper, flashes through your mind. This all occurs in seconds. The men are upon you. You know what you are going to have to do. When the lead guy is about twenty feet away, he lunges toward you with an upraised weapon of some kind. You have only seconds to respond before your skull is cracked open. Without hesitation, you draw your Glock, just as your dad trained you. You focus on putting the front sight on your attacker's chest and fire three rapid shots. As soon as you complete firing, you sidestep two paces to the left and look for another target. The other two guys are running across the median to the other side of the interstate. You line your sights up on the back of one of the fleeing men. You hesitate for a moment, then lower your weapon to the ready position. You scan all around for additional threats. Not seeing any, you remove the magazine from your Glock and insert the full magazine from your pocket. You place the other magazine into your left front pocket. You look down at the man lying on the ground. There is a spreading red circle on his chest. You look for his weapon. It was a short piece of pipe. It's on the ground outside of his reach. Seeing no other weapons, you holster your Glock. The man writhing on the ground looks up at you and gasps, "Help me. Help me." Your mind is racing. There is nothing you can do for him. Your small first aid kit does not contain supplies to treat a gunshot wound. Even if it did, you wouldn't know what to do. You make a hard decision. You look at the woman and say, "We've got to get out of here." Without saying a word to the man on the ground, you heft your pack and start to walk off. The woman quickly gathers her children and follows you down the interstate.

You don't look back as you walk. You hear the woman and children hurrying behind you. The adrenaline is starting to wear off and you're starting to shake. You start to walk faster. You've got to get away from here! Your mind is racing as you come to grips with the gravity of what has just happened. You just shot a man. You shot him! He's lying back there dying because you shot him! Bile starts rising in your stomach. You're going to be sick. The woman calls out, "Please, please slow down. We can't keep up." You stop next to a stalled Ford 4x4. You bend over at the waist and throw up what little there is in your stomach. Then the dry heaves begin. It feels as if your insides are going to come out. Your throat burns. Finally, you drop your pack to the ground and collapse to your knees and begin to cry. You cry hard with deep sobs. Why did this have to happen? Why?

You feel the woman's arms around you as she pulls you close. The sobs and feelings of regret won't stop. She says, "It's okay. I know you are hurting right now, but it's going to be okay. You saved our lives. Not just yours and mine, but you saved my children as well. Thank you. I will never forget what you did for us." Slowly, after a few minutes, you stop crying and pull away. You say, "Thank you. I've never had to do anything like this. Never! My dad taught me as a teenager how to shoot and defend myself. He would often say, "I don't want my daughter to have to depend upon a man for protection." I just never thought it would actually come to this."

The woman says, "My name is Mary." Referring to her children she says, "This is Mandre and Lucy." You smile and say, "My name is Jill. Pleased to meet you all." You pull a bottle of water from your pack and rinse your mouth and drink. You remember you promised them a protein bar. You pull two out of your pack and hand them to Mary, saying, "Here have both. I can't eat anything right now."

While sitting together, you strike up a conversation with Mary. She is a stay at home mom. Mary says, "I live not far from Exit 13. Only about three miles." You perk up, "Really? That's the exit I'm going to take. We can walk together that far if you want." Mary says in a pleading voice, "Oh, please let's do. I don't think I can make it alone. My husband, Bruce, is a police officer in town. I'm sure he's worrying pretty bad right now." "Well, if he's a police officer, he's probably pretty sharp. I bet he's tracking you down right now. Did he know where you were going yesterday?" Mary hangs her head, "No. We had a big argument yesterday morning. It was about nothing really, but it got heated and we both said things we shouldn't have. He stormed out of the house for work. I packed the kids and went to see my sister near Leeds. He called several times, but I didn't answer. I wanted to make him worry. I know he was calling to say he was sorry. He never could stay mad very long. Now, because I wanted him to suffer, he has no idea where we are, and if it weren't for you, my children and I would be dead on the side of the road. All because of my foolish pride."

"Well, Mary, I don't know what to say about that. But, we'll walk together as far as your home. We need to get moving, but before we do let's pray." You begin to pray, "Dear God, we thank you for your hand of protection. We pray you will see us safely to Mary's house and that Bruce will be okay. Father, I pray again for my baby girl, Lizzy, and my mother. Please place your hands of protection around each of us. In Jesus' name, Amen." You stand up and heft your pack. Mary and the girls rise. You take a good look all around, then continue the five more miles to the exit.

Chapter 4 Jack - Day 1 - *Realization sets in...*

It's early morning. You don't know exactly what time, as your digital watch isn't working. You didn't sleep well at all. How could you? The seat wouldn't even recline. No one with emergency services, or anyone else for that matter, has come by. In the distance, toward Montgomery, are a couple of stalled cars stalled with people standing around. Back toward Tuskegee, you don't see anybody. You start assessing your situation. Whatever has happened, must have happened over a widespread area, otherwise emergency services personnel would have passed by now. It is kind of early in the morning. You decide to wait another little while. If no one shows up, you'll start walking to the nearest exit toward Montgomery. It can't be more than ten or fifteen miles. You go to the fitness center twice a week, so you're in pretty good shape. Surely you can walk ten miles in a few hours.

Sitting in the front seat, you sip on the partial empty bottle of Dasani water and eat a Snickers candy bar. The only other food in the car is a pack of peanut butter crackers and an unopened bottle of Dasani water. You're going to be hungry and thirsty most of the day. At the next exit, you can buy whatever you need. You have nearly four hundred dollars in cash, plus a debit card, personal credit card, and work credit card. No doubt, at the next exit you'll be able to rent a room and get something to eat. Then you can sort this situation out. You just have to make it to the next exit.

You look around your car to see what useful items you might find to take with you. There doesn't seem to be anything useful in the glove compartment. In the center console, you find a nice LED flashlight. It's a really bright light. With fresh batteries, the thing shines a hundred yards or more. Melissa gave you this light for Christmas, this past year. You think of Melissa and your son. You wonder, if they are having the same issues with stalled cars that you are having here. You pull your laptop from the back seat and try turning it on again. Still nothing. Regardless, your laptop is coming with you. You have too much invested in it to just leave it. Inside the trunk of the car is a set of golf clubs, a small tote bag, a small first aid kit, a folding car sun shade and your luggage. The luggage has wheels on the bottom, but you can't even imagine pushing or pulling it over ten miles of interstate. Looking inside your luggage, you see more of the same of what you have on, nice business slacks, a white button-up shirt, socks, boxers, a toiletry kit, and a few other not so useful items. The laptop bag is large enough that it will hold the first aid kit and the toiletry kit along with the laptop itself. You reach into your golf bag and retrieve a number eight iron. Yes, this will make a formidable weapon and not a bad walking stick, though you cringe at the thought of it getting dragged along the road. Your golf shoes are in the trunk as well, but they aren't going to be of any use on a paved highway.

You've decided you have waited long enough. You close the trunk and lock the doors from the inside and then the driver's door with your key. Placing your bag strap over your shoulder and carrying your golf club in hand, you start at a brisk walk. You whisper a prayer, "Lord, please keep me safe and protect my family, Amen."

After walking a little over an hour you come across a teenage girl and a small child. They are sitting next to a stalled car. They both look haggard. The baby can't be much more than a year old. As you approach, the girl looks up and says, "Sir, can you spare some water for my baby?" You consider what she has asked as you think of your own situation. You've already drunk the half bottle of water and eaten the Snickers. You have just this one bottle of water and the peanut butter crackers left. You're thirsty yourself and it is far to the next exit. You look around and see what might be a small creek going under the interstate, but the water looks so nasty. You turn back and look at the girl then at the baby in obvious distress. You think about your own wife and son back home. Your mind races as you wonder if you'll ever see them again. You're a good person. You go to church every Sunday and sing in the choir. Your wife teaches Sunday School. You drop to one knee and offer the girl your bottle of water and say, "This is the only bottle I have, how about we just drink half of it?" She smiles and reaches for the bottle. That's when you hear the engine. You stand and look up. Yes! Help is on its way! You look around. Coming from the east you see two motorcycles. The two men stop as they reach where you are. One says, "Good morning. Looks like you folks are having a hard time of it. Is that your daughter and grandbaby?" You reply, "No, we just met. But yes, we are having a hard time. Could we ride with you guys to the next exit?" Both guys get off their bikes and walk closer. The first guy speaks again, "Well, I don't know. Let me think . . . ." Then something slams against your head. You fall to your knees. Stars are in your vision as you feel a heavy impact on your back and you fall on your face. You hear the frantic screams of the girl as your mind fades to black.

You're having a dream. Or is it a nightmare? You're at home in bed. Someone is trying to beat the door in. You think, "I need to get up and get my pistol." You move to the closet and pull the lock box from the top shelf. You can't remember the combination so you go to get your key. Where are the keys? Your mind is searching for the keys, yes, you remember now. You had your keys at the car on the interstate. The car? The pounding sound at the door slowly gives way to an intense pounding pain in your head. The pain brings you back to reality. You're not in your bed. Your eyes start to open. Things are spinning, but it's clear enough for you to see you're face down on the pavement of the highway. You hear a baby wailing. Your eyes slowly focus. You sit up and look around. You touch your head and feel caked blood. There is blood in your mouth. You turn to the wailing baby. The young mother is gone. The bikers are gone. You get to your knees and crawl to the child. You try to comfort the baby, but the loud crying continues. You look for the water bottle, but it is gone, as is your pack of crackers. You sit up. Your head hurts so bad! The crying of the baby is only making it worse. You must be going into shock. Water, you need water. Remembering the little creek, you slowly rise on wobbled legs. Walking down the shoulder of the road, you fall twice before reaching the fence blocking your way, but there is just enough room between the last fence post and the concrete culvert to squeeze though.

You make it to the creek and stumble in. The cold water jerks you to momentary alertness. You rinse your mouth out and drink deeply of the water. It tastes horrible, but you have to have water. You think about the crying child's need for water. Finding some discarded empty water bottles on the ground, you fill three with water—not realizing that when the electricity went off, it shut down all the sewer lift stations. The lift station a mile up the creek over flowed because the pumps didn't work. Raw sewage has been flowing into the creek since midnight. You get back up on shaky legs to take the water to the baby. You slip and fall, hitting your already throbbing head and pass out again.

Sometime later, you regain consciousness again. Your legs are too wobbly to stand, so you crawl to the fence and manage to squeeze back through. You crawl back over toward the car and the crying baby. That's when you see the woman, rather, the very young mother. She is naked. Her body shows signs of abuse and her neck is twisted at an odd angle. She is dead. You want to cry, but your head hurts too badly. You crawl around to the road side of the car. The cries from the baby are just a whimper now. He must have cried all he can. You open one of the bottles of water and hold it to the lips of the child. He drinks the water along with the bacteria from the contaminated raw sewage that has spilled into the creek. You keep giving him water until he cannot drink any more. He then lies in your arms and closes his eyes. You are injured, how bad you do not know, but you can't continue. You sit there and rest, holding the baby.

The consequences are going to be severe. The bacteria you and the baby have ingested will, in a few hours, cause uncontrollable diarrhea. Thus, further dehydrating your already dehydrated bodies. Unless you and the baby receive help real soon, you will be dead within 24 hours.

You close your eyes and think of your wife and son, hoping they are going to be okay. If you had only brought your pistol with you and maybe packed a few supplies, you might have made it home. Realization is sinking in. You will never see your family again. The baby's wailing has stopped and you fall asleep leaning against the car.

You feel hands shaking you. Your eyes open but only barely. A young woman is saying, "Mister, hey mister." You are unable to speak. You hear a man's voice, "His head is busted open. There is nothing we can do for him.

I can't carry him and we only have one bottle of water left." The woman says, "But the baby, we must help the baby." You feel the child being lifted out of your arms. You are unable to move or respond. The car door opens. The man says, "Here is the diaper bag. Change his diaper. It's overflowing." You can hear the baby crying and the rattling of cloth and diapers. Then the man kneels down in front of you. You can see him, but you're too weak to speak. He says, "Mister, I can't carry you. We are going to take your baby with us to the next exit. I will send some help if I can. I'm sorry. I wish I could do more." He pats you on the shoulder and stands. The last sounds you hear are the steps of shoes on the highway as they walk away.

Chapter 5 Jill - Day 1 - *A long slow walk…*

"We need to stop," Mary says. So, you stop. You're making your 10th stop since starting down the interstate. You've gone a little over 4 miles in 4 hours. This is killing you. You so want to make some progress down the road! But, don't want to leave Mary and the children by themselves. You're thinking at this rate, you might not even make it to Mary's house before dark. That would not be good. It's 3:30 p.m., and there is another mile to the exit, then another three to Mary's house. The math is obvious: One mile per hour, four miles to go – four more hours. That's if the kids and Mary can hang on. Mandre is 6 years old and Lucy is 5. They can't walk very fast or very far at a time. Mary is having to carry one at all times. You, well you can't carry the pack and one of the kids. You tried, but you just can't do it. So you're down to the walking speed of a child.

You open your pack and pull out a bottle of water. You started with eight and are now down to four bottles. You open the bottle and take a drink and pass the bottle to Mary. Mary gives each of her girls a drink, then takes a drink herself and passes the bottle back. The bottle is mostly empty as you put it back in your pack. You see what looks like college age guys and gals approaching. You instinctively stand up, not wanting to be sitting when they come by. They are approaching from the other side of the lanes, but as they approach, one of the guys walks over and says, "Hey, have you got any water you can spare?" You think about the few bottles in your pack and say, "No, sorry." The guy says, "Look, we saw you drinking water and we saw you put the bottle back in your pack. Come on, we're really thirsty." You reply again, "We don't have enough for ourselves and can't spare any. Sorry." The guy becomes agitated and steps closer. You draw your Glock, not pointing it at him but making it clearly visible. You say firmly, "We don't have any spare water!" The guy stops, raises his hands and backs away. He says, "Okay, uh, no problem." He rejoins his group as they continue to walk away and hollers, "Bitch!" You remain standing and watch them as they move on down the road.

Mary says, "Why didn't you just give him a bottle of water?" You look annoyed at Mary and say, "Mary, we have three bottles of water left. We've already drunk five bottles and we are only about half-way to your house. Do you want to make it home or not?" Mary sheepishly says, "Yeah, I do. Sorry." You consider Mary for a few moments. You feel sorry for her. Out on the road with two children and absolutely no supplies. You shake your head a little. Mary must be one of what your dad called "sheeple." People who are totally dependent upon others and just go where life takes them, never considering it might be taking them to the slaughterhouse.

"Mary, I've been wondering, with your husband being a police officer, why didn't you have any supplies in your car?" Mary hangs her head and sniffles. "That's what our big fight was about yesterday. You see, I just got my car the day before yesterday. It's a used car, but almost new. We unloaded my supplies from the old car and left them in the garage so we could trade the car in. It was late when we got back in, so we didn't load them back up. Well yesterday morning, Bruce insisted I load the supplies up before I went anywhere. I told him I was a big girl and didn't need him telling me what to do and the argument got out of hand. I left the supplies in the garage just to spite him." You shake your head. Pride certainly goes before the fall. "Well," you say, "that makes no difference now. We have to keep moving, if we are going to make it to your place before dark"

You reach down and shoulder your pack, say a short prayer and start walking again. Mary gathers the children and carries Lucy while Mandre walks. It's a slow go. A very slow go.

Chapter 6 Jill - Day 1 - *The end of a long day...*

You step onto the off ramp at the interstate exit, look up and say aloud, "Thank you Jesus. Thank you!" You look at your watch. It's 5:00. It's taken over an hour and a half to go the last mile to the exit. You look over at Mary and the girls. They are clearly in physical distress. You're worrying about them. Heck, you're suffering from the heat and sun too.

They are all red from sun exposure. You had given them all some sun screen after your first stop earlier in the day, but they had already been out in the open for hours before you came upon them. You pull the last water bottle from your bag and give them each a drink. This is it, except for the stainless steel bottle in its carrier. You know if you get into that bottle before you find more water you are going to be in trouble. You look over at Mary and the kids. You just don't know if they can go another three miles. You send a voiceless prayer: "Lord, please provide."

Everyone starts walking again. Just past the bottom of the ramp is a large Pilot station. Across from it is a Kangaroo station. Both are filled with stalled cars and lots of people milling around. Mary says, "Do you think we could go in and buy some water?" You respond "There is no way on God's green earth I'll go into that crowd." You keep walking. Just past the Pilot station is a Walmart Super Center. As you get close, it is obvious the parking lot is over half full of stalled cars. There is a very large crowd near the front of the store. You can hear angry shouts and raised voices, though it isn't clear what they are saying. You move to the other side of the highway, putting distance between you and the crowd. You look back over at Walmart and that's when you spot an overturned shopping cart at the back of the parking lot. An idea pops. "Mary wait here. I'll be right back." You move swiftly back across the road and toward the shopping cart. You stand it up. It looks like it's okay. With some difficulty, you get it across the grass and ditch back to the road.

The wheels turn smoothly. Again you say, "Thank you, Jesus!" You quickly take your pack off and place it in the basket. Mary comes over. She picks Mandre up and places her in the cart, then does the same for Lucy. You start pushing the cart down the road thanking God, as you are finally able to walk at a more normal pace.

You turn right off the main highway onto another road. Only two more miles! A lot more people are moving about. None approach or try to talk. Up ahead, you see a small Mom and Pop type gas-convenience station. The door is open and a few people are walking around. You tell Mary, "Let's try this place." As you walk in, the clerk, a Pakistani, says "Cash only." Mary walks in with the cart and says, "I have a debit card." The man pulls a pistol from under the counter and lays it on top. "Cash Only! And leave that cart outside." Mary's eyes grow wide. You say, "Okay, no problem. I have cash," and pull your emergency cash from your pocket for the clerk to see. He says, "Okay, but the cart must go outside." Speaking to Mary, you say, "Mary, take the cart outside and wait for me next to the door. It'll be all right and I won't be long." Mary takes the cart outside and waits by the door. You walk around the store. They are sold out of most everything. You pick up the remaining bag of beef jerky, a bottle of peanuts, three candy bars and a gallon of water. You go up to the clerk and lay the items down. The clerk has put the pistol back up. Using a pencil and a scrap piece of paper, he adds your items up and says, "Fifty dollars." You exclaim, "Fifty dollars!" He replies, "Take it or leave it. It really doesn't matter to me. Tomorrow it will be one hundred dollars." You only have one hundred dollars, but you need the supplies. You give him two twenties and a ten. He puts your items in a bag. You look at the counter and see one of the folding Alabama highway maps. It's got to have more detail than the one you have. You pick it up and place it on the counter. The clerk looks a little annoyed. He says, "Twenty dollars." You don't argue as you hand him a twenty-dollar bill. You have spent seventy of your hundred-dollar emergency money. You gather your things return to Mary put the items in the cart, and say, "Let's go."

Thanks to the cart, you have finally been able to make some good time walking. You cover the two miles to Mary's house in an hour. Mandre and

Lucy are asleep in the cart as you and Mary walk into Mary's drive. You stop as you look up and see a man sitting on the steps of the porch. His head is in his hands, as if he was crying or praying. Noticing your gaze, Mary looks at the steps. "Bruce!" she exclaims. She starts running toward Bruce, crying loudly. The man looks up in surprise, then jumps to his feet and runs to embrace his wife. They are both crying. You can't tell what they are saying. You just stand there watching, still holding the cart with the sleeping children. After a few minutes, Bruce and Mary release their embrace, turn and walk toward you.

Bruce glances at his sleeping children, then looks at you and says, "Thank you," as he grabs you and hugs you. He's crying again as he says again, "Thank you." He releases you, looks at Mary and says, "Let's go inside."

You are so tired. Your feet hurt so bad. You're sweaty and know you smell bad. You are so relieved when Mary says, "Let me show you to the guest room." You lug your pack as you follow. After entering the room, Mary points to the attached bathroom and says, "Bruce says the water is still on. Help yourself. I'll go find a candle. Wait, are you hungry? Bruce can fix something, I'm sure." You are hungry, but you're more tired than hungry. "No, not really. I'm just so tired. If you don't mind, I'm going to clean up and sleep." Mary says, "Okay. Make yourself at home. We can talk in the morning." She turns to leave, stops and turns around. She hugs you tightly and says, "Thank you, Jill. Thank you. If you had not helped us today, my children and I would be dead. You saved our lives. Thank you!" She lets go and walks away before you can say anything.

It's almost too dark to see in the bathroom. You fumble with the lavatory and wash your face. That feels so good. You hear Mary say, "The candle is on the dresser." You walk into the bedroom, and light the candle with the lighter Mary left. There is a nice soothing glow from the candle. You close and lock the bedroom door. Taking the candle, you return to the bathroom, stand in front of the mirror and remove your shoes. Oh that feels so good! Your feet have been so hot. You finish undressing, grab a wash cloth and move to the shower. Turning it on, you feel the warm water. Yes, this is going to be nice. You bathe yourself and enjoy the pulsing of the water, as it hits your tired and sore body. When you finish, you grab your undies, socks and bra and wash them. You hang them on the towel rack, then grab your pants and shirt, hanging them on the shower after washing them.

You return to the bedroom, pull on a clean pair of undies and the clean t-shirt from your pack. Before you crawl into the bed, you drop to your knees and pray. "Dear God, thank you for your hand of protection. Please continue to keep me safe and protect my mother and Lizzy. In Jesus' name, Amen." You crawl into the bed and lay your head on the pillow. This is the end of a very long and harrowing day. Before you can dwell over the day's terrible events, exhaustion overtakes you, and you fall fast asleep.

Chapter 7 Jill - Day 2 - *At Mary's home…*

Your eyes start to flutter as the sunlight shining through the shades hits your eyes. You're trying to remember where you are. You're lost and disoriented. You look around the room. It's not very large, but it is nice. You see what looks like a pack against the wall. Actually, it looks like the one you keep in your car. Finally, after a few moments, your mind comes back into focus. You're in a bed, at Mary's house, somewhere south on Hoover and AL261. Yes, oh my, the whole world has changed. You whisper a plea, "Dear God, save us!"

You start to pull the sheets off and rise out of bed. Your muscles scream, "Stay in bed!" Your body is sore and stiff all over from the previous day. Yet you sit up and swing your legs to the floor and stand up. Pain shoots through your feet and legs. You can't believe how sore they are. Your feet, your shins, and your calves all hurt like crazy from all the walking. Your back hurts from carrying the extra weight of your pack. Your shoulders are raw from the shoulder straps of the back pack. Your breasts hurt, too. Lifting your shirt, you look. Yes, the underwire bra you were wearing has made it raw underneath your breasts. That is not going to be good. You force yourself to take a few timid steps and start stretching. You are sore all over, though the stretching is limbering you up a bit. You walk to the bathroom and look into the mirror. Despite the sunscreen you put on yesterday, there is sunburn on your face. The sunscreen must have sweated off. It's going to be tough with the sun hitting your face again today.

You look in the mirror and turn the water on. There is still a flow, though much less than last night. You wash your face and try to do something with your hair—brushing it back and putting it into a pony tail. You've always had long blond hair and have suffered through all the dumb blond jokes. Most of them are way off base. You open the pack of peanut butter crackers and the partial bottle of water. Eating the crackers to curb the rumblings in your stomach, you walk over to the bed. After quickly making the bed, you sit on it and begin to ponder upon a plan for the day.

You pick your pack up and set it on the bed. Oh my, that hurts! You know it's going to be a rough day! Hopefully, walking will work out some of the soreness. You pull the map out and check your route. Looks like you have to go through Helena, then Brantleyville, before you get to Montevallo. Should you go through Montevallo or around it? You'll have to make that decision later. It'll be at least two or three days before you can get there anyway. Looks like you'll be hitting some smaller county roads south of Helena, but that's probably okay. There will probably be fewer people. You've decided the fewer you see, the better and then think, "Isn't that a shame."

You go to the bathroom and check your clothes. Everything seems dry enough, except the bottom of your pants. They are still a little damp near the bottom, but they will be ok. You go back to the bed and decide to inventory your pack. The pack itself is a multi-day hunting pack purchased at Academy Sports. It's kind of cute, camouflage with pink highlights. Well, at least you think so. Your dad rolled his eyes when he saw it, just like he did with your pink IWB holster. On the outside of your pack, you have a 32 oz. stainless steel water bottle in a water carrier strapped to the pack. You also have an emergency/tactical knife clipped to the pack webbing. This is one of those knives with a seat belt cutter, glass breaker and serrated blade. Hanging on the webbing are a few aluminum D-ring snap clips and some small elastic straps.

You start pulling the contents out of the pack. First, are the remaining empty water bottles. A total of eight bottles. At 135lbs, with the walking you will be doing, you will need at least that much water every day. You didn't even get half that much yesterday because you shared with Mary and the kids. You think about the gallon jug of water you bought. It's one of those milk jug type containers that won't carry in your pack. You could use it to fill your eight bottles, but you get another idea. You jump up, ouch that hurts, and go to the bathroom and turn the water on. The water is still flowing, but even slower than a few minutes ago. You grab your water bottles from the bed, rinse them out and refill them from the lavatory. You drink one of the bottles and refill it again. You return to the bed thinking, "I'll just give Mary and Bruce the jug of water." There is no way you'll be able to carry the extra weight, anyway, and you certainly aren't going to take the cart.

You next pull out your food pack. It's stored in a large zip lock bag. There are three complete stripped down MREs. You had four, but you, Mary, and the kids ate one yesterday. Three packs of single-serving Spam, three packs of single-serving tuna fish, three packs of peanut butter, three packs of Hardee's grape jelly, three protein bars and one 3600 calorie emergency bar. In addition, you have a small bag which contains six single-serving packs of instant coffee, creamer and sugar packets, four Emergen-C vitamin packs, four instant oatmeal packs, and some mustard and mayo packs.

You pull out your Stanley cook cup, complete with lid and camp cups. Stored inside the cups are a little squeeze bottle of cooking oil and another of honey. Some small utensils are attached to the cook cup. You've never had to use this cook set, but your dad insisted you put a cook set in your pack, and this is what was available at Walmart. You think of your dad and whisper a prayer of thanks, "Dear God, thank you for a father who insisted I prepare."

Next thing out is the hygiene kit. It contains two small bars of soap, a small bottle of body/hair wash, small tooth brush, a small tube of toothpaste, a small pack of wet wipes and a razor. You think about the razor for a moment, you hate leg hairs, but you're not shaving your legs this morning. In a separate zip lock bag you have a wash cloth, a roll of toilet paper and six feminine pads. You think about that for a moment. Your next period is in three weeks. Geez, you sure hope you don't need those before you get home. A small bag of clothes is next. Inside the bag of clothes are another pair of undies, socks, t-shirt, shorts, but the best thing is a sports bra. Yes! It'll be so much better than the underwire bra you had on yesterday. Actually, you don't think you could wear it again today. You certainly don't want to be braless. That creates problems of its own. A sleeping bag is at the bottom of your pack.

Underneath your sleeping bag is a zip lock bag containing twenty-five

9mm FMJ rounds. Your dad had told you to get hollow points, but they were a dollar a piece, the FMJs were only a quarter each. You should have listened to your dad. That reminds you to reload the Glock magazine. You retrieve the magazine and remove the hollow point ammunition. The magazine is four short. That's right, you shot three times, but your mind refuses to go there for now. There is also one round still in the chamber. You load four of the FMJs, then reload the hollow points.

In a back side pocket of the pack, is a small first aid kit and a mini-manual on survival and foraging, plus a hank of 550 paracord and a mini roll of duct tape and a dozen or so zip ties. The sunscreen and hand lotion is kept in this side pouch as well and a Kershaw folding knife your father gave you to keep in your pack.

In a side compartment, you remove an Esbit stove and a dozen fuel tabs, two Bic lighters, strike anywhere matches and an old medicine bottle with Vaseline coated cotton balls. You set one of the Bic lighters by your flashlight. In a second side compartment, is a small bottle of unscented Clorox to treat water, plus water treatment tablets, six coffee filters and a frontier emergency water filter.

From another outside compartment, you pull out a small LED high output flashlight that uses a single AA battery, and a larger Fenix LED flashlight that uses two AA batteries. This light has a belt holster. It was a gift from your father this past Christmas. You sure miss your father! You set the Fenix light aside. You also have a small LED headlamp that uses three AAA batteries. Next out is a bag of spare batteries. Six AAs and six AAAs. You pull the small emergency radio out and turn it on; nothing. It's dead. You remove the batteries and install two new AAs. Still nothing. You remove the batteries, put them back in the bag and set the radio farther to the side. The EMP must have damaged it. No need carrying a useless radio. You also remove the phone charge cable and toss it over by the damaged radio. From the compartment where you would insert a water bladder is a small 8'x10' silver and brown tarp.

You look at the items laid out. This is all you have, plus the jerky, peanuts and candy bars you left in the cart, to make it home on. It brings tears to your eyes. How, how are you going to make it home with only this? You get back on your knees and pray. "Dear Father, please provide! In Jesus' name, Amen." You get up, repack your bag and get dressed. You put the flashlight on your belt, the Glock in your waist band, the extra magazine in your left pocket and the Bic lighter in your right pocket. The knife clips into your left back pocket. As you complete putting everything back together, there is a knock on the door. "It's me, Mary. Bruce is whipping up some breakfast. It will be ready soon." You respond, "I'll be right down." You heft your pack with a moan and head for the door.

Chapter 8 Jill - Day 2 – *On the road again…*

Walking down the stairs, each step sends needles of pain through your legs and back. The stretches you did earlier are helping, but still your body has never before had to walk ten miles carrying a thirty pound pack. It's going to be tough making it home. Really tough. At the bottom of the stairs, you continue to the front door and set your pack against the wall. You walk over toward the kitchen where Mary and Bruce are. "It smells good," you say. Mary replies, "It does, doesn't it? Bruce is making eggs and bacon. Oh yeah, there is a pot of hot coffee on the stove." You watch Bruce for a moment. He is cooking over a propane Coleman camp stove. It's the two burner type. You walk over to the stove and pick the coffee pot up and pour a cup of coffee. Bruce says, "The creamer and sugar are in the little bowls." "Thanks. Just a little creamer for me," you reply. As you sit at the kitchen table next to Mary, Bruce starts passing out plates with eggs and bacon. It smells so good and you're still hungry. Bruce finally sets his plate down and sits. Bruce asks the blessing, then you all dig in. It is so good.

You look around. It's a nice kitchen, with beautiful wood cabinets. You notice lots of glasses and pots filled with water sitting all over the counter area. You say pointing at the pots, "That's a good idea. I hope my Lizzy and mom did the same." Your thoughts move to Lizzy, 'Baby, I'm coming home. I don't know how, but I'm coming home.' Bruce brings you back from you thoughts as he says, "Mary has told me all that you did. You are an amazingly brave and resourceful woman. Thank you for bringing my family home to me." You say, "I'm not really brave or resourceful. I just did what I thought I should do. That's all." Bruce says "Regardless, it was a good thing. What are your plans? You are welcome to stay with us, if you want. Even if only for a few days." "I can't. I have to get home to my daughter and mother." "Mary tells me you are from Clarke County. Isn't that north of Mobile?" asks

Bruce. "Yes it is. About 50 miles north. I live in Jackson. It's the largest town in the county." "That's got to be close to 180 miles. Do you think you can walk all that way?" Bruce asks. "I've got to, unless God sends another way. I don't know how I'll do it, but I have to do it"

Bruce studies you for a few minutes, then says, "I see you're determined to go. I can respect that. Given the same circumstances, I would do the same. I can promise you it's not going to be easy. What can we do to help you?" "Well", you slowly reply, "there are a few things, if you can. I need a ball cap, another light colored shirt and a roll of toilet paper, if you could." Bruce says, "I think we can help you with that. Anything else?" You think for a moment and say, "A ride home." Bruce smiles, "We might be able to help with that, too." Your eyes grow wide.

Mary leads you to the garage and points to three bikes. Your eyes are still wide, not knowing what to think. She says, "Bruce and I have been talking. We want you to pick one of these bikes for your journey." Tears start forming in your eyes. You turn to Mary and hug her and say, "Thank you. You may have just saved my life!" Bruce says, "You can pick whichever one you want, but I suggest you pick the red one. It's an old style single speed, but it has a large front basket you can put your pack in. What do you think?" You shake your head in agreement, walk over and hug Bruce. "You say I saved Mary and the kids yesterday. You have saved me today. I really didn't know how I would make it home. I really didn't. I prayed and asked God to provide and here you are giving me my life back. Thank you." Bruce smiles, saying, "Let me go over it and make sure every thing is ok. I'll check the tires and oil the chain, then it's yours."

You go back in with Mary. Emotions are still thick in the air. You pick up a pen and paper from the counter and start writing saying, "Mary, this is the address to my home. If you ever need to come there, please do." Mary smiled and says, "Thank you. Bruce says it may get really bad here. He's making plans for us to go to north Alabama with some friends. One of his friends has an old school bus that still runs. He's coming by tomorrow morning, so we are going to have to start packing."

You ask Mary if you can go see the kids one last time. You open the door and see they are still sleeping. They had a tough day yesterday. You walk over and gently touch their heads. You tell them goodbye and go back through the door. You return to your bedroom, for one last visit to the bathroom before you leave. Then you walk to the front door, grab your pack and go out onto the porch. Bruce has the bike ready in the yard . You walk over and put your pack in the basket. You have to steady the bike to keep it from falling over. Bruce says, "I put a small air pump in the basket. I'm sorry, but I don't have any tube patches." You smile and say, "Thank you. Thank you for everything." You push the bike over by the cart and load your water, jerky, peanuts and candy bars from the cart into the basket.

Your watch says it's 8:30 a.m. "Well" you say, "I guess it's time to leave." Mary comes over with tears in her eyes, she hugs you and thanks you again. Bruce gives you one final hug. You get on the bike and slowly start down AL261.

As you pedal onto the highway, you look both ways. It doesn't seem like anybody is out yet. But that's likely to change. Your legs are sore. It's been more than a year since you've ridden a bike. You pedal trying to get to that happy speed where there's less stress on your legs. You start thinking about what Bruce said. One hundred eighty miles. With this bike, you just might make it. Let's see. If you can average 30 miles a day that puts you home within a week. Home! You want to be home so bad. You hope Lizzy and your mom are okay and aren't worrying too much about you. Yet, you realize they are. You get a lump in your throat thinking about it. You ponder the day before. The walk down the interstate. Perhaps the worst day of your entire life. No, there was one day worse, but you refuse to go there for now. It's been less than two days since the world changed forever. You wish you would have had more time to talk to Bruce about it, but there just wasn't time. You hope they make it safely to wherever they are going.

This pedaling is tough on your legs, very tough. They are already sore from yesterday. You can't seem to maintain that happy speed. After what seems like a mile or so, you stop. The bike is certainly making your progress faster, but it's definitely not easier on your legs. There are people up ahead, walking toward you. You're a little wary, and decide it would be better to be moving than sitting still as they come by. You take another look behind you and start pedaling again. You pass a man and woman walking, breathe a "hello" and keep going. You stop again a little later and pull a bottle of water from your pack, take a drink, and decide to stop for a few minutes. You get three ibuprofen tablets from your first aid kit. You swallow them down and eat a Payday candy bar. Maybe this will give your legs some relief. They are so sore and your back hurts almost as bad.

You adjust your Glock on your hip. You still haven't found the sweet spot to carry it while pedaling. Looking both ways again, you see no one behind you, but several walking toward you. Wonder why the traffic seems to be one way? Hmm . . . must be because you're traveling faster than walking speed, so you're getting further ahead of anyone behind. You start pedaling again. A few folks ask you to stop and talk, but you respond, "Sorry, can't stop" and keep pedaling. You stop a little further ahead, when you see no one in front or behind. You have to take the Glock out of your waist band. It feels like it wants to fall out and you haven't been able to find a place for it to ride well. You take it off. It's too big to ride in your front pocket, especially with your legs pumping up and down. You unzip your pack and place it on top. You sure hope you can get to it quickly if you have to. The pack has double zippers, so you decide to bring each zipper up from the side and leave a small opening at the top of the pack. That might just work. You try reaching for your Glock. It's still a little awkward trying to get it out, but you have to leave it like it is. People are up ahead, coming your way.

There are more and more people on the road. Then you see it ahead. A road block. Two cars pushed across the road and what looks like men with rifles behind them. You stop, not sure about what to do. You ask one of the walkers, "Excuse me. What's up with the cars?" The person says, "It's a police road block, but it's not a problem. You can go into town." You approach the road block with some trepidation, wondering if this was a good idea. You can't remember from your map if there is another way around. It doesn't seem you have a choice.

You slow to a stop just in front of the road block. A man dressed in a police officer's uniform speaks, "Good morning, ma'am. What can we do for you?" You tell him you're just traveling through, trying to get to Clarke County. "Wow. Clarke County, that's a long ways. I used to hunt in Clarke County with a friend, but that's been a few years back. Don't guess that will be happening again anytime soon. If you're just passing through, stay on this road. There is a relief station along the way, south of the middle of town, where you can get something to eat. If you're planning on staying, ask for the relief camp, they are just setting it up. If you're caught wandering around town with no specific business, you will be arrested. You understand?" You say, "Yes, I do." Then he says, "Welcome to Helena," and passes you through with the wave of his hat.

With the way they have the cars set up, you have to go right through the middle, right by the police officer. As you pedal past, you realize this is the first sign of authority you've seen since the . . . . The what? What do you call it? EMP day? Is this the civilization changing event you've heard some talk about? Well it certainly seems like the crap has hit the fan. You decide to simply call it, 'The Day'.

Chapter 9 Jill - Day 2 - *In a hurry...*

As you pedal away from the road block, you notice the increasing number of houses. You've never travelled this way before. You always took AL5 to the interstate. It's shorter this way, just faster to drive the other way. The houses and layout remind you of home and the neighborhoods there. Home! You long to be home with Lizzy! The number of people walking in both directions increases. People on side streets are moving around, including a few on bikes. In the distance, you think you hear the sounds of an engine, but you can't be sure. Some of the stores appear to be open and have people going in and out. You think about it for a minute, but decide not to risk it.

As you approach downtown, there are dozens of people walking and milling about. You have to slow down, as people are walking on the road, as well as the sidewalk. You're barely able to keep enough speed to keep the bike balanced. You consider taking a side street, but remember the officers warning, "If you're going through town, stay on this street. If you're caught wandering around town with no specific business, you will be arrested." Arrested is the last thing you want to happen, but still the side streets would have fewer people. Maybe you could just go a block or two . . . BAM, somebody pushes you from the side. Your bike loses balance and you have to put one foot down to keep from falling over. A teenage boy grabs the handle bars of your bike. You holler, "No!" as you both struggle for control of the bike. You're about to lose and consider just grabbing your bag and giving up the bike, when the biggest black man you have ever seen steps forward and grabs the kid by his collar and nearly lifts him off the ground, "Boy, what are you doing!" he bellows, as he shakes the kid from side to side. The kid struggles and yaks back, but the big guy is relentless and won't let him go. He says, "You apologize to this lady or I'm going to shake the crap out of you." The kid, seeing he has no chance of escape, bows his head and says,

"I'm sorry." The big man says, "Boy, if I catch you bothering anybody else, I'm going to put my foot up your butt. Do you understand me?" The kid says, "Yes sir." The moment the big guy releases him, the kid dashes off. The big guy turns and says, "Ma'am, on behalf of the good people of Helena, I want to apologize for what just happened here." You smile, still a little nervous, and tell him, "Thank you." He says, "My name is Elijah. Are you staying here in town or just passing through?" You right your bike, placing it between you and the big man. You're still nervous, as you've never spoken to a man so large. You're wondering how to answer his question, not knowing his full intentions. Elijah, seeing your hesitation, says, "It's okay, ma'am. I understand if you don't want to answer. I'm just making conversation. I'm walking as far south as Miller Street. You're welcome to walk with me, if you want. Don't think anybody will be bothering you if you do." You decide to trust this man. You give a timid smile and say, "Yes. Thank you, Elijah. I will, if it's okay. I'm just passing through, going south. I'm just trying to get home. This whole thing, event or whatever it is, has got people going crazy. I just don't know who I can trust." He replies, "You can call me Eli. You're right to be cautious, very cautious. This event, or as I've been told, EMP, has changed the whole world. Our lives are changed forever. Law and order is soon to be a thing of the past. The bad of some folks is going to come out and the good of others will flow to the top. But this world is changed. And more changes are coming." "What do you mean?" Eli continues "You see," waving his arm around, "all this is fine and dandy until the food runs out. Then there won't be no relief station or relief camp. Whatever you do, do not go to the relief camp. That will be the absolute worst place a woman alone can go. You seem like a cautious woman. I noticed how you put that bike between you and me. And I've noticed how you keep looking at the opening in your pack, as if there's something in there you really want to hold. A knife or a pistol, I guess. But that's okay, you need to be cautious, otherwise in this here new world, somebody is going to take advantage of you." You stutter and respond, "You're right, Eli. I wasn't meaning to insult you and I do thank you for what you did and . . . ." Eli interrupts you, "I told you, it's okay. It's what I would expect. We are coming up on Miller Street, where we'll part company. A little ways down, you will find the relief station. It's in the Walmart parking lot. Apparently the manager at Walmart turned the entire store over to the city. They're cooking up all the perishable food and serving it as relief aid. That's only going to last another day or two." Eli stops at the Miller Street intersection and continues: "The food is going to smell good, and it is good. I had some myself earlier. But unless you're really, really hungry, I suggest you don't stop and keep moving out of town." Puzzled you ask, "Why?" He says, "If you want to keep that bike, you better not stop. Now good day to you and I hope you make it to wherever you're going." He turns on to Miller Street and continues to walk. You say, "Okay, I won't stop. Thanks again. Oh yeah, I'm sorry, my name is Jill." Eli stops and turns, "And a good day to you Jill." Then returns to walking down the street, not turning back around.

You look around. There are dozens of people walking in both directions. You get on your bike. Pedaling all the way to the left side, you continue southward. The number of people increases as you approach Walmart. You see the tents set up. Many people are coming in and going out from both directions. The barbecue smell is so thick in the air. It smells so good and you are really hungry. You've only eaten two candy bars and drank three bottles of water since leaving Mary's. Maybe you could stop quickly and get some food and come right out. But then, Eli's words come to mind, "If you want to keep that bike you better not stop." You need your bike. It probably means life or death to you. You pedal on past Walmart.

There are still a lot of people coming in from the south. Looks like most are turning in to the relief station. You wonder how long they can feed people before the food runs out. Two days? Three days? You really have no idea and you don't plan on being here to find out. You approach the south road block and slow down. The officer waves you through. He says, "Have a nice day," as you pass by.

After going through the road block, there are fewer people heading south. Seems as if more are trying to get into Helena than get out. You start pedaling. Your legs are still very sore, and you're hungry. You've got to find a place to stop and eat something, but there are still too many people watching. Finally, after what seems like forever, you come to a bridge crossing a creek. You look and there is no one in front and no one behind. You quickly dismount your bike and push down the embankment into the tree line close to the creek. You stop and look all around. Seeing and hearing nothing, you push further into the woods along the creek. You keep going until you can't see the road any longer, then stop and park the bike. Again, you look carefully all around. Seeing nothing and hearing nothing, you grab your pack and sit with your back against a large tree. You look at the tree and wonder what kind it is. You never were real good at tree identification. Guess that's why you didn't become a forester.

After getting situated, you open your pack and pull out an MRE. It says ravioli. You don't want raviolis right now. You pull out the next pack. This one looks better, beef brisket. You put the other back and get an MRE bread pack. You decide not to build a fire, to just eat it cold. You open both packs and start eating. It's pretty tasty, though cold. You're hungry, so anything would taste good right now. You decide to splurge and get a flavor mix out and pour it in your bottle of water. You finish your meal. It's cool under the shade of the trees. You hear the flow of the creek. Your legs are sore. You decide to rest for a few minutes. A short nap is all you need. You close your eyes and drift to sleep, listening to the running of the creek water.

Sometime later, much later, you awake with a start. You can tell it's late, as the light seems to be less. Darn! You wanted to be through Montevallo by dark! You hurriedly pick up your gear. You're down to three bottles of water. You look at the creek. It'll take a while to filter and treat five bottles of water. The three bottles with your quart stainless steel bottle and the gallon jug in the basket should be enough, even through tomorrow. You should find water again before then. You load everything in the basket, including your MRE trash, and push back to the road. At the tree line you stop. Not seeing or hearing anything, you push up to the road. The road is clear. Getting on the bike, you start pedaling. Despite the continued soreness in your legs and back, you pedal hard. You haven't gone this fast all day. The road seems to be flying under your wheels. You turn south on CR17 and keep pedaling. There isn't a road block at Brantleyville and you pass through without slowing. There are a few people out and about, but no one bothers you as you speed through. Whew! That took a load off your mind. Another mile and you have to stop for a brief rest. Seems like you've been riding a couple of hours since you got back on the road. CR15 can't be too far ahead. If you hurry, you might actually make it through Montevallo before dark.

While pedaling, you wonder if there will be a road block. Montevallo is a bigger town and a university town at that. You'll just have to see. But you've got to hurry. You head straight across the intersection onto CR15. This should go to AL119 and then into Montevallo. You turn onto AL119. You're making good time. You must have covered at least 15 to 20 miles since leaving Helena. You press on, pushing your already sore legs. Your behind is starting to get sore, too. Another sore spot, that's all you need!

Up ahead are two stalled cars. That's nothing unusual, except these are stalled close to each other in opposite lanes. They are blocking the outside parts of the lanes, forcing you to the middle. You slow a bit, but continue at a steady pace, looking around. Something doesn't seem right. Is that a snake in the road? You pull your feet up as you get close to it. Suddenly, it jumps straight up! It hits you in the middle of your chest. Your body is jerked clear of your bike as you slam to the asphalt flat on your back. All your wind is knocked out. Your head hits the asphalt, and your mind fades to black.

Chapter 10 Jill - Day 2 - *Darkness...*

Your eyes are starting to flutter. You don't know where you are. Someone slaps you on the face. You hear voices, they seem so faint. "Leave her alone, Hank. Let her wake on her own. We're in no hurry." "The heck you say, Earl, I'm ready right now." "Hank you'll get your turn soon enough, just like last night." The sound fades away and darkness returns . . . .

Your eyes open. "She's awake, Hank," you hear. Suddenly, you feel your arms outstretched. They're being held down! You come completely conscious. Ignoring the throbbing pain in your head, you scream, "Get off me! Let me go!" You struggle trying to free yourself, but to no avail. The men are too big and too strong. There are three of them. One holding each arm down and another between your legs.

The one between your legs smiles, "Did you like our little rope trick? It worked real well too, except we didn't intend for you to go out cold. Honey, we been waiting for you to wake up. Now, let the party begin!" You quickly look around, its dark, a fire is going. You don't see your pack or your Glock. You don't know where you are or how long you've been unconscious. You're brought back to the moment when the guy in front of you rips the buttons off your shirt, pulling it aside. You scream, "Stop it!" The guy smiles big, "Honey, I like it when you talk dirty to me," as he pulls out his knife. It has a huge serrated blade. It looks nasty and dirty. You lay still, looking at the blade. "That's right, honey, you just lay still for a few more minutes," as he slides the cold steel underneath your bra. You close your eyes expecting to be cut, but instead he cuts your bra apart, exposing your breasts. He sets the knife on the ground and says "Now, honey, you can squirm all you want," as you feel his rough hands all over you. You scream again and you try to free your hands. But, they are just too strong. You can't move. "That's nice, honey. They are really soft. Let's see what else you have down here." The other two guys egg him on, "Hurry up, Earl!" His hands slide down and start undoing your pants. You scream again and become frantic. You're fighting for your life. You can't move your arms, but you kick with your legs. Earl is laughing. "The more fight, the more fun!" You managed to get one leg free and over and your shoe catches Earl full in the face. Earl curses, as you see blood on his face. The other two guys start laughing. Earl looks straight at you, evil in his eyes. He grabs your throat with one hand and squeezes. He slaps you hard across the face. You're stunned. Stars are forming in your vision. You're hoping you'll pass out, but instead you lay there conscious but unable to struggle. Earl smiles and says, "Now, honey, you're going to get what's coming to you," as he undoes your belt and unzips your pants. You pray in a whisper, "Dear God, help me. Help me, dear God." Out of the corner of your eye, you see the guy on your left flinch and fall to the side. Earl stops and says, "What the fu . . .," as you see a red mist appear from the side of his head and he crumbles to the side. The guy on your right starts to stand, then falls across your chest. His full weight knocks the air out of your lungs, as you fade to darkness again . . . .

Chapter 11 John - The Day - *Nor the next...*

You're driving on the interstate near Leeds, listening to "Sweet Home Alabama," as you're ending your day, heading back to Clarke County. You've just finished a project at a small industrial plant north of Leeds. The project went well, should be a nice profit. Well, there will be when your secretary gets the invoice ready for your approval, then sent to the project engineer for his approval, then to their accounting department, for their approval then . . . . Well, let's just say about 45 days from now. This project had been cancelled until yesterday. The plant had an unexpected down day and wanted you there for starting some equipment. The window of opportunity for such things is very short and unexpected some times. It has certainly made for a long day, but they pay well.

You're ready for a few days off. You and your son, Will, are taking that long awaited fishing trip. You hear a rooster crowing on the sound system, as your phone syncs with the truck's audio system. Will's calling. You answer, "Hey bud, what's up?" "Hey Dad, you on your way home?" You respond, "Yeah, I'm just getting back on the interstate at Leeds, should be home around 8:30." Will says, "Okay, that little blow that came through last night knocked a tree down across the fences in back of the pasture. When I got home from school, a couple of cows were out grazing away. I got them back in before they could get to Uncle Robert's grape vines." You say, "Whew, that's good, otherwise I'd have to listen to Robert complain all summer. How big a tree and how much damage?" Will says, "It's not real big, maybe 12 inches, but it landed on top of one of the wood posts, busted it and broke the wire." You think, 'Aw crap. There goes the fishing trip. That'll take nearly a day to get fixed.' You say, "Can you stretch a couple of strands of barb wire across to hold the cows in? We can fix it tomorrow. Do not try to cut the tree off." Will replies, "I've already stretched the barb wire. Don't worry, I won't be using the chainsaw." You say "Okay, then if you want, I'll pick a pizza up on the way in and see you around 8:30ish." Will says, "Sure Dad that sounds good. Love you. Drive safe." "Okay son. I love you, too. Bye." You stop the call not realizing you wouldn't be picking up pizza that night nor the next nor the next nor . . . .

Styx's 'Sailing Away' shuttles up to play from your iPhone. Yes, one of your favorites. Your dad listened to them when you were a kid and the tunes for the 80s just grew on you. You didn't realize how much music was out there that you didn't like, until you got satellite radio. Over a hundred stations and you decided to just play music from your iPhone. With the auto-bluetooth sync up, it's just as easy as selecting a satellite station. About the only thing you listen to on satellite is the news, but even Fox News has become more 'talking heads' than news. You're going to cancel your satellite service when you get back to the office. Ought to save at least three hundred dollars a year. It's a few minutes after 4:00 p.m., so you decide to turn to Fox News to catch the headlines. This is what you hear "This is a Fox News Alert – Fox News has just learned, the United Sates is under immediate threat of . . ." then nothing. The radio dies, your truck dies, and the dashboard gauges die. The truck starts coasting down. Aw great! On the interstate and your truck dies! You shift to neutral and try to crank again. Of course it won't crank. These new trucks will only crank while in park. You stay in neutral as you pull to the side of the road and stop. Just what you need. You put the transmission in park and try to crank again. Nothing! It must be an electrical problem. All the electrical items of the truck have quit working. You open the door, pop the hood and step out. Checking under the hood the battery connections look good. You retrieve your digital voltmeter and check the battery. Darn, the battery must be dead on your meter, as it doesn't come on. But the light is on under the hood so the battery connection must be good.

You look at your watch. It's 4:15. Then it hits you, no cars have passed by. You look around. Cars are stalled everywhere. People are milling about. You rush back for your phone, it's dead. Oh crap! It's actually happened! Somebody has done it. Doesn't matter if it was the Russians, Chinese, or

Islamic Terrorists, somebody has struck the U.S. with an EMP weapon. You wonder if the whole US has been hit or just the eastern seaboard. That will make a big difference in the long term, but for now, to you in this moment, it makes no difference. Your truck is dead, every vehicle as far as you can see is dead. Cell phones are dead. You wonder if the electric grid is down. You look off the interstate at an intersection. The traffic lights are out.

Over 200 miles from home and dead in the water. You start thinking this through. You've been through this mental exercise before. You've played it out in your mind. You're not scared, but you are concerned. You look back to the side of the interstate. There, on the service road, is a bicycle shop. It looks like a small business and not one of the megastores. The sign says, 'Clyde's Bike Shop.' The door is open. Here is your chance. You have two hundred dollars in your billfold. That won't be enough for what you need. You open the back door and under the backseat, you open the metal box bolted to the floor. You pull out several anti-static mylar bags. You open the first one. It has your old iPhone and a LED flashlight in it. You turn both on. Yes! They power up. Still, no cell service. You open the next bag. This has a Magellan GPS device with maps of Alabama already loaded. Yes! It works. Two more bags, these are a little larger. You pull out two Baofeng two-way radios and turn them on. Yes! They work. You remove a night vision monocular (NVD), turn it on with the filter cap still on. Yes! It works. One more bag. This one has some small miscellaneous items, like a USB battery charger, and small backup battery. You'll check those items later. Those guys on the survival forums knew what they were talking about. The metal box worked like a Faraday cage and protected your devices. Plus one for your plan.

But those items weren't your main objective. You want a bike. At the bottom of the box, you pull out a Merchants Bank envelope with one thousand dollars in cash and a small draw string bag with four ¼ oz. gold eagles and twenty 1 oz. silver eagles. This is something you always load up when going out of town. Okay, your plan is set for the moment. Putting the money and coins in your pocket, you lock and close the door. The Glock 19 is in your waistband; from the console you get an extra magazine and put it in your left pocket. Closing the door you lock it the old fashion way, by inserting the key into the lock and turning it. You look around to make sure you have no threats, now off to the bike store.

Clyde's Bike Shop is almost right across from you on the service road. You look to the exit ramp about a half mile away. You consider, half mile to the ramp, another quarter mile down the ramp, then whatever distance it is to the service road and then to the bike shop–hmm . . . that's over a mile. You decide to just climb the fence and cross the ditch. You won't be able to come back this way if you get the bike, but hey, it'll help now. You walk to the fence and consider the best way to cross without breaking a leg or spraining an ankle. That would be bad, really bad. You climb the fence and are on the ground on the other side in just a few minutes. You look back at your truck, wondering if you should have brought your pack. It has been less than an hour since the EMP and people probably won't be getting desperate and going crazy for a day or two, so the pack and other items in the truck are probably safe for the time being.

You cross the ditch, noticing some people watching. They don't appear to be a threat, so you continue to the bike shop. As you walk in the clerk says, "The power is out and our computers are down." You tell him you will be paying in cash. The clerk perks up "Cash? All right, come right in. My name is Clyde. I'm the proprietor of this here business. What are you looking for?" You tell him you are looking for a quality cross country bike and a trailer. After thinking a moment, he says "I've got several options for you. If you're looking for quality, then I suggest this bike here. It's made of light weight titanium, has adjustable suspension, quick release tire clamps and 18 speeds." You look at the price tag—$395. Wow! But you say, "Okay. How about a trailer?" You follow him over to a row of trailers. He says "This one would work well, made of the same material and spring shocks. It also has a nylon top to help keep things dry." You look at its price tag—$225. Wow, again. Normally you would do a lot of research before making this kind of purchase, but that's not an option now. "Ok. I'll take both. I'll also need an air pump, a couple of tire repair kits, a water bottle attachment and water bottle, and a chain lock." Clyde thinks again and says "I've got all that." Clyde gathers the items together and walks to the counter. He starts writing your ticket and adds the cost. You see the total $720. Clyde stops, looks up and says. "Since, you're paying cash, let's just call it $700 and no tax." You pull out the envelope and pay him $700.

After finishing at the counter, Clyde helps you get things situated on your bike. You mount the pump and water bottle. After some small talk, you head to the door with your bike complete and trailer attached. Clyde follows and says, "Wonder what knocked the power out and how long it'll be out?" You pause and consider Clyde. Then respond, "I'm not sure, but I think we've been hit with an EMP weapon. I don't think the power will be back on for a very long time." Clyde shakes his head "Okay, whatever you say, but it'll be back on in an hour or so is my guess. Probably lost a major transformer somewhere." Not wanting to get into a debate about it, you say, "Yeah, you're probably right." You get on the bike and head to the road.

At the road, you stop and consider things. It's too late to get through town and into the country before dark and you really don't want to be traveling after dark, at least not yet. You look at your truck across the fence. You're going to have to pedal the long way around. Do you want to spend the night in the truck? How secure is that going to be with people, perhaps, walking the interstate during the night? What if someone comes looking for things in vehicles while you're sleeping in your truck? You really don't want that encounter. Further down the service road you see a Drury Inn and a Hampton Inn and, yes, right in between them, an old Family Inns of America. You turn down the road to the motels.

You pull into the Family Inn. The door is open to the small lobby. You chain your bike to a steel pole outside and walk in. There is a Pakistani behind the counter. "The power is off and our computers are down." You reply, "That's not a problem. I have cash and only need a room for one night." The clerk thinks for a minute and says "Okay, it's $75 plus tax." He puts a sheet of paper on the counter and a pen. He pauses, thinking; the power is out, the computers are down, the camera system is down, cash is being used. He pulls the paper off the counter and looks at you and says, "$75 please." You pay him and ask for a ground floor room. He hands you a key to room 114. As you walk out, he puts the money in his pocket.

You return to your bike. After stowing the chain, you pedal back up the service road to the off ramp. There are quite a few people walking now. All of them are walking down the off ramp, while you're riding up the ramp. A few give you an odd look, a couple try to talk. You don't like being rude, but you keep going without saying a word. You get to your truck and look around. Everything seems to be ok. Time to load up and head to the room. It's 6:45 p.m. You need to get moving. You don't want to be biking here in the dark.

Chapter 12 John - The Day - *Ready for the night...*

You take your bike and trailer to the off road side of the truck. There aren't many people walking past now and they are sticking to the middle of the road. That's good. You walk back around to the driver's door, insert the key and unlock the door, hit the power unlock button, and of course nothing happens. Duh! The electronic systems are shot in the truck. Guess in these newer trucks, the computers handle all controls. Wonder if they would work in a 1990 model? You don't know. You have to stay focused. You don't have much time till dark. You climb in the truck and try to unlock the other doors by hand, but as earlier, you can't get your fingers on the locks. You take your multi-tool from the holder on your belt, open it and use it to grab the door locks. You grimace as the multi-tool scratches up the door. You unlock each one, then exit the truck.

Looking around again, you move to the passenger side of the truck and open the front door. On the passenger seat, you pick up the Payday candy bar and pack of peanut butter crackers. You put the crackers in your shirt pocket and open the Payday. You're hungry and take a big bite. Tastes good. You get the half full water bottle from the cup holder and drink it all. Opening the glove box, you find the registration, insurance card, a state map and a few other papers. The same map is already in your pack, so you leave it. There is nothing in here really of any use right now. From the console, you pull out your second extra magazine for the Glock and two single magazine holsters for your belt. You clip both to your left hip, just behind your multi-tool. You insert this magazine, loaded with 147 gr. Remington hollow point sub-sonic 9mm rounds in the back holder. You retrieve the other extra magazine from you left pocket and insert it in the front holder. This magazine is loaded with 135 gr. Hornandy Critical Duty 9mm rounds. You pull out a small LED light. It's one of those single AA models. They are bright and cheap. You turn it on. It works. It's definitely going along. Thinking about it, you pull your Fenix light from your belt. It works, too. Good. You were really wondering if these LEDs would work after an EMP. You also retrieve nail clippers, note pad, pen and a USB thumb drive. You have no idea if the thumb drive will work, but it's light so you put it in your pocket. You consider the others items. There are duplicates in your pack, but for now you decide to take these as well. There are a few other things, but nothing worth taking.

You move to the back of the truck, looking all around. In the back you open your pack and remove the mylar bags from the metal box and put them in. From the floor, you pick up an Academy Sports bag containing 200 rounds of 9mm Winchester full metal jacket (FMJ) rounds. You place the ammo in the pack and, getting out of the truck, you move to the tailgate, open it and slide the cooler to the edge. Opening it, you pull the dozen bottles of water and four Gatorades out of the icy water and put them in the plastic Academy Sports bag. You close the cooler, the tailgate and place the bag in the trailer. Jumping back in the rear seat, you grab the six MREs from the box on the backseat and put them in the trailer. You grab the small, single man tent and sleeping pad from under the backseat and place them in the trailer. You look at your tool bag. There's no way to take the whole bag. Thinking, you grab the crescent wrench from the bag, go around to the driver's door and, reaching in, pop the hood. Looking around again, you proceed to unhook the positive side of the battery. You lay the wrench on the battery and close the hood. As you do you wonder, "Why did I do that?" Maybe, somebody might need a battery. Who knows why you did it, you just didn't want the battery to drain down. You go back to the truck. One more thing to do before loading the pack. You pull your laptop from its case. You just bought it two weeks ago. It took more than two days to get all the software loaded and set up. You set it on the floor board. You turn it on. Nothing happens, just as you suspected. You pick a hammer out of your tool bag and proceed to smash it to bits until you find the hard drive, then you smash the hard drive. You get your dead iPhone and do the same. They don't work, and you're not going to take them with you. As a matter of principle, you don't want to leave any of your data, private or business, lying around. You lock all your doors, pull your pack and close up. Putting your pack in the trailer, you walk around the truck one more time. It was a good truck. You've had it for two years. A Ford 4X4 STX. That baby cost you $50,000. Well, two years' worth of 0% interest payments, anyway. Now, it's just a marvelous piece of useless metal and plastic. You open the fuel door, place the key inside and close the door. You walk to the bike. Looking around, you pull out onto the road, heading for the hotel.

The trailer is heavy and it makes getting started difficult. You adjust the gears until you find a happy one and continue down the interstate. Driving down the off ramp, you pass a few people without speaking. It's getting dusk and you want to be off the road. Ten minutes later, you pull into the Family Inn parking lot. You locate room 114. Opening the door, you draw your Glock and clear the room. You don't want any surprises. You push your bike and trailer inside as it becomes darker outside. Closing the door, you set the deadbolt and door latch. You make sure the curtains are closed. Turning on your flashlight you point it toward the ceiling. The room is washed in white light. Pulling your pack from the trailer, you locate one of your emergency candles, set it up in one of the glass cups and light it. You place it by the mirror, trying to get as much illumination as possible. It's not real bright, but that's ok, you don't want anybody knowing you have light. You turn your flashlight back off and place it back in its holster.

Opening your pack, you pull three items. One is a tall nylon pull string bag, the other two are molle type equipment carriers. Out of the nylon bag you remove a Kel-Tec Sub 2k 9mm folding carbine. This carbine uses the same magazines as your Glock 19, which makes things simpler, especially for your purposes. You unfold the carbine and lock it into position. You remove the magazine and make sure the gun is unloaded. Out of the second bag, you retrieve a Burris Fast Fire III red dot sight. It's mounted on a quick detachable picatinny mount. You turn it on. You're in luck. It works. You wonder why, but you don't have a clue. You're just thankful it does. You mount it forward on the upper forend top rail. You reach up and unscrew the thread protector, exposing ½ x 28 threads at the end of the barrel. After placing the thread protector in the bag you just opened, you open the final bag. Inside is a Gemtech GM9 sound suppressor. You screw it onto the end of the barrel. You insert the magazine and chamber a round. You lay it on the bed beside you. You double check your billfold to make sure the tax stamp for the suppressor is there. You don't want any trouble with an overzealous police officer or federal agent. You pull one more item out, your night vision monocular (NVD) and set it by the carbine.

You take off your boots and blow out the candle. Returning, you lay back down on the bed. You pat the carbine next to you and the Glock on the night stand. You're tired. Your day started very early this morning. This is the first time your mind hasn't been busy developing and executing plans. You'll plot your route home in the morning, when there is more light. For now you lay back and relax. You start thinking of Will. You wonder if he's figured out what's going on. You have talked about this very event with Will before. You have plans and even an action plan written down. If he follows the plan, he should be fine until you get home in a week or so.

You pray to God, asking for his protection as you drift off to sleep . . . .

Chapter 13 John - Day 1 - *Heading home...*

Your eyes open. You don't need to look at your watch. Its 5:00 a.m., the same time you get up every day. The same time you've gotten up nearly every day as far back as you can remember. The same time your dad got you up every day as a kid. It didn't matter if it was a school day, Sunday, or a holiday. You were up at 5:00 a.m. Well, that's not exactly true. There were those days when Kathy kept you up late at night and those mornings when she kept you in till late, but there hasn't been one of those days in over two years. It's still dark in the room, with just a faint light seeping around the edges of the curtains. That's one thing you've always been impressed with in motel curtains, their ability to block out all light, regardless of the time of day. It's too dark inside to move around. You reach for your flashlight and turn it on low, point it toward the ceiling and wash the whole room with soft light.

First thing, you pick the room phone up checking for a dial tone. Nothing. You turn the lamp on. Nothing. You walk to the bathroom and flip the switch. Nothing. You walk back to the bed and retrieve your Glock from the nightstand. Tucking it and its holster into your waistband, you walk to the curtain and open it slightly. The dim light from the early morning seeps in through the opening. You look out, studying the surroundings and don't see anything out of the ordinary, except there are no street lights, no building lights and no traffic moving. Seeing nobody moving around, you unbolt the door and lift the latch. Outside it's eerily quiet. No sounds of traffic. You've never been in a city that you couldn't hear the sounds of traffic, regardless the time of day. Something else you sense, the faint smell of smoke. You had hoped you were wrong about the EMP and that things would be ordinary again. But they're not. The world has changed and it's going to get bad, real bad, just as soon as everybody else figures it out.

While you're standing looking around, another door opens two doors down and a man steps out wearing jeans, no shoes and no shirt. He says, "Morning," you grunt a "morning" back. He says "Looks like trying times ahead. What you reckon happened?" You're really not wanting to get into a conversation this morning. You have too much to do. You answer, "Not sure. Looks bad." The man lights a cigarette, takes a drag and says, "You know, I'm thinking it might be an EMP. I was talking with some co-workers last week, who call themselves preppers. Well, this seems like something they described. If it is, we're screwed." "Yeah it's scary for sure," you reply. "Where are you from?" The man says, "From Meridian. Now, how the heck am I supposed to get back to Meridian, Mississippi?" You consider him for a few moments, then reply, "How about riding a bike? I'm going to south Alabama and that's what I'm doing." He responds, "Yeah right, as if I could pedal a bike that far. No, I'm just going to sit here a few days and see what happens. The government will be around to coordinate things soon." "Yeah they might" you say, "but I wouldn't count on it. If you want a bike, there is a bike shop just down the road." He responds "Nah, I'm just going to wait it out a little longer. If things don't look up in a day or two I'll get a bike then." You say, "Best of luck to you," and go back inside. If this guy doesn't get a bike today, he won't be getting one period.

You lock the door, flip the latch, leave the curtain slightly open, and move a chair in front of the door. You decide to get the day going. You grab some clean boxers and socks from the pack and head to the shower. The water is cold. You rush through, washing your hair quickly. Getting out, you dry off and dry your hair with a towel. You get dressed putting your same pants and shirt on. You pick your Glock off the counter and tuck it and its IWB holster in your waistband. You run your fingers through you hair, combing it as best you can. You had a haircut right before coming to Leeds, so it ought to dry quickly.

You need more light, so checking through the window again, you open the curtain wider. The morning light begins to flood in. You decide to eat something before planning the day. Taking your Esbit stove out of your pack, you place it and a fuel tab in the microwave. You get your stainless cup and decide to fill it with tap water to conserve your water supply. You set the cup on the Esbit stove and light the fuel tab. While the water is heating, you pull one of your sustainment packs from your bag and retrieve a pack of instant coffee, creamer and two oatmeal packs. Looking around, you pick up two coffee cups from the bathroom sink. You pour the oatmeal into one and the coffee into the other. When the tab burns out, you remove the cup and pour half into the oatmeal and half into the coffee mug. You stir each with a spoon from your pack and sip the coffee while the oatmeal soaks. The coffee is warm but not hot. It certainly doesn't taste like a brew, but it's better than nothing. You check the oatmeal, it's ready, though a little dry. You needed more water, but you eat it like it is. Peaches and cream, not bad. Between bites, you retrieve an Emergen-C pack and a multi-vitamin. You mix the Emergen-C with a glass of tap water and use it to take the multi-vitamin. You know your diet is likely to be lean on essential vitamins for the next week or so. You clean everything up and put your equipment back in your pack. Now, for planning.

You pull out your map and the handheld GPS. Studying the map, you plot a route to help you minimize towns. But, first, you have to get through Leeds. You want to hit AL119 and take it down to Montevallo. Looks like the best thing to do right now is to get back on the interstate and take the next exit then work your way to AL119. You think about taking more street roads to AL119, but decide you're likely to encounter larger groups of people in more confined spaces. That is what you hope to avoid as much as possible. You trace your route on the map, using a red pen to make it easier to find while on the road. You turn the GPS on. It starts searching for satellites. Come on baby, come on. Finally it picks up a GPS signal. You program your route. The GPS figures 230 miles from your current location. So if you can average 40 miles per day, maybe more, you ought to be home in less than a week. That's good because it looks like you have enough food for nearly ten days, if you are careful. It'll speed your journey if you don't have to hunt or scavenge for food. You have about a two day water supply. As long as you can find running water along the way, you can filter it for use. You've planned for a situation like this. Your pack is filled with supplies to make this journey. Your plan is good. The key is the bike. The only way you can carry enough food to make it home is by using the bike. Without the bike, your trip will take much longer and your ability to carry food will be greatly reduced. Both would be really bad. You can't let anyone take your bike. Period. It could very well mean the difference between life and death.

You decide to change holsters for the Glock. You noticed yesterday the inside the waistband holster didn't ride well while on the bike. You pull a Combat Arms paddle holster from your pack and slip the paddle inside your pants. This won't conceal the Glock very well, but it is an easy to use and secure holster. You'll just put your shirttail over it. Later, out of town, you'll just carry it open. But for now, it's probably best to keep it hidden as much as possible.

You unload your carbine, remove the suppressor and red dot sight. You reinstall the thread protector, fold the carbine and put it back in the pack, but not inside the nylon bag. You want quick access to it. You put the suppressor and the red dot into the suppressor carrier and place it by the carbine. You then load up the NVD. Checking around, it looks like you have everything. You zip your pack and load it into the trailer. You head out the door. The guy a few doors down is dragging on another cigarette. He nods his head toward you as you mount your bike and head toward the road. You stop at the road and look all ways. It looks clear. You check your watch. It's 8:30 a.m. You start pedaling back for the interstate.

Chapter 14 John - Day 1 - *Officer Brunson...*

As you pass Clyde's Bike Shop, the door is open and Clyde is standing in the doorway. He waves and you wave back. He seemed like a nice guy. You hope he makes it. One thing you feel certain of, within two days he will either have sold all his bikes or somebody will steal all his bikes. It doesn't take long to make it to the on-ramp. You notice the Love's station has activity in the lot and around the door as you pass by. As much as you would like to use your money while it still has value, you just can't risk the stop. You can't risk your bike. You've got to keep your bike.

You pull up onto the on ramp. The incline forces you to change gears. Pedaling becomes easier but slower. This is going to be a workout. You wonder how sore you're going to be tomorrow. Your buns are going to be sore for sure. You make it to the top with the trailer in tow. This is going to be a tough ride home, but you thank God for providing the bike. You pass a lot of stalled cars. Most are off the roadway, as the drivers pulled them over as they slowed down. But there are still some here and there where the drivers just let them stop in the road just as they were driving. You've got a couple of miles to make the next exit. Full speed is impossible because of the stalled cars everywhere, but you're moving at a pretty good pace.

You look back every now and then to check your back. So far, so good. No problems. Guess there is a day or two before things really go crazy. Hopefully, by then, you'll be long gone from here. About fifty yards ahead, a man steps out from behind a stalled car and moves into the road waving his arms. Oh crap. He's not holding a gun so you think of speeding up and driving right past, but he does have one on his hip. He's also wearing a dark blue uniform with a badge on his chest. You bring the bike to a stop about twenty feet away. This isn't going to be good. Your adrenaline starts flowing. You force yourself to calm down. The guy says, as he walks closer, "I'm sorry, but I've got to have your bike. Official business. Please get off." You're stunned by what he just said. He wants your bike. Your adrenaline is really pumping. You continue to force yourself to stay calm. You say, "Officer, I just bought this bike yesterday. I've got to have it to get home. I can't let you have my bike." He says, "I'm sorry, but I'm going to have to take your bike. You can go to the station and file some forms and they'll compensate you when things return to normal." Yeah right. You respond, "Officer, there is a bike shop just a mile or so back that way. Why not just get one there?" He's getting a little agitated and says, "I don't have time for this crap." You notice then his badge says Gadsen Police Department. You're nowhere near Gadsen. Official Police business my ass. But it doesn't matter either way. You can't give up your bike. He quickly draws his Taser and says, "If you don't get off the bike, I'm going to tase you." Your mind quickly goes through some scenarios on how to get out of this. One thing is certain, if you make the wrong move you're going to get tased. If you get tased you're going to lose your bike, trailer and everything. At this range, the guy can't miss. Anger grows inside you. You force calm again and raising your hands a little at your side say, "Okay, officer." You get off the bike. He's walked right up to you, keeping his Taser raised and aimed. You ask, "Can I keep my trailer?" He responds, "Yeah sure, but hurry up." You turn your body as to start unhitching the trailer. Your gun hip is away from the officer. He obviously hasn't notice your gun with your shirt covering it, otherwise he would have pulled his pistol instead of the Taser. Out of the corner of your eye, you notice the officer seems to have relaxed some and lowered the Taser slightly. In a flash, you draw your Glock just like you've practiced a thousand times before. You turn bringing it up. The officer's eyes widen as he raises his Taser. You quickly step closer and with your left hand you grab his forearm pushing it to the left and away from your body. You hear the '*ping*' of the Taser release, as the probes pass by, only an inch from your body. You raise your Glock and stepping even closer, you put the muzzle in the man's neck. This all happens in a moment. Decisive, aggressive action, is what Col. Jeff Cooper wrote about in his book, <u>Principles of Personal Defense</u>. He was right. It worked here.

With your Glock to his neck, the officer becomes motionless. He says, "Please, don't kill me." You don't say a word as you reach for and unholster his sidearm. You put it in your left rear pocket. Then you command, "Drop the Taser." It clangs on the roadway. "Raise your arms," he complies. With his back toward you, and the gun still at his neck, you push him to a nearby car. You back away while holding the gun pointed at his head and say, "Cuff yourself to the door latch real slow." He complies and asks, "What are you going to do to me?" You respond by walking up and removing his can of MACE and tossing it aside. You then put the muzzle in his crotch, as you bend down searching for his backup weapon. You find it on the inside of his left ankle. You remove it, straighten up and back away. You then holster your own Glock. A few people have started to gather. You say, "This man just tried to steal my bike. Everyone stay back." No one appears to be armed and none approach. You turn back in anger to the officer and say, "Why? Why were you going to steal my bike? You're an officer from Gadsen. You've got no official business to take my bike. Why?" While saying this you unload his backup gun, a Glock 27 in 40 caliber. You pull the magazine and eject the chambered round from the pistol, letting it fall to the roadway. Then proceed to unload the bullets from the magazine letting them fall onto the ground before dropping the empty magazine. Pulling the slide back slightly, you push the take down bar downward and pull the trigger. With a slight push on the slide, both it and the barrel come off. You toss the frame to the ground. Then removing the spring and barrel from the slide you, drop them to the road as well.

The officer looks at you, with tears forming in his eyes. He says, "My wife is home, pregnant with our first child. She's due today. I was just trying to get to her. I'm sorry. I'm afraid for my wife!" You pull his duty weapon from your rear pocket. It's a Glock 22, a bigger brother to the Glock 27. You unload and disassemble it as well. Looking at his name tag you say, "Well, Officer Brunson that's a moving story, if it's true. So you wanted to steal my bike, not caring about me getting to my family. That's just pathetic and it pisses me off. Toss me those two spare magazines." He does and you unload them as before. He asks again, "What are you going to do to me?" You say,

"I ought to get your cuff keys and toss them in the grass. How much money do you have?" He looks confused, but responds, "What . . . ? I have a hundred dollars in my billfold." You pull the Merchants Bank envelope from your pocket and hand it to him saying, "Here is $200. Down the interstate at the next exit is a bike shop. With this and the money you have you might be able to get a bike. When I'm out of sight, you can uncuff yourself. If you uncuff while I can see you, I will shoot you. You understand?" The officer says, "Yes I understand. Thank you. I don't know really what to say." You respond, "I do. You're lucky I didn't kill you."

You hear a sound behind you and turn to look. A man has jumped on your bike and started off. You holler, "Stop!" He doesn't. Without hesitation you draw your Glock line the bright orange Trijicon front site with the fleeing man and fire three rapid shots. The first shot hits him in the tricep of his left arm shattering the bone. The second enters his back breaking ribs at his shoulder blade. The third shatters his T3 vertebra and severs his spinal cord. He slumps and he and the bike fall to the ground. You look around for more threats. You don't see any. You run to your bike. You pull and disentangle the man from it. Setting the bike back right, you check the trailer. Everything is still there. Looking around one more time, there is a stunned look on everyone's face. You holster your Glock, get on your bike and head off. You're back on plan. But you were wrong. It didn't take a couple of days for things to go crazy. They're crazy right now and you're right in the middle of it!

Chapter 15 John - Day 1 - *On the road...*

You pedal hard, trying to put distance between you and the scene behind. You look back. Officer Brunson is just standing there, looking in your direction. You wonder if he's going to come after you. No, he's not going to come after you. He wants to get home to his wife. Besides, he's got to put his guns back together. Then what? Chase you down on foot? No. He's going to uncuff himself, put his guns back together, reload his magazines then run down the interstate to get a bike. You'll never see him again.

But what if this isn't an EMP? A civilization changing event? You gave him a Merchants Bank envelope. How hard would it be to tie that to the registration on your abandoned truck? You shot and probably killed a man. Over what? A bicycle? The realization of what you've done and the crash from the adrenaline rush have you shaking. You have to stop. You look back, half-expecting Officer Brunson to be aiming his Glock at you but, you can't even see him. He must be at least a mile away. You feel nauseated and stop. You pull the water bottle from the bike. Taking a mouthful, you swish it around in your mouth, afraid to swallow for fear of throwing up. You spit it out. Your hands are shaking as you return the bottle to its carrier. You've got to get out of here! You've got to get out of the city! You've got to go now! You feel panic rising inside you. Panic can get you killed. You force yourself to calm down. You didn't kill that man over a bicycle. You killed him over your own life and that of your son. There was no other choice. If you had hesitated at all, he would have been beyond your skill to stop him. You would be stranded without a ride, without food, without water and without your essential gear and supplies. No, you didn't kill him over a bicycle. He tried to kill you by taking the only things that would keep you alive.

There's no more time for introspection now. That will be done later. Now, you have to get back to your plan. Nothing has changed. Keep your mind focused on what's at hand, worry about the other later. You whisper, "Lord help me," as you start pedaling down the interstate.

Nearing your exit, you see smoke over the city. There must be fires burning. The newer fire trucks, with their computer and electronic controls, probably won't work. If they were able to get a pumper out to the scene, they would probably deplete the city's stored water quickly making a bad situation worse even sooner. You take the off-ramp and see another crowded trucker service station. You don't stop. A few folks look your way, but no one attempts to interfere. You remember the route you planned and take the next right, then a mile further you take a left through a residential area. Clinton Drive will lead to AL119, from there you'll be out of the city and on toward Montevallo. There are two police officers at the intersection. They look at you. Inside you tense. You look at the one on the right. He nods at you, and you nod back, as you continue making your right turn.

Shortly, you turn onto Clinton Drive. There are houses on either side of the street. People are milling about and kids are playing in yards and on the street. It looks like a typical weekend morning. Things look normal. It's the first normal you've seen since yesterday. Too bad, it's not going to last. These people just don't have a clue as to what's coming their way. They should be out trying to buy supplies or a means of transportation. You hope they've thought enough to catch containers of water. Do they realize this is not a typical power outage? Phones don't work, the power is out, cars don't work, and the internet is down. You wonder how long before it sinks into the average person that the world as we knew it is gone.

Tough times are going to bring out the best and sometimes the worst in people, just like what you experienced this morning. But you refuse to let your mind go there for now. Kids playing some kind of round ball game in the street part ways, making room for you to pass. A little further, a little girl is out riding her bike. She waves as you pass. You smile and wave back. She falls in behind you, trying to keep up, but she falls further behind and soon gives up. This is a nice, peaceful looking neighborhood. Lots of oak trees shading the street. Things are going to be changing though, real soon. It's fortunate, if fortunate can be used, that this event occurred in early spring.

At least folks will have a chance to plant a garden, if they can find seed and tools for tilling the ground.

You turn onto AL119, feeling a little better. You pedal south, crossing the Leeds city limits. Soon the area is more rural and you feel even better. Few people are on the road. Then you hear an engine running, maybe two. From a dirt road, out shoot two 4-wheelers. Teenage boys are at the helm, with girls sitting behind them. They hit the pavement and turn south, laughing as they speed away. You look for a place to stop for lunch. Finally, there is a stretch with no one in either direction. You turn onto a dirt road leading into a pasture. Trees are on either side for a ways, then, after about a hundred yards, the pasture opens up. You move to the fence line and pull your bike into the thick brush, look all around and listen. Not seeing or hearing anything, you retrieve your pack, a couple of bottles of water and sit against a pecan tree facing the highway. The lower brush around the tree should obscure eyes from the highway from seeing you.

You're not queasy anymore. You've forced yourself not to think of the earlier events, but you are hungry. You pull a single-serving pack of Spam, MRE bread and a squeeze packet of mayo, slice the bread open and put the Spam inside. Squeezing the mayo, you make yourself a sandwich and bite in. Not too bad when you're hungry. You open a bottle of water and take a long drink. You should have been drinking more water, but your stomach wouldn't allow it. From your pack, you pull a small bottle of Milo water flavor. Coconut/pineapple is your favorite. You squeeze a little into your bottle and drink it down. Then, you open the second bottle and add a little to it. You finish your sandwich, and pulling a Walmart bag from your pack, you pick up the trash. Your watch says it's 12:30. Your GPS shows you've gone about 12 miles since this morning. Putting the GPS back in your right shirt pocket, you pull your iPhone from your left shirt pocket. Turning it on, you still have no cell service. No surprise. You set the alarm for 30 minutes and the volume at mid-level, then pull your cap over your eyes and drift to sleep.

You wake to the sound of a buzzing car horn. You look at your phone and turn the alarm off. Then you turn the phone off and put it back in your pocket. You realize you haven't reloaded your magazine. You dig into your pack and retrieve three 135 gr. Hornady Critical Duty 9mm rounds. You retrieve the magazine from your Glock and add the rounds. Holstering the pistol, you check your watch. Its 1:10, time to get moving, but first you pull a roll of TP from your pack. The call of nature . . . .

You're back on your bike, at the end of the dirt road, getting ready to hit the highway. You hear engine noise again. From the sound of it, it's not a 4-wheeler. You look north and coming fast is an old beat up blue and rust Chevrolet truck. Actually, it looks more rust than blue, maybe a late 70's model. As it approaches, the passenger hangs out the window and hurls a beer bottle at you, missing by several feet. Curse words fill the air. The truck slows, then turns around for another pass. You turn your bike and head back down the dirt road into the field. There's no time to retrieve your carbine. The truck pulls into the dirt road and stops. You can hear cussing and what sounds like arguing. They back out and head back south. You stop. Sitting on your bike, you listen. After not hearing anything for about 30 minutes, you ease out to the road. It's clear, so you start back south.

Having to worry about these idiots is just dandy. You pedal south, constantly looking all around and listening for the truck. You don't hear or see anything. About two hours later a wrecked 4-wheeler appears on the side of the road. It is one of the ones you saw earlier. There is a body on the ground. You stop and after looking all around, approach cautiously. It's one of the teenage boys. He's dead. He has a bullet hole in his chest. You wonder if it was those idiots in the truck that did this. What about the other kids, where are they? There is no clue. You check the kid for ID. You say to yourself, 'Allen Helms, I'm sorry I can't do anything for you.' You check the 4-wheeler. It's damaged beyond your ability to repair. You get back on the road, being more wary than before. After another two more hours, you start looking for a place to spend the night. You've passed a few houses along the way and really don't want to spend the night anywhere near one of them. Finally, a little before dusk you see an old hay barn on the side of a field. Checking to make sure the coast is clear, you pedal to the barn. After clearing the barn for any threats you pull your bike in and close the sagging door. This is going to be your hotel for the night.

Chapter 16 John - Day 1 - *Introspection …*

You back the bike and trailer between two round hay bales. There is a slight musty smell to the air. This hay must be left over from last year. Hopefully, it won't give you a sinus headache. You don't need one of those. You get your pack and ground pad and, spying a spot with lots of loose hay, roll your mat out and place the pad and sleeping bag on top. Trying to keep weight and bulk to a minimum in your pack, you had purchased a thin down-filled sleeping bag rated for 20F. It is small and weighs very little, but it offers very little padding. While there is still some light filtering in through the cracks of the barn, you assemble the components on the carbine. In addition to the suppressor and red dot, you also attach an infrared (IR) laser and a high output flash light. The IR laser is mounted under the barrel on a picatinny rail below the red dot sight. The flash light is mounted on the right side rail. Either can be activated with your fingers while holding the forend. All of the devices use quick detach, QD mounts. The whole idea behind this carbine is to keep it compact, readily assessable and quickly rigged with essential components. While the IR laser is invisible to bare eyes, it works well with the NVD. With the NVD on, you just put your laser on the target. No one without an NVD will be able see it. You and Will have done a few night exercises at the range with the weapon. With the NVD, IR laser and suppressor, the carbine makes a fairly stealthy nighttime weapon. You chamber a round and verify the safety, then lean it against the wall next to your sleeping bag. You pull out the NVD, attach it to the head gear and lay it next to the carbine.

You want something hot to eat but really don't want to build a fire in a hay barn. You decide to heat some water using the Esbit stove and a fuel tab and re-hydrate some freeze dried Mountain House chicken and rice. It's one of your favorites. You have three double-serving packs in your bag. A good thing about freeze dried foods is they are lightweight and tasty. They don't prepare as fast as an MRE, but they are lighter and do require water to prepare. Placing the stainless steel water cup full of water on the Esbit stove, you light the fuel tab. Within a few minutes the water is hot. You open the chicken and rice package and add the hot water. After stirring it well and sealing it back up, you let it sit for about 15 minutes while the water is absorbed into the food. While waiting, you decide to clean up a bit. Pulling a wash cloth and soap from your hygiene kit, you proceed to wash your face, neck, and arms. You drink another bottle of water while munching on a fruit trail mix bar. When the chicken and rice is ready, you open it and, using a spoon from your pack, proceed to eat. It's good, considering the little you've had today. Warm food is always better than cold food. Except of course for ice cream. You drink another bottle of water while eating. There are two plastic bottles and two 32 oz. stainless bottles filled with water remaining. Something is going to have to be done about water tomorrow. Before closing your pack for the night, you place your morning breakfast materials at the top. Coffee and oatmeal. Peaches and cream again.

You're tired, so you move to your sleeping bag and set the pack down for a pillow. Wonder how well that's going to work? It's getting dark, so you turn on a small battery powered glow stick, the kind that has multi-functions, like low glow, bright glow, strobe and even a pen light. Set to low it gives just enough light to see right around your immediate area, but not enough to be seen through the cracks. You strip to your boxers and socks, crawl into the bag, and search for the soft spot on your pack. You really should have figured a way to pack a pillow. You attach the Streamlight TLR1 light to your Glock. It is kept in the same pouch as the high output light you attached to the carbine. You lay the Glock in the sleeping bag with you, settle in, and make sure the NVD and carbine are within easy reach.

Now is time to review the day and a bit of introspection. It's time to put into perspective your thoughts and actions and decide if you have acted appropriately this day. What a day! You've never experienced anything like it. You've been training and preparing yourself for tough situations all your life. It's one of those things your dad ingrained into your mind. "Son," your dad would often say, "think about the things that could happen, the likelihood that they will happen, how bad it will be if they do happen, then plan accordingly." It's really just a personal application of SWOT analysis taught in business school. Contingency planning is something done in business all the time. Why those same people and countless others don't apply those same concepts to personal planning is beyond you. Burying your head in a hole in the ground has never been your idea of a good plan. You're a realist and a planner. You see what is in front of you and consider things that could happen, the likelihood that those things could happen, and the negative impact of those things. Then, you develop a plan taking all those things into consideration. You've watched the show Doomsday Preppers and while some are kind of interesting, most are extreme. You don't have to be a Doomsday Prepper to live a prepared life. That's the key—living a prepared life. With just a few minor adjustments, people could do so much now to make things better when bad things do happen.

This EMP event has not caught you completely unaware. You didn't know it was coming yesterday, if you had you would have stayed home. You have a plan. You have the gear and supplies to make it home. It's not by accident your pack was in your truck, it wasn't by accident your Glock was on your hip, it wasn't by accident food and water were in your pack and truck, it wasn't by accident your sensitive electronics were protected by a Faraday cage, it wasn't by accident you have clothes, cooking supplies, hygiene supplies, a carbine with suppressor and attachments, and it wasn't by accident you had the money to buy a bike. You are prepared. Fortunately for you, very fortunate indeed, the bike shop at the interstate was owned by an individual and not some superstore. The superstores would have all been shut down because of no computers.

You play the events of the day through your mind. The guy at the motel: As unprepared as he could be. He had an idea what happened, but no clue as to its full implications. He'll never see Meridian, Mississippi again. You wonder about his family and if they will ever know what happened to him. Will they survive without him?

You think about your encounter with Officer Brunson. He was a young man who was desperate, and a desperate man will do crazy and stupid things. He tried to use your respect for law enforcement to trick you into submission and steal your bike. Most people would have just given it up. Would you under similar circumstances, being desperate, do the same as he? You don't know. But you have gone to great lengths to prepare yourself and make sure you don't find yourself in desperate situations. You have no intention of allowing anyone to turn you into a desperate person. You consider how violent the encounter could have been had you not taken decisive, aggressive and prompt action. What if you had decided to carry your pistol open rather than concealed? You thought about it both ways before you left the Family Inn. You chose to conceal it as best you could. Would things have been different if Officer Brunson had seen your pistol? Yes, it would have. Instead of pulling his Taser, he would have pulled his Glock and disarmed you and you're pretty sure he wouldn't have left your Glock on the ground for you to pick up and put back together. That thought alone confirms the Provident Hand that led you to cover your Glock. Divine protection was with you this day. What made you give him the $200? Did you have pity for his situation? Maybe. But what prompted you to do it really? You're not sure, but something inside said "do it". It was the right thing to do.

You had compassion on Officer Brunson, yet you killed the next guy that got on your bike. Did you really have to kill him? Yes. You only had a few moments to stop him before he was out of range. There was no choice. But why not Officer Brunson? It's clear in your mind, if Officer Brunson had started off with your bike you would have shot him just the same. You wish you had not been forced to do it. What you did was the right thing to do, and if forced to, you will not hesitate to do it again.

One thing that has caught you by surprise is how soon things have become violent. You weren't expecting it so soon. It's only going to get worse. You were expecting, at least for a day or two more, scenes like the kids and neighbors BBQing in the neighborhood and playing. Yet, at the same time, you were expecting to see more people scrambling for supplies. Maybe they were and you just didn't see it. You were trying to avoid people as much as possible.

Something about that neighborhood still bothers you. What was wrong with it? Shouldn't those people have a little joy, considering the pain soon to come? Maybe, but there are going to be millions just like them who have no clue what is coming. Millions who will be dead within a month or two because most families have less than a week's worth of food in their pantry and less than a week of stored water. How many will live through this? Of course, they'll figure out how to get water from their toilet tank and hot water heater, but what are they going to do when that's gone? Do they know where to find water? Do they know how to treat the water they find? Considering most grocery stores only have about a three day supply of food on hand, how long before these families start to starve? Will the government step in and save the day? Maybe, but for how many? Can the government feed 350 million people when nearly all food production, processing and distribution have stopped? You don't think so. The government is going to take care of itself first, then attempt to control everything else. That's going to leave millions of people starving and desperate. Desperate people will do crazy and stupid and violent things.

You think about the kids on the 4-wheelers, out having fun and then the evil side of people, unbridled by law enforcement, raises its ugly head, stamping out a young life. Those idiots you encountered on the road probably killed that kid and took the others to do who knows what with. Those idiots aren't just idiots, they are evil. You hope you don't encounter them again, but something inside says you will.

You think about Will. He's been part of your planning for a long time. He and Kathy helped you develop many of your plans. Oh Kathy, sweet Kathy, how I wish you were still here. You push the sad thought of her death away. You can't go there. Will should be okay. He has supplies, equipment, energy sources and weapons available to him. You, along with some family and friends, have developed small scale farming on your respective properties. The fruits of which should be able to supply your food needs, as well as provide some to barter with or give to others. Yes, Will is going to be okay. If he's figured out what has happened, and he's pretty smart, he will probably try to get his girlfriend, Lizzy, and her mother, Jill, to come out to stay for a while. He had asked you about it when he and Lizzy became something a little more than close friends. You had agreed, but only under the condition he tell her nothing about it, unless some major catastrophe occurred. You think of Jill. You knew her back in high school. She was a good person. Kind of tomboyish, but cute. Actually she was pretty. She would have made someone a fine wife, but somehow she got involved with that dumbass, Clyde Baker. You never figured that one out.

It's only about 15 miles from your small community to Jackson, where Lizzy lives. In Repose you have a couple of vehicles, as well as other mobile equipment that will likely work. In your home library there is a manual you and Kathy put together: <u>EMP Event-Plans and Actions</u>. Will will be able to use that, along with the plans you've made with family and friends. You haven't been caught completely unprepared. That action plan, along with several other event-specific action plans were developed years ago and updated as your situation changed. You've taught him how to defend himself with a firearm. He's had hand-to-hand self-defense training. Family and friends are nearby; they are part of the plan. He is confident and has a strong mind and determination. Yes, Will will be fine.

You consider the Bible, the Book of Revelation and end time events and prophecies. You recall some of the teachings of Chuck Missler, Perry Stone, Jack Van Impe and your former pastor Scott Myers. Is this event part of that? Is this the event that takes America off the world scene? Or is this just another event soon to be a part of history? You're not sure. What you are sure of is this: you are still here, on earth, and as long as God leaves you here, you are going to do the best you can with the best you have to live and help those around you live. Events up to this point are clear: God's hand of Providence has been upon you. As Daniel Boone once said, "Know you're right and move ahead. Let the consequences take care of themselves." That's exactly what you plan on doing.

For now, you need to rest. You turn off the glow stick. The sounds of the crickets and grasshoppers fade away.

Chapter 17 John - Day 2 - *Plan for the day...*

It's 5:00 a.m. You're awake. The dim pre-dawn light weakly invades the barn. It's still too dark to move around. You lay there for a little longer. The night air was a bit chilly. You won't be sleeping bare chested tonight, that's for sure. If you were home, you would be up moving around. First order of business would be to brew the coffee and shower. After getting dressed, you'd have your first cup of coffee on the front porch swing. The early mornings have always been your favorite time of day. Seeing the day come to life and hearing the birds come alive have always made you feel good about the day. In the spring, you watch the colors go from gray to vivid green, with a splattering here and there of other colors as well. Kathy used to sit with you and enjoy these mornings. It seems so long ago, yet sometimes it seems like yesterday. She's been gone for more than two years now. It was tough, really tough, right after she passed. Truthfully, the void still hasn't been filled. Perhaps it never will be.

Finishing your first cup, you would go inside and walk to Will's room. Opening the door, you would walk in and ruffle Will's hair. On those mornings when he didn't want to get up, there were always the ice cubes. They worked every time. Usually, that's around 6:00. If time permits, you would have one more cup before leaving for work. Either way, you take a cup with you. Since Will got his driver's license, he's been driving himself to school, freeing up about a half hour every morning for you.

But you're not home and won't be home for at least several more days. There won't be any pizza to take home for supper either. How long will it be before you can have another hot pepperoni and sausage pizza? Maybe longer than your remaining lifetime. For now, more pressing things are at hand. Your neck is stiff. As you roll out of the sleeping bag the soreness in your legs comes alive. It's nothing compared to the pain in your rear end! This is going to be a tough day. You turn the glow stick on low. You've got to stretch or you're not going to be able to hardly walk. The stretches hurt, but the pain eases off some, as you limber up. Ibuprofen to the rescue, please.

You move to the corner of the barn. There is no grass, but you water it anyway. Now, time for the coffee. You set the Esbit stove up and add water to your stainless steel cup. You light the fuel tab and let it heat the water. While the water is heating, you munch on some granola. This morning will finish off your last two plastic bottles of water. All that will be left are your stainless steel bottles. Water is a high priority this morning.

The morning light is getting brighter as you sip the coffee. It's pretty good, considering you have nothing else. Eight more packs of instant coffee and creamer. You hope you make it home before the coffee runs out! Pulling the GPS out, you see there is close to thirty more miles to Montevallo. That ought not to be a problem, as long as you don't have any delays. There should be time to make it through the city, unless you get held up there. You can decide once you get there if you need to go around. You hope not, as it will add a lot of miles to your trip. One thing is for sure, you're not going to try and go through the city in the dark. So, the plan for the day is set. First, clean up and pack up. Second, find water. Third, bike to Montevallo. Simple enough—or so it seems.

You pull the little scrub pad and small bottle of dishwashing liquid out of the cook pack. Using a little of the remaining water, you wash your cup. You put a sling on your carbine and set it by the trailer. You have two more pairs of clean boxers and socks and one pair of pants and one more shirt. You put the clean boxers and socks on, but wear the pants and shirt from the past two days. You pack your dirty skivvies with the others from yesterday in a zip lock bag. You're going to have to do laundry before you get home. Getting dressed you re-holster your Glock, after removing the Streamlight attachment. The bag is packed. The trailer is packed. Looking at your watch, it's 7:00, and you're ready to go.

You pedal down the lane to the road, stop and listen, pull out your Vortex 10x50 monocular and glass the road ahead and behind. Seeing nobody, you hang the monocular around your neck. Pedaling onto the road, you feel pain in your sore legs. But the pain in your rear end is so much more!

After about six miles, you see a small creek flowing under the road. Glassing the road in both directions, you see nothing. Then, head down the bank and work your bike into the tree line. It's thick here, so it's difficult to get the bike and trailer all the way in. Once they're well hidden, you grab your pack and put all the plastic water bottles inside. Shouldering the pack you walk to the water's edge. Finding a place where the bank eases down to the water, you approach and set the pack on the ground. You place the bottles on the ground and remove the Katadyn water filter kit. Removing the filter from its bag, you place a coffee filter over the inlet hose and secure it with a rubber band. The inlet hose already has a large particle filter, but you add the coffee filter for good measure. Placing the discharge tube into one of the bottles, you begin to pump water. After filling one bottle you look at the water. It looks clear. You drink it down. The taste, well it's not bad, but it's certainly not Dasani either. You proceed to fill all twelve bottles. After removing the coffee filter and drying the pump, you repack it. With everything repacked, you're ready to hit the road again. Easing out of the tree line, you glass the road ahead and behind, and seeing no one, proceed to the road and head south.

There are a few people heading north. Most are on foot, but you have seen three bikes and one motorcycle. None have approached you or attempted to talk. You've pushed hard and covered nearly fifteen miles since your stop for water. You're hungry, having only eaten energy bars and drunk water. It's nearly 2:30; you must have something to eat. Spying a road going into the trees, you look around, seeing no one, proceed down the woods road.

You pedal a hundred yards or so, then pull into the trees off the road. You pull an MRE from the trailer. Southwest chicken and black beans. Okay, might not be bad, but it's going to have to be cold again as there is no time to build a fire. This meal also includes applesauce and a water flavor pack. You save the water flavor and get an Emergen-C pack and a multi-vitamin. You forgot to take these this morning. Finishing and packing the trash, you lean against a tree. You're tired again. You turn your iPhone back on and set the timer for 30 minutes. Just a short nap will make all the difference.

You awake to the low honking of a car horn. Turning the alarm off, you get up. You have to stretch again. Your legs are still sore. But your rear end is so much more! You put a few drops of Milo pineapple/coconut flavoring into a bottle of water and take three ibuprofens. Time to get going.

Approaching the highway, you again stop at the tree line. You listen and glass the road. You start lowering your monocular when you see a flash down south. You quickly replace the monocular to your eye. You see the rust bucket blue Chevrolet pickup turning south on the road about 300 yards ahead. Looks like the same truck driven by the idiots you encountered yesterday. Great, that's all you need, to have to deal with those idiots. You get off the bike and retrieve your carbine. You double check to make sure it's ready to go, then place it on top of everything in the trailer. Hopefully it won't be needed, but you want to be safe, just in case.

Heading down the highway, you approach the small road that the rust bucket pulled out from. You hesitate and stop looking up the lane into the small field and trees. About a hundred yards down is what looks like an old run down barn. Hmm . . . . You start to pedal again then stop. What about those kids? Did the idiots have anything to do with that? You don't know if they did or not. Should you go check out the barn? Why? It's only going to take time and there is probably nothing up there anyway. Besides, they could have somebody watching just waiting to ambush someone coming around. Or the idiots could just show back up while you're walking up there. Really, do you have any obligation to risk your life to go check a barn that probably doesn't have anything in it, but maybe a meth lab? What are those kids to you, that you should risk yourself for them? What about Will? What will happen to him if you don't make it home?

You know, none of the answers to those questions really matter. The only thing that does matter is doing the right thing. Your dad repeated this phrase many times: "All that is necessary for evil to abound is for good men to do nothing." You are a good man and you refuse to do nothing. Hiding your bike deep into the tree line across the highway, you retrieve your carbine and two extra magazines. You spot a fallen tree top about fifteen yards farther into the woods. Taking a picture with your iPhone, you walk toward it with your pack. You hide your pack in the top and come back to the highway.

You pause, look and listen. What you are about to do could mean nothing or it could mean life or death, including your own. The words attributed to Daniel Boone play back in your head, "Know you're right and move ahead. Leave the consequences to themselves." You pray for God's providential hand and set across the highway for the road.

Chapter 18 John - Day 2 - *At the barn...*

You semi-crouch cross the highway and enter the lane leading to the barn. On the left of the lane is an old fence line with trees and brush. On the right is open field. Feeling exposed, you get as close to the tree cover as possible and ease up the lane. Walking at a slow, determined pace, you make as little noise as possible and stay off the fallen leaves and sticks. You don't want to give anyone up there any notice you are coming. You hope you find nothing. This would be so much better if it was dark. If it was dark you could use the NVD and IR laser and take advantage of the covering night. You would certainly feel less exposed. Your clothes are earth tone colors, Khaki pants, that you wear every day, an olive drab fishing shirt, a tan ball cap, and Timberland boots. At least, they don't stand out like a flashing strobe.

The soreness in your legs and even in your rear end is unnoticed, as all your efforts are focused on making it to the barn unseen and unheard. You and Will have attended several tactical pistol and rifle training classes. Your favorites are those taught by Shootrite Firearms Academy near Guntersville. You even got to do a few drills with some of your law enforcement friends from the Jackson PD, but you know you are no combat soldier or SWAT team operator. No, you're just a regular guy who's tried to prepare himself for tough times. Well, right now is a tough time. You hope what you learned will keep you alive. On the good side, you chuckle, you have stayed at a Holiday Inn Express. Better keep things in focus.

Approaching a corner where the fence turns left, there is no more cover. There are twenty five yards between you and the barn. Twenty five yards of completely open pasture. You pause, studying the barn. You can clearly see where lots of new tire tracks have crushed the green grass. The tracks lead to the back of the barn. The front of the barn is solid, no doors, no windows, but lots of cracks. It wouldn't be difficult for someone to look through one of those numerous cracks and spot you crossing the opening. Adrenaline is starting to flood your body. You force yourself to remain calm. To get to the barn, you must cross the opening. There is nothing else you can do to get there. You can crawl, walk or run. Either that or you just turn around and go back to your bike and head south. But, you've already made that decision. You choose to semi-crouch, semi-run. The grass is soft, so your feet make no noise. You put your monocular in your shirt pocket to keep it from rattling. You check yourself for any other noise makers then start for the barn.

At the front corner of the barn, you pause. You can't get right next to the barn, because of the taller weeds growing at the walls. Dropping to a knee, you listen. Hearing nothing, you rise and follow the truck tracks to the rear of the barn. At the corner, you stop and drop to a knee again. Peering around the corner, it is evident the tracks lead into an open rear door. The door, actually doors, appear to have their top hinges loose as they sag to the ground. There is no closing those doors. Not now anyway. Studying the opening, your heart starts pounding as you rise and ease around the corner. Creeping up to the door, you stop again, listening for any sound. It's hard to hear anything with the pounding of your heart, yet you listen intently. Your breathing has quickened. You force yourself to calm and slow your breathing, but your heart is still racing. This isn't your job. This isn't what you do. You need professionals to enter this building. But you are all there is. You stiffen your resolve.

With your carbine raised, you slowly start cutting the corner, just like you were taught in those tactical classes, just like what your Jackson PD friends taught you. They are some brave souls is all you can think. Back on focus! It's not very bright deep inside the barn, but you don't turn your light on. You want to keep your presence a secret as long as possible. You're at the left door. As you start cutting the door, you're scanning the area to the right and then left, as more is revealed. As you break the 90 degree of the cut you see a body lying on the ground about twenty feet away. Looks like it might be the boy. You cut a little more and are stunned at what you see. Both girls are lying on the ground, naked. Their hands and feet are bound with duct tape and their mouths are tape closed. You almost lose it right there and rush in, but you know that would be foolish. You must clear the room of any threats before you can help those kids, if they are even still alive. You continue cutting the door and see a 4-wheeler, the remnants of a small fire and nothing else. You scan up, to make sure you haven't missed anything. Feeling the building is empty, except for the boy and two girls, you enter in.

You first reach the boy. His eyes are wide staring up at you. He's been beaten, that is obvious. His face is puffy and has lots of blood on it. You remove the tape from around his mouth and, opening your knife, cut the duct tape from his hands and feet. He rises to his elbows and starts backing away. You place your hand on his shoulder and look directly in his eyes. This calms him. You say, "Help me with the girls." You move quickly to the first girl. The boy moves to the other. There's no doubt they have been raped. You curse softly, wanting to kill those evil bastards. Removing the tape from her mouth, you talk reassuringly to her, letting her know you are there to help. She doesn't say anything. Her face is swollen. You cut the tape binding her arms and legs. She just looks at you, not trying to cover herself. She must be in shock. You see clothes scattered, some torn. You look at the boy, who is struggling with the duct tape. The other girl is crying. You tell him to come help this girl get some clothes on as you reach the second girl to cut the tape. She wails as the boy leaves her. Trying to calm her, you cut the tape releasing her hands and feet. She immediately goes into a fetal position. You look around quickly. Apparently those evil idiots left some blankets on the ground. You get two and throw one to the boy and wrap the girl in front of you.

You ask the boy what his name is. He says, "Johnny Helms." He nods at the girl he is helping and says "This is Rachael and that is Karen." You say, "Johnny, I have a pack in the woods across the highway. I'm going to go get it and bring it back here. I have some first aid supplies, food and water. My name is John." He looks up and says, "Okay," then rises and walks over to you. He extends his hand and says, "Thank you for saving us." You shake his hand and say, "Yeah, sure."

Heading back for your gear, you are very cautious, as you don't know when those evil bastards will be back. About half way down the lane, you hear the 4-wheeler crank up. Stopping and turning, you see it drive from around the barn. Johnny is driving with one girl in front and the other to the rear. They have managed to get their torn clothes on. As he pulls next to you he stops and says, "Thank you again, Mister. Me and my friends are going home right now." You watch him from behind as he turns north on the highway. At least that is opposite the direction the evil idiots were going the last time you saw them.

You think about the scene that just played before your eyes. The evil perpetrated by evil men. Those kids can't be much older than your son. You stop, bend over, and retch up everything. You have never before wanted to kill anyone. Sure, there have been some you wanted to give a good thrashing to, but never anyone you wanted to kill. That's changed. You want to kill those evil bastards!

Your hands are shaking as you cross the highway for your gear and bike. You go straight for your pack and reload your trailer, keeping the carbine strapped to your body. It's not going back in the trailer. It's staying with you till you get home. As you push your bike back to the highway, you stop and fall to your knees. You pray, "Dear God, help us. Help us all!"

Chapter 19 John - Day 2 - *She lives...*

Before getting back on the road you grab another bottle of water and down it. You've drank eight of your twelve bottles. You'll need more water tomorrow. Hitting the road, the sky is getting dark. Clouds are forming. It looks like rain, maybe a thunderstorm later. You need to find a place to camp. Preferably a barn, crib or something with a roof. Your single man tent is not going to keep everything dry. One thing is for certain, you're not staying anywhere near here. You have to put some distance between here and where you spend the night.

You pedal at a fairly good pace to find shelter before the rain, passing a few more houses and isolated pastures. Then you see what might be promising. It looks to be an old crib under some trees about 200 yards off the road. You pull your monocular out and study it. It's leaning pretty badly, but it looks like the roof is still on. A road heads in that direction going through a small patch of trees, so you turn into the road.

At first it doesn't register what you are hearing. The rumblings of a truck. The sound you've heard twice in the past two days. You quickly push your bike into the trees. Unslinging your carbine, you run to the road and hide in the bushes. Using your monocular, you see it. It's about 200 yards south and closing fast. It's definitely the rust bucket and those evil bastards! Anger rises inside you. It's time to kill these bastards. Part of you wants to open fire on the truck as it approaches. You have six Glock 15 round magazines. Ninety rounds. But you realize a 9mm carbine is no match for a moving truck. There are two people up front. There were three yesterday. Glassing it with the monocular you watch it as it goes by. They're driving pretty fast. In the back of the truck, you see the other guy and what looks like a red bike and a bundle on the bed of the truck. Then you see it. A head with blond hair sticking out from underneath a tarp. It's hard to tell, but you think the head belongs to a female.

Your anger rises even farther. This isn't going to happen, if you can help it. There is no question about it. No debate inside your mind. There is but one course of action. You follow the truck. By the time you get your bike and hit the highway, the truck is out of sight around a bend. But you have a good idea where they are going. If they go to the old barn and stay there you will find them. If they don't, you probably aren't going to be able to help whoever is in the back of that truck. You pray, "Dear God, send them to the barn. Lord, don't let them leave. Keep them there." You pedal hard.

You reach the barn road in about forty-five minutes. It's starting to rain a little. In the distance you can see flashes of lightning. No sounds of thunder yet, but you know it's coming this way. You pause at the road for a moment. Yes, it looks like they drove up here. The 4-wheeler tracks have been smashed with truck tracks. You can only pray they will still be there. You consider how you should approach. Should you hide your bike across the road again then sneak up? No, you sense urgency. If you don't get there in time, you might as well not get there. You pedal your bike toward the barn and stop where the fence turns left.

You study the situation and consider how you should approach. Looks like they went to the back of the barn the same way as before. It's starting to get dark. The glow of a fire can be seen through the cracks of the barn. You decide to approach the barn from the opposite side as before. You leave the NVD in your pack and push your bike along the fence for about twenty-five yards. You get your pack and move another fifteen yards down the fence and set the pack under some brush, then make your approach from the left side of the barn.

The sounds of arguing come from inside. You catch phrases, "We need to go," "We have time," "You'll get your turn." You move quickly toward the back of the barn staying well away from the sides. You don't want them getting any chance glances of you passing by. Then the thunder begins, not much just a few rumbles, but the rain is picking up.

Looking around the side, you see rust bucket parked outside the door and a fire just inside. There is a man standing watch near the pickup. You curse softly. You can't approach while he is there. You pray, "God make him move!" You study him for a minute. He's armed with what looks like an SKS rifle, more than a match for your 9mm carbine. There is no way you can win a fire fight with these guys. You have to use stealth and the silence of your suppressor, if you have any chance of coming out of this alive. You're waiting studying all options, when you hear, "She's awake Hank!" The guy at the door moves into the barn. Remaining still, you listen, then hear a woman's scream, "Get off me!"

You lose it right there and run toward the door, only to trip on some debris on the ground. You fall face first, your carbine underneath you. It knocks your wind out. You writhe on the ground, trying to regain your breath. You think you're making enough noise to wake the dead. The thunder rolls. It takes a minute or so to regain yourself. Your adrenaline is working overdrive and you force yourself to stay calm. You get back on your feet and make it to the corner of the truck then look in. All three men are surrounding the woman. You scan the barn for any others, but see none. It appears two men are holding her arms and one is in front. Her shirt has already been ripped open and her chest is bare. The woman is no longer screaming and appears to have ceased struggling. The man starts removing her pants and says, "Now honey, you're going to get what's coming to you."

You've determined your course of action. Raising the carbine, you put the red dot on center mass of the guy on the right and fire two quick shots. The only sound heard from your carbine is the working of the action as the spent case is ejected and another 9mm subsonic round is loaded. The guy pulling on her pants freezes, as you readjust your aim. He moves slightly as you fire two quick shots at him. The side of his head explodes. The third guy has managed to stand, looking confused as you place two rounds into his chest. He falls hard onto the woman's chest. The woman gasps loudly.

You quickly rise from kneeling and run into the barn. Not knowing if they have weapons on them, you are upon them in a flash. You quickly put two rounds in the head of the first guy and the second. Reaching down you pull the third guy off the woman. Blood is on her body and you pray you didn't miss and hit her. You throw the guy off. He hits the dirt floor with a thud and gasps, "Help." Raising your carbine, you put two bullets in his head.

Placing the safety back on the carbine, you kneel down beside the woman. She's not moving. You look at the blood then search for a bullet wound but see nothing. It must be bastard number three's blood. You check for a pulse. Yes, it's strong, but she's not breathing. Repositioning yourself beside her head, you tilt her head and check her air passage. Then, placing your mouth over hers, you give her three quick breaths. You watch her chest rise and fall with each breath. You pause. Nothing. You place your mouth back over hers and start rescue breathing. Counting between each breath. On the fifth breath she starts breathing on her own. Sitting back for a moment there are tears are in your eyes. She lives! Thank God, she lives!

Chapter 20 John - Day 2 - *Jill Barnes...*

You've been on an emotional roller coaster today. From anger, to fear, to self-doubt, to anxiety, to rage, to determination. Now with relief overwhelming you, tears fill your eyes, as you see this woman is still alive. But the time for emotions is not now. There is much to do. The storm is starting to rage outside. You push the feelings back inside, knowing there is no time to feel them now. Maybe later tonight, but for now you have to move.

You sit back up and look at the woman. You can see she's breathing smoothly by the rise and fall of her chest. The fire light is dimming, as the wood burns low. Shadows jump here and there. You shot each of those bastards two times, then two times again. That means twelve rounds. You had fifteen rounds available in the carbine and magazine. You are now down to three. You reach in your left pants pocket and withdraw a new Glock fifteen round magazine. Removing the magazine from the carbine, you insert the new. Now there are sixteen rounds available, one in the chamber and fifteen in the magazine. You pocket the nearly empty magazine in your right pocket.

Your mind returns to the woman. She has bastard number three's blood on her. You probably shouldn't do anything about that. You reach over and grab both sides of her shirt to pull it closed. You notice her bra is cut apart. Nothing you can do about that either. You feel and look for the buttons. They have all been ripped off. You pull the shirt tight overlapping the sides. As you let go it comes back apart. You grab the shirt again and overlap them again. This time the shirt only separates about three inches. Well, at least you got her breasts covered. You look around. You see a pack against the wall. It's a camo bag with pink highlights. Must be the woman's. You walk over and look in. There are a variety of supplies, female clothes and, what you were looking for, a sleeping bag. You pull the bag out. Yep, definitely a female bag. You pull the sleeping bag out of its compression bag and walk back toward the woman. Unzipping it all the way, it shapes into a blanket. You kneel down and wrap the blanket over her and tuck it in at the sides.

You stand up and walk to the fire. There is a wood pile to the right of the door. You had not noticed it before. You add two pieces to the fire. Picking up your carbine, you head back into the rain. Its full dark, the rain is hard and cold, fog is rising from the ground. You raise your carbine and turn the flashlight to high beam. Even with the 1000 lumen output, you can only see about fifty feet in front. You make the fence line but don't see your pack. Tracking to your right, you spot it under the bushes where you placed it. It's wet. Very wet. While the pack is water resistant, it is not waterproof. You hope the contents have not gotten wet. You didn't have time to put the rain fly on it when you started to the barn. You turn and track back along the fence until you come to your bike. You load your pack back in the trailer. You turn to look at the barn, but the fog is too thick to see it. Great! The last thing you need is to get lost in the fog. You look for the truck tracks. You can see them a few yards out and following them, return to the barn doors from the right.

You move your gear and everything into the barn. You add another piece of wood to the fire and set your bag close by to dry. You open your bag and remove the NVD that was sitting on the top. Whew! It's dry. You grab the head lamp from the bag and put it on, then walk to the truck and open the door. Inside, you look around. The keys are in the ignition. You turn the key over and look at the gas gauge. Half a tank, that's good. Lots of trash and beer cans on the floor. On the seat is what looks like a pink inside the waistband (IWB) holster. You remove the key and close the door.

Back inside, you are feeling the chill. The rain has cooled the air considerably. The wind is blowing and you are wet. You are cold, but can't do anything about it yet. You walk back to the woman and lean your carbine against the wall. You grab bastard number one by his legs and pull him to the far corner of the barn. You check his pockets and find a loaded 38 special snub nose revolver and six lead bullets. You pull his billfold from his back pocket. Harold Jenkins is his name. You also pull a buck knife out. You walk to the left corner, by the door, and drop the items. You do the same for bastard number two. His name is Earl Smith. He has a Hi-point 9mm with one magazine. You deposit those items with the others and return for bastard number 3. You pile him with the others. His name is Hank Jones. You retrieve a Glock 19 and a spare magazine. You look at the Glock a little closer and see the writing has been highlighted in pink. You turn and look at the woman asleep across the barn and smile. You know who this belongs to. You put the Glock and extra magazine next to your bag and dump the other items with the rest in the corner. Going back outside, you get the tarp from the back of the truck and start back. You pause at the truck door; opening it, you lean in and grab the pink holster off the seat.

Once back in, you drop the holster by your bag, then continue to the back and cover the bodies with the tarp. You find an SKS, an AK47 and a Mossberg 500 pump shotgun, on the floor or leaning against the wall near where the woman is lying. You eject the chambered rounds from each and put them in the pile in the corner. Your weapons need to be cleaned, but you're shaking so bad you decide to just use a Rem Oil wipe for now and clean them good tomorrow during the day.

You can't stop shaking. You have to do something or you're going to be hypothermic. From your pack you pull out the large heavy duty ziplock bag containing your clothes. You pull out a pair of pants, t-shirt, boxers and wool socks. You also pull out a small towel and some light weight camp flop shoes. Looking back at the woman, you see she is still asleep. You strip down and dry yourself as best you can with the towel. Your hair is soaking wet and you are shivering almost uncontrollably. You get dressed quickly and your shaking lessens. You've got to do something with your wet clothes. You pull a hank of 550 paracord from your pack. Securing it to a bent nail on the left wall, you stretch it across the corner to the adjacent wall. About three feet back from the wall, you put a loop in the line, then hang the cord around a board nailed in to the wall. You take the end and pull it back through the loop. You use this leverage to pull the line tight, then cinch it off. You quickly hang your wet clothes over the line. It sags deeply, but keeps everything off the ground.

You're hungry and cold. But more cold than hungry. You need to warm up soon! You get your ground pad from the trailer and your sleeping bag and ground mat from your pack. You roll them out, not too close, but not too far from the woman. Before getting in, you add two more pieces of wood to the fire. Then, on a whim, you retrieve your glow stick and returning to the woman, you turn it on low and lay it beside her. You turn toward your sleeping bag. You stop. Something dawns on you. You turn back around and look at her again. There's no doubt. That's Jill Barnes!

Jill Barnes! You can hardly believe it. How in the world did she end up here? You whisper a prayer of thanksgiving, "Dear God, thank you for sending me at the right time!" You're cold, very cold. Time for the bag. You return to your bag and remove your camp flops and get in. The down filling is warming and it feels good. The fire does little to heat the room. It's little more than a glow of flickering light. But it might help dry the outside of your pack. You were really surprised the water didn't seep through. Condor makes a pretty good bag.

Going over the day's events, how do you even describe it to yourself? You start the day with high hopes, end up freeing some kids, then fighting some evil bastards and saving Jill. Yep, that about sums it up. You understand desperate people will do desperate, stupid, and violent things. You don't approve, but you can understand it. Yesterday, Officer Brunson was a desperate man. You understand why he did what he did, but if he had gotten on your bike you would have shot him nonetheless. The second guy, you don't know about him, except he was trying to put you in a desperate situation and that wasn't going to happen. But these, these evil bastards, there was no reason other than pure evil for what they were doing. Killing and raping. There would have been more, no doubt. You wonder how many evil people like that are going to spring into action since law enforcement practically doesn't exist anymore. If this is a taste of things to come, it's going to be real bad.

You think of all the small events of the day and how they brought you to the big events, even to where you are now. There is no doubt God's providential hand was guiding you this day. His Hand of Protection was here. Your carbine is a nifty little compact rifle. Its intended purpose was to get you home, to allow you to protect yourself and secure small game. It was never intended to be used as an assault weapon. If any of those bastards had gotten their hands on any of their guns, they would have made Swiss cheese out of you. You know that. You were just a trip to the ground away from getting you and Jill killed. That fall saved your life. While you were lying on the ground trying to regain yourself Jill was being assaulted, but it was that full intent of theirs upon Jill that allowed you to get the jump on them. It's the little things that make no sense, except in its entirety, that make the difference between life and death. Now there's the truck. With the truck and the half tank of gas, you might be able to get home tomorrow. Tomorrow! Home tomorrow! That sounds so good.

Your thoughts turn to Jill. How did she find herself in these circumstances? What brought her to this place, at this time? She obviously had a pack, supplies and a pistol. You've known Jill for a long time, all the way back to middle school. You were three grades ahead of her, so you only saw her in middle school for one year, then three years later in high school for one year. But she seemed like a very capable and nice person. You've seen her around and even talked with her some since, but wow, here right now. You wish she hadn't got involved with Clyde Baker. You still don't understand that, but it's not yours to understand.

Your intentions are clear. You are going to do the best you can, with the best you have, to live and help those around you live. You'll do the same for Jill, if she wants you to. Evidently, God put you together with her for a reason, but that decision is up to her. For now, you've got to warm up and rest. You are so fatigued. You look one last time over at Jill. She seems to be resting peacefully. You close your eyes, and the sound of the rain puts you to sleep.

Chapter 21 John - Day 3 - *Waiting for Jill...*

The rain is falling softly now. It hasn't stopped all night. The morning air is cool and damp. You finally warmed up some time during the night. It's 5:00 a.m. and you're awake, just like every other day. There is no light from this overcast morning. You remain in your bag, enjoying the warmth after the chills last night. All that remains of the fire are a few red embers. Maybe you can use those to start a new fire shortly. Looking over you see the soft glow of the glow stick by Jill. From its faint glow, it's clear she hasn't moved during the night. It's still hard to believe you've run across her.

Lying there, you contemplate your plan for the day. You have to clean your weapons and find water. You need to study your maps and select a route around the cities and towns. If you drive a truck through one of them, the police may attempt to confiscate it and, depending on how many there are, you may have no choice but to let them have it. That would be a real let down. It's attitudes like that which have kept you from living in cities. Too often government thinks what you have belongs to them and you only have what you have because they allow you to have it. You just don't think that way.

Now your planning is going to have to include Jill. Is she traveling back to Jackson? Or is she going somewhere else? Either way you're not going to leave her alone. Two people together are stronger than one. You'll just have to talk with her about it when she wakes up. She was roughed up pretty bad. The reddening and slight swelling on the left side of her face and the red marks around her neck were evident last night. Things she undoubtedly got while you were on the ground struggling to regain yourself.

Jill was obviously prepared for something or was on her way camping. You didn't go through her pack except to get the sleeping bag, but you saw enough to know she had several days of supplies. The Glock 19 with pink highlights is no doubt hers. That's no surprise; she was always kind of tomboyish in school. Maybe that's why a few of the hot shot guys gave her a hard time. You know she's tough. She's practically raised Lizzy by herself ever since that dumbass, Clyde, abandoned her before Lizzy was born. But that was probably the best thing that could have happened to her. When she awakens you'll talk to her about her plans. You hope she is trying to get back home. It will make things much less complicated for you.

You think about Will. He should be ok. Everything is in place back home. Plans have already been made. If he follows them he should be ok. The only question in your mind is Lizzy. To what lengths will he go to find Lizzy? That part you just don't know. It's only been three days since the EMP, or the solar flare, or the whatever. What it actually was doesn't matter at the moment. Maybe later, but for now the results are the same. It left you stranded more than 200 miles from home. What should you call this event? You read a book back in high school, and again several times later, by Pat Frank, <u>Alas Babylon</u>. Your dad had read it when he was in the 9th grade. He insisted you read it, saying how much that book had shaped his thinking on being prepared. Well, you couldn't just read it once. In the book they referred to the terrible day that changed civilization as, "The Day." So, why not? Until something better comes along you'll call it The Day. Will has a good head on his shoulders and is a capable young man. What he has been taught will help keep him safe should things get tough for him.

For now, you better get stirring. The dim light from the morning is growing, though still not enough to function with. You reach and find the head lamp and put it on. Setting it on low, you get up and put the camp flops on, go to your pack, and retrieve your belt and holster. After putting them on, you remove the light from your pistol and holster it. You stow the light back in the pack, still amazed everything is dry inside. Now it's time to get the fire going.

You pull your fire starting kit from your pack and walk over to the wood pile. The wood is mostly broken limbs but there are also a few old boards. Everything is good and dry. Grabbing a few of the smaller limbs and a board, you lay them down close to the small but glowing red embers. You also get a handful of dry hay from one of the old bales. You kneel down and pick up the board. With your knife, you whittle a large handful of shavings. Then, using your Gerber scabbard knife, you split the board into strips about an inch wide. From your kit, you remove an old medicine bottle that is packed full of Vaseline impregnated cotton balls, get one of the balls, tear it open and lay it across the embers. It starts smoking, then a flame, you quickly add a little hay, but not too fast, you don't want to smother the fire. The hay is burning quickly as you add the shavings you whittled from the board. On top of that you add the board strips. You wait a few minutes for the fire to catch up and start burning the strips good. Then you add the small limbs. Too often people have trouble building fires because they get in too big of a hurry and smother it. You take your time. As the small limbs start up, you get a few larger pieces from the pile. There isn't much left in the pile, but you don't plan on being here very long. The fire is burning good now and lighting the barn. You can feel the heat and back away just a little.

You get your boots and set them by the fire. They are still very wet from yesterday. It would be so nice if they would dry out! You have wool socks and they'll keep your feet warm even when wet, but it would be so much better if they are dry. You check your other clothes. Your pants and socks are still wet but the others feel as if they have dried. You leave them to hang for a while longer.

By now its 6:00 and the light is increasing outside. The rain is steady, though light. It keeps the air cool and damp. Pulling your long sleeve t-shirt out of the bag you slip it over the one you are wearing to help cut the chill off your arms. It's time for the guns. You get your small pistol cleaning kit. You return and sit next to the fire on an old wood box you found in the barn. Your Glock is first. Unloading it, you disassemble it just as you did Officer Brunson's Glock 22. One of the things you like about a Glock is their simplicity of take down. You pull a Rem Oil wipe out of the kit and wipe everything down; the slide, the barrel, the inside of the frame and lightly around the guide rod and spring. You don't want too much oil, as it will attract dirt and dust. Reassembling the pistol, you check it for operation by working the slide a few times and pulling and checking the reset on the trigger. You check the magazine, then insert it into the pistol. You rack the slide to load a round. Removing the magazine, you add the extra 9mm round and reinsert it into the gun. You reach back to your pack and pick up Jill's Glock 19. Stripping it, you clean it just as you did yours. You notice she has an extra round, too. You wonder if she normally carries it that way or if she had to use her pistol under duress and do a tactical reload. You might ask her later.

You move on to your Keltec Sub2k carbine. Unloading it, you fold it. Pulling a 9mm snake from your kit, you add a piece of the Rem Oil wipe to it and pull it through the barrel. You check the action and clean it without disassembly. The disassembly of the carbine is a little more involved with some smaller parts and you don't want to chance losing a piece on the ground. You unfold the carbine and wipe the exterior. You also clean the red dot using a clean lens cloth and a wet lens wipe. You remove the Gemtech suppressor and disassemble it, wiping the insides down. After reassembling, you mount it back on the carbine. You reload the carbine and lean it against the wall. You go to your pack and retrieve the extra sub-sonic ammunition and reload your nearly empty magazine.

You turn your attention to the guns of the bastards. You wipe the Hi-Point down after making sure it was unloaded. You do the same with the snub nose revolver. You move to the long guns and wipe them down without disassembly. The AK47 looks like a WASR-1063 model, kind of on the low end, but serviceable. You wipe the SKS and shotgun down too. You lean all the long guns against the wall and set the Hi-Point on the ground next to them, then place the snub nose revolver in your pack.

Chapter 22 Jill - Day 3 - *It's John Carter...*

They are holding you down. You struggle, swinging your arms and legs. They keep grabbing you. You scream, "Get off!" and continue to struggle. There are three of them. Things are foggy in your mind, but you fight on. Suddenly, they fall off you, yet you continue to strike and kick to make sure they don't attack again. Someone is speaking. Did you hear your name? Your mind is spinning. You see a face, it's a kid's face. You're lying on the ground. You've been smacked around, but then it stopped. Someone pulled that guy off of you. You watch as they fight, until finally the bully runs away. Then the kid comes to you and says, "It's okay Jill, everything is okay," but it's not a kid. No, it's a man and he is saying "The bastards trying to hurt you are gone. It's okay Jill. You are okay." It's the kid from the 8th grade, but he wasn't in the 8th grade, no it's the boy from the 12th grade. No, it's not the boy, it's a man, yet it is the kid. Your confusion slowly diminishes as your mind comes into focus. Your eyes grow wide. You ask, "Is that you? Is that you John?" He smiles and says, "Yes, it's me." A flood of relief overcomes you. You don't understand. How can it be? How can he be here? You were being attacked and then went black. Now, here is John. You don't understand. "But why . . . I mean how are you here? I don't understand." A wave of nausea overtakes you as you remember what happened to you. You say, "I think I'm going to throw up," and sit up quickly, turning to the side as you heave. Your head is hurting pretty bad and it throbs from where you hit it on the asphalt. From the corner of your eye, you watch John walk away. A little pang of fear returns. 'Don't leave!' you want to scream. But he soon returns with a cloth, soap and a shirt. He gives you the cloth and says, "There is some water by your side. You may want to clean up and here is one of my shirts." Then, looking down you notice the blood on your chest. Your hand moves to your chest, searching for the wound, but you find none. John says, "I think the blood is from one of those bastards I shot last night." You look up, still confused. You start remembering, those guys had torn your shirt apart and cut your bra, but they didn't cut you. You flush as you realize you are completely exposed. You look back at John and say, "Um . . . Do you mind turning around?" He turns red and turns around. You quickly remove your torn clothing and wash the blood off. You start to put the shirt on. It's not your shirt. It's a man's shirt. It must be John's shirt; yes, he said it was his shirt. You look down at your chest and realize the cool air is going to make things awkward if you don't put a bra on. So you cover yourself with the shirt and ask, "Uh . . . would you mind getting me a bra out of my pack?" You realize you don't even know where your pack is. You don't even know where you are. You don't even know what day it is. You are relieved when he returns with your bra in his hand. He gives it to you as you flush again. He turns and walks to the fire.

You dress as quickly as your light headedness will allow. The shirt is big on you, but it's clean. You say, "Okay, I'm okay now." He returns and looks at you with concern, he hands you another bottle of water saying, "I have some coffee made. Would you like sugar and cream?" You respond, "Oh, thank you. Cream only." You drink the whole bottle of water. Your throat was parched. You don't remember when you drank last. Sometime before you fell off your bike, but you didn't just fall. You were knocked off. You watch John as he pours your coffee. You start to stand and wobble. John is quickly by your side offering support.

You take his arm. You feel weak, but his arm is steady. You look down at your pants. They are partially down. You pull them up and buckle your belt. You start crying as you remember what they were doing to you. Your thoughts come out as a whisper, as you cry, "Did they . . .," but you can't continue. You can't continue the awful thought. John seems to understand what you are thinking and responds, "No, Jill, they didn't. I got here in time." A wave of relieve overwhelms you. Just like before, John got here in time. Thank God! You lean your head onto his arm and cry. You look up into his eyes and say, "Thank you, John. Thank you." He leads you to the fire and you sit on a wood box. Somehow, you think everything is going to be okay, you feel safe. You watch him as he picks up a cup of coffee and hands it to you. You sniff it. It smells so good. You sip the warm liquid. It warms you as it goes down. The taste is wonderful. Your spirits are lifted. Yes, things are going to be ok. Smiling, you look at John and say, "There is nothing like the first cup of coffee in the morning."

John looks over as he sips his cup of coffee, saying, "Jill, everything is going to be okay." Then he asks, "What are you doing out here?" You respond by telling him you were traveling back home from a meeting near Birmingham when the event happened. That you walked with a woman and her two small children the first day. Having been given a bicycle by the woman's husband, you rode it the second day coming through Helena and Brantleyville. You were trying to make Montevallo when you were attacked. "I was in a hurry, not paying real good attention and I guess they clotheslined me with a rope. How I ended up here, I don't know, as I was knocked out when I fell from my bike and hit my head on the asphalt. When I regained consciousness those . . . those guys were holding me down. A few minutes later I passed out again. The next thing I remember is seeing you. I don't know how I got here or even where here is."

He asks you if you had trouble on the way, other than the three bastards. You say "Yes, on the first day. I had to . . . I didn't have a choice . . . I . . . I . . . I just can't talk about it." He says he understands and thought by the way your Glock was loaded that you had to use it. He then reaches over by his pack and picks up your Glock and its pink IWB holster and hands it to you. "I think this must be yours." You really like that holster. It was made by the Well Armed Woman LLC and cost about $45. The pink highlighting on your Glock you did yourself after your dad showed you how to highlight. You smile inside as you remember his eyes rolling when you showed him the hot pink fill you did the lettering in. It's actually pretty simple to do. Some hot pink nail polish dabbed into the recessed lettering then after drying you lightly wipe across the frame with non-Acetone polish remover. The highlighting remains. Looks cool. You smile as you take it. He gets up and brings your pack over and sets it by you. "I think this is yours, too." You smile again and say, "It is. Thanks." He says, "Maybe I should look at where you hit your head. Would you mind?" You respond, "Of course not. Thank you." He gets up and pulls something from his pack and walks behind you. He says, "Okay, I'm going to touch you. Is that okay?" You think, geez, you have already been touching me, why ask now. It dawns on you. Your contact before was you touching him; he didn't mind. He's wanting your permission for him to touch you. You smile, "Yes, John, I appreciate it." He moves your hair around and it stings a little. He says, "You have a nasty bump back here and a small cut that has bled some. I'm going to clean it." He pulls some gloves from what you suppose is his first aid kit. After putting them on, he cleans the blood away with an antiseptic wipe, then applies a small amount of antibiotic cream. He says, "Okay, I think you're good." You say, "Thank you."

He sits back down and looking at you says, "As to where you are, you're in a barn on AL119 about five miles north of Montevallo. And based on what you're telling me, you were attacked sometime yesterday evening. Probably, not long before I found you in the barn." You ask "John, what happened to the . . . you know the other guys?" He looks you straight in the eye, saying, "I had to kill them." Pausing to see your reaction, he continues, "They are over there in the corner, covered with a tarp." His gaze doesn't move as you look back, "Okay . . . thanks. Now tell me how you came to my rescue." As you expect, he downplays the rescue remark, looking away he says, "I just happened to be at the right place, at the right time." You think, 'yeah just like you're always at the right place at the right time.' He continues, "I was up near Leeds on The Day, you know the day of the event. I'm calling it, The Day until some better word for it comes around." You smile a little as you remember you called it, The Day yourself. Maybe his dad made him read that book, too. "I purchased a bike and started south the next day. I encountered those evil bastards the day before yesterday for the first time. I saw them yesterday coming out of this place. I thought they might be involved in murdering and kidnapping some teenagers, so I came up here. There were three kids. Two girls and a boy. All had been beaten and the girls, well, they were raped. I cut their bonds and then they left. As I was back on the road heading south, I saw the bastards coming this way with a person on back under a tarp. So I followed them back and well . . . I had to kill them. I didn't realize it was you until late last night. I'm just glad I was able to be here and stop them."

You smile and slowly standing, walk over to John and hug him hard. "Thank you, John. Thank you. You seem to make a habit of saving me." You pull back and look at him again. John looks transfixed and embarrassed at the same time. You continue, "You weren't just at the right place at the right time. You were the answer to my prayer for help. You, my friend, were God's instrument of my salvation. Thank you." You return and sit, noticing John being uncomfortable with all the praise. The movement has made the thumping in your head worse. But what else could you say and what else could you do? The man saved your life. He did more than that, he saved you from the most horrible thing you can imagine. It's not the first time he has intervened on your behalf. He's done it three times before. Somehow he just keeps popping up at the right time. You wonder . . . .

John says "I'm heading back home, too. I think it would be good if we travel together. There is a half a tank of gas in the truck. I think if we leave by lunch we might be able to make it home today. What do you think? Want to travel together?" You respond, "Absolutely! Somebody needs to protect you." He says "Good. Let's plot a route from here to Jackson." He pulls a map from his pack and, moving closer to you, spreads it out. "I think we should avoid going thru Montevallo, Brent and the other towns along the way. How about we hit this county road north of Montevallo then turn back south to HY25." You look it over "Yeah. I think that's a good plan. HY25 takes us to Brent. How do you want to go around Brent? Or do you think we can go straight through? I don't know the small roads around Brent or any of the other small towns until we get to Thomasville." John smiles and pulls out an electronic device and turns it on. You look amazed, "How is that working? I thought all electronics were destroyed." John smiles and says, "Well, I wasn't caught completely unprepared. I had stored some of my electronic equipment in a Faraday box in my truck. It protected this GPS and a few other items from the EMP." You ask, "A Faraday box?" John says, "A Faraday box is an all metal box lined with an electrical insulating material.

It is supposed to protect electronics from an EMP. I took an additional step of putting my devices inside anti-static bags, and well, it worked." He pulls up the GPS map and plots a journey all the way past Brent. He says, "We'll program the rest of the route as we get closer to Marion. Let's both study this route until we have it memorized. That way if something happens to the GPS we won't be lost on a back road." You say "Sounds like a plan to me."

Chapter 23 John - Day 3 - *Staying at the barn...*

You look over at Jill and say, "I'm starving. I bet you are, too. Since we've got a good fire here, how about I fix us some breakfast?" Jill says, "Yes, I'm hungry too, but my head and back hurt pretty bad. I don't know if I can help." You say, "I got it, don't worry about it. What if we get you propped up against the wall over there, while I fix breakfast? Then I'll get you some ibuprofen." Jill responds, "Yes, I think that would be good, but I don't want to be over there." She points to where she was lying yesterday. "If you don't mind, will you move me over to the other side of your stuff? I just don't want to be in that spot any more. I would do it but . . ." You cut her off, "Hey, no problem, Jill." You get up and pick up an arm load of old hay and spread it on the ground where she asked. You pile it thick and spread it so it won't be lumpy. You lay the blanket on the hay, then put your ground pad on top of that. Zipping up Jill's sleeping bag, you set it on top then walk back to Jill. "Hey, I've got enough in my gear to fix breakfast. How about we set your pack up against the wall so you can lean on it?" Jill says, "Yes, that sounds good." You place her pack against the wall, by the bed you made, and return to help her as she walks. She sits on top of the sleeping bag and leans back on her pack. She says, "Yes, that's better, thank you." Continuing she says, "My back is smarting pretty badly. Guess from hitting the pavement yesterday."

You move back to the fire and pull out your cook kit—an MSR compact stainless steel cook set. You remove it from its pouch and separate the pieces. Stored inside the kit, are a small bottle of canola oil, dish washing liquid, a scrub pad, a small hot pad, some beef bouillon and a small bag of dry rice. You set the contents aside, fill your stainless steel cup with water from one of the reserve water bottles and set it on a brick in the fire. You squirt a little oil into the fry pan and set it on the other brick. Reaching in your pack, you pull out a freeze dried Mountain House scramble egg two serving pouch. You also pull out a pack of single-serving Spam and a small ziplock bag of condiments. Opening the Spam, you place it in the fry pan and hear it sizzle. Yes, the temperature is right. After the water starts to boil, you open the egg pouch and pour the water in, stir then re-seal the pouch back up. Another fifteen minutes and you'll have scrambled eggs. You turn the Spam over, using your fork. Refilling the stainless steel cup with water, you place it back on the brick. Another cup of coffee won't hurt your feelings this morning. You get two MRE bread pouches out, cut them open and squeeze a strawberry jam pack into each one. Compliments of Hardee's, you say to yourself. Flipping the Spam again, it looks like it's almost ready. You fix two more cups of coffee using the camp cups. Getting up, you take a cup and a strawberry jam sandwich over to Jill. "Here get started on this and I'll have eggs and ham ready in a moment." Jill smiles and accepts the offered cup and bread. You can tell she doesn't feel well. You pull the Spam off the fire and cut it into little pieces. Checking on the eggs, you see they are ready. You pour the Spam in the eggs and mix them up. Using the extra pot from the cooking kit, you place half the eggs and Spam in it. You call over to Jill, "Do you want salsa?" With a look of surprise she responds, "You have salsa?" "Compliments of Sonic." She says "Yes." Picking up a pack of salt and pepper and the extra fork, you walk over and give her the pot.

Sitting next to her and eating from the pouch, you try to strike up a conversation. But you sense she's not into it, so you let it go. The eggs and Spam are good, real good. Jill finishes her plate and coffee. She smiles and looks at you, "That was good. Thank you. You're going to make somebody a fine housewife someday." You both get a chuckle. You reach for her plate and cup and walk back to the fire. It's getting low. You fill the stainless cup about half way and set it on the brick. You pour about a half a cup of water in Jill's camp cup and retrieve four ibuprofens. Walking back, you give them to her and she takes them. Then she says, "John, my head is really, really hurting, I need to lie down for a while. But, I . . .," she flushes, "I have to use the potty." You look out the door. The rain has slackened, but it's still falling. You look around the barn. To the back opposite the tarp covered bodies are several large round hay bales. There is about a four foot space between two of them. You suggest, nodding your head, "How about over there?" She nods and you help her up. You get your small U-Digit folding shovel and your roll of toilet paper and hand them to her. She takes the toilet paper, but says, "I'm not going to need the shovel." She walks to the back as you turn your attention to the dirty dishes.

You drain as much of the oil out of the fry pan as you can. Then add a few drops of dishwashing liquid to the now hot water in the stainless cup. With the small scrub you start washing the cups, forks and the pots, saving the fry pot for last.

Jill calls out, "John, I need some help." You turn and see Jill leaning against the hay bale. She says "Can you help me to the sleeping bag, I'm a little dizzy." You get a little concerned, thinking she may have a concussion. You walk quickly to her side and help her over. She sits down and you remove her walking shoes. You help her get in and she lies back. You touch her forehead but can't feel any fever. She says, "I'm going to be all right. I just need to rest and get rid of this headache." She closes her eyes.

You walk back to the dishes and dry them with one of the towels and repack the cook kit. You look over at Jill. She's been through a lot. She needs rest. It's probably best if she doesn't move today, even in the truck. You rub your chin, thinking. We'll just leave in the morning, if she's up to it. But that brings up a couple of other issues. First, the bodies. If you're staying here tonight, you have to move the bodies somewhere outside. Second, water. You're down to your last quart. You have to find water today. You know Jill has some water, but how much? You saw a few bottles in her pack when you got her sleeping bag and again when you got her bra. You find that bra puzzling. Jill has a pack that seems to be well prepared, yet that bra is more like one Kathy would wear for a night out, but not like the lace ones she would wear for a night in. It's obvious, it wasn't made for a lot of activity and sweating. So you wonder why she would pack one like that. Unless . . . . The cut bra she had on looked like a sports bra. Maybe on The Day she was wearing the one you found in the pack and she changed into the other for the journey home. Makes sense. But you'll never know because you're never going to ask.

You look back over at Jill. She's got to be pretty tough, but you already knew that. She seems to have a preparedness plan of some type. You consider her pack and the fact she's traveled, what thirty miles or so on her own; yes, she's strong all right. She had the courage to move. Fear didn't paralyze her in place. How many women, or men for that matter, would let something like this paralyze them into inaction? How many are just sitting in a hotel room, dragging on a cigarette, waiting for someone to come save them? The ordinary is where we live, it's comfortable. Serious thinking outside of ordinary makes many people uncomfortable. Too often people just push those thoughts aside. You've seen it before talking with friends. Good people, successful people, but refusing to consider "what if" ordinary is not ordinary anymore. You recall the events a few winters back, when Birmingham and Atlanta got completely shut down by the unexpected icing of the roads. Many people got stranded on the interstate. You heard the stories. Too many, far too many were totally unprepared, without a blanket, water, or even a flashlight. Fortunately, many found help by the next day, but what if the next day help had not come? How many, having gone through that harrowing experience, are still just as unprepared today.

One of the things that gets you the most about people not having at least some modest plans is the cost is so small considering the security you gain. People buy car insurance in case an accident occurs. They buy home insurance in case some catastrophic event destroys their home. They buy health insurance in case they get seriously sick or injured and they even buy life insurance to help protect those close to them in the event of their untimely death. When you think about it, most people will spend many thousands of dollars on insurance, but refuse to spend even a few hundred dollars on preparing for personal, out of the ordinary emergencies. Thinking of Jill, you know she wasn't prepared for an EMP type event, but nonetheless she was prepared for tough times. You, well you are undoubtedly an exception. You've been preparing yourself for tough times most of your life. It's what your Dad taught you. You've invested many thousands of dollars in an effort to make things not so tough, when tough times come.

You look outside. The rain has stopped. The rain! Why didn't you think about it last night or early this morning? There was your water supply! All you had to do was build a catch and you would have had all the water you needed. It would not have been difficult to do with your rain jacket or mylar emergency blanket and some paracord. Well, that opportunity is gone. You better start thinking more clearly if you want to make it home.

Your watch says it's 9:10 a.m. You better walk around the area, just to make sure no surprises are coming your way. You check your boots. They are still damp but they'll have to do. You put them on and pick up your drawstring bag. It's dry, so you put the coins back in and place the bag in your right pocket. You check your hanging clothes. The pants are still damp, so you leave everything hanging. You walk to the door and look around the sky. The sun is shining and there aren't many clouds, so you decide to skip the rain jacket and just grab your gloves. Putting your cap on, you pick up your carbine and monocular, then head out the door.

You scan the area and notice several thin tree lines. One is out back about 200 yards. Some others cut across the pastures. These are either going to mean a fence or a water branch. You'll have to check those out shortly. For now, you continue around the barn looking for anything out of the ordinary. Seeing nothing, you head down the road to the highway. This time you walk on the leaves to help mask any tracks you might make. The rain cleared all the truck and bike tracks. Getting close to the highway, you pause and listen. Hearing nothing, you proceed just a bit further so you can observe in both directions. Again, there is nothing. You retrace your steps back to the barn, being sure to stay on the leaves.

Now you have to do something with the bodies. You walk over to them, looking back to make sure Jill is still asleep, you uncover them. They are starting to swell a little. This is going to get nasty if you don't get them out of here soon. You lay the tarp out and manage to get the bastards' heavy stiff bodies on to it. It's a pretty good size tarp, so you pull the edges together and lace it together using some paracord. Nope. You can't budge it. The old rust bucket has a winch on the front. If it works, maybe you can just winch the bastards out.

Moving to the truck, you check the winch out. You insert the key and turn it over without cranking. You look around the truck, but can't find the remote. But you do find two AK47 magazines loaded with steel case ammo. Mounted to the bottom of the dash, you see the winch control. You push the switch to Out. Nothing happens. You push the switch to In. Nothing happens. Looking under the dash you see a spider web of wires hanging out. You don't want to get involved in repairing somebody's wiring mess. Going back to the front, you see the manual release and lock lever. You set it to release and pull on the cable. It doesn't budge. You give it an even harder jerk and it breaks free and the cable spools off. Okay, now you have to reposition the truck so you can pull them straight through the door.

You lay the loose cable back on the bumper and step in the truck. As you crank it, you're hoping it won't wake Jill. You really don't want her to see this. The truck is a rust bucket, but the engine fires right up. You reposition the truck so you have a clear path between the winch and where the bodies are. Turning the truck off, you get out and grab the winch cable. You look over at Jill, as you pull the cable into the barn, she's still asleep. You don't know how, but she is. You want to get this nasty business over before she wakes. You take the cable and attach it to a loop of paracord you previously attached to the tarp. Stepping back to the truck, you lock the winch. Cranking the truck, you slowly start backing up. Your eyes are glued to the pile in front of you. You ease back, not wanting anything to break or tear. You start looking for where you can take them. There is an old catch pen, but it's too close to the barn. The fence lines are either too close or too far. You don't want to just dump them in the field. Then, you notice a clump of small trees where an old piece of farm equipment has been sitting for a number of years. Small trees are growing around, in, and through it. It's about fifty yards away, so you drag the bodies over there. You don't have a good way to winch the cable back in, so you just wrap the slack around the bumper.

Looking back at the tarp, you consider what you've done. You don't feel any remorse and that scares you. The guy on the bike. You regret having to do that, you really do, but there was no alternative. You know in your heart you did the right thing, but you wish you had not had to do it. But these bastards, for these bastards you have no remorse. After seeing what they did to those girls and what they were trying to do to Jill, you have no regrets at all. In two days, you have killed four men. Is this how men slip into a violent, callous life? You know you are a good man. Your dad taught you to be a good man and you've worked hard to be a good man. This isn't going to change that. You'll fight to stay what you are, even if it means fighting yourself.

Chapter 24 John - Day 3 – *Standing too damn close...*

After parking the truck in front of the barn doors, you sit and look at your watch. It's 11:45 a.m. You aren't leaving today, that's for sure. You better go check on Jill. Her body took a pretty bad beating yesterday. She got clotheslined while riding her bike. Guess that explains the horizontal red mark across her upper chest. She landed on her back and hit her head on the asphalt, knocking her out. She was assaulted by three bastards. She has a bruise forming on her left cheek where she was slapped or punched. There is bruising on her neck where it looks like someone tried to choke her and a big man fell dead weight on her chest. She's got to have rest. No way are you leaving today, period, and probably not tomorrow. You go in and walk over to her. She seems to be resting peacefully. The sleeping bag rises and falls with each breath. Placing your hand on her forehead, you feel no fever. She just needs rest.

You have to attend to the water needs. You're down to your last stainless steel quart bottle. Opening it, you take a drink. Within one of those thin tree lines you saw earlier is probably a small branch, but you can't go check now. You don't want to leave Jill vulnerable and defenseless. You are just going to have to wait a little longer. Jill has some water, but you just don't know how much.

The small fire has gone out and the wood pile is almost depleted. Picking up sticks and limbs from outside will do no good, as everything is soaking wet from the rain. Looking around the barn you find a few dry boards lying around here and there. You gather them and, unfolding your Gerber limb saw, cut them in pieces about a foot long. Then, using your CRKT folding knife, you proceed to whittle two large handfuls of shavings. Then place the boards and shavings by the wood pile.

With some time to kill, you pull out one of the Baofeng radios, turn it on, and scan the shortwave frequencies. Nothing. You really didn't expect anything, as the range of your unit is very limited, especially with this short antenna. You turn it off. And decide to check the truck over more closely. The engine cranks good. You open the hood and check the oil. It's dirty but the level is ok. You check the water level in the radiator and it looks okay, too. Walking around, you look at the tires. They are pretty slick. Better not go too fast on these things. Opening the glove compartment, you look for an owner's manual, but the only things in there are the registration papers and an insurance card. You don't know how much gas is actually in a half tank on this truck. You're probably 150-160 miles from Jackson, with all the back roads you're going to be taking. It's probably not enough to make it all the way, but you'll run across stalled cars along the way. You passed quite a few coming south on AL119. If you had a syphon hose that would be nice and a fuel can too, but you don't have those things so you'll just have to figure something out later.

You pull Jill's bike from the back and check it out. The metal is shiny in places from the recent scrapes. The handle bars seem straight, chain checks okay and tires look okay, too. It's an older style single speed pedal brake bike, but it's solid. You bet her legs are sore from pedaling this all day. Jill must have carried her pack in the basket. This is what you'll use when you go check the tree lines for a water source. So, you load up your empty plastic bottles, empty stainless steel bottle, then pull your water filter kit out and set it in the basket too. As soon as Jill is awake and able to guard herself, you're going to look for water.

For now, you nibble on an energy bar, drink a little more water, and study the GPS route. The route around Montevallo is going to add miles and time. Going through Montevallo just doesn't seem like a good idea, especially with it being a college town. You may have to go through Brent. You're going to play that 'off the cuff' when you get close.

Your mind turns to supper for tonight. You have a few more freeze dried pouches, but think maybe you should use some of the MRE's from the trailer. You pull two out, hoping Jill will like ravioli or salisbury steak and potatoes.

You get both of your two-way radios and turn them on and set them for the same frequency. Doing a push test, you hear them both squeal. You'll give one to Jill and carry one yourself as you go looking for water. Now what else can be done till she wakes? Thinking of nothing at the moment, you sit down close to Jill and, using your sleeping bag as a pillow, lean back against the wall.

You hear it again. Something is moving around. You grab for your Glock, but your hand won't move. You struggle to free your arm, but nothing is holding it. You finally pull your pistol, but can't find your target. There it is, right in front of you, coming fast. You raise your Glock, but the trigger is stuck. You're squeezing as hard as you can, but it won't budge! It's almost on top of you when the trigger releases. You feel the recoil of the bullet firing and watch as it falls straight to the ground at the end of the barrel. Now, it's upon you! You start to struggle then, . . . your eyes open. You look around, Jill is getting a bottle of water from her pack. It was one of those nightmares. You've had them before. You don't know what they mean, if they mean anything at all, but they always scare you.

Jill looks over, "Are you okay, John? You were kind of twitching there for a minute." You rub your head, saying, "Yeah, I'm fine. Just a bad dream." You look down at your Glock, reassuring yourself. You have fired nearly 15,000 rounds through this pistol, without a single malfunction. Surely it's not going to put you down in your time of need. It hasn't so far. Looking at your watch, you see it's 3:00 p.m. You fell asleep earlier. Looking at Jill, you ask, "How are you feeling? How's your head?" "My head is fine. My back hurts like crazy and these bruises hurt, but I'm okay. I'm sorry I've held us up. I really am," she responds. "Hey, don't worry about it. You've been through a lot. You needed the rest. If you feel up to it, we'll leave early in the morning. If not, we can wait another day." She says, "Yes, in the morning will be great. I'm so anxious to get home and check on Lizzy."

She continues, "John, I'm almost out of water. I don't know how much you have, but I need to refill my bottles today." You say, "Yeah, I'm in the same boat. I'm down to about half in my last quart bottle. When I was moving about outside earlier, I saw some thin tree lines that may have some running water. I want to go check them out." She says, "I have a small personal water filter and some water treatment tabs. We can go check for the water whenever you want." You say, "I think it would be best if you stay here and watch over our stuff and the camp. I'll take your bike, if it's okay, and fill all our bottles. I have a manual filter pump. I should be able to do it in about an hour." She remains silent for a minute, as in thought, "Okay, but can you show me how to use one of the rifles? I've never used any like those before. Why not take the truck?" You answer, "I was thinking of leaving you my carbine. It's a 9mm and uses the same magazines as your Glock 19. The recoil is light and shouldn't hurt your back if you have to use it. Plus, with the red dot sight, it's really easy to aim. I'll show you how to use it in a minute. I'll take the AK. As far as the truck, I don't want to risk it. The ground may be too soft after the rain and I really don't want to risk getting it stuck."

She stands up and gathers her bottles and takes them to the basket on her bike. She looks around and says, "John, what happened to the bodies?" You say, "I took them out a ways while you were asleep." She says, "Thanks, I really didn't want to be in here with them any longer." She looks back over at you, "Thanks again, John, for what you did. I know that took a lot of courage. Thanks. Now, show me how to use your carbine and go get us some water. I'm getting hungry."

You get up and walk over to where she is. Letting her watch, you remove the magazine and eject the chambered cartridge. Moving a little closer, you show her the gun is unloaded. "This is a Keltec Sub2k 9mm carbine. It uses the same magazine as your Glock 19." You hand her the carbine. She says, "I haven't shot a rifle in a long time. I used to shoot pistols with my dad, but we didn't shoot a lot of rifles, other than a 22." You show her how to hold the rifle. "Grab the grip with you right hand and use your left hand on the forend. Pull it up close to your shoulder. That's right. Now, look down the barrel. You should see a little red dot." She moves it around a little on her shoulder, but says, "I can't see the red dot." You move behind her and reach over to help position the rifle. You are very close. "Tilt your head around until you . . ." You freeze for just a moment. You don't speak. You don't move. You smell her aroma. She doesn't smell like Jessica McClintock, no, she smells like sweat. Nonetheless, something stirs inside you. In that brief pause you realize, "I'm standing too damn close!" You remove your arm and step to the side a little. She looks up, puzzled, "Is something wrong?" Having regained yourself, you say, "No. I, uh, I think I forgot to turn the sight on." You step a little more to the side and front. Reaching over, you turn the sight on and say, "This is a Burris Fast Fire III micro red dot sight. To turn it on, you just push this button on the side. You can also adjust the brightness using this same button. Try it." She works the button saying, "It also turns it off." You respond "Yes it does, but let's just leave it on for now. It'll turn itself off after a while." She shoulders the weapon and says, "Yeah, I see it now." You say, "Normally, when using the suppressor, I use sub-sonic ammunition, like what I just took out, but I think it's best for now to remove the suppressor and use some self-defense rounds. Before we load up, go ahead and take it off safety and pull the trigger." She does and the snap of the firing pin being hit can be heard. "Now, rack the charging handle back. You can use either hand, but I prefer to use my left." You show her where it is located on the bottom side of the stock tube. She does and lets it go. It slams back into place. You continue, "Now it's ready to fire again. Go ahead and fire and recharge." She does, this time more smoothly. "All right, put it on safe and I'll remove the suppressor." She does and hands over the rifle. She asks, "Why are you changing the ammo and removing the suppressor?" "Since we are going to be apart, I want to be able to hear if you have to use the weapon. With the suppressor on, I might not be able to hear it. The self-defense rounds are more powerful than the sub-sonic ammunition. So, since I'm removing the suppressor, I wanted you to have the more powerful ammo." She says, "Okay."

While you're removing the suppressor, she asks, "How does the suppressor work?" You explain, "When firing a firearm there are three components to the noise you hear. The first is the mechanical noise inherent to the particular gun you are using. Like earlier, when you pulled the trigger and racked the charging handle. Those noises are inherent to this carbine and there really isn't much you can do about that. However, the larger two components of the noise are associated with the bullet breaking the sound barrier and the hot explosive gases contacting ambient temperature air as it escapes the end of the barrel. We can do away with the "sonic" boom by using sub-sonic ammunition that travels below the speed of sound. That's the kind of ammo I had in the carbine. The self-defense rounds are faster than the speed of sound, thus a sonic boom. The suppressor will not eliminate a sonic boom. The escaping gases can be caught inside the hollow chambers of the suppressor and then released at a cooler temperature, thus reducing the noise level. There is a little more to it, but you can think of it like a car muffler; only made for a rifle or pistol. This particular suppressor is a Gemtech GM9. You can use an oil filter with a barrel adapter to do almost the same thing for cheap, but the happy nut jobs in Washington say that's illegal and will put you in jail if you get caught. Of course, I'm not so sure any of that matters now." You hand her the magazine of self-defense ammunition saying, "Load up." She says, "Cool. Now go get us some water."

Chapter 25 John - Day 3 - *A misunderstanding…*

You start for the bike then say, "Wait, one more thing." Jill looks over inquiringly, as you walk to your pack and remove the two Baofeng radios. You walk back over to Jill and hand her a radio saying, "Here. You are supposed to have an amateur radio license to use these, but I don't guess it really matters now. I already have these set to the correct frequency. Turn it on and let's do a radio check." You push the PTT button. Jill's radio squeals, as your voice comes through the speaker. Then Jill does the same thing. "All right, I'll call and let you know what I have found when I get to the tree line. Then, let's contact each other every thirty minutes until I get back." Jill responds, "Okay."

Jill says, as you get on the bike, "If I can use your cook set, I'll warm us up some MREs." You hear the growling in your stomach as you say, "Great idea. My cook kit is in the side pocket." You get on the bike and head to the back tree line, looking around as you go. This single speed is a little harder to pedal than your mountain bike. The grass is thick and wet. As you approach, you look back at the barn. Jill is not standing in the doorway any longer. You reach the tree line in a short time. Just as you thought, there is a small stream flowing. The ground is a little boggy. You're glad you didn't bring the truck. You call Jill on the radio and let her know what you have found.

You maneuver the bike as close to the stream as possible, then get all the bottles from the basket and set them on the ground. You drink the last of the water from the stainless bottle, then remove the water filter from its pack. Like yesterday morning, you put another coffee filter around the inlet hose filter. Dropping it in the water and placing the outlet tube into one of the bottles, you start to pump. The stream isn't very dirty, and the water pumping into the bottle is crystal clear. There are a lot of bottles to fill.

Twenty-two plastic water bottles, your two stainless bottles and Jill's single stainless bottle. It's going to take a while and your arms are going to be tired.

Looking around again and back at the barn, you see nothing. You start to think about what happened back there. What made you feel so funny inside? Geez, she smelled like sweat! There was nothing there that should have meant anything to you. She hugged you this morning, and that didn't bother you. Heck, her breasts were bare in front of you this morning and last night, that didn't stir you either. So, why did a sweaty smell? You don't know. Something was different. You just don't know. You haven't been alone with a woman since . . . since Kathy died nearly two years ago. Maybe that's it. You better be careful, or you're going to make a fool of yourself. You've got to keep your mind focused on what's going on. You were just standing too close. That's all you can figure. Just too close.

You have about half of the bottles filled when you hear the radio, "Pumper, this is Barney. Do you copy?" Those were the call signs Jill assigned each of you before you left. You don't know where she came up with them, but they sounded okay at the time. You answer back, "Barney, this is Pumper. I am half complete. Everything is okay here." "Pumper, this is Barney. Everything is okay here. Out," was the return message. "Pumper, Out," is your reply.

You look around again, standing this time so you can see more. You kneel back down and continue pumping. You look at the land and woods around you. This is truly a beautiful place. The grass is green, and the water is cool. This would make somebody a great homestead. You think about Will and repeat what you've been saying and thinking. Will is going to be okay. Everything is going to be okay. You're almost finished filling the bottles when the radio squeals again. "Barney, to Pumper. Everything is okay here. Out." "Pumper to Barney, everything is okay here. Will be back in fifteen minutes. Out."

You return to the barn with the full water bottles. Jill has a fire going. You say, "Wow, that smells good." "You think so? I combined a couple of MREs to make a big meal. You hungry?" "Yes," you reply, feeling the gnawing pangs in your stomach. Jill motions with her hands, "Well, serve us a drink and let's eat!" You retrieve two water bottles and, going to your pack, pull your bottle of Milo's water flavoring. You look over at Jill with a raised eye brow, "Pineapple coconut?" Jill nods her head. Using your camp cups as small bowls, you each serve yourselves. Cheese tortellini and beef brisket mixed together, served hot, not bad. Guess she wanted something different than what you had laid out. "Jill, this is really good," you say between mouthfuls.

After finishing off a dessert of applesauce covered pound cake, you turn to Jill, "Tomorrow, if you're up to it, we'll leave in the morning. I'll go back to the stream before we leave and refill the bottles we use tonight and in the morning. Then we can load our bikes and head back south. If everything goes well, we should get to Clarke County by late afternoon. The tires on the rust bucket are in pretty bad shape so I don't want to go too fast." Jill says, "Why not load everything up tonight?" You respond, "I'm tempted to. I am anxious to get home like you, but I think it would be better not to load the bikes just in case something happens to force us to leave the truck here in a hurry." "Okay," she answers.

As you both clean up the dishes and pack the trash, Jill says, "John, I'm really worried for Lizzy and my mom, and I'm concerned for Will, too. All this mess we're going through right now, what are we going to find when we get home? I mean, what are people going to do? How are they going to live?" She looks up and you see real concern in her eyes. As you repack your cook kit, water treatment kit and water bottles you say, "I don't know, Jill. But, I think most people are ill-prepared for even minor emergencies, much less for something like this. It also depends on how the government responds. People who work together will have a better chance of making it, but the government could make things a lot worse if they intend to grab more power and control. I think it could get bad, real bad." You pause, not wanting to say how bad you really think it's going to get with thousands upon thousands of dead people in Clarke County, and a hundred million or more dead across the country, so you say, "Jill, I think Lizzy is okay. Will has a good head on his shoulders and I think she's in good hands." Fire sparks in Jill's eyes as she says, "Oh really? You think my Lizzy will just up and run off with your son?"

She stands, "Good night John. I don't want to talk anymore." Then, she walks to her sleeping bag and crawls in. You sit there stunned, thinking, "What did I say?"

You retrieve your carbine and unload the self-defense ammunition, then reattach the suppressor and reload the sub-sonic ammo. It's getting pretty dark outside. The fire is burning down. You decide to take one more look around outside. You get your NVD and head gear and start to leave, then stop. Turning toward Jill, you say, "Jill, I'm going to look around outside. I'll be back in a few minutes." She doesn't respond. You attach the IR laser to the carbine rail and turn the NVD on. Stepping out the door, you start looking around. You walk around the barn and then down to the paved road. There is a deer in the distance, but nothing else. You start walking back. Walking past the fence line, you look up. The sky is clear and the stars are bright. You always enjoyed just sitting in a lawn chair on a cool clear night and looking at the stars. There are so many of them, they seem to go forever. When you look up with the NVD you can see ten times as many stars. The stars you couldn't see with your bare eyes sprout out everywhere. The night sky is covered with them. You know God is still in control and that gives you comfort.

You walk back into the barn and over to your bag. Setting the carbine against the wall, along with the NVD, you remove your boots and your socks too, since they are damp. You place your Glock by your side and turn the glow stick to low. Turning, you look over at Jill. Her back is turned to you. "Jill, I didn't mean to say anything to upset you. I'm sorry." After a brief pause she says, "Good night, John. We can talk tomorrow."

You lie back and consider the day. You're going to make a fool of yourself if you're not careful. "God, please help us make it home. If tougher times are ahead, please give us the strength to handle them with courage and wisdom. In Jesus' name." Plans are set. Tomorrow you should be home. Then more decisions have to be made, but they'll have to wait their turn. You close your eyes and, as you're falling asleep, you realize you just prayed for "us." You better be careful . . . .

Chapter 26 Jill - Day 3 - *Many questions and no answers...*

You're mad as you walk back to your sleeping bag. "So he thinks my Lizzy will just up and runoff with his . . . his son! Not considering the fact that she is at home with my mother, nor the fact I'm not there for her to even ask. That just boils my blood!" you steam in your mind. You lie back down. You should have peed first. You're not getting up now and doing it, not while he's still moving in the barn. You hear him moving around, then John says, "Jill, I'm going to look around outside. I'll be back in a few minutes." You don't say anything. You're still too mad to talk. You hear him walk out and after a few minutes you get up for the potty. Only, the potty room has a dirt floor and hay bale walls.

Getting back in the bag, you consider the day. The fact that you're still alive is a miracle. The fact that it was John who saved you is another miracle. You shudder to think what would have happened if he hadn't come along. Your anger starts to subside. You've known John for years. He has never been anything but a gentleman. He has always treated you like a little sister; well, you're not his sister. You know Will is a good boy. You were actually excited when Lizzy started talking about her boyfriend and you found out it was John and Kathy's son. You knew John would teach him to be a man and Kathy would teach him to love. You never worried about his intentions toward your daughter. So, why did John's statement anger you so much? Does he know something about them you don't? You don't know. But you do know John is a good man. He's always been a good man. So maybe getting mad and in a huff wasn't the right thing.

"Oh, Lizzy, I hope you're safe, where ever you are. If you are with Will, I hope you both are safe," you think inside to yourself. You've got to make it home. You have to. John is your best chance of getting there; John and that truck. You reach for your Glock and place it inside your bag. At least you have all your gear, well, except your shirt and bra. They're rags now.

It's hard to believe things have fallen apart like they have. The things you've encountered and the people. Some are good people, but the evil is magnified in the bad. Without the restraining hand of police officers, bad people are running rampant. Is it this bad in the cities? Is it this bad in Jackson? What did John mean by "the government making things worse"? Why would they do that? You think about your own mayor, Jim Short, you never liked him very much, but he seemed like an okay mayor. You know the chief of police, Ben Hunt. He had been a friend of your Dad's for a long time. He's about John's age. How are they going to be able to respond to or even know about people needing help? What about food? You plead, "Dear God help us!"

You made some general preparations for hard times. There is a small supply of food on hand at home, maybe a month's worth. Will things get back to some kind of normal by then? Will food be back in the stores? What about work and money? You have a few hundred dollars in cash at home, but what is that if you're not able to go back to work? The EMP took the banks down, you're sure. No banks means your meager life savings are gone. So how will you buy food, even if food becomes available? You don't know. There is a growing fear inside, telling you things are going to get real bad.

John knows something and he's holding back. You can sense he is reserved. You know he's smart. He said this didn't catch him completely unaware. What does he know that he's not telling? Is he prepared for such a world as what we are finding ourselves in? His pack and his high-tech gear tell a story of a man prepared. What about Lizzy and Will? If they are together, what does that mean and how would John even know that? You have so many questions and no answers. You just know you have to get home.

What about John? Really, what about John? He saved you, that's true. He's intervened on your behalf before. But something seems different. He's always treated you like a little sister. Well, you aren't his little sister and you don't want him treating you like his little sister. You want him to . . . to what? You're not sure.

John walks in. You peek to make sure it's him. You hear him taking his boots off and getting in his bag. His bag that's on the hard ground because he gave you his ground pad. He says, "Jill, I didn't mean to say anything to upset you. I'm sorry." You have too many emotions flowing through you right now. If you start talking, you're going to start crying. If you start crying, he's going to come over here. If he comes over here . . . no, that can't happen. You catch your breath and reply, "Good night, John. We can talk tomorrow." You ask God for strength and peace and wisdom, then close your eyes . . . .

Chapter 27 Jill - Day 4 - *Catastrophe...*

John is moving around, but you're too tired to stir. Sleep was fitful and elusive last night. It feels as if you've only just closed your eyes. You slip back under. Finally, dreamless sleep . . . .

As your consciousness comes back to life, you listen with your eyes closed. You don't hear anything. John must be outside. You open your eyes. You're facing where John's sleeping bag was last night. Where John's sleeping bag WAS last night! It's not there. It's gone. You sit up quickly. Looking around, you don't see John's bike or trailer. Your bike is leaning against the wall where John parked it when he came back from getting water yesterday. Your pack is where you left it and the truck is still outside. A small fire is burning. You don't see John's pack. Has he left you? A pang of panic rises inside, you call out loudly, "John!" John come running inside. His carbine is in his hands and he pauses, looking around. He locks eyes with you and comes over, kneels and places a hand on your shoulder. "Jill, are you okay?" Relief overwhelms you and for a moment you want to cry, but you regain your composure. You look up at him and say, "John, I'm sorry about last night. I mean, about the way I acted. You didn't deserve that." John looks at you for a moment. You feel embarrassed as you haven't had a bath in what? Three days? You've got to look and smell terrible. John smiles and turns his eyes away, saying "Don't worry about it, Jill. We're both under a lot of stress and uncertainty. It's no big deal."

He stands and walks over to the fire and puts the last few pieces of wood on. "Coffee?" he asks. You smile, "Yes, that would be nice." "Well, I've got four packs left. Using these two, will only leave two more. I sure hope we make it home today." You reply, "I have a few in my pack." John walks over to his pack, sitting right next to yours. How did you not see it there earlier? It's a big tan pack. How could you miss it? He gets the coffee, creamer, his stainless steel cup and two bottles of water. After pouring one into the cup and putting it on the brick in the fire, he walks over and hands you the other bottle. You reach up and take it saying, "Thank you." "I'll refill them right before we leave," he says.

"Where is your stuff and your bike?" you ask. "I loaded the bike and repacked most of my gear. If you're up to it, I'd like to get an early start back. I don't want to push that old rust bucket. The tires don't look too good." You respond, "Yes, that sounds good to me. I need a few minutes, then I'll be ready." "Peaches and cream oatmeal or cheese grits?" he queries. "Cheese grits," you reply. "Ok, cheese grits it is," he says as he rises and returns to the fire. You get up. You're still sore all over. In fact, you can't seem to remember not being sore. What day is this anyway? You think. There was The Day, then the walk, then the bike and a few days here. Hmm . . . must be the fourth day since The Day. It seems like an eternity. Four days and you still have, what did John say? One hundred fifty miles or something like that. Before The Day the trip back from Birmingham took less than four hours. But you've got to potty again. You haven't seen John go to the bathroom at all. He must be taking care of his business outside somewhere. Guess that means you have the potty room to yourself.

You return to your bed and start to pick things up. You put your Glock back in your holster. The spare magazine is still in your pocket. You wonder if Mary and her husband made it to where they were going and if the girls are okay. You'll probably never know. You roll your bed and put it back in its compression bag. You reach for the ground pad, turn and look at John, then smile and roll it up and cinch the straps. The blanket, you leave. You don't want to be around it anymore. You put your things in your bag and set John's pad next to his bag, then join him over by the fire. He hands you one of the cups of coffee, then refills the stainless cup and sets it back on the fire brick. He picks his coffee up and sits on the ground nearby. You sip your coffee. It's hot and it tastes good. "There is nothing like the first cup of coffee in the morning," you say. "Yeah," John says, "I like my first cup on the front porch, watching the day come alive. Maybe we can tomorrow." We? What did he mean by 'we'? You're going to be in Jackson and he's going to be in

Repose, somewhere between Coffeeville and Jackson, or is that between Coffeeville and Grove Hill? Well, somewhere around there. You've never been there. "It's just a figure of speech. Don't read anything into it," you say to yourself. You say to him, "Yes, that sounds nice."

John says, "If you'll get your stainless cup, I'll put your pack of grits in it and add the water." You go to your pack and get your cup. Returning, he reaches for it and pours the dry grits in. He pours about half the hot water into your cup and then adds a pack of grits to the water remaining in his cup. You stir your grits and allow them time to absorb the water. As you eat, John starts talking, "Jill, when we get through eating, let's clean the cups and stuff up, then I'll go refill our water bottles. If you're sure you can travel, we'll leave right after I get back. Does that sound okay?" You say, "Yes. I'm anxious to get back home and see Lizzy and my mom. And John, I'm really sorry about last night. I know if Lizzy is with Will, she'll be okay." John smiles and says, "Don't worry about it, Jill. Everything is okay." You still wonder what makes him think they would be together. No need to go there now.

From John's cook kit, you get the scrubby and dish washing liquid, and using a bottle of water, you both clean the dishes. You set the stainless cups by the fire to dry. The others you dry with a cloth. You go back to your pack and get a wash cloth and a bar of soap and wash your face. It's so tender, especially your left side. There must be a bad bruise, though you can't see it. You put the empty bottles in the basket. John is removing the suppressor and changing the ammo just like he did yesterday. He hands it to you, along with the radio.

You turn the radio on and do a radio check. "How did you like my little play on words for our call signs?" you ask with a smile. John looks puzzled for a moment, then smiles, "Yeah, that's pretty good. I wondered why you picked those signs." He chuckles, then continues, "I'll call you when I get there and when I start back. Check with me every thirty minutes, as we did before, but I don't think it's going to take that long."

John gets on your bike and heads across the field. You set his carbine against the wall next to your pack. You think, "He's going to be gone for a few minutes, so I think I have time." You take your clothes off and using the wash cloth, the bar of soap and a bottle of water, you take a sponge bath. You hear him call, "Barney, this is Pumper. I have arrived. Everything is okay. Pumper out." You pick the radio up, "Pumper, this is Barney. I copy. Everything is okay. Out." You better hurry! You finish washing as fast and as best you can with a bottle of water and get your clean clothes out of your pack. Everything is fresh except your bra. You only have the one now. You bring it to your nose and sniff, you washed it at Mary's the other day and only wore it yesterday. It's just going to have to do, as there is no time to wash it. You finish dressing quickly, put your dirty clothes, along with John's shirt, in a Walmart bag and stuff them in your pack. You're putting your shoes on when John calls letting you know he's heading back.

When he gets back, he gives you a few water bottles for your pack and adds a few to his. He then puts the rest in the wood box and puts them on back of the truck. He puts the bike on back and closes the tailgate. He says, "Let's put our packs in the back next to the cab. That way if we have to leave the truck, they won't be too hard to get." He walks over and lifts his heavy bag with ease and puts it on the truck. You grab your pack. As you pick it up, you feel the pain in your back, but you shoulder it anyway. Making it to the truck, you throw it on back, but not with the same apparent ease of John. John goes back in and gets the guns and says, "These are all unloaded. The magazines are loaded, but a round isn't chambered. I'm going to put them on back by our packs. They'll just be in the way up front." Returning, he picks up his carbine and starts changing ammo and installing the suppressor. He takes a bottle of water and puts out the fire then says, "All right Jill, check the drawers and look under the bed to make sure we didn't leave anything." You laugh and say, "Let's go, John."

You both turn walking toward the truck. John starts toward the passenger side. You wonder, "Does he want me to drive?" You follow him, unsure what to do. He stops at the door, opens it and waits. You know what he's doing. "John, I can open my own doors. I'm not your little sister." John looks at you and smiles, "I know you're not my little sister, believe me. You'll have to open your own doors from here back home, as there will not likely be time for niceties. But for now, humor me." He motions with his arm for you to get in. So you do, and smiling say, "Thanks," as he closes the door.

John walks around and gets in the driver's door. He pauses and looks over, "I think we should pray before we leave. Do you mind?" "I really wish you would," you reply. John bows his head and prays, "Father, we thank you for your hand of protection you have provided us thus far. For the difficulties we face ahead, we ask for the courage and wisdom to face them without fear. May your hand be upon our children and our love ones and bring us back together. In Jesus' name we pray. Amen." You say "Amen." You smile to yourself, he's praying for "us."

John reaches for the ignition key, then stops. "Jill, there is something I want to talk to you about before we go." You look over at him, "Okay," not knowing what's on his mind. He continues "Those bastards back there. I pulled their driver licenses and checked their addresses on the GPS. While none of them are directly on our route out of here, the one called Earl, whose name is also on the truck registration, has an address not far from our route. I don't know if those bastards have any cousins or friends, but if they do and they see somebody besides one of them in this truck, we may have trouble." This must have been one of those things he's been holding back. You ask, "What do you think we should do?" John responds, "I couldn't find another route around Montevallo using the GPS. I don't know the back roads here at all, so I wouldn't want to just go try to pick a way around. I really don't think we have a choice but to stay with our plan and original route. Let's just stay on our toes. Okay?" You respond, "Okay, John, if you think that's best. I'm with you."

That's when you see it. That ugly, evil looking serrated knife, the one held to your chest. You shudder at the memory of it touching your skin. John is looking at you, seeing your distress, he says, "What's wrong Jill?" You say, "That knife. Please John, get rid of that knife!" He says, "Yeah, sure. I found it on the floor in the . . . ." His eyes grow wide, "Oh my, Jill, I'm sorry, I wasn't thinking." He picks it up and throws it out the window into the fence line. "I'm really sorry, Jill. Are you okay?" "Yes, I just never want to see that thing again. Never!"

After a pause, he says, "All right. I just wanted to make you aware we may have trouble, hopefully not, but we might. This is what we're fixing to do right now. I'm going to ease the truck up and stop just short of the fence and tree line, then I'm going ahead on foot to glass the road. If it's clear, I'll return and we'll hit the road. If there are any problems, we will either wait or return to the barn. Either way, I want you to pay attention to me and be ready to move if I say so." "Okay, John. I'll follow your lead."

John pulls the truck ahead and stops as he described. He gets out with his carbine and heads to the road. Moving into the tree line, you see him take a knee and start scanning both directions with his monocular. He gets up and walks quickly back. Getting in the truck, he says, "Looks clear. It's 8:30 a.m. If everything goes well, we should be home before dark." He puts his seat belt on and puts the truck in gear. As he pulls out onto the highway, you chuckle. He asks, "What's so funny?" You point at the old seat belt and say, "Do you think that's really necessary? You're only going to drive thirty miles per hour." He says, "Yes I do, and you should put yours on, too." You roll your eyes and, smiling, you buckle in. You watch the sides of the road as you feel the truck lurch slightly as John shifts through the transmission. It's a good thing he didn't want you to drive. It's been a long, long time since you've driven a manual transmission. Home! Home before night! You are so anxious to see your Lizzy!

John says, "We are looking for Smithfield Road. It should be up ahead on the right, in about two miles. Montevallo is about five miles ahead. Keep your eyes open and don't let me pass it up." "Okay." He says, "Your Dad gave me my first speeding ticket back when I was in high school. He also gave me a ticket for no seat belt." You reply, "Yes, I know. He told me. He also said one day you would come and thank him." "Really?" John says, "I did go see him a few months back and did exactly that." "Yeah, he told me that too." You ask, "John, last night you said you thought Lizzy would be with Will. Why did you . . . . Lookout! There's a truck coming through the woods!" John curses softly as he shifts gears and gives the truck more gas. The truck surges forward. You're about to pass the road from the woods when you hear the POP, POP, POP of gunshots and holes appear in the windshield in front of John. You hear metal tearing and glass breaking. The truck suddenly slows and lurches into the left lane. You're being jarred by the suddenness of it all. Steam and smoke are coming out from under the hood. You turn toward John, he's slumped over the steering wheel with crimson blood flowing down from the side of his head. "John!" you scream. From the corner of your eye you see the truck pulling alongside of you. In that instant things seem to slow down. You are filled with anger and rage. "They've killed John!" you scream inside. You turn toward the oncoming truck reaching for your Glock. The truck is almost right beside you as you start pulling your Glock and raising your arm. In a moment, just an instant of time, your eyes meet those of your attacker. You see the same hatred in his eyes that you feel inside, then suddenly, a shocked expression on his face as his truck collides with yours. The impact of the collision slams you into the door and your head hits the frame hard. Stars appear in your vision, as you lose grip on your Glock and it falls to the floor. John is now lying to the side; his shirt is covered in blood. The impact has sent your truck off the road toward a large culvert. The front of the truck lurches into the void where the culvert opens into the shoulder of the road. With a crash, the truck nose dives into the water, hitting on John's side. Water splashes inside, hitting you in the face. You and John are being slung around like rag dolls, only being held in place by the seat belts as the truck rolls and rights itself. Your mind is foggy. You hear people running to the door. You hear them say, "Oh no. It's not them! Mark, it's not them!" You're facing John, as he lies motionless across the seat. You whisper so low, "John, I . . . ." But your mind refuses to form any more words. The last sensation you have is of hands pulling on your body.

Chapter 28 Jill - Day 5 - *How can it be...*

Birds are chirping outside. You hear them singing their beautiful morning songs. Slowly, you open your eyes. You're lying on your left side, your head resting on a soft clean pillow. You're looking straight through an open window. The curtains are tied back, yet they move in and out as a gentle breeze comes through the window. You don't move except for the blinking of your eyes. It seems so peaceful here. It reminds you of the Bed and Breakfast where you and Lizzy stayed in North Carolina a few years back. Why are you here? How did you get here? Oh, John! John's gone! He's gone! Tears start filling your eyes. The beautiful, peaceful day seems no more. Yet you do not stir. Grief overwhelms you, as the tears flow. "God, I don't understand. Why did you send him back into my life, just to snatch him away? I don't understand." You start having regrets. You wish John had not found you. At least he would still be alive. What about Will? Another flow of tears stream down your cheeks. I'm so sorry, Will. I'm so sorry, Lizzy, I've tried. I've tried to make it home. You hope she is with Will, as you realize you may never see home again.

Your eyes start looking at the room. It's a nice room. Obviously, a woman prepared this room with pastel colors and flower decorations. There is carpet on the floor and a dresser along the wall. Next to the dresser, leaning against the wall is your pack. Your shoes are neatly set beside your pack. Determination rises back inside you. You ARE going to make it back home. But how? Oh John, I need you as I've never needed you before! How are you going to make it when someone as capable as John doesn't? You think about what John has done for you through the years, how he's intervened on your behalf, even to the point of violence. You remember back in high school, him standing back up after defeating Clyde. He had blood on his face. He walked over to where you were sitting after being shoved down by Clyde. Kathy was there with you, her arms around your shoulders. John knelt down and asked, "Jill, are you okay?" The same words he asked this morning or whatever day it was. You whisper, "Thank you, John." Now, because he helped you again, he is gone. He is gone! You continue to silently sob.

But something is amiss. Your mourning stops and all your senses are alert. You still haven't moved. But you sense you're not alone. You listen, but you discern nothing. Then . . . something . . . something shakes the bed. Oh no, no, no, no! This isn't going to happen! You're going to die first! You start to turn quickly, but every bone and muscle in your body screams, STOP! Yet you turn, though slowly. There is a man in the bed beside you! "Oh Dear God no!" Your mind is racing. You frantically look around, searching for a weapon, but see nothing.

You slowly turn further around. You can see him now. He's lying there without a shirt. You quickly glance at yourself. Your shirt is on. You look under the covers. Your pants are on. You look back at the man. Your eyes grow wide. Tears blur your vision. You reach up and wipe them away. But how can it be? How can he be here? What does it mean? The man beside you is John!

You wipe the tears away and try to clear your vision. It is John. It's him. He has a large bandage around his head. He looks pale, but it's him, no doubt. You extend your arm, despite the pain, and touch his cheek. His head is partially turned toward you, as you gently touch him. His face is warm but not hot. You feel the stubble on his chin. John was clean shaven when you left the barn. This can't be the same day. You look into John's face. "Dear God, thank you. Thank you for saving John's life." You rest your hand on John's shoulder, close your eyes, and drift back to sleep.

Later you awaken still facing John and your hand resting on his shoulder. There is movement beyond the closed bedroom door. There are two doors in this bedroom. The one you hear the noises from is on the opposite side of the window. Maybe a hall, but you don't know where you are or whose house you are in. The last thing you remember was people trying to kill you and John, but if they were going to kill you, why place you here? Why treat John's wounds? You look at John again. He hasn't moved. His skin is slightly pale, probably from all the blood he lost. You see his chest rise and fall with each breath. Strong, steady breathing. His bloody shirt is gone, and his chest is bare. You see strong shoulders and strong arms. John is not a big man, but from what you see, there is no doubt he is a strong man.

You hear movement again and some voices. You sit up and almost cry as the pain is terrible, but you force yourself up and out of the bed. You still have your same clothes on. The only things removed were your shoes and your holster. You check your pocket; yes, the extra magazine and knife are gone, too. That makes you nervous. If they weren't going to hurt you, why would they take your gun? You have no idea where you are, how you got here or why you are here. You move to your pack, feeling pain with each step. You unzip your bag. No Glock. You look for the knife you always keep on the outside webbing of your pack. It's gone, too. You look around and on the opposite wall you see John's pack, with his boots neatly arranged by his pack. You quickly check it for weapons. None. Even his scabbard knife he keeps on the shoulder strap has been removed from its sheath. You go back to your pack. Digging down, you check one of the small pouches on the inside of your pack. Yes, there is your folding Kershaw knife your father gave you to keep in your bag. You put it in your pocket and slip your shoes on.

You need to go to the potty bad, but you can't, not knowing where you are and who is on the other side of the door. You look at John one more time, then head for the door. You try the door knob and it turns. Gently turning it, you slowly, very slowly open the door a crack and peek through, but all you can see is what looks like a hallway. You open the door further. It doesn't creak. That's good. You open it far enough to walk through. There is no way you're just going to poke your head through. Your dad had told you that was the fastest way to get a cracked skull if someone was on the other side. You ease through. Partially in and partially out. There are voices coming from your right. You scan the hall. It dead ends just a few inches to the left of your door. Across the hall, you see another door just to the right of yours and then another a little further down. They are both shut. It looks like, to the left, the hallway ends at a large room. You can see the back of a couch. You hear the voices again.

Slowly, you creep into the hall. Your body is raging in pain, but you force yourself to move. You remove your knife from your pocket and hold it behind your back in your right hand. You grip the handle with your thumb resting on the blade, ready to open it quickly. You ease down the hall. Your heart is racing and adrenaline is coursing through your body. The pain seems to be less. The sounds seem to be coming from the right side at the end of the hall. You creep further down. You're near the corner. The hall is shorter on the left side. You see a great room of some type. It has a fireplace, couches, chairs, two recliners and a TV. There is a bookshelf lining one wall. You look at the decorations and picture frames. It seems like a homey place. Christian type decorations are many. It gives you some comfort, but you still don't know why you are here.

It sounds as if the voices are in a low conversation. Maybe three, two men and a woman, but you can't tell what they are saying. You ease to the right corner and look around. You see them, an older man and woman and a middle age man. They are in a large kitchen that adjoins the great room. The men are sitting at a bar with their backs to you. The woman is leaning from inside the kitchen. She looks up and raises her hand to her face and says, "Praise the Lord. Praise the Lord, you are up!" She straightens, and the men turn and start to rise. You shrink back into the hall. You hear the woman, "You men be still. She's scared." You hear her walking toward you talking, "It's okay honey, we aren't going to hurt you. I'm so glad you are up walking. My name is Betty." She comes around the corner and looks straight at you, "Honey, I know you are scared. You've been through a lot, but we aren't going to hurt you, dear." She reaches out with an open hand. You look at her uncertainly. She has a kindly face. A woman, maybe in her sixties, older than your mother. You bring your right hand from behind your back. The woman looks at your knife, but doesn't back away or move her extended hand. You pocket the knife and stepping forward take her hand. Oh, how you wish you were with your mother! You step closer and the woman draws you near and gives you a gentle hug. The tears flow, you can't stop as you sob into this woman's chest. She wraps her arms around you and gently, like a mother, smooths your hair and says, "Go ahead and cry, honey. It's okay. Just go ahead and cry." You do. The days of stress, the days of uncertainly, the days of worry and the constant threat of harm have not found relief until the loving arms of this older woman embrace you.

Your tears flow for what seems like forever, until all have been shed. You withdraw from the embrace. The woman holds you at arm's length. You see the two men, their eyes look red and puffy. You look back at the kind face in front of you and say, "I have to use the bathroom." She says, "Of course, dear," and walks you back to your room.

Betty quietly opens the door to the bedroom and peeks in before opening it all the way. She walks through, as she leads you to the guest bathroom. She whispers, "I do hope your husband will wake soon, too." She opens the door to the bathroom and turns on the light saying, "Honey, the towels are in the cabinet underneath the sink. Shampoo and soap are in the shower. Let me know if you need anything, dear." You smile and say, "Thank you," as she walks out. You realize she just called John your husband. You start to tell her he is just your friend, but pause. You remember all the religious decorations you saw earlier and wonder whether if she knows you aren't married, they'll put you in separate rooms. You don't want to be separated from John, not for now anyway. So you refrain from correcting her.

You close and lock the door. After taking care of what your dad always called, "the paper work," you walk back to the lavatory. After washing and drying your hands, you look into the mirror. Your hand goes to your mouth and you gasp. This is the first time you have looked in a mirror in days. Your eyes begin to fill with water again. You hardly recognize the person looking back. Your hair is oily and matted in places. There are dark bags under your eyes. A blue knot is just above your right temple. The whole left side of your face is a ghastly black and yellow. There are bruises around your neck. Each individual bruise made by the fingers of your attacker when he choked you is visible.

You start undressing, first removing your shoes and socks, then your pants and now, your shirt. Lastly, your bra and undies. You look back in the mirror. Your upper body is covered with bruise marks. There is a horizontal burn mark all the way across your chest, just above your breasts, from the rope that unseated you from your bike. There are bruises on your arms, your ribs, a big black and yellow splotch across your upper back. Even your breasts have bruises. It's no wonder you hurt all over. "Dear God, thank you for keeping me alive," you whisper.

There is a light tap at the door. You pull your shirt up from the floor and cover yourself and say, "Yes?" Betty says, "Honey, I've brought you some clean clothes. I'll just place them on the bed. When you get ready, come to the kitchen for something to eat." "Thank you, Lord, for this precious lady!" you whisper to yourself. You drop your shirt to the floor, pushing it along with your other dirty clothes to the wall. Opening the cabinet, you pull out a large plush towel and wash cloth. They are soft. Obviously they haven't been used much. You move to the shower, place the large towel in the hanger, open the stall door, and turn the water on. Yes, there is hot water! You adjust it and step in. The warm water flows over your body and slowly seeps away some of your pain. You look at the shampoo and body washes. The first one you pick up is an Old Spice body/hair wash. You smell it. You like the smell, but not on you. There is also a bottle of VO5 shampoo and Bath and Body Works cucumber and melon body wash. The body wash smells light and fresh. Yes, this will do nicely. You wash your hair, taking extra care around the knot above your temple and the tender spot where your head hit the asphalt. The cucumber and melon smell is refreshing after the sweat smell you've had for nearly four days. Four days? You don't even know what today is. Has it been four days, or five days, or more? You don't know. You're going to have to ask Betty.

Drying off, you walk back to the mirror. It's fogged over, so you remove your towel and wipe it off. You look at yourself, considering what you have been through the past few days. It is truly amazing you are not in worse shape. If it hadn't been for the training your father gave you as a young woman, you would be dead. If it wasn't for the pack he insisted you keep up to date in your car, you would be dead. If it wasn't for the bike Mary's husband gave you, you would probably be dead. If it wasn't for John, you would be dead. If it wasn't for Betty and these people in this house, you would be dead. You see it clearly now. God has been with you your whole journey, intervening at the proper time to keep you alive. That gives you comfort. God is your protector. You will see Lizzy again. "Thank you, God. Thank you," is your short prayer.

Picking up the towel, you wrap it around yourself again and slowly open the door. You look at John. Good, he's still asleep. You gather the clothes Betty left on the bed and return to the bathroom. There is a pair of jeans. They are a little smaller than what you normally wear, but you've probably lost weight considering what you've been through. A turquoise pullover shirt, white ankle socks and white undies. But, the best item is a comfortable looking white bra! You check the size. Yes! It's going to be good. You put the undies and bra on, then think of drying your hair. You look for a hair dryer but don't see one. You're looking for a hair dryer? Really? A hair dryer? After an EMP attack and you're looking for a hair dryer? Then it dawns on you. There was hot water for the shower! The electric lights are working! They are working! You go to the light switch and turn it on and off. Yes! It works! The power is back on! Things are going to be normal again! You quickly finish dressing, brush your hair softly, put it in a ponytail using a hair band you found in the top drawer, then exit the bathroom.

You walk over and check on John. Smiling you whisper, "John, everything is going to be okay. I'll have that cup of coffee with you on the front porch soon." You walk out the door and close it slowly.

Chapter 29 Jill - Day 5 - *Jill are you okay…*

You walk down the hall. Not as timidly, as you did earlier. Despite your pain, you actually have a smile on your face. You feel happy again. Yes, everything is going to be all right. You walk into the kitchen and see Betty. She smiles and says, "Honey, you look like you feel much better now. Would you like some coffee while I fix you some breakfast?" "Yes, thank you, with cream," you reply. She pours your coffee and hands you a large mug and a bowl of creamer. You sit at the bar and stir cream into your coffee. The mug is warm in your hand. You bring it to your lips and carefully sip. Oh my. It's so good! You look around the kitchen. The cabinetry looks beautiful; it reminds you of some you saw that Pugh's Cabinets had made back home. You look at the appliances and granite counter top. You'll probably never have anything like this. It's beautiful. Betty says, "How do you like your eggs?" "Over medium, if it's not too much trouble." Betty says, "Oh dear, it's no trouble at all." You watch her walk over to the gas range and crack two eggs into a cast iron skillet.

The aroma of the kitchen reminds you how hungry you are. When was the last time you had a home cooked meal? It was back when your own mother cooked a very similar breakfast before you left for your meeting in Birmingham. You think of your mother, how gentle and sweet she has always been. Your dad, though a wonderful father, was sometimes rough around the edges. But not your mom. She had a way of bringing calm to most any situation. You watched that rough exterior of your dad calm down many times with the touch of your mother's hand upon him. Even when you had to tell your parents you were pregnant, your mother was able to calm your dad. But even she wasn't able to calm him when he found out Clyde was the father. He was so upset he left the room and left the house. Later, he came and wrapped his arms around you and hugged you close. Your dad would often say, referring to your mother, "Never underestimate the power of a good woman. With a cutting look from her eyes, she can send a strong man to his knees. But, with the gentle touch of her hand she can invigorate strength and courage into an otherwise defeated man." Well, it must only work on good men, because it certainly didn't work on Clyde.

Betty puts your eggs on a plate and spoons some grits from a pot on the stove. She opens the oven and removes a pan containing a few biscuits and bacon. She adds those to your plate and brings it to you. Handing you a fork, she sits on a stool across from you. "Go ahead, honey, and eat up," she says. You smile and say, "Thank you," but you pause and briefly close your eyes and thank God for this food. The food tastes so good. Oh, it really does and you're so hungry! You force yourself to slow down. You don't want to show bad manners.

Betty says, "If you'll get me the sizes of your husband, I'll see if I can't find him some clean clothes for when he wakes up. I don't think he can wear anything of George's, but I think I can round something up." You have a tinge of guilt as you hear her call John your husband again. You realize you don't know what size clothes he wears. John's not a big man, but he's not a small man either. Maybe he's about the height of your father, just not quite as thick. You'll have to check his clothes to see what size he wears. "Okay Betty, I will. His name is John." Betty smiles, "Yes, I know dear. My husband, George is his name, checked his license when you were brought here. We placed it in the top of your husband's pack. We didn't find any identification on you. So honey, I don't even know your name." You blush, "I'm sorry. My name is Jill. Jill Barnes." Betty looks a little surprised, but says nothing. You realize what was just said. John Carter and Jill Barnes. While it's not unheard of for a woman to keep her maiden name upon marriage, you have always thought it was strange and showed a lack of commitment and respect for the marriage. You remember it took nearly an act of congress to get your name changed back from Baker to Barnes after your divorce. You shudder at that thought. You say, "Betty, I don't want to deceive you. John is not my husband. He is a very dear friend. Maybe something more, I'm not sure." You tell Betty of your journey and your relationship with John through the years. You tell her about the barn and those evil men. You tell her how he arrived at just the right moment to save your life by killing those evil men and that he stayed with you until you recovered enough to travel. She listens intently and smiles, "Well, I thought something like that might be the reason you were in that truck. It sounds like you two are crossing paths for a reason." "Betty, I know this may sound unusual to you, and John and I are not intimate, but please don't put us in separate rooms. At least not until he is able to get around on his own." She pats your hand and says, "Don't worry dear, you can stay just like you are until you want another room."

"Betty, I don't know what day it is, or where we are, or even how we got here." Betty smiles and tells you what day it is. You realize you must have been unconscious for at least twenty four hours. That makes this day five after The Day. She continues, "We are in the country a little north west of Montevallo. As far as how you came to be here, Mark, George's nephew brought you here. I'll let them tell you the circumstances, if you don't mind." You think, "I've heard that name before." But you can't place it right now. You say, "Well at least things are getting back to normal with the electricity back on. I didn't realize just how dependent we are on electricity until it's been out for a few days. Do you know if the phones are working too? I would like to call and check on my daughter, Lizzy and my mother." Betty just looks at you, and after a pause, asks, "What do you mean getting back to normal?" You say, "You know, with the electricity back on. Surely it won't be long before the phones are working, too." Betty looks at you with sympathy in her eyes. She reaches back over with her hand and holds yours, "Honey, the electricity is not back on. If what George says is true, it's not coming back on for a very long time. I'm sorry you've got your hopes up. George has a generator and some other things he uses to make electricity. The power from the power company is not back on." You sit there, stunned. The great hope that things were getting back to normal fades away. You think with a sigh, "John, I guess we won't be having that cup of coffee on the front porch any time soon."

While you and Betty are talking, the kitchen door opens from outside.

Setting your coffee cup down on the counter you turn to look. A big, older man is stepping in. Behind him, though obscured by the first man, looks like a younger man, maybe about John's age. Betty says, "Jill, this is my husband George. George, this is Jill. This other young man is our nephew, Mark." You look at the man clearly. Your eyes grow wide! "What is this!" screams through your mind. This is the same face you saw looking at you with hatred in his eyes! This is the man who attacked you and John! You stand up quickly from the bar knocking the bar stool over and it clangs loudly on the tile floor. You start backing for the hall to retreat to the bedroom. Betty moves from around the bar and walks toward you, "Honey, I know you're confused. Please let me explain." You reach in your back pocket and bring out your knife, ready to open it if any one approaches. Betty stops. You say, "What is this! Don't come near me! I know who this is! This is the man who attacked us!" Desperation builds inside you and without thinking you holler, "John!" The men look stunned and don't move or say anything. Betty's eyes start to fill with tears, "I'm so sorry, Jill. I'm so sorry. It was all a mistake. They thought Earl was in that truck." You look over at the man. There are tears in his eyes, too. You don't know what to think. You pray, "Dear God, oh dear God, what do I do?"

From behind you, down the hall you hear the bedroom door jerk open. John comes staggering out. In a weak, but firm voice he asks, "Jill, are you okay?" He staggers forward, with his left hand reaching for his head. Again he says, "Jill, are you okay?" In his right hand is a pistol. In an instant, you consider all the ramifications of what you've just heard and what that pistol in John's hand means. He's ready to fight, though he isn't able. You make your decision. There really is no other one you can make. You move quickly to John. "Yes John, I'm okay," you say in a calm voice. He says, "Where are we? What happened? My head hurts so bad." You move closer to him. You put your knife back in your pocket and with one hand, you touch him on his chest saying, "I'm okay, John. Everything is okay." John's look shows confusion and he says, "I don't understand." You move even closer, "I know, John. I know you don't. I will explain later. But for now, please trust me. Everything is okay." He looks down at you and says "Of course, I trust you."

You reach for the pistol and say, "Let me have this, John." He lets go, and you put it in your front pocket. "Now, let's get you back in bed." You move to his side and place his arm around your shoulder, as you help him down the hall. He is losing strength, and his weight is becoming too heavy. You call out, "Betty, please help me, but only you." Betty comes to you and takes John's other arm, and the both of you return him to the bed.

In the bedroom, it takes both of you to get John situated in the bed. He lies back on the pillow and closes his eyes. Betty says, "I think he has a concussion. He needs rest, but we also have to get some liquids into him soon, real soon." You look over at Betty and say, "Okay, whatever we need to do, I will do. But first, tell me what's going on."

Betty moves from the bed and in a lowered voice says, "It was all a tragic mistake. The man that owned that truck you were in, raped Mark's daughter and another girl two days ago. They also beat a neighborhood boy and killed his brother. Mark and some of the men went out looking for them. They saw the old rusted up truck that Earl always drove and when they did, they attacked it. It was too late when they saw their mistake." Betty looks into your eyes, "Mark is devastated by what has happened. He is a good man and he is so sorry for the mistake he made. He brought you and your husband here, because I'm a former ER nurse." You notice she is calling John your husband again, but remain silent. She continues, "You were banged up pretty bad, but I didn't see any major injuries on you. Your husband, though, he was in pretty bad shape. He had a bullet wound from where a bullet skirted alongside his head. It didn't penetrate or damage his skull, but it did leave a nasty head wound and they always bleed so much. I cleaned his wound and stitched him up. But, he also must have hit his head pretty hard, giving him a concussion. We would have taken him to the hospital, but we've heard they were turning patients away, and thought we could give him better care here. He's going to be all right, Jill. He just needs some rest." You look at her, amazed at what she just said. You answer, "Mark's daughter must be one of the girls John freed before he saved me. John killed those men. We were using that truck to get home." Betty raises her hand to her mouth and says, "Oh my! Thank God for your husband."

You take the small pistol from your pocket. It looks like a Glock, though you've never seen one this small. You run your finger along the slide. Yes, you feel the slight raise of the ejector, indicating a round is in the chamber. You place it in your waistband just behind your right hip. Betty watches you, but doesn't say anything. She heads to the door, stops and turns. There are tears in her eyes again as she says, "Please don't kill Mark, he has a wife and two daughters." You walk quickly over to Betty. You embrace each other, as you both cry.

Chapter 30 Jill - Day 5 - *I forgive you…*

You are both still sniffling as you exit the bedroom and walk down the hall. You stop as the hall opens into the great room. Betty stops with you, with her arm still around you. George and the man both rise. You look at the man and you can't help it, you start to cry again. There are tears in the man's eyes, his face is contorted as in pain. He takes a step closer, then stops and says, "Ma'am, I'm so sorry. I am so, so sorry." Betty says, "Mark, Jill's husband is the man who freed your daughter." The man starts sobbing out loud. You look at him. You've never seen a man cry like this before. It shakes you. You have compassion for him, but you have no comfort to give him. John is lying in the bed, severely injured. No, you have no comfort for him. You simply say, "I forgive you, and I'm sure John will, too." The man sobs more, but after a few minutes he regains himself and says, "Thank you. I think I should leave now. When your husband is awake and able, I will come face him." He tells Betty and George goodbye and nods toward you and walks through the door. You look over at George; he is wiping tears from his eyes, too.

George says, "Betty, some coffee please. I need something to ease these shattered nerves." Betty says, "Yes, of course George. Jill, would you like to help me?" You say, "Yes," and follow her into the kitchen. She prepares the coffee in the percolator and sets it on the gas stove. After a while it starts to percolate. She says, "I always let mine percolate for about ten minutes. If you like it stronger, you can always let it go longer." You say, "Whatever you fixed earlier was great." Betty says, "Well, that's the way I did it. Would you open the pantry door over there? I think there is an unopened bag of chocolate chips. Would you get them so we can have something to munch on?" You go over and open the pantry, expecting to see a small closet, but instead you see a fairly large room. It's stocked full of food, paper products and other household essentials. Your eyes grow wide with amazement. You have never seen so much food and supplies outside of a store. You look at the door and see the chocolate chips. Getting them, you return to Betty. She hands you a plate, "Put some on here, honey. Thank you."

Betty says, "While this coffee is percolating, why don't you go see if you can get John to drink some apple juice. The glasses are in the cabinet by the sink, and the juice is in the door of the fridge." You walk over and get a thick tumbler from the cabinet and pour it about three quarters full. You start toward the bedroom and Betty says, "Try to get him to drink all of it if he will, but don't force him. I'll check his bandage later." You say, "Okay." and head for the bedroom. You open the door and walk over to John. He is asleep. You place your hand on his shoulder. His eyes open. He starts to rise and you say, "I have some juice for you. Can you drink it? You really need to." He says, "Yes. I am thirsty. Thank you." He takes the glass and slowly drinks it without saying a word. He hands the glass back to you and asks, "Jill, what's going on? What happened and where are we?" You respond, "We were in a very bad accident and you were severely injured. These people, George and Betty, have taken care of your wounds and allowed us to stay here for a while." But you really don't know how long a while is. "Betty told me we are north west of Montevallo." "North west of Montevallo? Hmm, we didn't travel far then, did we? I'm sorry, Jill. I just can't remember anything after pulling out on the road from the barn. What happened?" "I'll explain everything soon, I promise. But for now, you need rest. I need you to recover and regain your strength so we can go home." He lays back down and says, "Okay, Jill," and closes his eyes. You look at him for a minute to make sure he goes back to sleep. You had not intended to call out his name earlier. It just came out. You were in need and you called out to who? The only person outside your family who has ever come to your aid. He did it again this morning, despite his pain. "What is happening, John? What is happening?" You ask yourself, but find no answer.

You return to the kitchen. Betty and George are in the great room drinking coffee. Betty says, "Help yourself, dear." You place the glass in the sink, then fix a cup of coffee. You walk into the great room and sit in a large cushioned chair across from where Betty and George are sitting. You look around the room again. This time paying more attention to the details. Yes, this room has seen a lot of living. Not wear and tear, but it's obvious good people lived in this room. You sip the coffee. Yes, it's good. George says, "I don't want to drown us all in deep emotions, but I want to tell you how sorry I am for what has happened to you and John. Without making excuses for Mark, I will say he is a good man. Betty has told me some of your story. It looks like you have had a really rough time. You are safe here. No one is going to hurt you or your husband. I promise you that. You are welcome to stay here as long as you need or as long as you want. When you do, if you do, want to leave, we will not try to hold you back. Mark has had all your things gathered from the . . . the wreck and brought here. Your packs are in your room. Your other gear is in the garage, though some of it is in pretty bad shape. Your guns, we gathered all your guns, at least I thought we had, and they are in a safe place. I'll return them to you as soon as I talk with your husband. You can keep the one you have, if it'll make you feel better." You think, "These are good people, they truly are." After having encountered so much evil over the past few days, George and Betty give you hope. "Thank you both. I know without your help we would be dead. I can't care for John with the little we have. Thank you. I know as soon as John is able we will want to travel back home. He has a son and I have a daughter back home, expecting our return." He looks a little puzzled so you continue, "I've told Betty, and I'm sure she has just forgotten, John is not my husband. He is . . . is . . . I really don't know how to say it . . . a very special and important friend to me. I won't willingly part from his side, at least not until we return home." George says, "Okay. That's fine. You are both welcome in our home." Betty says, "I'm sorry, Jill. It just seemed like the right word to say." You smile, "Betty, there is no harm done, but John will really be surprised if he wakes up and finds he has a wife." You all chuckle a little.

"Betty, I wasn't trying to be a snoop earlier, but when you asked me to get the cookies, I couldn't help but notice the largest pantry I have ever seen." George says, "Well, Betty and I have been sensing for a very long time that things weren't just right in this country; that hard times, some very hard times were on the horizon. Oh, we didn't know we were going to get hit by an EMP, but we knew it was a possibility. We've taken steps through the years to prepare for hard times, such as we have right now. Part of those plans were to have a significant amount of food stored. What you saw in the pantry is part of our preparations. When you walk outside, you'll see most of the rest, at least food wise." You ask, "Didn't that cost a small fortune? I mean, that is a large pantry." George smiles, "That's what a lot of folks think, and maybe that's what keeps them from preparing for difficult times. In truth, if you eat what you store, then there is really no cost to it. Actually, you save money. Yes, initially, depending on how long you take to build your food reserves, it requires more money upfront. But it's really not a cost, it's an investment and an insurance policy." You ask, "What do you mean?" George continues, "From the insurance perspective consider this. Why do you buy insurance? In case something bad happens. Right? You don't buy insurance in case something good happens, well I guess it is a good thing when children are born, some of them anyway." Betty slaps George on the shoulder, "George!" George continues, "As I was saying, investing in a food reserve is the same thing, except it may be even more important to your life. Well, in our circumstances it is. Our home insurance is useless right now. Our car insurance is useless. Who is going to payout the life insurance proceeds if I die? Our food insurance is going to pay us now. If we were like so many unprepared people, with maybe a week's worth of food, do you think we would be able to help you like we are? No. In order to truly help others, you must first help yourself. If you have nothing, you have nothing to help others with."

You say, "Yes, I understand what you are saying. Wish I had been more forward thinking. I have about a month's worth of food in our home. But how do you see it as an investment?" George smiles even bigger, "You see, the food I bought last year that we are using today cost less than it does today. Well, at least before the EMP. For now, let's don't consider the EMP. If I invest one thousand dollars and put it in a CD at the bank, what kind of interest rate do you think I would get? How much at the end of the year would that thousand dollar CD be worth? I can tell you, because I have some. The current suppressed interest rate is around a quarter of one percent. At the end of a year, my thousand dollar CD will be worth one thousand two dollars and fifty cents. So I've made two dollars and fifty cents by investing in a bank CD. Cometh the tax man. Since the two dollars and fifty cents is interest income, it gets taxed at twenty eight percent. So, after taxes, I end up with a gain of one dollar and eighty cents. I loan the bank one thousand dollars for a year and I profit one dollar and eighty cents. Sounds good doesn't it?"

"Now, consider food inflation has been at least six percent every year, despite the bogus numbers published by the government. If I took that same one thousand dollars and invested it in the food I will need, then the value of that food at the end of the year when I will actually be using it is one thousand and sixty dollars. Since I will be consuming the food and not selling it, there is no tax on this increased value. Investing one thousand dollars in a food reserve earns me sixty dollars. Investing one thousand dollars in a bank CD earns me one dollar and eighty cents. You can do the math and compare the profits from both." "Wow, I never thought of it like that. I wonder how many people would have thought differently if they had considered what you just said. Me, I guess, I always thought of it as short term insurance. You know like for hurricanes and if I lost my job and my income was reduced for a while," you say.

You think out loud without realizing it, "I wonder if John has thought about these things. He told me this event didn't catch him completely unprepared, but I don't know what that actually means." George says, "Judging, from what I have seen of his gear, mind you I didn't go snooping, he seems to be prepared better than most. In fact, at least with his gear, better than anybody I know." George continues, "When you walk outside, you'll see where our real food reserves come from. The breakfast you ate this morning, except for the flour and coffee, came from outside. It's not hard to be prepared, but it does take a mindset and a determination to be so. It doesn't just happen."

You say, "I am still very tired and weak and emotionally spent. If you don't mind, I'm going to lie back down. I can help you around here later, Betty, if you'd like." Betty says, "Of course dear, we understand. You have to be a very strong woman. I think most women would have given up. John is fortunate to have you stay by his side for your journey home. Go get yourself some rest."

You get up and walk to the bedroom and take some ibuprofen for the pain that is still wracking your body. You consider the roller coaster of emotions you've experienced today. You can't even begin to describe it to yourself. It has left you mentally exhausted. You remove your shoes and hair band. You look at the Glock. It's smaller than any you've seen before. There is just enough light in the room to discern the slide engraving. You remove the magazine and eject the chambered round. It's a Glock model 42 in 380 auto. It's small and very compact. The magazine has a capacity of six rounds and has five cartridges in it. You point, aim and fire the unloaded weapon several times to get the feel of the gun. The trigger is the exact same as you have encountered on the other Glocks you have shot. You put the ejected round into the magazine, insert it into the pistol and load a round. After verifying the round has loaded, you put it back in your waistband. You get your pack and place it front of the nightstand. Opening the top you place the Glock inside with the muzzle pointed down. You take a deep sigh and crawl into the bed. John is in that bed. A few days ago it would have been a completely foreign thought for you, but today, in this time, it just seems natural. You sense a bonding occurring. You don't know what kind. Maybe it's because of the circumstances that you find yourselves in. Maybe when you arrive home everything will be as before. You don't know. But for now, you need each other. You won't be leaving his side. Not now and maybe . . .

Chapter 31 Jill - Day 6 - *I don't snore...*

You open your eyes. The light is dim, as with the waning of the sun. You're facing the window and the birds are chirping their music again. It sounds almost as if it was the break of day. You roll over and reach out to touch John. He isn't there. He isn't there? Did something happen to John? Where could he be? You sit up, still very sore, and look around. There, sitting in the chair, is John. You quickly get out of the bed and move to his side. "John, are you okay?" you ask, "What are you doing out of bed?" He smiles and says, "Jill, it's 5:30 a.m. I'm always awake at 5:00 and having a cup of coffee by 5:30. Besides, you snore." Your mouth falls open. You try to speak, but words won't come out. Sitting on the table beside the chair is a John Deere coffee cup about half full of coffee. John's finger is inside the handle, and he has a big silly grin on his face. You try to speak again. Finally, the words come out, "I don't snore!" A little harshly you ask, "Where did you get that coffee?" John asks, "Are you always in this bad of a mood in the morning? Here have some of my coffee. Maybe you'll be more companionable." "John!" you say in exasperation, "what is going on!" "Jill," he says, "I think you must be confused. It's 5:30 in the morning." You slump down to the floor, next to the chair. You were so exhausted you slept through the afternoon and night without waking. You've been so worried about John, seeing him up and talking is almost overwhelming. "John, I . . . I've been worrying about you. You were hurt so bad. I . . . I . . ." John bends slightly over and reaches down and touches the side of your face. Smiling he says, "Thank you, Jill. I am hurt. I am hurt bad, but I'm going to be okay. My head still hurts, but at least my mind is clear. My strength has not returned. I'm going to need a few more days for that. I've talked with Betty briefly this morning, hence the coffee, but I still don't know what happened or where our guns are." You look up at him, then rise and walk to the night stand. You reach inside your pack and retrieve the Glock. You walk back over to John and hand it to him. John looks at it for a moment, then says, "You keep it on you. It's our only defensive weapon we have right now. Don't let anybody take it away from you." Reaching into his pocket he says, "Here is the extra magazine." You reach for it and put it in your pocket. You tuck the Glock in your waist band, turn and say, "I have to potty." You stop at the bathroom door and look back at John, saying, "And I don't snore!"

Your clothes are all wrinkled and your hair is disheveled. You really want to take a shower, but really need to talk with John first. How is he going to take it? You don't know. Walking back into the room, you look at John, he's putting things back in his pack. You had forgotten you had seen a lot of his stuff on the floor beside his bag when you and Betty put him to bed. The Glock must have been hidden in there somewhere. "John, I need to talk to you about what happened." He stands up slowly and says, "Yeah, Jill, I don't remember anything, really. I'm sorry for wrecking the truck and getting us hurt. I hope the truck is okay and we can still use it." He sits back in the chair and you sit on the edge of the bed across from him. You look across at him, "John, it wasn't your fault. You remember those cousins you were worrying about?" He says, "Oh crap, did they ambush us? How did we get away?" "Well, no, it wasn't them." He asks, "Well, who then?" You reply trying to figure how to explain it without becoming too emotional. "You remember the girls and boy you found and freed? One of the parents and some other men came looking for Earl and his gang. They saw the old truck and thought it was Earl and attacked us. They realized their mistake, but it was too late." John stares blankly for a moment, "I can understand that, but those idiots, they should have made sure who they were attacking! Look at me. I'm so weak and I know I've lost a lot of blood. What did I do, other than set his daughter free? How did we get here?" You think of what John just said. His good deed almost cost both of your lives. "When they realized their mistake, they tried to help us. Betty and George's nephew brought us here. They treated your wounds and have agreed to allow us to stay here as long as we need." "What about the rest of our gear and our guns?" John asks. "George says our other gear is in the garage and he's put our guns up in a safe place and will return them after he talks with you." Continuing you say, "John, I think it was a horrible mistake. I met the man who did this and he is truly distraught and sorry. I never watched a man cry like he did. I truly believe he is sorry." "How long have we been here?" John asks. "This is the third day," you answer. "Crap," John says, "the cities ought to be about to fall apart now. People are going to be on the move, a lot of people. It's going to make our trip even more difficult." "You really think so?" "Yes, I do. I'll regain what strength I can today, then we need to hit the road tomorrow. Let's see, this is our third day here? Hmm, that makes it six days after The Day. Maybe two more days to get home. That's my best guess, anyway."

He looks over looking directly into your eyes. You quiver slightly as you look back into his blue eyes. He says, "Jill, thank you for caring for me. Thank you." Blushing a little, you smile, "It's okay, John. You did more for me. I'm just so glad you are up. I truly am." "And Jill," John says, "I'm truly sorry for allowing us to be ambushed. I should have been paying more attention, though I don't remember any of it." You say, "It's okay, John. It's not your fault. Everything is going to work out." Though on the inside you have no idea how any of this will work out. Then continuing, "Let's go see if we can talk Betty into some breakfast."

Chapter 32 John - Day 6 - *A small voice...*

Before leaving the room for breakfast, you stop Jill, saying, "Jill we've been through a lot since we left the barn. About much of which I know nothing, but if you don't mind, let's pray." "Yes, John," Jill says, "please do." You go to one knee beside the bed, Jill follows suit. Bowing your head, you pray, "God, for Your great hand of protection, we thank You. I don't know what all You have done, as is often the case, nonetheless I thank You. Thank You for these kind people who have helped us. Please allow us to continue our journey soon. Protect our children. In Jesus' name. Amen." You hear Jill whisper "Amen."

You stand and Jill does, too. She says, "Thank you, John. Thank you for doing that. Now let's go eat." She opens the door and enters the hall. You are right behind her. You take notice where she tucked the Glock, just in case. She tucked it in her waist band in the same position you carry yours, just behind her right hip. Those hips . . . You've never paid much attention to them, but this morning, for some reason, you do. Pleasantly curved, is the first thing that comes to your mind. The second thing is a pang of admonishment, as you think to yourself, "You don't have time for this. Neither of you. You have to get yourself and Jill back home safely. Then . . . we'll see." But, you can't help it. You have to look one more time.

As you reach the end of the hall way, you see a big, older man. The man says, "John, my name is George. It's good to see you up and about. I know you have a lot of questions. But, Betty has a fine breakfast cooked and it's hot. So if you don't mind, let's eat first." You smell the food and your stomach says, 'don't argue,' so you say, extending your hand for a shake, "Sure, George. I do have a lot of questions, but they can wait a little longer." You study the man as you move to the table. He's a big man, maybe in his late sixties or early seventies. Obviously, a hardworking man used to outdoor activities. You hold the chair back for Jill. She's probably going to fuss, but this is what your dad taught you to do. You recall one of his talks, "Son, always, under all circumstances, be kind to women. Never think their delicate feminine ways are a sign of weakness. Because in truth, they are stronger than men. The fact that any of us are born is evidence of that." You sure would like to see your dad right now.

You sit next to Jill. Betty brings a plate of food and sets it before you. Your plate is covered with fried eggs, grits, bacon and biscuits. A large tumbler of milk is before you. George asks the blessing on the food, and you start to eat. You notice what you are eating is not store bought food. You can tell the eggs are yard eggs, the grits have been milled by a small grist mill, the bacon is thick, smoky and still has the rind on it. Yes, this breakfast probably came from outside that kitchen door. You say, between bites, "Mrs. Betty, this is so good. It reminds me of home." Betty smiles and says, "Thanks and don't be bashful. I have plenty more on the stove and George doesn't like to eat left overs." You smile, "Yes ma'am. I'll do my best to keep George from having to eat left overs." You turn toward George and ask, "Did you raise the pigs, or is there a local pig farmer around?" George cocks his head and asks, "What makes you ask that?" "Well," you say, "This is thick cut smoke cured bacon. Hickory I would say. Not the smoke flavored stuff from the store. And those grits, they were milled at a local grist mill is my guess." George smiles, "Yes, everything here is from our small farm or our neighbors. Everything except the flour. Nobody around here has planted wheat in a long time." George continues, "I can tell you're an observant man. That's good, real good. If you want, later I'll show you around."

After your third trip back to the stove, you tell Betty, "Ma'am, I'm sorry, I tried, but I just can't eat anymore." Betty brings coffee to the table. You should have brought your mug from the bedroom. You'll have to go get it later. The coffee is hot. Turning to George you say, "George, I appreciate everything the both of you have done for me and Jill. We've been through a lot. It's good to see there is still good in this world." Looking at Betty, you ask, "What happened to my head?" George says, "I don't know what Jill has told you, but son, you were shot in the head. You are fortunate to be alive."

You sit, stunned. You were shot in the head? Why didn't Jill tell you that earlier? You see her looking down. Her eyes are getting moist. You ask, "How bad is it?" afraid of the answer you will receive. Betty says, "John, I'm not going to sugar coat it. You had a nasty gash, and you lost a lot of blood. That's why you feel so weak. But the bullet did not hit bone. I was able to sew you up nicely, and when your hair grows out, I don't think anyone will be able to see the scar." You say in a low voice, "Thank you."

George says, "Let's step out to the garage. I know you want to see your gear. But I'm going to warn you, some of it is pretty damaged." You all get up and walk to the garage through the side kitchen door. Next to the far wall you see your tent, sleeping pad and a box containing some water bottles and MREs. You walk over to the box. Looks like four MREs and six bottles of water. You pick your GPS from the box, it's cracked and coming apart. The likelihood it will work is slim. You turn it on. Nothing. You'll try new batteries later. But the loss of this is a hard blow, a really hard blow. Then, you see the pile of bent metal near the garage doors. Your and Jill's bikes are twisted and bent. You let out a curse. There is no way to fix those things, no way at all. Then a load of bricks hit you. The bikes being twisted like they are can only mean one thing. "George, the truck. Where is the truck?" you ask with a shaking voice. George says, "John, I'm really sorry. The truck is a total loss. It rolled down an embankment, completely crushing the front end. I'm truly sorry." The bricks are piling on. Your mind is reeling. The enormity of the implications are clear. That bastard, whoever he is, has killed you. Your plans and preparations mean nothing, as in a brief moment some bastard has taken it all away. You're one hundred fifty miles from home, with less than a week's worth of food between you and Jill, no transportation, with a serious head injury. It'll be days before you can carry your pack. Days! Then what? Walk you and Jill to your deaths? Maybe with the GPS you could have taken to the woods and navigated around questionable areas. But you don't even have that now. You look over at Jill. She's looking at you. You ask George, "Where are our guns?" George says, "John, they are in a safe place, and I'll give them to you, but first I want you to talk to Mark, he's our nephew, and he brought you here. After you talk to him, I'll give them all to you." You say, "Okay George, I'm in no position to make demands." You look at George and then Betty. They both have concern in their eyes. You look at Jill. She is weeping. You turn and walk back to the bedroom, cursing silently as you go.

Jill follows you into the bedroom. Your mind is still reeling and the weight of the bricks you feel upon you is overwhelming. You sit in the chair. Jill sits on the bed across from you as before. She asks, "What are we going to do?" You look over at her, still unsure of yourself, "I'm not sure. As soon as I have enough strength to carry my pack, I should start back south. Maybe in three weeks, or so, I can make it home," you respond. "Jill, I'm not sure we can actually make it home on foot. It's going to be very dangerous. Things are only going to get worse. I think you should stay here and let me go alone." Jill jumps to her feet asking, "Are you abandoning me, John!" Her words sting. You look at her and rise from your chair. You walk to her. Her arms are across her chest. She is looking straight into your eyes. You want to hold her, but you're not sure if you should. She is trembling. You reach out and pull her to yourself. She leans on your chest, as you wrap your arms around her and hug her tight. "Jill, I will never abandon you. I want you to live." She pushes away, looks back up at you and says firmly, "I will not part ways from you, John Carter. I will not. Where you go, I will go." She turns and walks out the door.

You sit back in the chair. Your body is still weak and you are tired. The enormity of what has happened, your destroyed plans and your weakened condition have caused you to despair. How are you going to keep the both of you alive until you make it back home? You don't know. You have got to figure something out. But first and foremost, you must shake these foreboding thoughts from your mind. There is no time for them. It's not just your life anymore. It's hers, too. As long as God allows you to remain, you will do the best you can, with the best you have, to live and help those around you live. You owe yourself, Jill, Will, Lizzy and your other family and friends nothing less. You rise and walk out of the room. Jill is in the great room, sitting in a big chair. Her feet are tucked up in the chair. She has a paper towel in her hand, dabbing at her tears. You walk over and kneel by the chair.

"Jill, I'm sorry. Of course we'll go together. We need to plan. We will make it, but it's going to be hard, very hard." You reach over and squeeze her hand. She holds tightly to you. You say, "I'm still weak. After I've rested some, let's sit down and plan our course of action." She smiles and says, "Yes, John, get some rest, then let's make our plans."

You return to the bedroom and lie upon the bed. You need a bath. But you are just too spent right now. You look up at the ceiling, considering everything that has happened up to this point. You should have been stranded back on the interstate, but you weren't. You should have been killed at the barn, but you weren't. You should have been killed from the ambush, but you weren't. You're still alive. You think of Will, "Will should be okay. If he follows the plan, he should be okay." What about Lizzy? If she's with Will, she should be okay, too. You pray, "Dear God, if ever I needed you, I need you now." You drift into sleep.

Sometime later you awaken, alone in the room. You have got to have a bath. You check your pack. Your dirty clothes have been removed. You have a clean t-shirt, boxers and a pair of clean socks. That is all of your clothes. Jill must have removed your other clothes. But, you had two shirts. You wore the first one for what? Three or four days? Now a t-shirt. What happened to your other clean shirt? Did you leave it somewhere? Your mind searches back. Yes, at the barn you gave it to Jill to wear. She only wore it for a day. Maybe it's in her pack. You'll ask her later. The t-shirt will do for now. You walk into the bathroom and flip on the light. It doesn't work. You try it again, it still doesn't work. Guess George's generator has quit working. Maybe you can help him with it later. You close the door, but it's too dark to see. With it open you have just enough light to see with. You look back into the bedroom, yes the door is closed. You get a towel and wash cloth and turn the shower on. Stripping down, you step into the shower. You see the Old Spice and, trying to keep your head from getting wet, you bathe. Getting dressed, you walk out. The bedroom door is still closed. You feel naked without your Glock. What's up with this "meet Mark before you get your guns?" Who is this Mark? Is he some kind of leader to a small group? You don't know, but you're in no position to make demands yet. Before you leave you will have them, even if you have to pull the Glock from Jill's hip to get them. For now, you need these people. They have been very good and kind, but it just seems like they are holding something back.

You go to the floor and, wanting to gauge your recovery, you start doing pushups. You get to twenty before your strength leaves. You have a ways to go, a long ways. You exit the bedroom and walk down the hall. There is plenty of natural light coming through the windows of the kitchen and great room. You see George and Betty at the two ends of the table. Jill is sitting with her back to you. Almost across from her is another man, about your age. You don't recognize him. Jill, sensing your arrival stands up and asks, "Would you like a cup of coffee?" You say, "No, not right now. Thanks." You motion for her to sit and you help her with her chair, then sit next to her, directly across from the man.

It's quiet for a moment. Then the man speaks, "My name is Mark. Mark Anderson." The man has a frank expression on his face. He continues, "My daughter, Karen, is one of the girls you rescued from the barn. I want to thank you for what you did. It was a brave and honorable thing. I can't truly express my appreciation and gratitude." You sense there is something more going on here. The man takes a deep breath and continues, "I am also the man responsible for what happened to you and your wife. I made a very bad mistake and it has cost you dearly, I know. I am truly sorry." Your mind starts processing his words, "So this is the bastard who has killed me and Jill!" This bastard has destroyed your plans, destroyed your means of getting home and shot you in the head! You feel the anger start to rise inside you. You killed a man for trying to take your bike. You would have killed Officer Brunson if he had taken your bike. You killed those evil bastards for what they were doing to Jill. Here, right in front of you, is the bastard that has done all those things! You may never see your son again. Lizzy will never see her mom. Jill is going to die, because this bastard 'made a mistake'! Does he think 'sorry' means anything to you when he's taken your very life! You feel a darkness invading your soul as your fury mounts. The man continues, with an expressionless face, "I know there is nothing that I can truly do to make this right." He reaches behind his back and pulls out your Glock and holster and sets them on the table in front of him. The grip is pointing toward you and the barrel toward himself. You hear a gasp of air come from Jill and Betty. From the corner of your eye you see a stern expression on George's reddening face. Looking at the Glock, Mark says, "I took this off your hip when we brought you here. It's just like it was. It hasn't been unholstered. I have one just like it, but not needing it today, I left it at home. I brought yours in case you felt a need for it." He looks up at you with no outward expression of emotions and slides your Glock across the table in front of you. He sits back, with no expression on his face and folds his hands. You reach for the Glock. It's definitely yours. Your hand molds around the grip, with your extended index finger, you release the pistol retention and slide it from the holster. You run your finger across the slide, feeling the ejector is slightly raised, indicating a round is in the chamber. You slide your finger down to the frame, just above the trigger, and pause. This bastard across the table from you, is he expecting sympathy from you? This man who's stupidity is going to cause your and Jill's death! You think about what will happen to Jill after you are killed. The fury inside is overwhelming. You grip the Glock harder. You're going to make this bastard pay! As the rage and darkness envelope you, you hear a small voice from somewhere deep inside, it's just a faint whisper, "John, John, you are a good man. You must fight to remain what you are, even if it means fighting yourself." At that moment you feel a trembling hand touch your arm. You glance over at Jill. There are tears and a pleading expression in her eyes. Your eyes are locked for a moment. Her gaze is penetrating. The darkness inside starts to fade, and the burning fury subsides. Sanity returns. You loosen your grip on the Glock. Looking the man straight in the eyes, you holster your pistol and place it on your hip. Then say, "I hope your daughter can recover from what has happened to her." Betty's hand is covering her mouth as she weeps. Jill leans her head in your arm, and the red in George's face lessens. The man says, still without expression, "Yes, she will. In fact, she wanted to come thank you herself, but I told her to wait."

"Mark, I don't know what it is you want from me. If it's forgiveness, I grant it. But the fact remains, you have killed us." For the first time, the man's eyes falter, and a pained look appears across his face, "I know," he states simply, "But, I've been trying to figure a way to get you some transportation. There is a guy around here who has an extra 4-wheeler. I've tried to buy it from him, but he won't take cash, and he says I have nothing of value to him. He did say he wanted an AK47, plus silver and gold. I was thinking, if you could part ways with your AK, I could combine it with the silver I have and maybe some from other folks around here, and maybe I can get the 4-wheeler for you." You smile slightly, "Well Mark, maybe you didn't kill us after all, if you can get me the 4-wheeler and enough fuel for one hundred and fifty miles. I have the AK, an SKS, a Hi-point pistol and these." You reach in your pocket and pull out two quarter ounce gold eagles and ten one ounce silver eagles and place them on the table. Jill looks up at you with a puzzled expression on her face as if to ask, "Where did you get these?" You smile and say, "I told you I wasn't completely unprepared." Jill smiles back.

"Mark, I need a 4-wheeler big enough to carry me and Jill and both our packs and enough fuel to make it to Jackson, in Clarke County. If you can get me that, you may save our lives. Use whatever you need of what I just told you. If there is anything left, I also want to trade for a 22 rifle and some ammo and a few other things. Let me know what's left, then I'll tell you what we need." Mark stands and asks, "Will you trust me with these things?" You say, "Yes, I will Mark. George, will you return my guns so I can give Mark the ones we talked about?" George says, "Yes, of course" and leaves to get the guns. Mark stretches out his hand. You reach out yours. You shake hands. He says, "Thank you." You respond, "You're welcome." You might just like this bastard after all.

Chapter 33 Jill - Day 6 - *Don't let him fall...*

You sense the turmoil inside John as Mark says, "I am also the man responsible for what happened to you and your wife. I made a very bad mistake and it has cost you dearly, I know. I am truly sorry." Though you don't truly understand what the mistake is going to cost you, you know John does. The fact he wanted to leave you here tells you he thinks death awaits you on the road. Mark continues, "I know there is nothing that I can truly do to make this right." Then the gun appears. You gasp. Is he going to kill John? Your hand reaches for the Glock on your hip. If he starts to unholster that gun, you are going to kill him. Your course is set, if he tries to hurt John, you will kill him. You hear no more of Mark's words. You watch him closely. He slides the gun toward John. Your eyes grow wide with fear as you watch John unholster the pistol. You watch his finger as he checks to see if it is loaded. Mark is just sitting there. You pray, "Dear God, reach inside John. Don't let him fall! Please, God!" You must help John. You reach with your trembling hand and touch his arm. He looks at you, and you see the rage and fury in his eyes. There is nothing you can say in words. All you can do is reach out to John with your eyes. Your eyes lock with John's and plead with him. You both look deeply into the other. Then a transformation seems to take place inside him. The hate subsides from his eyes. The real John. The good man reappears. He holsters his pistol then says, "I hope your daughter can recover from what has happened to her." Relief overwhelms you. Your head falls to John's arm. You pray, "Thank you, God. Thank you for saving this good man. Thank you for bringing him from the precipice of self-destruction."

You listen, as John and Mark talk. Maybe there is some hope. John says, "Well Mark, maybe you didn't kill us after all, if you can get me the 4-wheeler and enough fuel for one hundred and fifty miles. I have the AK, an SKS, a

Hi-point pistol and these." You watch John reach into his pocket and pull out some gold and silver coins and place them on the table. You look up at John amazed. He smiles at you and reminds you of what he's told you before, "I told you I wasn't completely unprepared." You smile. "Thank you, God, for putting this man back in my life."

Betty gets up from the table, still wiping her eyes. You follow her to the kitchen. She looks at you and says, "God is so good. He is so good." She embraces you close. You pour a cup of coffee and add some cream. You walk back to the table and see John and Mark shaking hands. As they part, you look up at John and hand him the cup of coffee. He smiles and says, "Thank you."

Chapter 34 John - Day 6 - *A walk around the farm...*

Going outside with George, you tell him you can work on his generator if he needs you to. George smiles and says, "There's no problem with the generator. We only run it eight hours a day, in order to conserve fuel. From 5:00 a.m. to 9:00 a.m., and from 5:00 p.m. to 9:00 p.m. This gives us enough run time for the freezers and allows us to do our chores around the house and farm before dark. We have enough diesel for our farm equipment and eight hours of generator usage for about a year. If fuel supplies are not available by then, we'll have to figure something else out." George stops, turns, and says, "John, take a look around. Tell me what you see." You slowly look around. You see the pastures, the livestock, and the bird yard. There are barns of various sizes, tractors and various pieces of farm equipment. You see a large LP fuel tank and not far from it, a diesel fuel tank. A small building that looks like a pump house is around back of the house. There are some pecan trees around the house, offering shade. A small postage stamp fruit orchard, with about a dozen trees, is to the south side of the house. Just outside the kitchen is a small vegetable garden with some young plants growing. You see potatoes, pole beans, squash and other vegetables. A gravel road runs between two pastures on its way to the county road, about one quarter mile away. You say, "I see quite a few things. I see a well-planned and organized small farm. In the pastures I see a renewable food supply with the cattle and sheep. Breakfast is in the bird yard. Further back, I see planted fields, with what I'm going to assume is feed for the stock. I see the equipment and fuel supply necessary to work something on this scale. I see a dead truck, a dead car and a dead new tractor, none of which may ever work again. What I don't see is bacon. Looks to me George, with what you have here, you can sustain yourselves for a very long time, if someone doesn't come along and take it." George says, "We've considered that, too. Our community has banded together. We have manned road blocks on the two county roads coming in, and we have a roving crew of guards. It does stretch our ability to take care of our farm needs, though. I swap hamburger for bacon with my neighbor."

Walking back to the kitchen, George stops you. "Son, before we go in I've got something to say. Mark is fortunate you are a good man. I sensed you were struggling trying to decide what to do with that pistol. I thank God, Jill was there to save you and Mark. You better not let go of that woman. Mark is going to do everything he can to get the things you talked about. I'm going to tell you, and you probably already know, even with a 4-wheeler, you are going to have a very hard time." You say, "George, you and Betty are two of the nicest people I have ever met. I have a son and Jill has a daughter counting on our return. Actually, my community is much like yours here. We can only survive as a community, and as a part of that community, I must return." George says, "It's 5:00. I better go crank the generator. Let's meet back inside," as he turns and walks off.

You walk into the kitchen. Jill and Betty are still drinking coffee. Betty asks, "Has George gone to crank the generator? When the lights are back on I want to look at how well your head is healing." You say, "Yes, ma'am." The lights come back on and Betty gets her safety scissors. Coming to you, she says, "Sit in the chair so I can reach your head." After you sit, she cuts the bandage off. She inspects the cut and stitches and declares, "Everything looks good. Let's keep it open. Tomorrow, if you are of a mind to, you can wash your hair." She leans back and looks at you, then gently pulls you to herself, like a caring mother, and says, "Thank you, son. Thank you." She pats you on the back, then turns and walks back into the kitchen.

After the evening meal, George starts a conversation saying, "John, are you a religious man?" You reply, "If you mean by religious, am I a Christian, then the answer is yes." Jill says, "I am, too. I don't think I could have made it without God's help." George continues, "I thought the both of you probably were just by the way you act. Granted, I've only known you for just a few days. What do you think about the events happening now? Do you think they are end time related?" You start off slowly, really not wanting to get into a deep religious discussion, "It could be related, probably is related, but I don't know for sure." You pause for a moment then say, "What I do know is this: While God leaves me on this earth, I am going to do the best I can, with the best I have, to live," and looking at Jill you continue, "and help those around me live." Jill looks back at you. Her face turns red, and she smiles. George thinks for a few minutes then says, "You know, that pretty much sums up what we all ought to be doing all along."

"If you ladies will excuse me, I'm going to go lie down. I still feel tired and weak." Betty says, "You go right ahead. You should be getting a lot of your strength back in the next day or two." You return to the bedroom. Looking at your watch, you notice it is nearly 8 p.m. Sitting in the chair, you remove your boots. Retrieving your toothbrush, you go to the bathroom to brush your teeth. You look in the mirror and see the wound in your head. A half inch over and that bullet would have shattered your skull and scrambled your brain. You whisper, "Thank you, Jesus." It's going to leave a scar, a pretty big scar, in fact. But perhaps, Betty is right, maybe your hair will conceal it as it grows out.

You return to your side of the bed and set your pack up in front of the nightstand. Opening the top, you place you Glock inside. You undo your belt and start taking your pants off. As you unzip you pause, realizing "This isn't going to work." You wonder if you should roll out your sleeping bag on the floor. The bed sure is a lot softer than the hard floor. Just make sure you keep your pants on and don't roll to the middle. You take your belt off and zip your pants back up.

Chapter 35 Jill - Day 6 - *Jill talks…*

You watch John as he walks down the hall. He looks tired. Betty says his strength should be returning in the next day or two. That will probably be about the time the 4-wheeler gets here, if Mark can make the deal. You help Betty clean up the kitchen, then follow her to the great room. You sit in the same big chair you were in this morning, with your feet tucked into the seat. So much has happened since this morning! George asks, "Jill, tell me about your family." You tell him about Lizzy at home and your mom living with you since your dad died two months ago. "If it hadn't been for my dad teaching me how to use a weapon and how to defend myself, I would have been killed on the interstate the day after the EMP. My dad saved my life, even though he is no longer here," you say with a smile. "I think you would have liked my dad. He gave John his first traffic ticket in high school. He came home and told me about it saying, "One day, that boy is going to come and thank me for giving him that ticket." I was pretty mad because just the week before, John had come to my rescue, forcing a twelfth grade bully to leave me alone. Kathy, John's girlfriend at the time, was right there helping me, too." "Well?" George inquires, "Was he right?" You smile again, "Yeah, actually he was. A few months before my Dad died, John came to see him and told him that ticket probably saved his life." You're not going to be telling the rest of the story, though, that your father also said, "Jill, that boy would be a good husband" still calling John a boy.

"So you've known John for a while then?" Betty asks. "Yes, most of my life, actually," you reply. "John . . . I guess John always treated me like a little sister. Always nice and kind through the years, and intervening during certain times. That bully he made leave me alone when I was in the ninth grade, well, that bully kind of made an about face after that. He was always asking me out on a date and doing little nice things, but I rebuffed all his advances.

His meanness was still too fresh on my mind. Well, about seven years later, I was home from college. I went to a party at a friend's house. There was Clyde, putting on the charm. That night I got drunk for the first time. I had sex for the first time. That night I got pregnant with Lizzy. Clyde said he wanted to do the right thing by me, and we got married. It wasn't long, though, he decided a pregnant wife was not what he wanted at all. It came to a head later, when we were in the Walmart parking lot. Clyde was having one of his yelling fits, screaming and cursing me for tricking him into getting me pregnant, saying all kinds of vile things. He knocked me to the pavement just as John drove up. John is not a real big man, especially compared to Clyde, but John was a fighter. While Kathy was helping me get up off the ground, John whipped Clyde so bad he left town. He came back not long before Lizzy was born, just to deliver divorce papers. As far as I know, he has never seen Lizzy." Betty says, "I'm sorry, dear, you've had such a rough go of it."

She asks again, "What about John's wife, Kathy? Where is she?" You begin, "Kathy was a very good person. She always treated me nice, kind of like a little sister, too. She and John are both three years older than me. She and John got married not long after John finished college. A couple of years later, Will was born. Kathy was a good mother, she really was. She died in a car accident about two years ago. A drunk driver ran a red light and hit her car. She died instantly."

"Oh dear!" Betty says, "You both have had a really hard time with things. Maybe despite these terrible times, God has brought you two together for a reason." "Maybe . . . I'm not really sure. We need each other right now, and I know I can trust John to do the right thing. What happens when we return home, we'll just have to see."

George asks, "Do you two live close to each other?" You answer, "No, not really. I live in Jackson. Jackson is the largest town in Clarke County. John lives in a small community called Repose, not far from town. I think he has some type of small farm, but I've never been there. But we live close enough our kids go to the same school. It's ironic. They are boyfriend and girlfriend."

George says, "It's after nine. I better go turn the generator off. Good night, Jill." You reply, "Good night, George. Think I'm going to go lie down, too. Good night Betty." You rise from your chair and go to the bedroom. John is in the bed, lying on his back with his hands behind his head. You can't tell if he's awake or asleep. The only light is the faint glow of John's glow stick on the night stand on your side of the bed. Guess John must have put it there. You pick it up and go to the bathroom and brush your teeth. You comb your hair a little, a useless gesture you know, but you feel better doing it.

Returning to the bed, you place your Glock in your pack and empty your pockets onto the nightstand. You remove your shoes and ease into the bed, trying not to wake John. Easing your head on the pillow, you hear in a low voice, "Jill, I can sleep on the floor if it makes you feel more comfortable." On the floor? Is he serious? "No, John, everything is good." A few moments later, John says, "Thank you for saving me earlier, at the kitchen table. I had almost forgotten who I was. A darkness had overcome me. Thank you for bringing me back to the light." You say in a soft voice, "You're welcome, John. You are a good man." You remember the words of your father: ". . . the gentle touch of a woman's hands . . . ." The last thing you hear as your eyes close is the gentle but strong breathing of the man next to you.

Chapter 36 Jill – Day 7 - *A talk in bed...*

You start to stir as you listen to the morning songs of the birds outside. You look out the window, watching as the day comes alive. Maybe this is the reason John likes getting up so early, to see all this. You could probably get used to it, too. You start stretching, as you roll from your side to your back. Making the usual stretching moans, you swing your arms around and they hit someone on your right. Startled, you see John still lying in bed. He shouldn't be here; it must be getting late for him. "John, are you okay?" you ask, as you roll to your side facing him. "Yes, I'm good," he replies. You ask, "What are you still doing in the bed? Isn't it kind of late for you?" John says, "Yes, it is a little later than normal. It's close to 7:00 a.m. I'm normally long up by now. I've been awake since 5:00. I've just been lying here, thinking about the events of the past few days and what we have yet to encounter. I've also been thinking of Will and Lizzy. I think they are okay, Jill. If Will follows the plan, they should be fine. You know today is Thursday. Last Thursday was The Day. One week and we are still one hundred and fifty miles from home."

"John," you start, "I've been wanting to ask, but things keep getting in the way. Why do you think Lizzy and Will are together?" John answers, "Jill, I told you this event didn't catch me completely unprepared. I didn't know we were going to be attacked when we were, or even certain it would ever actually happen. If I had, I would have just stayed home. But . . ." He rolls over facing you, "An interesting thing is . . . the project I was working on had been cancelled a month ago, but the afternoon before The Day, I got a call telling me it was back on go. It had to be completed on The Day." You think, "I didn't find out about my meeting in Birmingham until the night before The Day." John continues, "If I had not completed that project on The Day, I would not have been there to help you. I'm really glad I was there Jill, I really am." A shudder runs through your body as you consider what John just said. It's almost like God was looking out for you every step of the way, making plans for your deliverance even before you left home. That thought gives you comfort and confidence, though the road be hard ahead, you will make it home. You will see Lizzy and your mom again.

"But, that doesn't answer your question," John says and continues, "Jill, I've been preparing for hard events like this for a very long time. Will has been a great part of that planning. About six months ago, Will asked me, if things got really bad, if he could invite Lizzy and you to our small farm, at least until things got better. I agreed, under the condition he not say anything to Lizzy about it unless something really bad happened. Well, something really bad has happened. So I think he has probably gone looking for Lizzy and you. Of course, he would ask your mother as well." You lie there not knowing whether to be angry for John and his son making plans for you and Lizzy without even consulting you or to be thankful that Lizzy is probably in a safe place right now. What is he saying? Is he wanting you to move to his farm? Isn't he being presumptuous thinking you and Lizzy would just jump at the opportunity to move in with him and Will? But those dark thoughts fade as you remember, John has never been anything but good to you. Maybe God has been making plans for you all along. You respond to John, "We'll see John. Let's get home. Then, we'll see."

"Jill, I think we should hold off on planning our trip back until we find out if we have the 4-wheeler or not. But a little later this morning, I think it would be a good idea if we inventory our supplies and packs. That way we'll both know exactly what we have." "Okay, John, but do you think we can have coffee and breakfast first? I'm hungry." He says, "Yes, of course. I need that first cup pretty bad, too." You rise and put your feet on the floor. You're still a little sore, but nothing like a few days ago. You walk to the bathroom. As you reach the door, John says, "Jill," you pause and look back, "you didn't snore much last night." You retort, "I don't snore!" as you close the door.

As you enter the kitchen you see John, George and Betty sitting at the table. Betty says, "I left your plate on the stove, honey, to keep it warm." You feel the coolness of your wet hair on your neck. You just had to have a shower before you came to breakfast. You feel refreshed. "Thank you," you reply. At the table John holds your chair out for you to sit. You smile and say, "Thank you." John sits back down and you pick up on the conversation. John is saying, "George, I can help you around the farm, if you need me to. My place is a lot like this. I really don't want to be a free loader." George says, "John, we have everything covered. Please, don't ever think of yourself as a free loader. You and Jill are our guests and you need to recover your strength. If I need something, I will ask. Okay?" "Okay, George," John replies. George says, "Sometime today I want to take you to see an old friend of mine. He's down the road a piece, but inside our watch area. I found out this morning he has some shortwave equipment that survived the EMP. Jill can come along too, if she wants." John says, "Yes. I really would like to know what's going on across the country. I wonder how bad it is in the big cities and what the government is doing." "I and a few of the boys have some things to do at the back field this morning. Why don't we go over some time this afternoon?" George says. "Okay," says John.

Speaking to Betty you say, "Betty, I need to wash some clothes today. Is there a better place than the lavatory?" Betty smiles, "I've been doing ours in the large double sink on the back deck. I'll help you if you like." "Thank you, Betty, that would be nice." Betty says, "How about after ten this morning. That should give your clothes plenty of time to dry in the afternoon sun." You help Betty with the kitchen, then, after fixing two cups of coffee, you return to the bedroom. John is on the floor. You quickly set the cups down. "John, are you all right?" John says, "Yes, just trying to gauge my recovery. Fifty pushups. I'm about fifty percent."

You say, "I brought you another cup of coffee. Are you ready to inventory our packs?" John says, "Yes, let's start with mine." He picks his up from the floor and sets it on the bed. You notice it isn't with the same ease as the other day. Guess he's not back to a hundred percent, like he said. He says, "I'm going to unload everything, then we'll inventory." He starts unloading his pack. There is a lot of stuff in that pack, all kinds of stuff. Some of it you recognize, some you have no clue as to what it is. You see a bottle of vanilla spray he laid on the bed. Picking it up you gaze over at John, "John?" as you shake it for him to see. He says, "For my feminine side." He smiles broadly, "Actually, it's a pretty good mosquito repellent." "John, where did you get the idea for putting all this stuff in your pack? I never would have thought of a lot of this stuff."

John says, "I built my pack based on the survival axiom of threes, or the progression of threes, or the matrix of threes, or the pyramid of threes or the hierarchy of survival. Some folks call it different things. But the meaning is the same. The axiom goes like this:

You can survive:

Three weeks without food

Three days without water

Three hours without shelter

Three minutes without air

Three seconds without a defensive weapon

You sit on the edge of the bed and ask, "Can you explain that to me? I've never heard of it before." John says, "Based on what I just said about survival time, what do you think is the most important item?" You answer, "Based on three seconds it would be a defensive weapon, but I thought water was the most important item." "Well it can be, if you don't have any and haven't had any for three days. These are all generalizations of course. There was a study done a number of years ago regarding violent assaults. Most assaults are initiated against their victims within twenty-one feet. The amount of time for a person committing an assault to reach you twenty-one feet away is about three seconds. You have three seconds, maybe even less, in order to defend yourself from great bodily harm, perhaps even death. That's why it is so important to have your weapon on you at all times." You consider what John just said. At the Interstate, yes the guy initiated his assault about twenty-one feet away. By the time you had drawn your pistol and shot him, he was almost upon you. If your pistol had been in your pack, you would have been killed.

John begins again, "Air: we all have to have oxygen to survive. That is one of the reasons it is so important to learn to swim. If the air around us contains contaminants, then we need to remove them from the air before we breathe.

One of the best ways is with a military grade NBC mask and canister filter. NBC stands for nuclear, biological and chemical. You've seen these in lots of movies I'm sure. The problem with an NBC mask and filter is it is bulky and heavy. For me it takes up too much space and adds too much weight to be included in my pack. Instead I carry several N95 dust masks. These are small, lightweight and can be found at any Walmart or Lowe's. Well, they used to be, but probably not now."

"If you find yourself in a hostile environment, such as, extreme cold or heat, or even rain, you must be able to find or build a shelter. Exposure is one of the major causes of death for those who get lost in the wilderness. Shelter includes, your clothes, rain gear, jackets, tents, tarps, and any other items that can be placed between you and a hostile environment."

"It's important to keep your body hydrated. Without water, your internal organs will start to shut down and your brain will fail to function properly. Ultimately, within three days without water, you will die. An average person requires around 128 ounces of water per day. Some more, some less, depending on body size and physical activity. Water weighs eight pounds per gallon. For most people, carrying more than a day or two supply of water would be difficult, so we must have the means to collect and purify water"

"Food is important, though we can actually go a long time without food before we starve. It's important to carry some food with you and have a means for preparing the food for your consumption. An average male needs around 2000 to 2400 calories of food per day. An average woman needs around 1600 to 2000 calories of food per day. But food is also heavy. A can of Dinty Moore's Beef Stew is much heavier than a package of Mountain House Freeze Dried Beef Stew, for the same amount of calories. So you can see, all calories aren't the same."

"As we inventory my pack, you will see how I've attempted to address each of the items in our Axiom of Threes. Bear in mind that weight and bulk are very important things to consider when building a pack. So in a lot of cases, you are going to see mini sizes of items. You want to get started?" You say, "Yes, let's do" as you reach for the paper and pen.

Chapter 37 Jill - Day 7 - *John's Pack...*

John says, "Since we started talking about what I call The Axiom of Threes, let's just go in that order on our inventory. I'll repack when we are through, so the most frequently needed items are near the top. Is that okay?" You say, "Yes, sure." Seeing all this stuff has gotten you kind of excited. John continues, "OK, let's go over the most critical category from our Axiom of Threes, personal defense." Looking over at your writing, John says, "Yeah, that's a good idea keeping the list by category. Here we go."

"Personal Defense

One Glock 19 with night sights and laser guide rod

One Kel-tec Sub 2k Gen 2 with fold down rear sight and removable front sight

Six Glock 19 magazines, 15 round capacity

Eighty-eight rounds 147gr. sub-sonic 9mm ammo

Ninety-seven rounds 135 gr. self-defense 9mm ammo

Two hundred rounds 115 gr. full metal jacket 9mm ammo

One Glock 42

Two Glock 42 magazines, 6 round capacity

Twenty-five rounds 95gr. self-defense 380 ammo

One extra threaded barrel for the Glock 19

One Streamlight TLR1-HL rail mount light for the Glock 19

One IWB holster for the Glock 19

One paddle holster for the Glock 19

One Burris Fast Fire III red dot sight with quick mount for the Sub2k

One Fenix PD35 flash light with quick mount for the Sub2k

One Crimson Trace IR Laser sight with quick mount for the Sub2k

One Magpul MS3 sling for the Sub2k

One Gemtech GM9 9mm sound suppressor, works with the Sub2k and Glock 19

Two copies of BATFE approved form for the suppressor

Two Blackhawk single magazine pouches

One 9mm gun cleaning kit

Pouches to hold the items when not mounted to the carbine or pistol

One Gerber 7" sheath knife

One CRKT 3" folding knife

One no brand rescue knife

Knives are an absolute, last resort item. They have more useful functions than self-defense. I think that's it. See anything I missed?" You say, "Gee John, I had no idea you had this kind of stuff. What's the Tax Stamp for?" "Oh, boy," John says, "Don't get me going on that or we'll never get this done, but the short answer is the federal government, in its infinite wisdom, regulates suppressors and requires you to complete applications and pay a $200 tax fee. After holding your paper work for about six months, you'll get your license for the suppressor in the form of a Tax Stamp. The Tax Stamp must follow the suppressor wherever it goes. There is more to it than just that, but I gave you the short version. The really crazy thing about this is, for twenty-five dollars, you can buy an adaptor for your threaded barrel and a ten dollar oil filter from NAPA, and do almost the same thing I spent nearly a thousand dollars doing. But that's supposedly illegal. It probably doesn't much matter now, though." You ask, "The extra barrel for your Glock, would it also work in my Glock?" John says, "Yes it would, but we would have to modify your IWB holster to accommodate the extra length of the barrel."

"What about your night vision gear? Should it be listed here?" John says, "I guess so. It has other uses too, but yeah, sure, list it here. By the way, don't let me forget to show you how to use it. The unit I have is an OPMOD PVS14 Gen 3. It's one of the upper end models. Back before The Day, you could buy Gen 1 devices for around four hundred dollars from Amazon.com. They aren't nearly as good as a Gen 3, but they are relatively cheap. Are? Ha!

I bet $10,000 wouldn't buy a low end Gen 1 device today." You say, "I don't think most people ever thought about these things. I know I didn't." "Don't take me wrong, Jill, I'm not faulting anybody for anything. I chose to learn certain skills and acquire the gear I thought would give me the best chance to make it back home in case of something like this. I hope what I've done is enough." You say, "I do too, John." He looks back into your eyes, "Jill, Will knows most of these things, too. Lizzy is going to be okay." You smile and turn away before you tear up.

"Okay, let's move on to air. I don't really have much here, as I didn't think I could justify the weight and bulk of keeping an NBC mask in my pack. Sometimes I carry one in my truck, depending on where I'm going, but I felt the risk was pretty small coming up here, so I left it at home. I do have three N95 masks. The one's I have include an exhale port to make them more comfortable to use. Back before The Day, you could purchase these at Lowe's and the standard N95 mask, even at Walmart. If we get into an area with lots of smoke, or other items in the air, we can use them." You say, "My dad had me pack a few in my pack, too." John looks back over at you and says, "I liked your dad, Jill. He was a good man and I know he's taught you some good things. It's evident, from the fact you've made it here, that there is a lot of him in you." You smile and say, "My dad liked you, too."

John says, "Now, to shelter. Let's see what we have.
 Shelter
One sleeping bag
One ground pad
One camouflage tarp
One ground mat
One set rain gear
One pair camp flops
The clothes on my back
One cap
One pair Timberland work boots
Two mosquito head nets"

"Is there anything I'm missing?" John asks. You respond, "What about the tent in the garage?" John says, "Yes, I missed that. One one-man sleeping tent." You realize he said "one-man" sleeping tent. That ought to be interesting if you have to use it. No need worrying about it now. Just cross that bridge when and if you get to it. John says, "I need to get another shirt. By the way, do you still have my shirt I gave you the other day?" You blush at the thought of those awkward moments a few days ago, "Yes, Betty and I are going to wash clothes a little later. Thanks for letting me use it. I'm going to make another list of things we need. We can add to it as we go along." "That's a good idea," John says, "I also have some paracord and other miscellaneous items to help build a shelter, but let's just list it under a separate heading further down the list."

John says, "Moving on to water. Ready?" You nod your head.

"Water

Two 32-ounce stainless steel water bottles full of water

Six 16-ounce plastic water bottles in the garage

One Katadyn water filter pump

Six coffee filters

One bottle water treatment tabs

One small bottle of concentrated bleach with instructions

One small bottle of water flavoring, about half full

One pouch to contain the equipment"

"With this setup, as long as we can find water, we'll have no problem making it safe to drink. Finding water here in Alabama should not be a problem. There's a branch or creek every few miles along our way. We'll certainly cross one, at least once, each day. We could treat months' worth of water with these supplies. I think that's it. See anything I missed?" "No," you say, "Looks like that's it. I like the idea of the water flavoring. Sometimes treated water doesn't taste so good." John says, "That's for sure."

"Now to food," John starts picking up some packs, "Let's list the calorie content next to the item. That way we can see the total calories we have available.

Food

Four MREs in the garage 6,000 cal

Three packs freeze dried entrée's 2,600 cal

Two Spam packs 500 cal

Three tuna fish packs 450 cal

Three MRE wheat bread packs 540 cal

Three peanut butter packs 750 cal

Two cheese spread packs 360 cal

Four millennium energy bars 1,600 cal

One Datrex emergency ration 3,600 cal

Two grit packs 300 cal

Two oatmeal packs 300 cal

Two instant coffee packs

Two hot chocolate packs

One dozen multi-vitamins

Four Emergen-C packs

One lot of miscellaneous condiment packs

"Some more miscellaneous items, like hard candy, mints, and gum, but that's about it. How many calories does that make total?" John asks. You add the items up from the list and say, "Seventeen thousand calories, and based on what you said earlier, that gives us about four days. Though I have to say that Datrex emergency ration bar doesn't look too appetizing." John says, "It's okay in a pinch, but you certainly don't want to eat it unless you have to."

John says, "Let's list the rest of this stuff." You say, "All right let's do it." John continues calling out the items:

"Cook kit

One MSR stainless steel cook set

Two plastic camp cups

One camp utensil set

One stainless steel cup

One cleaning kit with dishwashing liquid and scrubby pad

One camp towel
One hot pad

Hygiene Kit
Three-quarter roll of toilet paper
One pack wipes
Small bar soap
Two wash clothes
One shave kit, razor is in the bathroom.
One small bottle Old Spice body wash/shampoo
One Old Spice small deodorant tube
One tooth brush, in the bathroom
Two small tubes tooth paste"

He stops for a moment and says, "I hope you like Old Spice." You blush and say, "Actually I do, though I prefer to use something else on myself." Now it's his turn to blush and say, "Yeah, I don't think I would like this on you either. Back to our list," John continues to talk:

"Power Kit
One folding solar charger kit
Four rechargeable CR123A batteries
Four rechargeable AA batteries
Six rechargeable AAA batteries
Four CR123A batteries, non-rechargeable
Six AA batteries, non-rechargeable
Six AAA batteries, non-rechargeable
Two CR2032 batteries for the Fast Fire sight
Six 357 batteries for the electric glow stick
One multi-battery charger
One wall charger adapter
One car charger adapter
One USB charging cable

"John, do you think the car charger is going to work? Mine quit working after the EMP." He says, "I'm not sure. Mine stopped working, too. I haven't tested this one. Normally, I wouldn't keep anything I didn't know for sure if it worked, but I think, in this case I will." Then he continues.

"Fire Kit
Three magnesium fire starters
Three lighters
One box strike anywhere wet/dry matches
One pack vaseline impregnated cotton bales
One Esbit stove
Nine Esbit stove cubes"

"Lighting
One head lamp
One high output AA LED light
One pocket high output AAA LED light
Four keychain squeeze lights
One Fenix TK12 LED light, this one stays in a holster on my belt
Two chemical glow sticks
One electric glow stick
Two emergency candles"

"We listed the gun lights in the Personal Defense section, but we could use them for other things too, but I don't think that will be necessary."
"Medical
IFAK – Individual first aid kit
ITK – Individual trauma kit
Various over the counter medicines"

"Miscellaneous
Two BaoFeng radios, complete with earbuds, mics and spare battery
One Gerber short machete
One knife sharpener

Seventy-five feet paracord, left about twenty-five feet at the barn

One folding limb saw

One string saw

One small camp shovel

Two nail clippers

One small roll duct tape

Ten tie wraps

One Gerber Multi-tool, this one stays in a holster on my belt

One signal mirror

One alarm whistle

One Alabama highway map

One small notebook

Two ink pens

One iPhone 4

One Silva compass

Twenty-five feet snare wire

One small bottle bug spray

One small bottle vanilla spray, for my feminine side

Two hand warmers

One lens cleaning cloth

One magnifying glass

Two emergency mylar blankets

One small tube sun block

One small sewing repair kit

One mini-fishing kit

Two pair maxi flex gloves

Various D clips and straps

A small New Testament

A small bag of miscellaneous items."

"Did I miss anything?" John asks. "I don't think so, but that's a lot of stuff, John. How much does all that weigh?" He says, "The stuff that I normally carry in my pack comes up to fifty-six pounds. If I have to carry the other MREs and water, it's going to add a few more pounds. If we have the 4-wheeler, weight won't be a big issue."

"John, can I ask how much did all this stuff cost?" John smiles, "All I'm going to say is, a lot. It cost a lot. If you count the personal defense items, then many thousands of dollars, but anybody could have built a kit, maybe not on this level, but still pretty good, for a lot less. Priorities; mine were to be prepared for unexpected events. Let's pack all this back up so you'll also know exactly where everything is in my pack." You say, "Okay, then we can do my kit. It doesn't have near this amount of stuff."

Chapter 38 Jill - Day 7 - *Jill's Pack...*

"All right, John, let's switch roles and I'll unload my pack." John takes the pen and pad you are handing to him. You unload your items on the bed. It's not near the amount and type as what John has and it makes you feel a little embarrassed. "John, I guess I'll start like you did, with personal defense. Are you going to make a separate list for me, or just add this to your list?" John says, "We are in this as a team, right? So everything I have in my pack is now ours, not just mine. We should consider yours the same way. But, it's still important to know what we have in each of our individual packs. I'm going to draw a line down the page, just to the right of where you wrote my bag inventory, and add yours. That way our items will be listed together, yet separate at the same time. Sound okay?" "Yeah, it does. I like that." Taking a deep breath, you say, "Personal defense."

"Personal Defense

One Glock 19, complete with pink highlights

Two magazines

Twenty-seven rounds of 135 gr. self-defense 9mm ammo

Twenty-five rounds of 115 gr. full metal jacket 9mm ammo

One IWB holster, pink

One rescue knife

One CRKT folding knife

One Kershaw folding knife

One small can of MACE"

"Okay, that's it. My folding knife is just like yours. My dad gave it to me for Christmas a few years ago." John says, "That's a good knife. I like those pink highlights. Did you do it yourself or have it done?" You say, "My dad taught me how to do it, and I did it myself." Looking at John and smiling, you ask, "You want me to highlight yours in pink?" John laughs, "No thanks, my feminine side stops with the vanilla spray." You say, "It doesn't look like much compared to yours." John says, "Well compared to mine it isn't, but don't compare it to mine. What you have here is a good defensive setup. Staying on your toes, this can get you home. But I think with the amount of ammo you have, I would have gotten all self-defense rounds and skipped the FMJs." "That's what my dad said, but I wanted to save a few dollars. The FMJs were cheap." John picks up your holster and looks at it, turning it in his hands. "This is a nice holster, not my color, you understand. If we put my threaded barrel in your Glock, we would have to cut a hole in the bottom to allow for the extra length. I don't think we should swap barrels since you're already used to the setup you have. Besides, the suppressor is mostly going to stay on the carbine." You say, "Sure, I was just curious earlier, that's all. I don't want to swap barrels."

You say, "Air. I have two N95 standard dust masks. That's it. Plus, I can swim and hold my breath until you can save me." Smiling, you look over at John. He just rolls his eyes.

"On to shelter," you say.

"Shelter

One sleeping bag

One gray/brown tarp

The clothes I have on my back, but I'll have our other clothes this afternoon

One pair walking shoes

One ball cap"

"That's it." John says, "This works, but I think I would have added a ground matt. You know, something to keep the moisture from the ground from seeping up into your bag. Of course, you could use a mylar blanket to block water moisture. With some paracord, you could build a decent shelter with what you have. Combined with what I have, I think we'll be okay." You think, "I bet he hasn't thought about the implications of the 'one-man' tent yet." You say, "Yeah, I do, too."

You start on your water related items. "All right, John, on to water."

"Water

One 32-ounce stainless steel water bottle

Two 16-ounce plastic water bottles

One package water treatment tabs

One small bottle unscented bleach

Six coffee filters

One Frontier emergency water filter"

"That's it for water. Now for food."

"Food

Two complete stripped down MREs 3,000 cal

Two packs single-serving Spam 500 cal

Two packs single-serving tuna fish 300 cal

Three packs of squeeze peanut butter 750 cal

Two protein bars 400 cal

Four single-serving oatmeal packs 600 cal

One emergency ration bar 3,600 cal

Six single-serving instant coffee packs

Small bag of condiments

Small bottle canola oil

Small bottle honey"

"That's it." John says, "Hmm . . . that totals to 9,150 calories. Combined with mine, gives us 26,150 calories for about six days." You're thinking, "I sure hope we get home before we have to eat the emergency ration bars."

"Moving on," you say,

"Cook kit

One Stanley cook cup

Two camp cups

One utensil set

One stainless steel cup

One small bottle dishwashing liquid

One small scrubby

Small camp towel"

John asks, "How do you like the Stanley cook cup? I had thought about getting one." "To tell the truth John, I've never used it."

"Hygiene Kit

One and a half rolls toilet paper

One pack of wet wipes

Two small bars of soap

Two wash cloths

One small bottle of body/hair wash

One tooth brush, in the bathroom

One small tube toothpaste

One small hair brush

One small bag of miscellaneous items"

"That's it for that. You know, I don't see my razor. I must have left it at Mary's. Darn!" But, your eyes grow wide as John reaches out and picks up your small bag of feminine pads you had intentionally not mentioned. He says almost to himself, "You know, you can use these for bandages." You snatch the pack out of his hand, as your face grows red, and say, "That's not what these are for!" John's face begins to turn red and he says, "Yes, of course, I was just thinking . . . thinking out loud. Sorry." You guess you'll let him off the hook, but the little bugger doesn't stop there. He says, "Jill, when I left Leeds, heading home, I thought I would be home in four or five days. We're at day seven and we haven't even made it to Montevallo." "Yeah, so?" you say, still a little annoyed. He continues, "If we get the 4-wheeler, and can leave here in a day or two, and it takes us three to four days to get home, it's going to be nearly a week from now." You say, "Okay," not knowing where he's going with all this. "But," he says, "if we have problems, it could take us longer." "So, your point being?" He looks up at you and asks, "Do you have enough of those pads?" Your face really turns red. What business is it of his if you do end up on your period? In a highly annoyed voice you respond,

"What business is that of yours?" He reaches out with his hand and covers yours and says, "Jill, you better write that on our needs list. You know, whatever you're going to need. Just in case." Why does he have to think of everything! Is he always thinking days, weeks ahead? As you think about it, your annoyance dissipates. He's only thinking of you. Why else would he even bring something like that up? Most guys would avoid that subject like the plague. "Thanks, John, you're right. I will."

"Back to other things," you say quickly.

"Power Kit
Six AA batteries
Six AAA batteries"

"Fire Kit
One Esbit stove
Twelve fuel tabs
Two bic lighters
One magnesium fire starter
One pack strike anywhere matches
One small medicine bottle of vaseline coated cotton balls"

"Lighting
One LED head lamp
Two high output AA LED lights
One emergency candle"

"Medical
One small first aid kit
One small pack various over the counter pain medicine
One small bottle sun block
One small bottle lotion"

"Miscellaneous
One nail clipper

Various D clips and straps
Twenty-five feet paracord
One small roll duct tape
Twelve zip ties
Two mylar emergency blankets
One mini-survival manual"

"That's it. That's all I have." John smiles, "that's a pretty good kit you put together, Jill, pretty darn good."

Betty comes to the open door and knocks, saying, "Jill, honey, if you're ready I'll help you with the clothes." "Okay, give me about five minutes." Betty walks back to the kitchen. You look over at John and ask, "John, do we have enough to make it home?" He says, "I had plenty of reasons for making it home," pausing, he looks at you, "and I have even more now. I promise you, I will do everything I can to make sure we make it home safely." Though he didn't really answer your question, he gave the answer you needed. You smile and say, "I believe you will, John."

Chapter 39 John - Day 7 - *The Honda ATV...*

Watching Jill as she walks out the door, going to find Betty, you think to yourself, "That is one heck of a woman." "Dear God, we need your help to make it home. Help me not to falter. Give me courage, wisdom and strength not to fail Jill, Will, Lizzy and our other family. In Jesus' name. Amen."

Things have got to be getting pretty bad now around the large cities. More people are going to be on the road, trying to find relief in more rural areas. People are going to become more desperate. Desperate people do desperate things. More people means more predators trying to take advantage of them. This is the time, you think, roving gangs are going to start developing. You use the term "gangs" loosely. Gangs are going to be groups of people wanting to do nothing but steal, murder, rape and pillage. Some might look like some inner city gang, others might be wearing camouflage hunting shirts. If you don't encounter some on your way home, you'll be surprised. That's why you've decided to travel at night. Using your NVD, IR laser and suppressor will give you an advantage at night you wouldn't have during the day. You wonder how many of those evil gangs out there have bought NVDs, too. Probably not many, unless they were organized before The Day. Those are going to be the most dangerous ones right now, those organized before The Day. You've been to the online forums. You've seen the discussions. Many have accumulated weapons and training, intending to use those assets and skills to steal the other things they need. You can't afford to risk confrontation with these groups. No, you've got to go slow, deliberate and quiet. If you do have to take action, it must be fast, aggressive and decisive.

The wildcard, you think, is going to be the government. Is it going to slam the hammer down, oppressing everyone attempting to create order? Or . . . or what? Is it going to completely collapse? The military? What is it going to do? Roving gangs are one thing; a roving rogue military unit is another. What you think the government should do will be exactly what they won't do. You hope not to see anybody with the government, period. You walk to the bathroom. Time to wash this grease mop hair.

Jill walks back into the bedroom. She looks over at the table where you are sitting and adding to the "Need Item" list. She looks over your shoulders, saying, "Whew, that was a job washing clothes by hand. Is this what we have to look forward to for the near future?" You look up, slightly perplexed, realizing you haven't made any plans for being able to wash clothes after an EMP attack. "Hmm . . . wonder what else I missed?" you think to yourself. Jill says, "What?" You shake your head, "Oh, nothing." She looks at the list and says, "That's getting long. How are we going to pay for all this?" You smile and reach in your pocket and bring out two gold coins and ten silver coins. She says, somewhat surprised, "I thought you gave those to Mark?" "I didn't give Mark everything I had. I told you I wasn't completely unprepared." She says, "Yes, you did, and you're full of surprises." She sniffs your hair and makes a funny face saying, "You actually don't stink this morning."

Betty knocks on the wall beside the open door saying, "Mark is here." You both get up and walk down the hall. Entering the kitchen, you see Mark sitting at the table with a cup of hot coffee. You look at your watch. It's 11:00 a.m. Mark has a smile on his face as he stands up. That's a good sign. He says, "Good morning, John. Good morning, Jill," as he extends his hand and shakes yours. He continues, "I've had some success. I was able to trade for a 1998 Honda Rancher 400. It's a little old, but it's still in great shape. It's a 4x4 with front and rear racks. It has a full tank of gas and I was able to get two five gallon cans of gas. I need to take it to George's shop while he's running his generator and attach a bracket to the back, to hold the fuel cans. The cans are the old, metal military type cans. Oh, yes, I was also able to get you a Ruger 10/22 with three ten round magazines and a small 325 round brick of bullets." You say, "Wow, Mark, I wasn't sure you would be able to do it. Thanks. You have the Honda outside?" "Yeah, it's out there," he says, pointing with his thumb back over his shoulder. "One more thing", he reaches into his pocket saying, "I had these left over," and places five silver coins on the table. He continues, "Sorry, man. I wish I could have brought all of it back, but the only thing the guy wanted that I had was silver coins and I just didn't have enough myself." You smile, "Not a problem. Actually, I have a few more items I would like to get if they can be bought or traded for. I left the list in the back. I'll be right back."

You pick the list up from the table in the bedroom and look it over. You call out, "Jill, can you come here a minute?" Jill walks in and you say, "Look over this list and see if we need to add anything." She picks it up and scans through it. She says, "Do you think we will be able to get all this?" You reply, "Probably not, but I think it's worth a try." She looks it over again, saying, "It looks complete to me, if Betty will let me keep the clothes I'm wearing. I'd really like to have two bras." She looks at you and blushes. You walk back to the kitchen with Jill behind you. You hand Mark the list. "Check this out and see what you think. If you can't get any of this, it's not going to be a major problem for us." Inside you think, "Not getting those pads could be a major problem." Mark scans over the list, occasionally remarking about the items, "Tarp 12x16, brown or green. Shouldn't be a problem. Tire repair kit. I've got that in my shop. Two large men's shirts. I've got that, too. One woman's shirt," looking up at Jill, he says "that shouldn't be a problem. Freeze dried food." Betty says, "We have plenty and will share whatever you need." Mark continues, "Feminine . . . ," he looks back up at Jill and they both blush a little, "that shouldn't be a problem. These other items don't look like a problem either." You say, "Do you think the remaining silver coins will be enough?" Mark reaches for the coins and slides them closer to you, saying, "This list isn't going to cost you anything. Let's go out and look at your rig."

Walking through the kitchen door, you see George coming up. Everyone gathers at the Honda. You walk around it. The tires look good. You pull the dip stick. The oil looks clean. Mark says, "The guy had some oil and a filter, I changed it before bringing it over." The seat is intact. You get on and crank it up. It starts easily. You drive it around a little and bring it back and park it. You say, "I think this is going to work. You did good Mark, real good."

Mark has a smile on his face. You say, "I do want to take all the light bulbs out, except the head light and remove or cover all the reflectors. The plastic of the 4-wheeler is green. That's good. It won't stand out like a sore thumb in the woods." Mark says, "I can handle all that for you when I mount the bracket to hold the fuel cans. Uncle George, you don't mind if I use your shop later do you?" George says, "No, Mark, I don't mind at all. Betty, this old man sure is hungry. Have you got anything to put a smile on my face?" Betty says, "Yes, y'all come in. Meatloaf sandwiches and ice tea."

As everyone heads to the kitchen, you and Jill fall behind. She's walking beside you. You look over and say, "I think this is a good start. I'd like to leave tomorrow night." She looks up with a puzzled look, "Why tomorrow night? Why not tomorrow morning?" You answer, "I want to use the darkness as cover. Using the NVD, I should be able to drive without a problem, though I won't be able to drive very fast and may have to stop frequently to give my eyes a break." She says, "Okay, I can understand that. Why not tonight?" You reply, "I don't think we can be ready by tonight. Mark still has to mount the bracket for the fuel cans. I want to drive the Honda around a little and make sure it's not just going to die right after we leave. I also want you to get some driving time and we need to get you some trigger time on the Ruger. Besides, I still don't have enough strength. I think I need one more day." She replies, "All right, John, whatever you think is best. I'm with you." For some reason, hearing those words causes you to smile as you open the kitchen door for her to walk in.

George says, "Betty, as usual you fixed another fine meal. You fellas, if your wives become as good a cook as my sweet Betty, you will be blessed indeed." You say, "Amen!" before you realize what you are saying. You don't have a wife. But no one seems to have paid what you said much attention.

Afterwards, you say, "Mrs. Betty, this was another fine meal. It surely was. You and George have been good to us. I know God has blessed you both with loving hearts." Jill says, "Oh yes, you both truly are good people." You continue, "Since we now have a means of transportation," looking over at Mark you say, "Thank you. Since we now have a means of transportation, Jill and I plan on leaving for home tomorrow night. Mark, if you're able to get the things on that list by then, I would appreciate it." Betty says, "Oh my. Are you sure you're ready? I mean, son, don't you want to give yourself a few more days to heal?" "Mrs. Betty," you say, "I have thought about this a good bit. The longer we wait, the more trouble we are likely to encounter along our way. Things in the bigger, and even small cities, are going to be getting pretty desperate. Folks are going to be fleeing to the rural areas looking for help. It's only going to get worse. I'm too weak to leave today, but I think tomorrow I should be strong enough to travel." Jill says, "We so need to get back to our children, Lizzy and Will, and my mother. We just don't truly know what we will find when we get home. We must leave soon." Betty says, "Yes, I know. But in these past few days, I have grown to love you both as my own children. I know you must leave. I pray God will bless your travels and keep you safe." She rises and heads into the kitchen. Jill gets up and follows her.

George says, "John, I know you are an intelligent and capable man. Have you really thought this through? You both can stay here as long as you want. Maybe let things settle down a little, then return home." You reply, "Yes, I've thought it through. The road is going to be hard, heck we might not even make it. But our children are there; we must return home. Unfortunately, George, I don't think things will be settling down for many months. It's only going to get worse, much worse." Mark says, "I understand. I would do the same thing. Before you leave, could I bring my wife and the girls over just to meet you? They all want to meet you and your wife, especially Karen." You say, "Yes, that's good Mark, anytime. But I want to leave after dark tomorrow. And Mark, Jill is very special and dear to me, but she is not my wife." Mark looks surprised. He says, "Are you serious? Sure seemed like she was to me."

You steer the conversation in a different direction. You say, "For us to leave tomorrow, there are several things we must do. First, we have to get the Honda ready. Second, we need the items on that list, if possible. Mark, you said you could take care of both." Mark says, "Yes, I'll take care of the Honda this evening and get these other things tomorrow." You say, "I appreciate it Mark, I really do. Third, I want to take the Honda out for a ride to see for myself everything is functioning properly. George, I think Jill and I could use it to ride to your friend's house when we go check out his HAM radios." George says, "Why don't we go in an hour? Say, 3:00?" "Sounds good," you say, "Fourth, I need to let Jill shoot the Ruger and drive the Honda." Looking at George you ask, "Do you have a place we could shoot?" George says, "Yes, just drive to the back of the pasture. You'll see a little shooting bench set up with steel targets on into the woods. That's where we practice." You say, "I'd like to take Jill sometime tomorrow morning. Then it's packing our gear and hitting the road after dark."

Jill and Betty are in conversation, though you can't tell what they are saying. You're tired again. You walk back to the bedroom and retrieve your iPhone and set the timer alarm for 45 minutes. Then, removing your boots, you lie back down.

The road ahead is going to be fraught with danger. Here, in this little enclave of community farmers and friends, you have been isolated and protected. But, that's going to change when you leave this place. In fact, it will change whether you leave or stay. People are going to become desperate. Across the country, millions will be leaving urban areas thinking they can find food or refuge in more rural areas. What they don't realize, is that most rural people depend upon the same grocery stores and supply chains that urban people do. The art of self-sufficiency has practically died across America. It will take time for those skills and the mindset to be relearned, time that many people don't have. Millions are going to die from starvation. Millions are going to die from lack of medical care. Millions are going to die due to violent encounters. Yet you see potential hope. What rises from the ashes may be stronger than the stubble that covered the land. It's going to be hard; really, really hard.

You have to go through or around several small towns. The largest is Montevallo. George says he can give you a map of back roads around Montevallo. That's good. Then you must go through Brent, Marion, Safford, Catherine, Pine Hill, Thomasville and Grove Hill before you make it to Jackson. What are you going to find when you get to Jackson? Have the citizens been able to hold things together, or is it going to be in complete chaos? How are the perpetual government dependents going to be able to survive when someone isn't there to provide for their needs? How are those in nursing homes going to survive when there is no more electricity? In this coming new world, those who can't or won't provide for themselves are simply going to die. If what you think is correct, there are going to be thousands of people dying in Jackson and its surrounding areas. You hope there is something left when you get there. You have some ideas to help the area transition to a new normal, but something has to still be there when you make it home. What about your own community of Repose? Will your friends and neighbors implement the plans, so carefully, laid out? If they do, your community has a chance.

What about Jill, Lizzy and Jill's mother? Will you be able to protect them? There is just so much to consider, so many different scenarios, many of which have no positive outcome. "Dear God. We need you now. We all need you now" is your plea. You're tired, really tired. This injury has taken its toll on your strength. You hope by tomorrow you will have regained enough to leave. Either way, you must leave. But, now, you need the rest.

Chapter 40 John - Day 7 - *The national news…*

The room is shaking. You hear rumblings. Is it an earthquake? The sounds become more distinct as the shaking continues. "John, John, get up you sleepy head, it's time to go." You open your eyes. It's Jill. She's standing next to the bed, leaning over and gently shaking you. Why? You sit up quickly, almost bumping heads. She says, "Hey! Watch it!" as she dodges your head. She continues, "If you don't get up, George and I are going over to his friend's house without you." The cob webs clear from your mind. "Yeah, sure. Is it 3:00 already? I thought I had set my alarm." Jill says, "Look out the window. Does it look like 3:00 to you?" Turning, you look through the window. It's getting dark. It's getting dark?! You jump from the bed, bumping into her. You grab her as she falls back, saying, "I'm sorry, Jill. What time is it?" Jill is laughing, almost as if she's having fun. You realize your arm is still around her, and she is off balance. Setting her upright, she is right next to you, your arm still around her waist. The laughing stops as she looks up at you. A lump enters your throat. Your mind is reeling again, 'Damn it, this isn't the time for this!' you admonish yourself. You remove your arm, and the moment is gone. She says, "Are you always this playful when someone wakes you? It's 7:00 p.m. George says he's ready to go and can't wait any longer. You did set your alarm. After you didn't wake up while it was spewing out that awful loud old car horn noise, we decided to let you rest. George cranked his generator up early for Mark, and the ATV is ready. We can follow George over to his friend's place, but you've got to hurry it up!" "Okay, I will. Why did you let me over sleep by so much?" Jill says, in a softer tone, "John, you needed rest. Let's go." After putting your boots and Glock on, you grab your carbine, IR laser and NVD and follow her down the hall, attaching the IR laser to the bottom rail of the carbine as you walk.

George says, "About time there, son. We almost thought you changed your mind. Mark just finished up with your ATV, that's why we woke you up. Go check it out, then we can leave." As you and Jill head to the door, Betty says, "Hold up." You stop and look over at her. She hands you a cup of hot coffee and a large slice of homemade cornbread. You smile thinking, this sweet lady is so much like your mom was. You're nibbling on the cornbread and walking a little slower in order not to spill the coffee, as you head out the door. The Honda is just outside. Walking around it, you see all the reflectors have been removed and all the bulbs have been removed. There is a rack out the back with two five gallon jerry cans held in place with bungie cords. Removing your flashlight, you shine it at the Honda and walk around again. Good, no reflective light. You shake the fuel cans; no rattle. Looks like Mark placed some kind of padding between the two cans. Smiling, you look over at Jill saying "This is going to work." Getting on, you crank it up. It's much quieter than it was. Mark must have done something to it. You drive it to the shop and back. At the house, you ask Jill, "Will you tell George we're ready to go? Then come back and get on." Jill says, "Yes." When she returns she excitedly gets on behind you saying, "I haven't been on a 4-wheeler since . . . since high school. This is going to be fun." You reach back and pat her on the knee.

George drives his golf cart down the lane, then turns right at the county road. You follow behind, not able to really gun the Honda because of the slow speed of the golf cart. Jill is sitting behind you. Her hands are resting on your shoulders as she steadies herself. About half a mile down the road, George turns left into a wooded lane. Another half mile, the trees open to a large pasture with a white wood frame house sitting on a hill. You see three tall shortwave antennas standing not far from the house. One must be close to one hundred feet tall. As you pull up, a large German Shepherd barks and comes running toward you. You feel Jill tense. The dog stops short and continues barking. An older man steps out on the porch. He hollers, "Rusty! Come here, Rusty! You folks come on in, I'll close Rusty up." Rusty runs to his master and goes into the house. Shortly, the man returns alone. Jill gets off the Honda and you follow. Joining George, the three of you approach the porch. George starts the introductions, "Frank, these are my friends, John and Jill. John, Jill, this is my longtime friend Frank." Frank reaches out with his large hand and shakes your hand, "Nice to meet you, John, and your lovely wife, Jill. Y'all come on in. You are certainly going to want to hear what I have been finding out." You look at Jill and she looks back at you. You both just shrug. Seems everybody around here thinks you are husband and wife.

Once inside, Frank says, "Just set your rifle against the wall over there. I've been using solar for a number of years. All my chargers, batteries and controllers are in the metal building behind the house. Don't know if that's what saved them or not. My newer radios were all damaged, but I had an older unit stored in the shed as well. I set it up and have been hearing some amazing things. Amazing."

Frank says, "First, late on the day after, the President gave a speech. My older equipment does not have recording functions, but it went something like this. He said the nation had been attacked by an EMP device. That the NSA, CIA, FBI, Homeland Security and the Military were working diligently to find out who launched this attack. In the meantime, he said, we didn't need to jump to conclusions and prejudice our thoughts against any group of people or religion. In fact, he signed an executive order declaring attacks or the incitement of attacks or statements deemed to be inflammatory against Islam would not be tolerated. Those that violated this new Executive Order would be arrested and held indefinitely based upon other Executive Orders, previously issued, that were being implemented. He suspended the Bill of Rights and all other Constitutional rights until things return to normal. He also declared martial law. The personal ownership of vehicles, fuel, guns, gold, silver and food supplies longer than three days, was prohibited and he gave citizens one week to turn the contraband items over to local law enforcement officials. He asked that neighbors keep an eye on their fellow neighbors and report any person they suspected was in violation of these new rules. All travel on public highways, other than by walking or bicycle or other non-motorized equipment, would be prohibited after seven days."

Jill starts to tear up. George's mouth hangs open. This is not completely surprising to you, but you didn't think the idiot in charge would go this far.

You say, "That's just incredible. How does the idiot think he's going to enforce these dictates?" Frank continues, "There's more. Using existing agreements which state and local law enforcement agencies signed to receive federal grants, he federalized all state, county and local law enforcement agencies. Each state will be reporting to a liaison from The Department of Homeland Security. These liaisons will be in place within the seven days he talked about earlier. He went on to say the military would report to the Director of Homeland Security until command units from the UN could arrive and take control of the situation."

You say, "War is coming. It looks even worse than I feared. In addition to the nightmare cause by the EMP, we have the chains of the federal government to fend off. Incredible. If the military turns against us, it's going to be tough in deed."

Frank says, "But that's not all of what he said. He also said that this event would be used as an opportunity to correct many injustices, including redistribution of money, redistribution of land and leveling of all pay scales. People would not be allowed to accumulate more than they need until after everyone in their districts have all their needs met. He also said that special aid camps run by FEMA were going to be setup and people would be relocated to the shelters in a timely manner where their needs could be taken care of and their skill sets could be evaluated. He went on to say the Constitution was a flawed instrument, written by greatly flawed men and it would be updated for a new modern day world view."

George is silent for a moment, then asks, "Is he saying he is going to take our farms? Our property that we have worked so hard to turn into something productive? Is he saying he's going to confiscate all this?" as he waves is arms all around. Jill says, "How can he do this? How? Why would our soldiers allow him to do this?"

Frank stands up. He says, "There is even more. Let me fix you all a glass of cold tea first." You all walk to the kitchen. As you pass by a door on your left, you can hear Rusty whining to get out. In the kitchen you, Jill and George sit while Frank pours the ice tea. You drink yours. It's good; not too sweet but plenty cold.

Frank starts again, "Two days later, let's see, that would be day three since the attack, the President was again giving a speech, this time from in front of the White House. He was talking about the new powers being given to Homeland Security, when all of a sudden gun fire could be heard. People were screaming and cursing. You could hear explosions in the background. Then, after about thirty minutes . . . I was glued to the radio, I couldn't leave . . . after about thirty minutes, General Trevor of the Joint Chiefs came on the air. He was saying that he, and certain other military generals and commanders, along with certain legislators, had taken action to secure and protect the Constitution and the Republic. The President, his entire cabinet and others who assisted him in carrying out orders detrimental to the Republic and against the Constitution were arrested and being kept in a secure area, pending prosecution at a later time. In the meantime, the Joint Chiefs would govern the nation until a new government could be instituted."

After a brief pause, Frank continues, "General Trevor nullified all executive orders issued by the president. He said the military would protect the country from outside threats and try to avoid getting involved in internal strife. He ordered all National Guard forces that had been federalized, to place themselves back under state control." Jill says, "What does all this mean?" You say, "Hope. At least some hope that America may survive."

Frank says, "But wait, there's more. Yesterday, as I was monitoring a BBC news broadcast from South America, they reported the US had nuked Iran and North Korea. They also reported some major clashes at the US-Mexican border between the US military and the Mexican military." You ask, "Frank, when do you normally pick up these broadcasts?" Frank responds, "It depends on the atmospherics. It's possible I'm missing a lot." You ask, "Any more, tonight?" Frank says, "Maybe; I'll be scanning nearly all night." You're trying to process the implications of what you just heard. You just don't know what it all means.

"Frank, if I give you a set of frequencies, can you call? I have a friend, near my home, who has a shortwave that we use as a group. If you can contact them, we might be able to get some help. At least we can find out how things are at home." Jill's eyes light up, "Oh, yes that would be wonderful if you could." Frank says, shaking his head, "I wish I could. The reason I bought the newer equipment was because my transmitter went out on this unit. All I can do is receive, sorry." Jill looks very disappointed. You say, "Thanks anyway, Frank."

As you leave the house, you stop at the bottom of the steps. You turn to Jill; it's too dark now to see her features. You say, "I really don't know what to make of all this. I really don't." She says, "Just get us home, John. Just get us home."

Chapter 41 John - Day 7 - *A starry night...*

You hear George coming down the steps behind you. He says, "I had no idea so much was happening." You say, "George, bad things are coming to your community. Maybe not from the government, but bad things are coming. Make ready." George says, "Yes, we will. And the trouble from the government might not be over. Who knows, the powers in play right now might want their own dictatorship." Jill says, "Yes, it's scary isn't it? I just don't understand what all this means." You say, "George, I know the way back. Jill and I are going to take the ATV out and see how she handles at night. It might be a little while before we make it back. Do you have anything special you want us to do to identify ourselves when we return?" George responds, "Na, just knock on the door. We'll see you. Be careful."

You mount the ATV. Jill follows, as before. "Jill, I'd like to drive around a little to get the feel for driving the ATV with the NVD on. We'll take it slow. Tomorrow, when I take you shooting, we can open it up and also give you some driving time. Is that okay?" Jill says, "Yes, that's fine. I'm game, if you are." You say, "How about help me with this headgear for the NVD. Let's see if we can get it on without bumping on my head wound. It still smarts a bit." Jill says, "Yes, I can help you." You loosen the straps and start putting the head gear on. Jill has her flashlight on. It must be in her mouth, as you feel both of her hands guide the straps over and around the gash in your head. She says something, but the flashlight is still in her mouth and you can't understand. She takes it out and says, "How's that? It's not rubbing is it?" You tighten the straps down and say, "No, I think this is going to be okay. You ready?" Jill says, "Yes, let's go!" You clip the NVD in place on the headgear, turn it on and adjust the focus for about twenty-five yards in front. You say, "Here we go," as you place the ATV in gear and give it the gas.

Depth perception is not very good with the NVD, and it takes some getting used to. Especially making turns onto side roads. You're getting the hang of it. You're just not going to be able to drive very fast and it's going to tire your eyes. You turn into one of the large pastures and drive toward the middle. Stopping the ATV, you say, "Jill, help me remove this gear." Jill says, "Okay, but what are we doing way out here." You say, "This may be our last peaceful night for a very long time. I thought we might just enjoy it." Jill says, "Yes, sure," as she helps you remove the headgear. You say, "The sky is clear. See how many stars are out? Isn't it beautiful and amazing?" as you lay your head back. She looks up and says, "Yes it is. There are so many of them. I've often wanted to just find a big field somewhere at night, lie back and just gaze at the stars." You say, as you get off the ATV, "I want to show you something." Jill says, "Okay, what?" You say, "Turn around. No, stay on the ATV, just spin around on the seat. Yeah, that's right. Now, sit as far toward the back as possible." Jill complies and adjusts herself as you direct. She has her legs crossed, sitting on the very back edge of the seat, facing backwards. "Here," you say, "let's put the NVD on you." You help her put it on. "Now, lean back." Jill says, "John, what are you doing. You're making me nervous." You respond, "I don't mean to. Just trust me. You'll see in just a moment." She says, "I do trust you." You smile and say, "Okay, then just ease back. I'll help you." Jill says, "Ouch, my head is hitting on something." "Hold on, just a minute," you say. You start removing your shirt. Jill says, "John?" "Trust me," you say as you fold your shirt and place it under her head. "Now, place your feet and legs to make yourself comfortable. Now watch this." You reach over and turn the NVD on. Jill catches her breath, "Wow, John, this is amazing! So many more stars. This is simply amazing!" You show her how to adjust the focus and say, "You like it?" Jill says, "Yes, I do, though I didn't know what you were up to there for a few minutes. This is wonderful. Thank you." You say, "Just lay back and enjoy."

Still lying back and gazing at the stars, she says, "John, your place, isn't it a small farm or something like that? Does it look anything like this?" You think for a minute, trying to figure out how to describe it. You look at Jill lying on the ATV. Something has happened to you over the past few days. You're seeing things you've never noticed before. You're feeling things you haven't felt in a very long time. You say, "Jill, I'm not sure exactly how to describe it. It's a small farm, that's true. We have cows, sheep, chickens and ducks. There are a few ponds. But, it's really more than that. It's complete because of the community we live in. Many like-minded individuals live there, individuals who work together to achieve a common goal. I think you would like it out there, Jill, I really do. The main thing is it's safe. Well, as safe a place as you will find in Clarke County."

"John, do you have places there like this, where we can get a good view of the night sky?" "Yes, I do, Jill." You wonder if she's deciding if she and Lizzy are coming to your place. Jackson is going to be a tough place to be. You think there are some things you can help the people there with, but regardless, it's still going to be tough, real tough. She continues, "John, what do you think things will be like when we return home? Please don't patronize me. I'm not some little dainty pretty girl and I'm not a ditzy blond either. I can handle the truth, and don't you ever give me anything but the truth." "Jill," you say, "I think it is going to be worse than anything you can imagine. There is not enough food in Clarke County to feed the people of Clarke County. People are going to be dying from lack of medications, lack of food and disease. Desperate people are going to do desperate things. It's going to be bad." She says, "Didn't you say you had some ideas to help make things better?" You say, "I do, if they haven't already thought of them. But regardless, people are going to be dying on a scale never before seen in this country. Violence is going to be an everyday occurrence. The police, if they are still intact, and I hope they are, because without them recovery will be impossible, but the police are not going to be able to protect you as an individual. They couldn't do it before The Day, and they certainly won't be able to now. I think you and Lizzy will be safer with us, in Repose." Jill says, "Let's make it home, then we'll see. I can't say right now." You say, "Okay, Jill."

You look at her again, the starlight silhouetting her body. The form is perfect. Why you never noticed before amazes you. "Jill, let's head back. We have a busy day tomorrow." You walk over and extend your hand. Jill reaches for your hand and you pull her up. She removes the NVD and says, "Hop on, cowboy, and take us home." You laugh and climb on the ATV. She helps you put the headgear back on, and you drive back to George and Betty's home.

Chapter 42 Jill - Day 8 - *Target practice…*

You feel the bed move. A man has been sleeping in the bed with you for almost a week. It seems so strange, yet it feels normal at the same time. You stir and look over. John is on the floor. You hear his faint counting, "sixty-seven, sixty-eight, sixty-nine, seventy." John stands and starts stretching. He looks over at you. "I'm sorry. I didn't mean to wake you. Go back to sleep. You may not have another soft bed for several days." You just lie there watching him. This man in front of you, this man is willing to die for you. It is so clear to you, now. Staggering down the hall, he came to your aid. It must be true. 'Greater love has no man than that he is willing to lay down his life for his friend.' Yet, he remains restrained. You wonder why. You smile, maybe soon when you get home, he'll say what he wants. Tonight, tonight you head home. You are so ready, yet some fear enters your mind. "Dear God, bring us home. Bring us home soon. Amen," you whisper. John says, "I'm sorry, I couldn't tell what you were saying." You say, "How are you, John? Are you up to leaving tonight as planned?" John says, "I'm close to seventy percent. I think that's good enough. Do you think you'll be able to take these stitches out for me in a couple of days?" "Yes, I've talked to Betty about it. She said the day after tomorrow would be the right time." He asks, "Are you going back to sleep, or getting up?" You start twirling your finger through your hair and say, "I think I'm going to just lie here for a while if you don't mind." John answers, "I don't mind." John closes the door as he enters the bathroom. You hear the sounds of morning activities from within. You think, "I could get use to this." You know there has to be more; you'll just have to see. You aren't home yet. John walks out and into the hallway.

Lying there you think of Lizzy and your mother. You hope they are with Will. If things are going to be as bad as John says, you really hope they are in

Repose. But, perhaps, in a few more days you will be home; then you can decide what you should do. You sit up and place your feet on the floor and rise. Hmm . . . you don't feel much pain. You walk into the bathroom, picking up some clean clothes as you go. Removing your clothes, you look in the mirror. The bruising, though still evident, is starting to fade. The one on your face has changed to a yellowish color. That's a good sign. The mark across your chest where the rope knocked you from your bike, it's still there. You shower and redress. You dry your hair as best you can with a towel, and then brush it out. Looking in the mirror, you realize you haven't worn any makeup in over a week. You spent a lot of money through the years at Dillard's buying makeup and perfume. Clinique and Estee Lauder were your favorite brands. Wonder what perfume John likes best? Poor guy, all he has gotten to smell is sweat, but he hasn't complained yet. That's a good sign, but of course he wouldn't, anyway. Maybe makeup is a thing of the past. You'll just have to wait and see.

You slip your Glock inside your waistband, after putting your shoes on. You walk down the hall and join George, John and Betty in the kitchen. It looks like they have already eaten. Betty says, "Dear, I placed a plate for you in the oven." You open the oven door. There are the familiar bacon, eggs and biscuits. Getting a cup of coffee, you sit next to John and say, "Thank you, Betty. This is good, real good just like always." Betty says, "You're welcome, dear." "John," you say turning and looking up at him, "if you'll put some clean clothes on and give me those dirties, I'll wash them and hang them to dry before we go shoot." John smiles, "That's great, Jill. Thanks." John gets up and starts back to the bedroom. He pauses, "Jill, where do you want me to put them?" "Just set them with mine, on the floor in the bathroom. I'll get them as soon as I finish with breakfast."

John returns, wearing clean clothes. He has his only button-up shirt on, the one he loaned you that day. It's an olive-drab kind of color, an earthy color. He says as he passes by, "I've got a couple of things I want to do to the ATV, but I can help you first." "No, I've got the clothes. Go do whatever it is you're wanting to do." There is no way you're going to let him wash your undies and bra. No way.

With the clothes hanging to dry, you start looking for John. He's still at the barn with the ATV. You walk over. "Hey, Jill," he says, "Look at this." You walk over look and say, "Okay, what is it?" He says with a slight frown, "This is a swivel mount for our forward cannon?" You say, "What?" John smiles just a little, "for the Mossberg pump shotgun. It's going to ride clipped to this mount. That way if we have a problem and need to clear some space, it'll be ready." You say, "I hope we don't have to use it." John says, "Yes, me, too. Are you ready to go? If so, let's go get our guns and gear." "Yes, I'm ready," you say as you turn back toward the house. Walking to the house, you pass by the clothes line. John pauses, which causes you to pause. He looks at you with a little mischievous grin, "Are those your little bitty panties on the line?" You turn red and punch him on the arm. Turning you walk back to the house without saying a word.

You make it to the shooting bench. John insisted you bring your pack, though he didn't tell you why. Getting off the ATV, you both approach the bench. There are several white metal targets spaced out in the trees. Some are closer than others. They are all about the size of a sheet of notebook paper. John says, "Okay, let's go over a few safety rules. First, always keep your gun pointed in a safe direction. Second, consider all guns loaded unless you have visually checked them yourself. Third, always keep your finger off the trigger until you are ready to shoot. Fourth . . . ." But you interrupt him, "John, I'm not a school girl. I've been shooting guns since I was ten years old. My dad taught me to use the Ruger 10/22 and his old rifle is in my closet." John says, "Yeah, sorry, I know he did. Just habit I guess. You and I haven't been shooting together and well . . . I . . . ." "Don't worry about it," you say. "Keep your sunglasses on, and put these ear plugs in," John says. He reaches out and hands you the three loaded ten round magazines for the Ruger. Then he adds, "Load up, and put these all down range on target." You load the gun and say, "Range is going hot!" You start firing, putting the first ten rounds into a single swing target. The next twenty rounds you scatter amongst all the targets. John reaches for the empty magazine and reloads it, just like he did the others. He says, "Let's try this. There are six targets. From left to right, we will call them one through six. When I call out a number, I want you to put three bullets into the target. On the third target I call out just empty the magazine, which should require four rounds. Then switch magazines and we'll continue until all three are empty. Ready?" You reply, "Yes." John says, "Range is going hot! One!" You send three, small twenty-two lead bullets into target one. John says, "Four!" You switch aim and put three bullets into target four. John says again, "One!" You adjust your aim, and put the remaining four rounds into it. You replace the magazine and John continues his calls.

John says, "I think you've got that down pretty good. This Ruger is going to be your "go to" rifle. If you need a gun, besides your pistol, this is the one you are going to go to. We'll keep it strapped on top of your pack on the rear rack. Now, I want you to put a few rounds through the carbine, then I'll take a turn." You ask, "Are we going to use the suppressor?" John says, "Yes, but not with the sub-sonic ammo. We'll just use the FMJs for now. They won't be completely silent, but they won't be as loud as without the suppressor. Let's save the really good stuff in case we need it. We'll just shoot the FMJs for practice. I've already removed the sub-sonic and self-defense ammo from the magazines. They all have the FMJs. I've loaded five of my magazines with the FMJs. I'll keep the sixth one loaded with self-defense ammo, just in case. I'll keep it in my pocket. If you'll give me your spare magazine, I'll load it with FMJs as well. Unload your pistol, and put that magazine in your pocket." You say, "Okay" and proceed to unload your Glock and remove the self-defense ammo from the magazine. You say, "John, I'm just going to unload the magazine that was in my gun. I'll keep the other in my pocket." He says, "Yeah, that makes more sense doesn't it." He hands you the rifle, stands behind you, and watches as you turn the sight on and position the rifle. He reaches over and says, "Here," as he gives you the magazine and moves a little closer. He's helping you position the rifle on your shoulder, so you can find the red dot sight. You sense his breathing is just a little heavier. You look up at him. He has a different look on his face. You ask, "Are you all right, John? Do I smell bad or something?" His expression changes and he moves back a little. Smiling he says, "I'm good. I wouldn't describe your scent as bad." "Really?" you query. "Yes, really. Now, turn around and shoot." You shoot the carbine, then shoot your Glock.

When John's turn arrives, he moves away from the bench. He puts one magazine in the carbine and one in the Glock. He places the other two in his magazine pouches. He loads each weapon. His carbine is hanging by its sling in front of him. He looks at you, and moves two more steps away. He asks, "Are you ready?" Seeing you nod your head, he says, "Range, going hot." In a flash, he raises the carbine and starts firing rapidly, double tapping each target until the magazine runs dry. Dropping his carbine to his side, he draws his Glock and continues the double tap. When the pistol slide locks back, he ejects the empty magazine, allowing it to fall to the ground, then inserts the new and racks the slide. He does this all in one swift, steady motion. This time he is moving towards the targets as he begins double tapping again. He moves from target to target, getting closer and moving side to side. When his magazine runs dry, he reloads again. This time his double taps are being taken as he takes back and side steps toward you. When the slide locks back, he stops and says, "All clear." He then removes the empty magazine and releases the slide and holsters his pistol. You have never seen anyone shoot so fast and on the move, too. You're dumbfounded. You thought the movies were all fake stuff, but maybe some of it was real. You look at John in astonishment as he walks back, picking up his empty magazines. You say, "John, I've never seen anything like that before. I'm amazed." He says, "Jill, I've been practicing for many years and thousands of rounds. Will has, too. If we find ourselves in a violent encounter, our actions must be quick, aggressive and decisive. Our actions must be overwhelming. Can you do that?" You think, "Yes, I can do it. I've already had to do it." You say, "John, if I have to I will do it. I won't shirk from your side. You can count on me." He looks directly into your eyes for a moment and says, "I believe you can."

You say, "I think Mark is bringing his family over for lunch." John says, "Okay, but before we go, load up one of your magazines with FMJs and run your pistol again. I'm going to move back to the ATV and reload my magazines." You load up the FMJs, then stepping from the bench you look at John to make sure he is ready, then say, "Range, going hot." In a deliberate, smooth motion you draw your Glock and double tap each target until your slide locks back. Walking back to John, you say, "That wasn't as fast as you." John says, "No, it wasn't, but you hit your target each time. Accuracy is more important than speed. Now, get on and drive us back to the house."

Chapter 43 Jill - Day 8 - *Leaving for home...*

You see four bicycles as you drive up to the house. Three are girl bikes, and one is a boy's. The boy's bike has a wagon attached to the rear, on a swivel. You always wondered why girl and boy bikes were made different. Was it because in the days when bikes were so prominent, that women all wore dresses? Did the low cut intend to make it easier to ride a bike in a dress? You don't know, as you've never ridden a bike with a dress on before. You think of your cousin, Jerry, back in your early teens. He was standing and pedaling hard when his foot slipped and he landed hard on the horizontal bar. You watched as his bike fell over and Jerry lay on the ground in a fetal position, racked in pain. It scared you. It took him nearly fifteen minutes before he could stand. Even then he had to push his bike home. That darn horizontal bar. Wouldn't it have been better for him to have a girl's bike? It's one of those silly things you'll never understand.

You park the ATV and John says, "You did good, Jill, real good. Wished I had thought about letting you drive last night with the NVD." You say, "Looks like Mark's family is here." John says, "Yes, it does," as he gets off the ATV. He reaches back his hand to help you off. He looks into your eyes; you look back into his blue eyes. Something is happening. "Jill, before we go in . . . ." But the moment and words are lost as the kitchen door opens and George walks out saying, "Lunch is ready. Betty has fixed up a fine meal. Come on in and meet Mark's family." John turns his head and says, "Great. We are on our way." He holds your hand as you get down. You both grab your packs and rifles, and walk in the door.

Just inside the door you set your packs and rifles against the wall. You see Mark with his wife and girls standing close by. Mark starts, "This is my wife, Melissa, daughters, Karen and Lynn." Turning slightly, he says, "These fine people are John and Jill." As he speaks, Karen runs quickly to John and embraces him. She is crying. "Thank you! Thank you so much." John is starting to tear up, something you've never seen before. In fact, everyone's eyes are tearing. You look at Melissa. Her hand is covering her mouth as she leans into Mark. John hugs Karen and says, "You are very welcome. You are a beautiful young lady. I hope your friends are okay, too." Melissa walks over and hugs your neck. She says, "We are so sorry for what happened, and so thankful for what your husband did for our Karen. Thank you so much." The emotions are high. You find it hard to swallow and speak, but say, "I'm so thankful that John was there. I truly am. I hope everything will be okay with Karen and the others." Melissa says, "Yes, she is going to be okay. She is a strong girl, much like her father. We are truly so sorry for what happened. We really are." Melissa cries even harder as she squeezes you tight. After a few moments, she moves over to John. She looks up at him with an expression you can't describe. She reaches her arms around John's neck and pulls him down. She hugs him tight and whispers something in his ear. Then after a few seconds, she releases him and, with tears still running down her cheeks, she returns to Mark's side. George clears his throat and says, "Why don't we all take a minute to freshen up and then let's come eat this fine meal while it's hot?"

John picks up his pack and carbine and heads to the bedroom. You follow suit. John sets his pack and rifle next to the wall and straightens up, taking a few deep breaths. You walk over and stand in front of him. You reach out and pull yourself to him. You embrace each other. As your sobbing subsides, you look up at John and say, "Thank you, John, for being a good man." John's eyes are moist as he takes another deep breath and replies, "Thank you, Jill." He hugs you close, then says, "Let's clean up and go eat, before I fall to the floor and start bawling." You smile and say, "Yes, let's do."

The meal is excellent. Pot roast, baked bread and all the fixings. The mood is no longer heavy with emotion, but light with conversation, like a family gathering. As you sit there watching the interactions of each person and the gaiety of the atmosphere, you wonder if John is really right about what is happening outside this enclave of family farms. Yes, you encountered some bad people, very bad people. But here, right now, everything is normal.

You hope John is wrong, you really do. Because right here, all around you, is life, a good life. You glance up at John. This could be a perfect life, but something tells you this is all going to change, and change real soon. You almost feel guilty, sitting here with new friends, eating a normal meal, while you know in your own town people are hungry. You reach out and grab John's hand and squeeze it. He looks over and smiles. At least you have each other for now. You'll just have to see what happens when you return home.

You help Betty and Melissa in the kitchen, as the men move to the great room talking. You can't hear what they are saying. Melissa says, "I have something for you." She walks into the great room and picks up a bag and returns. She says, "Here. You and I are about the same size. I hope everything fits." You open the bag and see a complete set of clothes. The pants are khaki and the shirt an earthy color. She says, "I was going to give you something a little brighter, but Mark thought this color would be best. I hope you like it." You look up and smile saying, "Yes, Melissa, this is great. Thank you." In the bottom of the bag is a zip lock bag packed with feminine pads. With a light smile on your face, you look over at John and whisper, "Thank you." But by far, the best thing is the sports bra!

Finishing up with a cup of coffee, you overhear John and Mark talking. John says, "Mark, I don't know how you guys are set up for security, but I hope you realize when people figure out what you have here they will be coming. You need to decide now, what you will do then." Mark says, "Yes, we've been discussing it. We're pretty out of the normal travel lanes, so we are hoping we won't get many visitors. We have some road guards at the main county road keeping people from coming in. It's working so far." John reaches into his pocket and pulls out the five silver coins Mark had returned. He hands them to Mark and says, "Mark, I know you used all your silver to get these items we needed. Keep these, if you will. I have more at home." Mark looks up, "Okay, thanks man."

Mark and his family leave. You, John, George and Betty are on the front porch waving bye. The moment just seems so surreal, when considering what is happening not far from here. As you go back in, John looks at his watch, saying, "It's after 2:00. I think I'm going to try to take a nap so I can be rested for our night travels." "Yes, John, I think that's a good idea. I think I will too, but I want to talk with Betty a little more." You watch John as he walks away. You, Betty and George sit in the great room. You climb into the same large chair you have sat in the past few days. Tucking your feet underneath, you say, "Betty, George, I want to thank you both so much for what you have done for us. We will never forget your kindness. I know if it weren't for you, John would be dead. You both are like my parents and I love you both." George says, "Jill, we were glad to help. I know you must leave and we both, Betty and I, have been praying for you and John and your families back home. If things ever get back to some kind of normal, we would like to come see you and John at your place. John gave me his business card with his address. He also wrote yours on the back." Betty says, "Yes, Jill honey, it has been wonderful having you in our home. I wish things were different, I really do. Today just seemed so right. I hate to see you leave, but I know you must return home." After a few more minutes of chatting you say, "I think I should try and take a nap, too. I don't really know what to expect later tonight." George says, "I think that would be a good idea." You rise and walk to the bedroom.

As you walk into the bedroom, John is lying in the bed. His eyes are closed and he appears to be asleep. You take your shoes off and remove your Glock, and lie down trying not to wake him. You are going home tonight. Tonight! You're excited and scared at the same time. John said he thought it would take three to four nights of travel to get to Jackson. He just can't drive very fast with the NVD. His NVD is a monocular; it only covers one eye. When he's wearing it, one eye is looking into the NVD and the other into darkness. It's probably going to give him a headache if he has to wear it for hours. You pray, "Dear God, bless us. Bring us home safe."

You open your eyes. You must have fallen asleep. John is still sleeping. You look out the window; it's still daylight outside. John said he wanted to leave around 10:00 tonight. When you asked why so late he said, "I want to give anybody traveling on the roads ample opportunity to set up camp and settle down. Perhaps it will lessen our chances of encountering anyone on the road." You lie there for what seems an eternity, but are unable to go back to sleep. You look over at John; his watch says 6:10. You must have slept for two hours. You can't just lie here any longer. You ease out of bed and head to the bathroom.

It's going to be a while before you're able to have another shower, so you decide to take one last advantage while you can. Standing in front of the mirror, you undress and rub your foot along your leg. You feel hairs, lots of hairs, a week's worth of hairs! You can't ever remember having this much hair on your legs. You shudder slightly, look in the mirror, then at the lavatory. John's razor is sitting on a hand cloth. You think about the hairs on your legs, and the single man tent, then you think of John. You reach for the razor saying softly, "Just in case."

The shower felt good. The shaved legs feel even better. John is gone. He must be doing something with the ATV. At least he made the bed before he left. You sit in the chair and put your shoes on. You hope you cleaned all the hairs out of John's razor. Your dad used to get mad at your mom when she would use his razor. She would often say, "You'll appreciate it later." When she said that, dad always stopped complaining.

You pack all your gear up and put your Glock on your hip. You look around the room, seeing if there is anything else you might do or pack up. Betty already insisted that the towels be left on the floor in the bathroom. You told her you wanted to wash them before you left, but she insisted she would take care of it. It looks like John has all his gear packed, too. Everything, except what's left in the bathroom. On the dresser you see the GPS unit. You walk over and pick it up. You have to be careful, as it is falling apart. John didn't say anything about having tested it with fresh batteries. You get four AA batteries from your pack and put them in the GPS. Crossing your fingers, you push the power button and smile as the screen lights up. Even though it has several cracks, the screen is still easy to read. Now for the duct tape. Your Dad used to say the only thing duct tape would not cure was the common cold. You're fixing to find out. You unroll about twelve inches and using your knife, cut it off the roll, then slit it lengthwise to make two pieces. Holding the GPS together, you tightly wrap the duct tape around the seam. Then turning it over, you use shorter pieces of the slit tape to secure the battery cover. You look at your handy work and think, "Call me MacGyver." You turn it back on. Yes! It's still working. Turning it off, you set it on John's pack. He is going to be surprised.

You walk into the kitchen. Betty is there. She's preparing two plates of left overs. She looks up and smiles, saying, "Honey, I thought you and John might want a bite to eat before you go. The coffee is fresh, too." You smile, "Yes Betty, thank you. Where's John?" Betty says, "He's outside loading up some things Mark brought." You say, "I'll wait for John." Betty stops what she is doing and walks over saying, "Honey, I know it is truly a sad tale of events that have brought you two together, but, sometimes God works in mysterious ways to bring us comfort. I think you and John are right for each other. I really do." You smile, "Thank you, Betty. Maybe we are. We'll have to see what happens when we get home." John walks in. You both look up. "Are you two ladies conspiring against me or something?" You respond, "Or something. Come, Betty has prepared a plate for us."

After the meal, John says, "It's 8:45. I'm going to take a shower and finish packing my things. I'd like to leave at 10:00, if that's still okay with you." You say, "Yes, I'm really ready to get going. I have all my things packed. Just place your towels on the floor with mine. Betty won't let me wash them." John says, "Okay. It won't take me long." What is it about men and showers? Your dad could always be in and out of the shower in the amount of time it took you to wash your hair.

You hear John whoop. Walking back to the bedroom, you ask with a smile, "What's wrong?" He's holding the GPS, smiling, he looks up and says, "You did good Jill, real good. This may help save our lives." He still has a smile on his face and is shaking his head as he walks into the bathroom. You return to Betty, taking your pack and Ruger to the great room. About twenty minutes later, John brings his pack and carbine and sets them next to yours. You ask, "Where is the shotgun?" He says, "I've already mounted it on the ATV. I've loaded all the other things up as well. All that is left is our packs, rifles and our bottoms."

George walks in and hands John a small package saying, "Some things you might find handy." John looks inside the bag. Nodding his head he says, "Yes, they might," then closes the bag. Betty brings coffee for everyone.

George pulls out a hand drawn map. He says, "John, this is the sketch of how to get around Montevallo. There are quite a few turns, but all the roads have name signs, at least they did the last time I drove it a few months back, all except for this dirt road right here." He points it out to John. "This road is a cutoff road and does not have a sign and neither does the other end. There are several small logging roads spurring off of it. Just stay on the main road and you'll be fine." John says, "This is great, thanks. I hope we can make it past Brent before morning, but I really haven't figured how to get around it yet. This little lady right here," he nods at you, "has fixed our GPS, so I may give it a try. If I can't find a way, we'll wait and go through early in the morning. I don't want to try to sneak through town during the night. They may have road guards who are jumpy."

John looks at his watch. It seems like you've only been talking at the table a few minutes, yet he says, "It's 9:45, let's load everything up." Standing from your chair, you walk over and pick up your pack and Ruger. Taking them to the ATV, John straps your pack to the rear rack, then straps the Ruger crossways on top of your pack. He straps his gear to the front rack and hands you a radio saying, "Keep this with you until we make it back home, just in case." Betty and George walk out to the porch. John says, "If you don't mind, we are going to pray before we leave." Everyone bows their heads and John prays, "Dear Heavenly Father, there is so much uncertainty and peril in our path ahead. We pray for your protection. Give us wisdom and courage to handle the trials we must face. Please bless our families back home. Bring us safely to them. Thank you for our dear friends, George and Betty. Please bless and protect them. In Jesus' name. Amen." You all say, "Amen."

John mounts the ATV. You climb on behind and help him put his NVD headgear on. Betty walks up and hands you two small bags, saying, "I packed you some lunch. The other bag has some other useful items." She kisses you and hugs you and John. George walks over and hugs you, and then firmly shakes John's hand saying, "Be safe, son. One day we will meet again. Take good care of Jill." John smiles, "Thanks, George. Thanks for everything." Looking back at you he says, "I will do everything I can to keep her safe." With a wave goodbye, John drives the ATV into the darkness.

Chapter 44 Jill - Day 8 - *On the road again...*

John turns right at the end of the lane and continues for about two miles. He is still trying to get the NVD situated where it won't rub on his stitches yet remain in place. Approaching CR10, John slows down. He asks, "Can you see up ahead, the fire?" Looking, you say, "No, I don't see anything." He says, "The NVD is picking it up good. We are still about a half mile away. Having a fire, like they are, is a really bad idea. It makes them an easy target to spot." Wow, you don't see anything, yet. It's still pretty dark, with only the stars and slight cloud cover. John is approaching slowly, so as not to startle anyone there. He stops about a hundred yards away and, using a flash light, he flashes the code as George instructed him. Receiving no response, he flashes again. Finally, someone at the road block flashes back. John approaches slowly. He flips his NVD up as the ATV pulls up to the guards. There are two guards. One has a shotgun and the other a scoped bolt action rifle. The fire light dances across their camouflage clothing. The older of the two says, "Hi, you two must be John and Jill." John says, "Yes. I'm John. This is Jill." The guy says, "I'm Randy. This other goof ball is my son Michael. George told us to expect you." John asks, "Have you seen many people walking down the road?" Randy says, "No, not really. We did see a group of six walking north about 6:00 p.m. But other than that, we haven't seen anybody." John says, "That's good, we're going south so we shouldn't encounter that group. What kind of shift are you guys working?" Randy says, "We pull a 24-hour shift. We get relieved at 6:00 a.m." John says, "Wow, that's a pretty long shift. How do you stay awake?" Michael speaks up, "It's not bad. We don't do nothing but sit around. If we get tired, one of us naps in the car." John asks, "Have you heard anything about what's going on south of here?" Randy says, "Those folks passing earlier today said something about seeing some militia or military looking guys driving around, but they didn't bother anybody." John says, "Well, good luck to you guys. We're going to be moving along." Randy says, "Safe travels." You wave at them as the ATV turns south on CR10.

John's driving about ten miles per hour. He says we'll turn right about seven or eight miles ahead onto the dirt cutoff road. George said the road was to the right, just past the old Methodist church. Your hands are on John's shoulder. That's the most comfortable position you have found, and it helps keep your chest off John's back. You lean in closer as John starts speaking, "What did you notice about the road block back there?" You think for a few moments. "They didn't seem to be very alert; maybe it's because of their long shifts." John says, "You are right, they aren't very alert, and you are right, the long shift probably has something to do with it, but that's not all." "What do you mean?" John says, "First, the whole road block is set up in a bad location. It's near the bottom of a small hill; you don't want the low ground, if you can help it. Second, the road block consists of one car across the road and nothing off to the sides; not a very effective block at all. Third, they have a fire going. It's a signal to everybody around as to where their location is. It also hampers their ability to see in the dark. Fourth, neither of them had flashlights mounted on their guns. Fifth, yes the lack of sleep probably made them less alert, but I bet it's more lack of discipline than anything else. Napping in the car! Geez! The whole thing smells haphazard. They are going to be in trouble if somebody really tries to get in." This troubles you. You ask, "Do you think George and Betty are going to be in danger?" "I'm afraid they might, unless trouble comes incrementally and allows them to learn before it gets bad. Bad trouble, right now, would be a disaster for them." You pray softly, "Dear God, please protect our friends. Open their eyes as to what they need to do. Amen."

About an hour later, John slows down and says, "I think this is the old church right up ahead." You look, but really can't see much more than the outline of a building. It's just too dark to tell much about it. John says, "St Paul's United Methodist Church, that's it. Let's look for the first dirt road, to the right. You want to stretch your legs?" "No, I'm good." About ten minutes later, John slows again. He stops and says, "I think this is it." He slowly navigates the ATV onto the dirt road. It's in fair condition, with some wash board grooves here and there. It causes John to drive even slower. You ask him what he sees around. "Just road and trees. I've been looking for any sign of fire or light, but I haven't seen anything." After a little over an hour, there is a paved road. There are no signs. John stops just short of the road, saying, "This must be Marvel Road." He eases the ATV onto the pavement. Then, shortly, pulls over to the side. You ask, with some concern, "What's wrong?" He says, "There is a small field off to the side here. You've been fidgeting for the past ten minutes, so I figure you need to make a stop. Besides, my eyes need some relief." You feel your face grow red. Was it that obvious? You were waiting as long as you could, but he's right, you need to go pretty bad. Those bumps were not too easy back there. Getting off, John reaches back and helps you off. Your legs are stiff, and your back is sore from maintaining the same position for so long. John says, "I'm going to turn the NVD off. It's pretty dark, so you can go anywhere really." You don't like this. True it's dark, too dark to see very far or very much, but you still don't like it. You walk off a bit and look back. You can't see John or the ATV. Finishing up, you start back, but you've lost your sense of direction. You call out, "John, where are you?" John says, "Over here," as he shines a small light for you to walk toward. When you get back he says, "I'm glad you didn't use your flashlight. Let's don't use them unless we absolutely have to. Here, take this key chain light. It won't shine far but it will help you walk around. Try to keep your hand around it and only let out the minimal amount of light you need." You take the light and say, "Thanks." He reaches into his pack and pulls out two energy bars. Using another keychain light inside his pack, he asks, "Blueberry or cherry?" "Blueberry." He asks again, "Want to share, or do you want the whole thing?" "Sharing is fine with me." He breaks the bar in half and hands one piece to you and starts munching on the other piece. You ask, "John, what time is it?" John looking at his watch, says, "Jill, it is now 12:30. Good Saturday morning to you." "I can think of some other things I'd rather being doing on a Saturday morning." John says, "Yeah, I can too, but I've got to stay focused." Now what does he mean by that?

John turns the ATV back onto Marvel Road and says, "We've got about twelve more miles to go, or something close to that, before we hit AL25 south of Montevallo. Our next turn is south on CR65. That should take us into AL25." "Okay, at least we're getting closer." The miles seem like they are only crawling by, but you are very glad you aren't having to walk. Very glad indeed. The night air is slightly cool, maybe the upper 60s. The ATV is really quiet. You don't know what Mark did to it, but John sure was happy to hear how quiet it was. John has been silent for a while. Your head falls forward and lands on John's shoulder. You say, "Sorry." A few moments later your head falls again. You say, "Sorry." The next time, your left hand slides from John's shoulder and you face plant into his shoulder. "John, I'm sorry I can't stay awake." John says, "It's okay, Jill. Go ahead and get some rest. I'm okay." "Are you sure?" "Yes, I'm sure." You just can't help it; you're too tired and sleepy. You've tried to keep off John's back, but it's no use. You take your hands from his shoulders, wrapping your arms around him and lean fully into his back. You make yourself comfortable, laying your head on his shoulder. You hope he doesn't mind, because you're just too sleepy to do anything else.

John is squeezing your leg. He's saying something. What is he saying? "Jill, wake up." You finally come to your senses and ask, "What is it, John? How long have I been asleep?" "There is a fire on the side of the road up ahead. Be alert."

Chapter 45 John - Day 9 - *Roadside campfire...*

As you leave the field behind and continue on Marvel Road, you start thinking of your new found friends, hoping they will be okay. They really don't have a significant security plan. Anybody, who really wanted to, could go right through their impromptu road block and be amongst the farms and homes in a matter of minutes. You wish you had known how poorly they were set up. You might could have helped them with some ideas. The whole time you were there, you didn't see a gun on Betty or George. In fact, prior to the road block, the only gun you saw besides yours and Jill's, was the Glock on Mark's hip. That won't be enough to defend a community. The guards talked about rumors of military looking guys roaming around. That could be good, or it could be very bad. If they are community minded and trying to keep things secure, that's a good thing. If they are out roving, looking for a good place to set up operations, it's going to be bad for your friends, very bad.

You feel Jill's head fall to your shoulder and she says, "Sorry." Her head falls again and she repeats, "Sorry." You can't blame her. You're tired too; there is just too much on your mind, otherwise you'd be nodding off. You feel her hand slide from your shoulder and her face falls harder. She says, "John, I'm sorry I can't stay awake." "It's okay, Jill. Go ahead and get some rest. I'm okay." She asks, "Are you sure?" "Yes, I'm sure." You feel Jill remove her hands from your shoulders and wrap her arms around you. Then, she snuggles in close and lays her head on your shoulder. She feels warm and soft. It's pleasant; a type of pleasant you haven't felt in a very long time. You smile to yourself. Jill is a beautiful woman, sandy blonde hair and green eyes. It has certainly been hard refraining from reaching for her these past few days. She is beautiful in her complete form. Why you haven't seen it before is something that continues to amaze you. The events that brought your paths together seem to have been guided. But, you can't let your mind linger in these thoughts, no matter how pleasant they are. You have to stay focused. You need to get yourself and Jill home safely. Once there . . . you'll just have to wait and see.

You think back on the poor security setup George and Betty are depending on, and cringe. Your own community of Repose is small, with only about 300 people. It's situated between US43, US84 and AL69. There is only one county road that travels through the area. There are several small county roads inside the community, but only one that passes through. Some years ago at the Repose Volunteer Fire Department BBQ, you struck up a conversation with some community friends. The conversation drifted into preparedness in general. Later, as the BBQ was winding down, five men approached. They wanted to meet up and talk about things some more. It was agreed. Soon you were meeting every two weeks, and the number grew to its current number of twelve. Three years ago you all agreed to start pooling some resources and skills to help survive as a community, in case of some catastrophic event, including this very event. In addition to pooling resources and making plans, you each prepare as individuals and try to get as many in your community to prepare as possible, some without even knowing it. Talking someone into raising chickens or planting a garden wasn't too difficult to do. These types of things only enhance a person's preparedness, even if they aren't doing it to be prepared. Enhancing personal preparedness enhances community preparedness.

You realize you're fortunate to have been successful in business, and your resources to prepare have been greater than most. You also realize some in your group of twelve have very little, yet they prepare as best they can. It's a mindset that transcends financial, social, gender and racial barriers. As a group, and as individuals, plans were made, responsibilities assigned and schedules set. Kathy was key. She really was. Key to keeping you on track. But why didn't you, or even Kathy, think about washing clothes? But maybe Kathy did make some plans. You'll have to check when you get home. If not, it's going to be a difficult chore. Two of the more important aspects of your plans were physical security and operational security. Physical security for the community in the way of well-planned, armed check points and patrols. Operational security by keeping a tight lid on who knew about your actual preparedness plans. There are many others aspects as well, including setting up communications.

The warmth from Jill's body has turned into sweat. She's tired, really tired. She didn't even wake when you made the turn onto AL25. Soon you're going to have to stop. Your eyes are hurting from the two different light levels. The bright green hue of the NVD for your right eye, to deep darkness for your left eye. You sense a headache coming, despite the three Tylenol you took at your last stop. It's now 2:15 in the morning. You've seen a few camp fires way off to the sides in fields and woods. Not many, but you've been watching one particular fire more closely as you approach. It's pretty evident that it is right on the edge of the road. Why would anyone set up camp right on the edge of the road? They are either ignorant to the dangers, or they want to ambush someone traveling by. You've been fortunate not to have seen anyone traveling, but this fire has you concerned. You're going to have to check it out before driving up to it. You slow the ATV down about a half a mile back. Maybe it's half a mile. It's really only a guess. Time to check things out.

You speak softly to Jill, "Jill . . . Jill . . ." She doesn't respond. You reach back and squeeze her leg, "Jill, wake up." She starts stirring. It's taking her a minute to gain coherency from her deep sleep. Finally, she asks, "What is it, John? How long have I been asleep?" You say, "There is a fire on the side of the road up ahead. Be alert. Jill, you've been asleep for quite a while, more than an hour. It's 2:25. I'm going to have to check it out on foot before we drive by." You see a small opening in the trees to your left on the opposite side of the road from the campfire. You drive in and turn the ATV around to face the road.

Jill starts stretching her arms, then places her hands back on your shoulders. "Oh, John," she says, "I'm sorry. I think a drooled on your shirt." You thought there was something wet back there besides sweat. "Don't worry about it, I may return the favor sometime. Let's get off and walk back to the road." You both dismount. Putting the sling of the carbine around your neck, you test the IR laser. Yes, it's good and bright with the NVD, invisible to the naked eye. You say, "Here, hold my hand. It's too dark to walk around without probably tripping." Jill takes your extended hand. You approach the road and stop, scanning both directions. You lead Jill to the road and ask, "See the fire up ahead?" She says, "Faintly." "This is what we are going to do. I'm going to use the NVD to go up there on foot and see what's up. I need you to stay here with the ATV and our gear. We'll keep in contact using the radios. If you see anything suspicious, call me. When we get back to the ATV, I'm going to give you an earbud and a small mike for the radio. I'll check in with you as I can. If you need to call me, do so, but if I can't respond verbally, I will simply key the mike three times. Under no circumstances are you to leave here unless I specifically ask you to." She responds, "But what if you get hurt and need me?" "Jill, under no circumstances are you to leave here unless I ask. I'm serious. If you come up there and I don't know you are coming, I could mistake you for a bad guy. Don't do it. If I get hurt, or for some other reason don't return, stay here until daylight and make sure no one is around before you leave." She says, "All right, John, I won't follow unless you call for me, but I'm telling you right now, I'm not leaving this place without you, no matter what you say. Period." You study her face. She looks pretty in the green hue of the NVD. You smile, knowing she can't see your expression. "You know, you look pretty with that set expression on your face. Especially, with the green tint of the NVD. Kind of reminds me of the Wizard of Oz." She crinkles her nose and says, "Don't be worrying about whether I'm pretty or not. You go up there and come back here or you'll see the witch side of me." You say, "Here, take the NVD," as you unclip it from the head gear, "study the surrounding area, the road, and lead us back to the ATV." She scans around, then takes your hand and leads you back. At the ATV you say, "Now, study the way back to the road. If I call for you to come, you need to do so without light, if possible. I know you won't be able to see very well, but I think it will be safer. If I see otherwise, I will let you know." She hands you the NVD. You give her the ear bud from your pack and help her get it inserted into the radio and attached to her ear. You clip the NVD back in place, and say, "Remember, don't use your flashlight. If you have to use a light, use the keychain light I gave you. Let's use the same call signs you gave us at the barn. I'm Pumper. You're Barney." She says, "Okay." "One more thing, Jill. Just in case, keep these for me." You hand her the gold and silver coins from your pocket. She closes her hand around the coins, then hugs you and says, "Come back to me, John Carter. You come back." You say, "I will. I promise," as you turn and walk back to the road.

Stepping onto the pavement, you consider should you cross the road and approach through the tree line, or go straight up the road? If you follow the tree line, there could be ample opportunities to trip and fall, perhaps making a lot of noise. The gen 3 NVD you have is really good, but it's still not daylight. If you walk along the pavement, you could be opening yourself up to being seen by someone else with an NVD. If those at the fire have an NVD, it's likely to be a gen 1. While they are better than nothing, they will most likely whiteout due to the campfire. Your gen 3 is autogated; it'll adjust itself and not over intensify the image. But, what if they have a gen 3? If they have a gen 3, and understand its capabilities, they would just wait without a fire and simply clothes line somebody passing by, similar to what happened to Jill. You decide to cross the pavement to the same side of the road as the fire and follow on the edge of the pavement. You say a silent prayer, "Dear God, grant me strength and courage. In Jesus' name, Amen." Your boots are almost completely silent. When you get close to the camp, you will slip into the woods if you have to.

You're moving at a brisk but silent walk. The road is clear, front and back. You're about fifty yards away when the radio crackles in your ear. "Pumper, this is Barney. I hear a vehicle approaching. Now I see headlights behind you." Seeing the lights, you whisper back, "If they stop, or shine a light in your direction, call me immediately and I'll return. Don't move. Just stay still. Pumper out." You turn into the woods and quietly enter. You sit behind some thick brush and wait. Your wait is not long. The truck drives right by and stops at the campfire. You find it strange. They leave the truck lights on and you can hear the doors open. People start speaking. They sound like some young men. "Well, well, how are you folks doing tonight? I see we have the Mr. and Mrs. and your two darling little children. It's nice to meet you.

My name is . . . well . . . it doesn't matter what my name is. I see you have helped yourselves to our firewood and we have come to collect our pay." You hear a man speak, "What do you mean?" You start easing closer, very slowly. The first guy speaks again, "That firewood you've been burning. Didn't you see our sign? There it is, right next to our, now, half gone wood pile. Didn't you just help yourself like the sign said? Well, now we've come to collect payment, just like the sign says."

You've approached within twenty-five yards. The low brush is thick where you are and you don't want to risk making more noise. Leaning against a large pine tree, you kneel and find a spot where you can see through the brush. You turn the IR laser on, position the carbine through the opening, and scan what is before you. You see a man, a woman and two small children standing on one side of the small fire. On the other side, between the truck and the fire, are two men, if that's what they can be called. They both have shotguns in their hands. They are just dangling, not pointing at anything in particular. The man speaks again, "We're sorry. We didn't know the wood belonged to anyone. We can refill your wood pile in the morning, before we leave." The first guy laughs, "So, you think it's just that easy? The sign was clear. It said, 'Help yourselves to our firewood, we will collect pay later.' There the sign is; I know you saw it. So we are here to collect our pay." The man says, "I'm sorry, it was our mistake. All I have is twenty dollars. You can have it." The guy says, mockingly, "Money? Money? Why the hell do I want money? It ain't worth nothing." The man says, "We don't have anything else." The guy says, "You don't. She does. Now, little lady, why don't you just come over here and pay your debts?" The second guy is gushing, "Oh yeah, come on over here!" The man says in a trembling voice, "No, we can't do that. That's not going to happen." The guy's tone changes, "By gosh, she is going to pay one way or the other. Either she comes and pays on her own accord, or we'll beat the crap out of you and those whiney brats, and she'll pay just the same!" The woman speaks for the first time, "If I do, will you go and leave us alone?" The guys laugh, "Of course, little lady; all we want is our pay, then we'll leave you fine folks alone." The woman says, "How many are there of you?" The guy is smiling, "Just me and Jimmy here. Just come on over here by the truck, and we'll get this over with." The woman speaks again, her voice not trembling, but seemingly resigned to her fate, "Do you have water? We haven't had any water in nearly a day." The guy says, "Jimmy, throw them four bottles of water. After you pay up, I'll give you four more." The woman speaks again, "Food. Do you have any food? At least some for my children." You sense strength in this woman. She knows what's going to happen, yet she is still looking out for her children. The guy responds in an irritated voice, "What do you think we are, a grocery store? No, I don't have any food. Now you come over here and pay up, or we'll take it out on the kids first! But, we aren't cruel men. Jimmy, throw those two brats a candy bar." The man speaks, "Lisa, don't do it. Don't do it." The woman turns to him, "Tim, this is your fault, your fault for what is about to happen. I tried to get you to leave a week ago and you refused. I tried to get you to go around Brent. You refused and we lost the 4-wheeler and our guns. I tried to get you not to stop here, yet you did and . . . and . . . ." She turns to the first guy and says, "Okay, but on the other side of the truck. I don't want my children to see." Jimmy is clapping his hands. The guy says, "Okay, little lady you come on over here. Jimmy, you shoot that spineless excuse if he makes any moves. When I'm finished, you can have your turn." The woman walks toward him.

Your blood is boiling, but do you have any obligation to these people? If you risk your life and something happens to you, what will happen to Jill? You could just slip back to Jill and wait until these bastards leave. You think of what was going to happen to Jill at the barn. Would you have wanted somebody to stop and help her, even if a stranger? The words play in your mind, "All that is necessary for evil to abound is for good men to do nothing." You are a good man. You refuse to do nothing. Your mind is set. There is no doubt what you must do. This is not going to happen. That spineless husband is useless, but you're not going to let these bastards have their way. You speak loudly and firmly, "Stop, drop your guns and raise your hands, or I'm going to blow your stinking heads off!" Everyone freezes. No one speaks. Your IR laser is dancing on the guy's head. If he raises or turns that shotgun, you are going to kill him. You are going to do it. You speak again, "Drop those damn guns, now!" The guy speaks, "Come on now mister, we're just collecting on a little debt. We weren't going to hurt nobody. Come on down and you can have some, too . . . ." He spins and raises his shotgun. You pull the trigger in two rapid successions. The 147 grain 9mm Remington Golden Saber sub-sonic bullet exits the barrel at 990 feet per second. It travels the seventy five feet in less than one tenth of a second. The first bullet punches through the guy's right eye. The second follows quickly behind, and punches through the middle of his forehead before his body can start to crumble. A pink mist spews out the back, as a golf ball size hole opens up in the back of his head. The one called Jimmy is covered with the guy's brains. He drops his gun and screams, "Don't shoot! Don't shoot!" The woman is frozen in her tracks. The kids are crying. The man stands there with his mouth hanging open.

You say in a stern voice, "Nobody move!" You move out of the brush, toward the camp. The woman gasps. The kids scream and run to their daddy. The man still has his mouth hanging open. Jimmy is crying, "Please, don't kill me. Please don't. Honest, we weren't going to hurt anyone. Really, we weren't!" Flipping up your NVD, you walk over, with your carbine at the ready position, and scanning each person. You say, "Shut up! Shut up, now!" You move closer to the bastard and he falls to the ground begging. You put the carbine on his forehead and ask, "Are there any more of you? If you lie to me and I hear something coming, I'm going to kill you!" The bastard is shaking; you see a wet spot at his crotch, as he says, "No, it was just Billy Ray and me. Honest. I swear. Please, don't kill me! Please, I beg you. Don't kill me!" You say, "Shut up or I'm going to kill you right now!" With the carbine still on his forehead, you reach down and pick up the shotgun. It looks like a Mossberg pump 20 gauge. Making sure it's on safety, you toss it far to the side. You say, "Ma'am, why don't you tend to your kids?" She shakes out of the daze, and walking over to the campfire, picks up the water and candy bars and goes to her children. You call Jill, "Pumper to Barney. Everything is ok. Please drive down. Use your light only if you have to, turn it off after getting here." Jill responds, "Copy, Barney out."

Jill approaches with the ATV. It's not audible until it's about twenty five yards away. Mark did good when he silenced that thing. She stops and gets off the ATV. Spotting you, she walks over. She catches her breath as she sees the guy dead on the ground. She nods at the other guy, "Is he dead, too?" "No, not yet. Take your Ruger and hold it on his head. If he moves, pull the trigger." Jill walks over and does what you asked. You walk over to the wood pile and add the remaining wood to the fire. The blaze brightens up. You walk over to the truck, open the door, and reaching in to turn the lights off, see a nearly full roll of duct tape on the dash top. You get it and walk over to Jill and say, "I don't want to be here very long." To the bastard on the ground, you say, "Hold your hands out!" He does, and you duct tape them together from the elbows down. You then command, "Pick up your feet!" You duct tape them from the knees down. "Jill, use your light. See if there is any food in the truck. If it is, bring it out to these people. If not, get one of our emergency ration bars. Jill says, "Okay."

For the first time, you walk toward the family. The man immediately stands up and speaks harshly, "Why did you kill that man! He wasn't going to hurt us. He said he was going to leave. You didn't have to kill him. You're a murderer!" That's more than you can take from this spineless excuse for a man. You swing your right fist, and it lands on the side of his chin. He crumbles to the ground. Surprisingly, the woman just looks at the man on the ground, says nothing and does nothing. "Jill is getting you all some food. My name is John. How did you find yourself in this situation, and where are you going?" She says, "My name is Lisa. Thank you for what you did. I have an uncle, and other family, living in the country above Montevallo. I tried to get Tim—he's my useless husband—to leave our home the day after the EMP. He refused, saying everything would be back to normal. He finally agreed when our neighbor's house was set on fire the day before yesterday. We all loaded up on the 4-wheeler. I tried to get him to drive around Brent, but he said it was too far to do that. At Brent they confiscated our gun and 4-wheeler. They escorted us to this side of town and gave us each two bottles of water and one candy bar. Then they said, "Goodbye and don't come back." I knew we shouldn't have stopped here. Especially, after reading that sign, but we did. I guess you heard what was said?" You say, "Yes, I heard everything." She says, "Please, don't judge me. I was only going to do what I had to do to keep my children alive." You say, "I don't judge you, period. I think you are a brave woman. What is the name of your Uncle?" She says, "My uncle's name is George and my aunt's name is Betty. I have a cousin named Mark that lives close by, too."

Jill walks over and says to Lisa, "Here," as she hands her the emergency ration bar, "my name is Jill." Before Lisa can speak you say, "Jill, this is Lisa, George and Betty's niece." "What?" Jill exclaims. Lisa looks confused and says, "What's going on?" You say, "I'll let Jill explain, but first what do you want me to do with him?" pointing at Tim, still out on the ground. Lisa asks, "Can I have the truck and one of the shotguns?" You say, looking at Jill, "Sure, no problem. But what about him?" Again you nod toward Tim. Lisa looks like she is thinking, "I can't leave him here. He will only tell whoever comes along where we went. Can you tape him up and put him in the back of the truck?" You smile, this woman is smart and tough, "Yes, it will be my pleasure. Jill, you and Lisa bring each other up to speed. I'm sorry we don't have much time to socialize. I want to be leaving in twenty minutes." Jill says, "Okay."

You walk over to the bastard on the ground, turn him over, and pull his billfold. The name is Jimmy Jackson. He has a Montevallo address. "Jimmy, you are a low down bastard. I ought to kill you. But, instead, I'm going to leave you on the side of the road, right here with this other bastard." He starts crying and cursing. You say, "I can put an end to that, too." You grab the duct tape and put four wraps around his mouth and head. Then, with your knife, you make a small cut at his lips for him to get air. You lay him right next to his dead friend. Walking over you pick up the "Help yourself" sign and drop it on his chest. You pick up the other shotgun, set the safety, and place it and the first shotgun on the dash inside the truck. You check the fuel gauge. It's half full. That should be more than enough to make it to George and Betty's house. In back of the truck there is a half case of bottled water. You load Tim into the back of the truck. He has regained consciousness and is struggling and trying to speak, but the duct tape keeps him secured and his mouth shut. What a useless, spineless man.

You replace the magazine in your carbine and walk back to the girls. The adrenaline rush is crashing down. You're feeling weak and nauseated. "I'm sorry we can't stay and talk. Did y'all bring each other up to date?" Jill says, "Yes, but I do wish we had more time." "Yes I know, but we really don't." Looking at Lisa, you hand her the hand sketched map from George. "Lisa, I wish we had more time, but we have to get out of here. This is a map George gave me that got us to this point from his house. If you follow it back, you can avoid Montevallo and maybe hold on to this truck. Here is a note I've written for Mark and George. It's important they get it. Don't stop for anybody, for any reason. If you have to, just run them over. Here is a 38 revolver. Do you know how to use one?" Lisa says, "Yes, actually; that's just like the one I had that the Brent police took." You say, "Okay then, let's get everybody loaded up and get moving."

Chapter 46 Jill - Day 9 - *Talking with Lisa...*

You are completely amazed. How do things like this happen? George and Betty's niece! Looking at her, you're guessing the clothes Betty gave you were Lisa's. You say, "Lisa, I'm so glad you and your children are okay. John is a good man. We met George and Betty a few days ago. They helped us a lot." Lisa looks, as in thought, "Thank you, and I'm so glad your husband was here. He is a good man, much better than this thing I have here." She nods toward Tim, taped up on the ground. She continues, "We live on the other side of Brent. I tried to get Tim to go over to Uncle George's the day after the EMP, but he refused. He said I was overreacting and the government would have things back to normal in a few days. Things started getting really bad about five days after. People were running out of food. We were running out, too, only eating a bare minimum. The day before yesterday, a gang attacked our next door neighbors and burned their house. It was only then that Tim would agree to leave."

Lisa pauses for a minute, giving each of her children a piece of the emergency ration bar. She nibbles on a piece and says, "Thank you. We haven't eaten anything since yesterday morning. Do you know what time it is?" You think for a moment, you're not sure, and say, "I'm not sure exactly. It must be getting close to four." Lisa continues, "We drained the water from our hot water heater, and from the back of the toilets, and put it in bottles. There wasn't much water left when we decided to leave. We only had maybe a day's worth of food left. The 4-wheeler was packed. It didn't have a rack or anything like that. We had to tie everything on. The kids had to ride on the seat with us. I asked Tim to drive around Brent, but he refused. When we got there, we were met by armed men who said they worked for the police. They said the President had ordered that all firearms and motorized vehicles be confiscated from civilians. When Tim asked them how we were going to be able to get to my Uncle's, they said it wasn't their problem. They also said we couldn't stay in town. They escorted us to the city limits, gave us each two bottles of water and a candy bar."

Lisa nibbles some more and helps her children drink more water, then continues, "I told Tim we shouldn't stop on the side of the road; we needed to camp in the woods. But he said there was a nice pile of wood right here someone had left for us to use. After reading the sign, I thought it was a trap. I should have been more forceful, but I guess it was a good thing, since your husband showed up. Now we have a chance of getting there with the truck. I really thought we were going to die trying to get to Uncle George's." She looks up with tears in her eyes. "I was only going to do what I had to do. I want my children to live. I thank God for your husband!" You smile, you thank God for John, too.

You watch John as he loads Tim into the back of the truck. How is he still going? He has got to be exhausted. He goes over to the ATV and takes out a notepad and starts writing. The twenty minutes is fast approaching, and he is going to want to leave. You saw him drag the other guy over by the dead body. You wonder if he killed him. No, he didn't. John is not a murderer. You ask Lisa, "Why did you ask John to tape your husband up?" Lisa chuckles, "You better ask your husband. Of all the things your husband did tonight, that was probably the best thing for me. But what about you? Tell me, where are you traveling to, and how did you come to meet my uncle?" "John and I are trying to get back home to Jackson, in Clarke County. We've had a pretty tough go of it. We have both been traveling since the day after The Day. I see John coming. Your Aunt Betty can tell you more about how we met." Lisa looks up, watching John come closer, and says, "At least you have a real man to travel with. Be thankful for that." You are thankful.

John approaches and says, "I'm sorry, we can't stay and talk. Did y'all bring each other up to date?" You say, "Yes, but I do wish we had more time." John says, "Yes I know, but we really don't." Looking at Lisa, John hands her the hand sketched map George gave him. John says, "Lisa, I wish we had more time, but we have to get out of here. This is a map George gave me that got us to this point, from his house. If you follow it back, you can avoid Montevallo and maybe hold on to this truck. Here is a note I've written for Mark and George. It's important they get it. Don't stop for anybody, for any reason. If you have to, just run them over. Here is a 38 revolver. Do you know how to use one?" Lisa says, "Yes, actually; that's just like the one I had that the Brent police took." John says, "Okay then, let's get everybody loaded up and get moving."

You help Lisa load up her kids and the few possessions they have. John opens the door for her to get in. Good ole John. You guess some things will never change. Lisa starts to get in, then stops and turns to John. She hugs him hard for a moment. Then, releasing him and wiping a tear from her eye, she says, "Thank you. You have saved my family. I will never forget what you and your wife have done for us. I pray God will keep you safe." She gets in the truck and waves "bye" as she turns onto the pavement.

John puts the campfire out, then mounts the ATV. You climb onto the ATV behind him. As you touch his back with your hands, you feel his body shaking. "John, are you okay?" His body continues to shake. It's too dark to see his face. "Jill, I'm not a cold blooded killer!" You sense his need and say, "John, you are a good man. You did what you had to do. Lisa and her family will live because of what you did. I know you are not a cold blooded killer. You are the best man I have ever met." His shaking diminishes. He says, "Thank you, Jill. Thank you." He gives the ATV fuel and you resume your journey toward home.

Over his shoulder John says, "Jill, it's almost 4:00. We can't make it around Brent before daylight. Based on what Lisa said, we can't go through Brent either. We need to find a place to camp for the day. I need to rest." "Of course, John. Find us a place and let's set up camp." About fifteen minutes later, John stops the ATV and says,"Wait here; I want to check this small path off the road." He dismounts and walks down the embankment. A few minutes later he returns and says, "I think this will work. I'm going to drive into the woods and see what we find." He turns the ATV and heads down the embankment. You can't see very well, but it seems as if the underbrush is thick around the path. Further in, the underbrush is thinner.

John turns into the woods, drives a hundred yards from the path and stops. He says, "If it's okay with you, let's set up camp here. It's not too thick." You say, "Looks good to me," though you really can't see much at all.

John says, "Let's wait for a little daylight before we set up camp. It'll be easier. It shouldn't be much longer." You say, "Yes, I think that's best. I couldn't really help you in the dark. Are you hungry? I forgot about the lunch Betty fixed for us." John says, "Yes, I did, too. I'm starving!" You open the bag. Inside are four roast beef sandwiches and a bunch of chocolate chip cookies in a zip lock bag. You pull out two sandwiches and hand one to John, "There are two more in here, too. Plus, Betty packed some cookies." John removes his head gear and says, "Thanks." As you finish half of your sandwich, John says, "Can I have another one?" "Wow, John. You really are hungry." You pass him another sandwich. You both eat in silence. John is leaning back on one side of the ATV and you are leaning back on the opposite side. A faint brightening of the sky begins. "Jill, this is my favorite part of the day, when day breaks and nature comes to life. Listen for the birds, as they sing their beautiful songs." You lean back and listen. Yes, the birds are singing sweetly. It was nicer hearing them from the soft bed at Betty's, but it's nice here, too. John says, "If I can have two cookies, that will finish me." You hand John two of the cookies. You've just finished your first sandwich and decide to have a cookie, too.

"Jill, we've only come about thirty miles. The long way around, to bypass Montevallo, took a lot of time. I hope Lisa can follow the map and makes it to George's." "Yeah, me, too. She seems like a very nice person. She said, 'I was only going to do what I had to do'; do you know what she was talking about?" John is silent for a moment, then answers, "I do, Jill. But I can't say it. I just can't. Please don't ask me to." You think, "That's weird," but then you realize what Lisa meant and say "Oh!"—glad that John can't see your blush in the dim light. "Okay, John, if it bothers you, you don't have to say." "Jill, that woman has strength and courage beyond what most men have. She reminds me of you, but, thanks to God's guiding hand, she didn't have to do what she thought she had to do." He reaches back and squeezes your hand.

"John, I asked her why her husband was taped up and she said to ask you." John responds, "I have no respect for spineless men, and even less respect for spineless men who try to hamper real men. His mouth bought him a ticket to na-na land. The duct tape was her idea. You heard that part. He wasn't a man. He was a male." You think for a moment. You are glad you have a real man as a traveling companion.

John says, "Will you help me set up the tarp?" You say, "I'm your partner. Tell me what you want." You can see his smile in the dim light. He says, "You are my partner. So partner, I'll get the tarp, you get some paracord." You start digging in your pack and retrieve your paracord. You ask John, "Do you think this will be enough?" Looking over at you he says, "I think it will. If not, we can get some from my pack." He takes the paracord from your hand and ties it to a tree about four feet up. He stretches it to another tree and shows you how to put a loop in the line so you can use it as a tension point. Then, handing you the cord he says, "Tighten it up." You pull the cord around the tree, then back through the loop in the line. You pull the cord tight and the line cinches tight. "Now," he says, "put some hitches in the line while it's tight. That's it. Now, tie the end off." John grabs the tarp and unfolds it. He says, "Help me put this across the line." You help him stretch it across and then tie the center grommets to the line using paracord. Next, you help John tie the left bottom off to some trees. Together, you move over to the right side and pull it tight, then tie it off as well. John has you tie the ends using the second grommet from each end. This forms flaps for the front and back. He then gets his ground mat and rolls it out on the ground under the tarp. He asks, "Can you hand me the tent?" You get it and bring it to him underneath the tarp. He shows you how it is set up. It's super easy. Once you set it up, you see it's going to be a close fit for the both of you. John says, "Get your sleeping bag," as he gets his and his ground pad. You follow him under the tarp. He unrolls the ground pad in the tent. Your heart is starting to beat a little faster. Then he reaches back for your bag and rolls it out in the tent. Your breathing is becoming a little more difficult. It's obvious you are going to be real close in that tent, body to body close. He takes his bag and rolls it out. Next to, but on the outside of the tent! You think, 'That little bugger was thinking of that one-man tent when he asked for the tarp!' Oh, well, you needed to shave your legs anyway."

"Jill, one of us needs to remain awake at all times to keep watch. I can take the first watch, if you want me to, but I am so tired." "Of course, John, I think that's a wise thing to do. I'll take the first watch. Get some rest. You deserve it." John says, "Thanks, I really am tired and my eyes hurt. Keep my carbine with you. If you want to heat some water for coffee or whatever, use the Esbit stove. Let's only build a fire when we are both awake, in case the smell draws attention. Wake me when you need a break. Good night, Jill." "Good night, John. Don't let the bed bugs bite." He laughs and pulls out a mosquito head net and puts it on. In a matter of moments, he is sound asleep.

You decide on some coffee. You're pretty tired yourself and need the caffeine. You clean an area of leaves and anything else that might burn, and set up the stove. You place a cup of water on top and light the fuel tab. While the water is heating, you get your camp cup and open the second bag Betty gave you. It has a large zip lock bag of instant coffee, and another of creamer. There are also six oatmeal and six grits single-serving packs. "God bless you, Betty. God bless you!"

Time seems to drag when you have little to do, and that's exactly what you have to do right now. You pull out your road map to see if there is a way around Brent. There just doesn't seem to be enough detail. You wonder if you can use John's GPS. You get it from his pack and turn it on and study the onscreen instructions. You find Brent on the road overlay and begin searching for a way around. You think you may have found a way, but it's going to be a big detour and add lots of miles. You don't know how to set way points in the GPS, so you retrieve your notepad and pen. There wasn't a route to the east of Brent, so you search for one to the west. It might be in the same area where the gang is that attacked Lisa's neighbors. Better tell John about that. This is seems to be the best route: From AL25 turn on to US82 and pass over the north side of Brent. Then, turn south onto Ingate Pass Road to Bear Creek Road. Bear Creek meanders south to Dull Road, which in turn meanders south to AL5 about ten miles south of Brent. John might be able to find a better route, but this might help him as he plots a course. If the drive is like last night, you won't be able to get much further than the south side of Brent. You hope you don't run into any more trouble along the way.

While waiting for John to awaken, you check around your gear and the ATV for something to do. You check the fuel and get the fuel can from the back. "Geez! This thing is heavy!" You pour fuel into the tank, spilling some. Maybe you better let John handle this next time.

You look over at John as he sleeps and speak to him silently, "John Carter, what is happening to us? Are we both too afraid to say?" What is happening to Lizzy right now? Is she safe with Will back at John's place, or are she and your mom still in Jackson, having to ward off gangs like in Lisa's neighborhood? What about the city and county governments? Are they going to be confiscating vehicles and guns too? If they try to, there are going to be lots of dead civilians and dead police officers. You just can't imagine all the rednecks freely giving up their guns. Taking someone's vehicle is a death sentence, too. You think the Sheriff and the Police Chief in Jackson are smarter than that, but you're not sure about the other towns. You know a couple of police officers from Thomasville from their visits to the Physical Therapy Clinic, where you work as a Physical Therapist, but you don't know how they stand on following orders to oppress people. What about the National Guard? There are three units in Clarke County. What are they going to be doing? Will desperate people from Mobile migrate as far north as Clarke County? There are so many unanswered questions. So many!

You pray, "Dear God. Please, dear God, bring us home safely. Protect our community. Thank You for Your protection. In Jesus' name. Amen." You know God has been with you from the beginning. The fact you are still alive makes that evident. Without Him sending people like John and Betty into your life at the right time, you would be dead. God must have a plan for you of some kind. You look over at John again. "Maybe God's plan for me includes you too, John."

A car horn startles you. It's in the distance, but you haven't heard one in so long. You stand and pick up John's carbine. Yes, it's faint, but you hear it; a steady stream of car horn. You hear John stirring. He must hear it, too. He sits up and stretches. Looking at you with a smile, he turns that darn iPhone alarm off! He gets up and puts his boots on, then walks over. You say, "Good morning, sunshine. Why did you set an alarm?" He says, "I knew I was too tired to wake on my own, and I knew you were tired too, so I set it for four hours so you could get some rest, too. Maybe I should have set it sooner." You look up with a smile, "No, John, you shouldn't have set it at all, but since you're up, let me show you a route I've found around Brent." You hand him your notepad. "You may find a better route; this was the best I could find. Oh yes, a big thing, before I forget, Lisa is from the west side of Brent. She said their community was attacked by gangs." John looks at your notes, then at you, and says, "Did you use the GPS for this?" You answer, "Yes." He smiles and shakes his head saying, "You are an amazing woman, Jill Barnes. With no manual you were able to figure out how to use that thing." "I couldn't figure out how to set way points, so I couldn't plot the course in the GPS. You're going to have to do that, if you want to use this route. And you are right, I am amazingly tired. I'm going to crawl into the nest you made for me and go to sleep. In the bag over there, Betty gave us some instant coffee and some other things. Help yourself." You crawl under the tarp and start to enter the tent. Pausing and turning, you smile and say, "John, if you want to heat some water for coffee or whatever, use the Esbit stove." You see John smiling and shaking his head as you close the tent door. You remove your shoes and Glock. What the heck, you think, as you remove your pants and slide into your sleeping bag. Your eyes close, and reality disappears.

Chapter 47 John - Day 9 - *I'll still have them when we get there…*

The water is hot. You pour it into your camp cup and stir in the coffee and creamer. This truly is a wonderful gift Betty gave you and Jill. The first cup of the day; it's always good. You are still tired, but not sleepy. You are glad Jill is getting a chance to rest. She didn't sleep much the day before. You pick up her notepad and study the route she laid out. She figured out how to use the GPS on her own. That's a sign of quick intelligence. It took you half an hour, with the instruction manual, before you could figure out how to make the darn thing work. You better be careful around this woman; she may outwit you. You turn the GPS on and trace out the route Jill selected. Yes, it does make a by-pass around the west side of Brent. It's going to add a lot of miles and time. You scan the GPS highway overlay for any connecting roads to the east of Brent and you find nothing as useful as what Jill has routed. You bring the map back up for the route Jill planned, and set the way points. It's a wonder she didn't figure that out, too. All these extra miles will probably require more fuel than you have. You've seen a few abandoned cars along the way and may be able to get fuel from others along your route. You would have stopped last night and tried a few cars except you didn't have anywhere to store the gas. After you refuel the ATV, you can syphon fuel into the partial full can.

You look over at the tent, underneath the tarp. You don't know what you are going to do if she parts ways with you when you both arrive back home. You want something more, but not now. Right now could get you both killed. Maybe when you get home, if she'll have you. You just don't know. But for now, you can't let your mind and emotions get cluttered. Too much depends upon being able to focus and think clearly. Jill needs to get home to Lizzy and her mom. You need to get home to Will, your father and community. You really hope she'll come with you; you really do, but not like this. You won't be able to handle this tension back home. It has taken all your will power to refrain from reaching for her. You have got to get her home safe; that thought, and that thought alone, has enabled you to keep yourself in check.

You walk over to the ATV and remove one of the fuel cans. It feels light. Something is not right. You checked those cans before you left George's. They were both full. You look for any signs of a leak, but can't find any. There must be a pin hole about half way up the can, or something. You mark the can so you won't fill it above its current level. It's a wonder you didn't smell the leaking fuel. You bring the can to the fuel tank and open the lid. The tank is full. A smile spreads across your face. That woman has been thinking again. She is definitely one to ride the river with. You replace the tank cap and return the can to the back of the ATV.

You pull out your solar charger and cables, get the rechargeable batteries from the NVD and go looking for a sunny spot. You have to go all the way to the path to find a spot with enough sun light. It's far away from your camp, and you really don't like to leave it here, but there is no alternative. You set it up as best you can to conceal it, and position it to catch the most sunlight. Being the woods are so thick, you won't be able to get but a few hours of sunlight. But every bit of charging, even a little bit, is better than nothing.

Sitting at the camp, your mind starts to wander, thinking about home and the challenges that are ahead. It's going to be tough, but with Jill's help, you can make it. Your subconscious alerts your mind. You've been hearing a sound approaching for a while; it just didn't register on you. The sound is getting louder, and it seems to be headed for your camp. You are alert now. All your senses are concentrating on this one thing. It sounds as though there are several people walking through the leaves. You better wake Jill. It's almost 1:00 p.m.; she's had a little rest. You quietly crawl under the tarp and open the tent. There she is, asleep with the sleeping bag open. This is exactly what you didn't need to see. Focus! You lean over to Jill's ear. "Jill, wake up," you whisper. You reach for her shoulder and give her a shake. She finally starts coming around. Her eyes are looking into yours. You hold your finger over your lips and say, "Shhh. . . somebody or something is moving toward the camp." Looking up at her legs, you say, "You need to get up and get dressed, quietly. I want you to be ready in case we have to take action." She whispers back, "Okay," and starts getting dressed as you exit from under the tarp.

The sound has stopped. Maybe they are setting up camp somewhere close by. Jill approaches by your side. "What is it, John?" You say, "Whatever it was has stopped." Jill's eyes perk up, "I hear it. There must be more than one person." Your thought exactly. "Jill, let's back away from the camp quietly." As you start moving backwards the noise intensifies. They're rushing the camp. You say, "Ready yourself, Jill," as you raise your carbine. The noise is right behind the tent; now it's coming around the side. Now . . . it's . . . an . . . armadillo! You and Jill both start laughing, in relief. Then you say out loud, "This could be supper." Jill wrinkles her nose, "Really? What does it taste like?" "I've only eaten it once. It tasted like chicken." Jill rolls her eyes, "John, everything tastes like chicken. Any better description?" You say, "No, it's been a long time." Jill says, "Okay, I'm game. Maybe we can roast it on a fire, but you have to clean it." You smile and say, "Okay, partner." You put the red dot sight on the front of the armadillo and squeeze the trigger.

Cleaning the armadillo carcass is a first for you. You've never cleaned one and never seen it done. But hey, who's watching? You look over at Jill. She's building a fire. You pause and watch her. It looks like she's gotten some dry leaves and placed a vaseline cotton ball on top. She strikes her magnesium firesteel over the cotton ball. After a few strikes, the burning magnesium ignites the cotton ball. She then adds a few leaves, then twigs, then bigger sticks. Obviously, it's not the first time she's built a fire. You better get finished before she starts inspecting you butchering a butchering. The flesh of the armadillo on its back is white. You strip it out and wash it down with some water. You're glad George gave you the six gallon jugs of water. It's going to make things a lot easier not having to stop and treat water every day. You cut a few long but skinny tree limbs and skewer the armadillo. Walking over to Jill, you see the fire is going good. Using the dry limbs like she is, the fire makes very little smoke. She is already setting up the sticks across from each other to hang your armadillo sticks on. Retrieving your condiment pack, you salt and pepper the "Dillo Stick." Jill says, "How about some grits to go with our gourmet?" You smile. "Yes, I think that would be nice. I'll get a couple of wheat breads. We're going to make this into a regular meal. Maybe something to rival Mrs. Betty's cooking." Jill looks over at you and rolls her eyes, "No, John, this is not going to rival Betty at all!"

You are sitting side by side, with Jill leaning against a tree. The Dillo Stick is pretty tasty, but Jill is right. It doesn't rival Mrs. Betty's cooking, not by a long shot. "Jill, our first dinner date, and I have treated you to gourmet, not even found on the menus of New York restaurants." Jill laughs, "Well, John, it's actually not bad, not bad at all. It kind of tastes like . . . chicken." You both laugh. After cleaning up, you say, "Can you rest anymore? We have a few hours before we can leave, but I would like to take the tarp and tent up before dark if we can." She says, "I'd rather you rest first. If I get tired on our way I can always drool on your shoulder." "Okay, I am still tired. I'll set the alarm for two hours." Jill says, "Can you use anything other than the car horn?" You smile and say, "Yes, I can." You remove your boots and Glock and crawl back into your bag.

It seems like just a few minutes when you hear a rooster crow. He crows again, then again. Then a stick hits you, and you hear, "John wake up and turn that rooster off. I think I liked the car horn better." You turn it off. The battery is down to ten percent. You're going to have to use the battery boost from the solar charger to charge it, but that will have to wait until tomorrow. You shut the phone down. Guess if you miss any calls, they can leave a voicemail.

You retrieve your hygiene kit and wash your face. Feeling the stubble on your chin you decide to shave. You wet your face and put the gel on. You raise your razor for the first stroke, then suddenly stop. Pulling it from your face, you look at it closely. "Jill," you say, "did you use my razor?" You look over at Jill. Her face is turning red, "One day you may appreciate it." Then she gets up and walks away. You wonder what she means by that. Oh well, you glide the razor across your cheek.

Walking back to the path to retrieve the solar charger, Jill walks with you.

It's had a few hours to charge, but with the angle of the sun and the height of the trees, the charger is in the shade now. You pick it all up and repack it in its case. Walking back, you say, "Jill, I checked your routing on the GPS. I think it's probably the best way. I've set the way points in the GPS. I can show you how to do it later. The gangs, I just don't know about them. I don't know their hours of operation. Did Lisa say what time her neighbors were attacked?" "No, she didn't, at least I don't remember her saying anything about time." You say, "I still think the cover of darkness is our best protection right now. We'll travel like we did last night. If we see any signs of trouble, we'll pull into the woods." Jill says, "Okay, I'm with you."

You break camp, reload all your gear, then wait. It's starting to get dark, so you get the NVD out and the GPS, turn the GPS back on and check the way points. Yes, they are all there. As you and Jill sit with your backs to a tree, you watch her head nod off. Good she needs more rest, but she's likely to have a neck ache. It's 8:30 and very dark. You'll let her sleep a little longer before waking her to leave. You pray softly, "Dear Father, please bless our journey. Grant us courage and wisdom as we face each new obstacle in our path. Thank You for the blessings of life. In Jesus' name, Amen"

It's 9:30. You want to leave a little earlier than yesterday. You wake Jill. She comes around, rubbing her neck. She asks, "What time is it? Is it time to go?" "Yes, it's 9:30." Reaching down you help her up. "Use your keychain light, take care of whatever business you need to, then we'll leave." You're sitting on the ATV when Jill returns and climbs on behind you. With the NVD on you maneuver back to the path, then to the road. Stopping at the road you scan both directions thoroughly. "By the way, you have nice legs." Jill says, "Don't worry about my legs; just get us home. I'll still have them when we get there." You give the ATV fuel and continue your journey home.

Chapter 48 Jill - Day 9 - *With a loud bang…*

As he steers the ATV on to the highway, John says, "By the way, you have nice legs." You feel yourself blushing. Maybe shaving your legs wasn't a bad idea, after all. You say, "Don't worry about my legs; just get us home. I'll still have them when we get there." You like that he noticed, but there is no time for that, not now anyway. You need to get home. John has to stay focused or neither of you will make it. That darn armadillo nearly made you wet your pants! But he got his payback in the end; tasty, too.

There are cars stalled on the side of the road up ahead. John slows the ATV and says, "Jill, we need to get some fuel. I'm going to check these cars out." "Okay, what do you want me to do?" He says, "There is really not much you can do right now. If you don't mind, just stay on the ATV in case we have to leave in a hurry." "No problem." John dismounts and gets the syphon hose Mark provided. He walks slowly up to the car, with his carbine at the ready. He looks inside the car, then moves over to the adjacent car and repeats the same thing. He whispers into the radio, "Barney, everything looks clear. I'm going to see if I can get the syphon hose into the tank." He's not that far away. He could have just spoken, but maybe he's wanting to be quiet. You push your mic and say, "Copy." It's not so dark you can't see his movements, but it is too dark to see more than just outlines of what's going on. He speaks on the radio, "No-go on car one. Moving to the next car." You watch him. He is now at the car in front of you, doing something near the fuel door. You hear a "ping." He must have had to pry the fuel door open. He stands there for a few minutes, doing what you guess is trying to get the hose into the tank. He comes back over to the ATV and says, "No go; both have anti-syphon devices. It's going to be a hit and miss on these things. A lot of newer cars have the devices installed." You ask, "Why were we using the radio?" He says, "Two reasons. One, I want to remain as silent and as invisible as we possibly can, even when we think no one is around. Second, we need to practice this now, while we are in the middle of nowhere, so we'll be comfortable with it when it really counts." "Sounds like a good idea." John says, "Oh yeah, thanks for filling the fuel tank." "No problem. We're partners, right?" John says, "Yeah, we are. Let's move on down the road. We are going to be hitting US82 in a little over an hour."

After turning onto US82, John says, "There's a group of cars up ahead. Let's try them, and maybe we'll have better luck than the last four we've checked." John stops a little ways before reaching the cars. He approaches them on foot. Again you can only see faintly what he is doing. He said there were four cars up ahead, but you can only see the outline of two. The radio says, "Car one, clear. Moving to car two." You reply, "Acknowledged." This radio lingo stuff is new to you. Should you have said something different? You guess if John doesn't approve, he'll tell you. The radio crackles again, "Car two, clear. Moving to car three." "Acknowledged." John has moved beyond what you can see. Car three must be further apart than the others. It's taking John longer to check in. You are about to call him when you hear, "Car three is occupied. Returning to you. Pumper out." Your heart rate quickens, and you feel the slight increase of adrenaline. What does this mean? Is there going to be trouble? John didn't say anything about trouble. He didn't say to prepare for anything. You see his shape approaching. He's walking briskly, but not running. As he gets to the ATV, you ask, "What's going on?" "There are some people in car three. My guess, teenagers. We'll just ease by and look elsewhere for fuel." You asked puzzled, "Teenagers, how do you know they are teenagers? Are they armed?" Getting on the ATV John says, "There are two bikes parked next to the car, and the windows are all fogged up. Judging by the sounds I heard, I figure it's a teenage boy and girl." You ask, "Could you hear what they were saying?" He turns his head back and says, "Jill, I didn't hear any words. Just sounds you might expect a boyfriend and girlfriend to make late at night, in the backseat of a car." You feel your face grow red, as the realization of what he is talking about hits you. You say, "Oh . . . okay. But isn't that dangerous out here? I mean, if you can walk up on them, couldn't anybody else?" John says, "Maybe, but what can

I do about it? I can't go up to the door and knock on the window and say, 'Hey kids, get dressed and take this somewhere else.' I might get shot." You say, "I see what you mean, but still, we ought to do something." You jump off the ATV. John asks, "Jill, what are you doing?" You pick up a large chunk of wood you see on the ground and say, "Improvising. When you drive by, I'll let them know how unsafe that car is." John starts laughing, saying, "Okay, but I'm not stopping." John eases down the road, actually he's driving a little faster than normal. As you come by the third car, you toss the wood. It hits the hood of the car with a loud bang. Looking back, you see a flashlight dancing inside the car. You sense John is silently laughing along with you. Maybe they got the message. You think for a moment, as you speed on down the road, 'I've never been in the backseat of a car like that.'

After a few more miles on US82 John spots another car. He stops and says, "Same procedure." "Yes, sir." John dismounts from the ATV and walks up to the car. He is scanning all around the car and inside the car. He has his carbine at the ready. On the radio, he says, "Barney, everything is clear here. I'm going to try the fuel tank." You say, "Roger." Is that the right word to say? You know you've heard it being used on TV before. You can see John at the side of the car. He calls back, "Barney, I've got the hose into the tank. Can you see well enough to bring the ATV?" You say, "Copy, Pumper. Bringing the ATV." You drive slowly up to where John is. He gets the partially empty fuel can off the back and sets it on the ground by the car. After inserting the tube into the fuel can, he starts squeezing and releasing the pump bulb. After a few moments he says in a low voice, "Got it." It doesn't take long to fill the can; then he tops off the fuel tank on the ATV. With everything stored back in its position, you proceed on down the highway.

Everything seems quiet. The stars are out bright. John is not talking. The lull of the ATV engine is making you sleepy again. You don't wait for your head to fall this time. You take your hands from John's shoulders, snuggle closer and lay your head on his shoulder, hoping you don't drool this time.

Chapter 49 John - Day 10 - *There goes the neighborhood…*

For the last few miles, all the cars along the way have been destroyed. All the glass has been shattered; windows, windshields, rear glass, lights and mirrors, nothing was spared. You've counted fourteen so far. It gives you an ominous feeling. It won't be long before you'll be turning onto Ingate Pass Road. Something inside is telling you there is danger ahead. You've got to be alert and aware.

Jill's been asleep for about an hour and a half. Looking at your watch, you see it's 1:30. You are glad she is getting some rest. She didn't sleep much during the day. It's better she get the sleep taken care of now, so maybe she can be more alert later. You just hope she doesn't drool all over your shirt again. Sweat, you don't mind. Drool . . . yuck. Stopping for the fuel cost you a lot of time. Hopefully, after making it around Brent, you'll have a straight shot to Marion. Then, you can decide what to do there.

As you turn down Ingate Pass Road, you start picking up a faint whiff of smoke. The further you go, the stronger the smell becomes. You're starting to see more houses, but still have not seen or heard another human. As you continue to travel, on your left you see a home set far off the road with a large fire blazing in the yard. There are people around the fire. It sounds like a party. You ease the ATV to the far right side and reach back and squeeze Jill's leg. She finally wakes and you tell her, "Shhh . . . be alert, there may be trouble ahead." You hear shouts and laughter and, occasionally, a woman's shrill voice. You're beginning to wish you had not come this route. After passing around a bend in the road, darkness envelops you again. The sounds are fading behind, and you're driving a little faster.

You are beginning to think you've put it all behind you—when you hear Jill say, "John, a vehicle is coming behind us." Spotting a woods road to your right, you dart the ATV for it. It's too late. They have spotted you. Hearing the truck gun its engine, you give the ATV more fuel. It's dangerous driving this fast on a narrow road in the dark, even with the NVD. Your heart is racing. The lights from the truck are shining into the brush on the left, as it hasn't made the turn onto the woods road yet. You take a chance. Turning off the road to the right, you quickly maneuver deeper into the woods. "Jill, keep your head down low behind my back." Limbs are slapping you; it's just so thick here. After about fifty yards, you turn back toward the highway and drive a few yards. You quickly dismount and grab your carbine and the shotgun. You speak quickly, "Jill, I need you to do exactly what I say. I'm going to scout up ahead to see where they went and if they are coming back anytime soon. I need you to stay here. Do not leave this spot." Jill starts to protest, "John, that's not fair. I need to help . . . ." You say, "Jill, if you had an NVD you could help, but you don't. I have got to move fast. Please, stay here. Do not turn your light on for any reason. I'll be back, I promise." You turn and walk into the woods, pull the GPS out and set a way point. Then, changing screens, you view the path back to the woods road. It's hard to read the screen with the NVD, especially with the backlight turned way down, but you think you can see it well enough.

You make it back to the woods road and start jogging in the direction the truck took. It's stopped not far ahead. Someone is shining a light out into the woods. You hear them talking. "Where did they go? I know they turned down this road, and the one on the back is definitely a woman." The other bastard says, "Let's go. We've got to make it to the other house for the raid." The first bastard says, "If we catch her, we get to go first. I'm tired of being at the back of the line." You're about forty yards back, directly behind them in the woods. They're scanning to the front and sides of the truck. They don't scan to the back. You quickly study the scene. It looks like a Ford truck, and it's facing into the woods. There is one bastard standing on the floor board in the driver's door, and one doing the same on the passenger side. Surprise is your most useful tool. You turn the IR laser on, and walking quickly, you approach from behind and stop about twenty five yards back. Putting the IR laser on the driver's head, you pull the trigger. The clank of the carbine operating is nearly all the sound that is made. The driver falls. The other bastard looks over, "Roy, you okay?" You put two rounds into his head. He falls to the ground. You scan the area again; then seeing nothing else, you quickly walk closer to the truck. You approach the driver's side. The bastard is dead, no doubt. Then, cautiously, you approach the passenger side. He's dead, too. You do a tactical reload on the carbine magazine, removing the one with three rounds missing and inserting a fully loaded one.

Moving back to the driver's side, you turn the truck and its lights off. Scanning inside, you see a box of 9mm ammo and put them in your pocket. There is also a very nice looking hunting rifle; it looks like a Remington 700. You can't read the caliber engraved in the barrel with the NVD, but there are three boxes of 7mm-08 ammunition. You sling the rifle over your shoulder and pick up the ammo. Underneath the ammo is a sheet of paper with writing and a map sketch. You look at the map for a minute. It looks like a sketch of maybe this community. Some houses have a circle with an X on them; one has a circle. You put it in your pocket and move to the bastards on the ground. Each has a Hi-point 9mm pistol. You leave the pistols on the ground, after retrieving the ammo from each. Using the radio, you call Jill, "Barney, this is Pumper. Everything is okay here. Return shortly. Will advise as I get close. Out." You hear Jill's voice, "I copy Pumper."

The long hunting rifle makes it a little more difficult walking through the woods in the dark. You make it back to Jill. She says, "It looks like you did more than scouting." You say, "Yeah, I didn't have a choice. They were here to hurt us; especially you. The opportunity to put them down was there and I took advantage of it." Jill says, "I know, John. I support whatever you did." You place the shotgun in the rack and study the rifle a little more. Opening the bolt you see it's loaded. Removing one of the rounds, you compare it to one from the 7mm-08 ammo boxes. Yes, it's the same. You've read a lot of good things about this cartridge, though you haven't shot one. You wonder if the scope is sighted in. It was probably stolen from one of the houses around here.

"Jill, sit down here beside the ATV, and let's look at this map." She says, "Okay, but unless you're going to turn a light on, all I can see is a piece of paper." You flip up your NVD and pull your keychain light out. Shining it on the paper, you and Jill both look at it. Jill is a quick thinker; she says, "John, this looks like a hand sketch map of a community of houses. Probably, right around here. These Xs are probably houses they have already ransacked. I bet this O is the next on the list. The address marked is 8968 Ingate Pass. Did you notice any of the addresses as we were driving?" You say, "Yes, I did. The one with the bon fire was 6688, and the numbers are increasing in our direction of travel. I don't know if we should continue down this road. Those guys seemed to be in a hurry to get to the next raid." Jill says after a few moments, "John, if they are preoccupied with raiding a house, could we just slip by in the dark?" You think a few moments, "We might, I don't know. We can try it, but we could also find ourselves in a lot of trouble." Jill says, "What are our other options?" You say, "The way I see it, we can go back and try to find another way around, or we just go on through and prepare ourselves for the worst. Staying here is not an option." Jill says, "I think we should try to go through. We may not be able to find another way around. Even if we did, it may be just as bad." "I agree. Let's be ready for action." You reach down and help Jill up. This woman is definitely a thinker. Jill says, "John, why don't we take the truck?" You consider what she has asked and say, "I think it would be more difficult to use the NVD through the windshield of the truck. I tried it at home and nearly wrecked. I'd probably have to go slower than I am now. Plus with all the reflectors and lights it wouldn't be very stealthy. Right now, I think out best course is being as invisible as possible." She says, "That makes sense. I'm glad you're thinking of these things."

You're driving a little fast for the NVD, and it's definitely going to give you a major headache. After another mile you start hearing gun fire up ahead. Your instincts tell you to turn the ATV around and go in the opposite direction, but Jill is right; the next route you find could be just as perilous. "Jill, stay on high alert. What side of the road was that house?" She says, "It's on the right side." You steer the ATV to the far left side. The gun fire is sporadic but getting louder. You slow down as the woods turn into a clearing. You see it. Jill gasps. The house is starting to burn. Gun fire is being exchanged between the occupants and people taking cover behind two old trucks. The truck lights are pointed at the house. Jill asks, "John, is there anything we can do?" A woman screams. "I don't know, Jill. We could get killed right here." Jill prays, "Dear God, please show us a way!"

Two people ahead are running across the road. They are both armed and jumping into the ditch. They are aiming toward the house. "Jill, there are some people in the ditch aiming toward the house. I'm going to pull the ATV into the woods, on the opposite side, and see what's going on. Stay with the ATV in case we have to leave quickly. Be ready to pick me up." She says, "Okay, John, I'll be ready." You grab your carbine, the hunting rifle and the boxes of 7MM-08 ammo. You crouch as you run toward the ditch. As you approach you say, "Don't shoot." Both men jump in surprise. You move into the ditch beside them. "My name is John. We need to do something real quick, or those folks are all going to be dead." The woman scream again. One of the guys says, "That's my cousin's house. His wife and two daughters are in there with him." You sense they have no plan, so you take command. "Are you guys any good with those rifles?" They both say they are. You say, "I'm going to move to the ditch on the other side of the drive way. When I start shooting, pick a bad guy and start shooting." They agree. You crouch and run across the driveway. The house is about a quarter engulfed in flames. It won't be long before no one can stay inside. You see a man hanging out of an upstairs window. A woman is in the yard and men are standing around her. You watch the two girls run from the house. They run for the woods, but are quickly overtaken by two of the men. You count six men. That means six bastards who have to die. Your NVD will be of no use with the scope, so you flip it up, open two of the ammo boxes for easy reach, pick a target through the scope, and start firing. After your third shot, you hear shooting coming from your right. You guess they finally got the nerve. You hit two of the bastards with your shots. The other four bastards fall to the ground as the guys on the right are deadly accurate. You call out, "Take head shots and make sure they are all dead." After about ten minutes, all is quiet except the burning of the house and the screams and sobs of the woman. You get up and cross back to the other side of the driveway. The men look up. The first guy says, "Thank you, we are going to check on the family." You say, "You're welcome," and head back to Jill.

When you reach the ATV, Jill swings her arms around your neck and squeezes you tight. She says, "Thank you, John. Oh, thank you." You hug her back. The softness of her body ebbs the tension inside you away. After a few moments, you say, "Jill, let's go. I don't want to be here any longer." She releases you. You stow the guns, then continue your journey home.

Chapter 50 Jill - Day 10 – *It's not a fair question...*

You watch John as he runs across the road to the ditch. You want to help, but he's counting on you to have the ATV ready in case you must flee in a hurry. You begin to pray, "Dear God, please bless and keep John safe. Help increase his courage and wisdom. In Jesus' name, Amen." Rifle shots close by startle you. You want to call on the radio, but hesitate, not wanting to distract him. The firing increases. You pray again. After what seems like forever, the shooting stops. You see John coming to you. Relief overwhelms you and you wrap your arms around him. You feel relief he is safe, and you feel safe with him beside you. His strong arms return your embrace. Your fears and worries begin to subside. After a few moments, John says, "Jill, let's go. I don't want to be here any longer." With reluctance, you release him. Mounting the ATV, John pulls back onto the paved road.

Passing by the house, you see it is completely engulfed in flames. It is bright and you can feel some of its heat all the way up here. Two men, a woman and two young girls are at the end of the drive. They wave John down. He stops, but keeps the ATV running. He flips up the NVD, as light from the enormous fire is illuminating everything around. You notice his hand is not far from the shotgun. The guy says, "Mister, I don't know who you are, but if you had not come along, I don't think we could have saved Mandy and her daughters. My cousin is dead." John says, "My name is John. This is Jill." Before John can protest, you get off the ATV and approach the woman. She is crying and clearly going into shock. You say, "John, I think she's going into shock." John dismounts the ATV and retrieves an emergency mylar blanket from his pack. He walks over and wraps it around the woman and gives her some water. He asks the man, "Do you have a place you can get her in bed?" The man says, "My name is Randy, and my place is about a half mile back up the road, down a long drive." John says, "Why not let your friend run back and get one of the trucks and drive Mandy to your place? She needs to be kept warm and her feet propped up." The girls walk over to their mother; one must be about twelve and the other ten. They wrap their arms around her, and it seems to bring her comfort. Randy says, "Yes, that's a good idea. Charles, would you go back and get one of the trucks. Get the keys out of the other one, too. They had three trucks. I don't know where the other truck is." John says, "The other truck is down a woods road, back the other way, with two dead bastards beside it. How long have they been preying on your community?" Randy says, "They've been here a few days. I tried to get the people around here to band together, but the only one I could get to agree is Charles, my next door neighbor. I don't have much, but you two are welcome to come to my home for the night. Not sure if I can feed you breakfast." John says, "Thanks, but we are going to be on our way. We're traveling south, trying to get home." Charles arrives with the truck. Randy helps the woman into the truck as the kids climb on the back. He says, "Thanks, again. There is no telling how many lives you saved tonight. I pray God will bless your journey home. Charles, let's go." The truck pulls out onto the highway and heads in the direction of your travel.

John just stands there for a few moments, looking in the direction of the truck. "Jill, if these people don't band together, this will just happen again in a few more weeks." He turns to you, "I don't know what we are going to find in Jackson when we return. I hope they have a better handle on things than what I've seen since The Day. Repose is going to be much different than this, I promise you. We are going to survive as a community." You say, "I hope things are better, too, much better." You both get on the ATV and start back down the road. As you travel you see several houses have been burned to the ground. Why couldn't these people do what John just prompted them to do? Take action! Is the conditioning of always having someone else take care of your needs still so strong that people refuse to act, even for their own welfare? All these houses, burned. Yet right here, with John's prompting, three men put an end to it in less than half an hour. Why could they not have already done this? Leadership and personal drive is lacking in this place. John is right; they probably won't make it much longer before they become victims again.

You bet one of these houses belongs to Lisa. What are they doing for food? Are they just waiting to run out before they make any plans to get more? You realize, right where you are, on the ATV with John, you are better off than anybody you have met, maybe even better off than George and Betty.

You travel for nearly two more hours and make AL25 without any further incidents. John says, "Jill, it's almost four. I know there is still at least an hour before daylight, but I'm so tired, we have got to stop and make camp. My eyes are hurting pretty bad, despite the three ibuprofen I took an hour ago." You can feel the weariness in John's shoulders as you rest your hands on them. "Yes, John, find us a place to spend the day." After about twenty minutes. John says, "I'm going to try the small road ahead, to the right." "Okay." He turns down and you enter the woods. He stops the ATV and dismounts, saying, "Jill, let me check the road for tracks." He studies the ground for a minute or two then says, "It doesn't look like anything has been down this road in a while." He gets back on and continues down the road. He turns to the right, through the trees, and zig zags around obstacles. He stops the ATV and says, "This looks like as good a spot as any. I think we must be about a hundred yards from the dirt road."

He dismounts and helps you off. "Jill, I'm so tired. I've got to lie down for a few minutes before I can set up camp. Do you mind?" "Of course not, John. I know you're tired. Pick a spot and roll out your sleeping bag. Let me have the NVD, and I'll keep watch while you sleep. When you wake, we can set the camp up together." "Thanks, Jill, I appreciate it." He gets his sleeping bag and rolls it out. He hands you the NVD and his carbine, saying, "Wake me if you need to. I'm going to set my alarm for one hour. That should allow me enough rest to help set up camp." He lays down on his bag without removing his boots or his Glock. He is almost instantly asleep.

You walk over by his side and sit for a few minutes, thinking about all the things this man has done, and been through, the past few days. You say in a low voice, "No, John, you're not going to get a wake up alarm in an hour." You reach over and pick up his iPhone. The battery level is at eight percent. The screen is locked and password protected, so you simply hold the power button until it shutdowns completely. Speaking softly, you say, "John, my friend, you are going to get some well-deserved rest."

You put the NVD on and adjust the head straps. John's head is bigger than yours. He's going to have to readjust it when he puts it back on. It's wet with John's sweat, but you don't mind. You're sweating, too. Turning it on, you look around. This really turns the darkness into a green hued dusk. The focus is manual and set for a certain focal range. If you want to see close, you have to adjust. If you want to see far, you have to adjust. You can see where this would give you a headache if you had to wear it for a long period of time, especially if you need to focus on objects with large distances between them. You take time to reflect on the past two nights and whisper, "Thank you, Jesus, for your guiding hand." You hope the rest of the journey will not be as difficult and perilous, but something inside says it will be.

The sun is starting to rise. Birds begin singing. This is the second day in a row you have broken the morning in while John sleeps. What does the early morning look like from John's porch? He says it's nice. You may have to see for yourself. You're hungry. Not wanting to use too many of the dwindling fuel tabs, you decide to eat an MRE dessert and fix a cup of coffee, using only one fuel tab. The first cup of coffee of the day is always good. You still think about that front porch. No need to dwell on that now; you have to get there first.

You look over at John. He hasn't moved at all. He must be completely exhausted. You decide to set up camp yourself. You helped him yesterday and he did a good job of explaining what he was doing. You unpack the tarp and the paracord and find a few trees spaced about right. You tie the paracord around one tree, then stretch it to another. The pull loop you put in yesterday is not exactly in the same place, but it will do. Putting the tail through the loop, you cinch it tight and tie it off. Next you get the tarp over the line and tie off both sides. Standing back, you survey your work. Not bad. You roll out the ground mat, then set up the tent. Getting John's ground pad and your sleeping bag, you place them inside the tent. You start to set the pad up for John, but you know if you wake him he will not go back to sleep and he'll just refuse the pad anyway, insisting you use it. No man, other than your father, has ever put your interest above their own. You like this. It makes you feel . . . feel . . . loved. You don't know how else to describe it. Maybe you are reading things wrong with John, but you feel loved—something you haven't truly felt from any man other than your father. You look over at John and silently ask, "John, do you love me?" You know it's not a fair question, not now, anyway. Maybe when you get home. Regardless of whether he loves you or not, you feel loved.

You prepare a place for a fire, then gather the wood, set the stakes and place the kindling. All you have to do is use your firesteel or your Bic lighter to light the fire. You'll wait for John to awaken before lighting it. You wish the camp was close to a creek. You would love to shave the stubble off your legs. It catches inside your pants and you don't like it. You think of John's comments from yesterday, "By the way, you have nice legs." You smile; maybe there are other benefits, too.

You think of setting up John's solar charger and charging the batteries for the NVD, iPhone and GPS, but you would probably have to walk back to the road to get enough sunlight, and you're not sure you could find your way back. You could try fueling again, but it might be better to let John handle those heavy cans. You don't need gas all over everything.

You think of Lizzy and your mom. You pray they are with Will in Repose. John believes his community is safe. How can he be sure? But you trust John. You trust him with your life, and even more. You walk over to John and look down at his watch. It's 10:35. He's been asleep for nearly six hours, and he hasn't moved at all. You wish you had your watch, but you lost it after you got knocked from your bike. It's then when you hear the voices.

You hear a man's voice say, "Cassandra, pedal hard! Faster!" Then you hear a loud truck. It must be on the dirt road. You hear men hollering, though you can't make out what they are saying. This is something John needs to know right now.

You kneel beside John. He's obviously still in a deep sleep. You start speaking to him and shaking his shoulders, "John, wake up. Wake up, John." His eyes start to open, but you can tell he hasn't made it back to reality yet. You become more urgent, "John!" Finally, he becomes aware and sits with a start, "Jill, what is it?" "John, this is important, listen carefully. I let you sleep through. It's almost 11:00 a.m. A truck with some men hollering just drove down the dirt road. It sounds as if they are chasing two other people. You can hear their voices." John rises to his feet, looking in the direction of the noises. He says, "Yes, I can hear them. Jill, I need to check this out. Please, get yourself ready to leave and prepare to fight if we have to. I'll call you on the radio." "I will. John, be careful." John picks up his carbine and GPS and heads into the woods.

Chapter 51 John - Day 10 - *Please protect Jill...*

As you proceed into the woods, you set a waypoint in the GPS. The battery is at twenty-five percent; that should be enough. When you do make it back to camp, you're going to make sure you have spare batteries in your pocket. That's something you should have already thought about. You can hardly believe you slept for nearly six hours. Jill should have woken you up. You're tracking toward the noise. The sounds you hear seem to indicate conflict of some type. You are so tired of the conflict, the constant struggle and the killing. Why can't people just act right? Why are there so many evil among us? You guess that has been an age old question since the days of Noah.

Up ahead is a wash in the ground. It seems to be following toward the sounds. You enter the wash. It's about three feet deep, with pine trees growing on each side. This is good, as pine needles make very little noise. You crouch as you get closer. The sounds are becoming more distinct. It is obviously a lot of male laughter, filled with vulgarities. It looks like the area you are entering was once a gravel pit but has been abandoned for many years. As the trees thin, the brush thickens on both sides of the wash. You can see the opening ahead. There is a truck and people moving around. You creep closer. The wash makes a turn to your right and seems to parallel the opening about twenty-five yards away. You approach slowly, and as quietly as possible. You stop at a good spot, with just a small opening in the brush. The trees are very thin between you and the group of people you see ahead. Their words are distinct now. You observe everything, soaking in every detail you can.

In front of you is one of your greatest fears, the very thing you have been dreading. There is no greater danger to you and Jill than what you see ahead. There is a black man, maybe in his early forties, with a machete. He is swinging it in a menacing way. Close by is a black woman about the same age. There is fear on her face. She's trying to stay away from the swinging blade. But those two are not your greatest fear. There, surrounding them, are five white men. They are laughing and taunting. They make occasional aggressive gestures, causing the black man to react with his machete. The men laugh each time. The men range in age from what appears to be early twenties to late thirties. One is a massive man, not fat, but a huge, powerful man. They each have the same camouflage clothing. They each have the same insignia patches. They each have a side arm on their hip. They each have the same combat tactical vest. They are each holding an AK47. These guys are a group of organized and trained evil bastards. Your greatest fear, and greatest threat, is right before you.

The oldest seems to be the one in charge, as you have heard him issue instructions that others have followed. He says, "Leroy, I think we've had about enough of this part of the game. I don't want to be here all day playing with these two. We have to be above Montevallo by dark. Take that toothpick from Sambo, before he chops the head off that sweet thing he has with him." The other bastards laugh again. Greater fear fills the eyes of the man and the woman. Leroy hands his AK47 to the bastard next to him and walks into the circle. He is a mountain of a man. The black man is about your size and he stands no chance. Leroy makes a few feigns, and the black man reacts with machete swings. The woman stands behind him. She is pleading for them to just leave them alone. She should just save her breath and strength, though that likely won't help her live past the next few hours. The black man is obviously getting tired. When he swings the machete again, Leroy quickly advances and grabs the arm holding the machete, and with one massive sledge hammer of a fist, he hits the man on the side of his face. The man crumbles to the ground like a rag doll. The woman screams and falls to the ground, reaching for the man. Maybe he is her husband, but you'll never know. Leroy picks her up. She is flailing wildly. Leroy slaps her viciously across the face and she collapses. The older man starts cursing, "Damn it, Leroy! Don't kill her!" You see the woman moving again, though she doesn't seem to be fully conscious. The man speaks again, "Okay boys, time for a little more fun." You see and hear the ripping of the woman's clothes.

There is nothing you can do, nothing at all. There are five of them, each armed with pistols and AK47 rifles. They are obviously trained to work in a group. No, if you intervene, you will be killed and Jill will become a play toy for them. You shake your head. Inside you plead, "Dear God, can't you destroy these evil bastards?" The good man inside you wants to come to the aid of the woman and the man, but there is more than your own life at stake. You want Jill to live. You head back toward your camp with a heavy and sorrowful heart. The woman must have regained complete consciousness, as you hear her screams and pleas. The vulgar laughter of the bastards only grows louder with each scream. How do men become so evil? They weren't born that way. How is it they can rape and torture and kill? They need to die. You pause for a moment and look at your carbine. It's no match, you can't do it. Continuing back to Jill, you call her on the radio, "Barney, this is Pumper. I'm returning to camp." Jill says, "Copy."

At the camp, Jill looks at you and asks in an urgent tone, "John, what is happening? What is happening back there?" You look at her, unsure how to answer. The woman's screams and pleas change in tone and tenor. You know what is happening. Jill's eyes grow wide. She knows, too. "John, can't we do something?" "Jill, there are five heavily armed, and probably well trained evil bastards assaulting a man and a woman. They all have pistols and they all have AK47s. There is nothing I can do." You look at your carbine, and repeat, "There is nothing I can do." The woman's screams and pleas persist. Your moral fabric is being torn. You look at Jill; she is starting to tear up. She says, "John, I can fight. I can fight with you!" How can you tell her what you feel? You want to fight, but you want her to live. Both can't happen. She asks again, "John, is there any way? I trust you with more than my life. Tell me, is there any way?" Your mind is racing as you rapidly run through scenarios in your mind. They all end with you dead and Jill brutally raped and tortured. You see no way. The screaming stops. You look at Jill; there are tears in your eyes, too. The screams begin again.

Inside you plead, "Dear God, show me a way!" You hear a faint small voice inside saying, "Fear not, for I am with you. I will not leave you, nor will I forsake you." You feel Jill touching your arm. You look over at her. She is looking directly into your eyes. "John, I trust you more than you will ever know. Whatever you decide, I am with you. Whatever you do, I will not leave you, nor will I forsake you." You are a good man. Jill is a good woman. You both refuse to do nothing. "Jill, we can try. I don't know if we can succeed, but we can try, but Jill, it may cost us our lives and maybe more." She looks steadily into your eyes, "I will fight with you and I will fight for you." You nod your head, "Okay, let's move quickly, we can't keep her from being raped, but we might be able to save her and her husband's lives. We'll take our packs, and the shotgun, too. Bring your Ruger, magazines and ammo." She reaches down and picks up her rifle and says, "Yes. I will." You see the Glock and the radio on her side. "Follow me, quietly. No matter what you see happening when we get there, you must not make a sound. Jill, do you understand?" She says, "Yes, I won't let you down."

You crouch as you enter the wash, looking back; Jill is doing the same and following you. At the spot where you were before, you motion for Jill to get down. She does, and you both remove your packs. You slowly look around. The scene has changed some. The woman is on the ground about twenty yards away. One man is kneeling by her head, another is on top of her. Those damn evil bastards! The black man is being held between two of the other bastards, a little further away, past the truck. The leader is the only one with an AK in his hand. The others are either leaning against trees or the truck. The black man's face shows signs of a brutal beating. You sit back down and whisper close to Jill's ear. "This is what we are going to do. Right in front of us is the woman being assaulted by two of the bastards. I need you to take those two out with your Ruger. Do it just like we did with the targets. Head shots. Shoot the first three times, then move to the second, then back to the first. Understand?" Jill says, "Yes." You continue, "I'm going to move back around through the woods to the other side of the truck so I can get a shot at the other three. When I get into position, I'll click the radio mic three times. When I do, count to five, then start shooting. Do you understand?" Jill says, "Yes, I do." You say, "It's going to take me a little time to get to where I need to be. No matter what you see, do not do anything until you get the signal from me. If you do anything before I contact you, we will both be killed. Do you understand?" She says, "John, I'm with you. I won't let you down. I promise." You say, "I'm going to leave the shotgun here for a backup for you. If anybody approaches, switch to the shotgun. Let's radio check." You click yours three times. She gives you a thumbs up. She repeats what you did. The radios check good.

You start to rise, but then sink back down. You look directly into Jill's eyes for a moment. You may never see those beautiful green eyes again. You place your hand behind her neck and your forehead on hers. There is so much you want to say, but there is no time. You say softly, "Jill, I . . . I . . . ." The screams become louder. Your mind becomes refocused on the task at hand. "All right, Jill, remember, the bad guys are all white. Don't shoot the black man or the black woman. Now rise up but not all the way." She does and her hand covers her mouth. Her eyes are wide as the scene unfolds before her. You squeeze her shoulder. She looks over at you. You give her a thumbs up. She gives you the same. Her expression changes from fear and horror, to determination and anger. You head back into the woods, looking for a way to cross over without being seen.

Once you are across the road and about ten yards in, you work your way toward the opening. There is no wash here for cover, and the brush is low and patchy. You position yourself about twenty-five yards from the three bastards. Two of them are holding the man. The leader has his AK in his hands. He walks over and slaps the man again. He hollers over at the bastards assaulting the woman, "Hurry up, damn it! All this screaming is giving me a damn headache! Carl, when you get through, knife her!" It's now or never. You position your carbine. The red dot is on the leader's head. You click the mic three times, then count to five. The instant you hear the sounds of the Ruger, you pull the trigger on your carbine. The bastard's head explodes and he falls to the ground. You swing to the bastard on the right, but now there is a struggle. All three men are moving. The black man is fighting back, fiercely. You take a couple of shots, but they are wide. Finally, the black man is able to knock the bastard on the right to the ground. The black man and the other bastard struggle together as they fall to the ground on the left. You start firing at the one on the right. Your first few shots miss, as the man is moving rapidly. He pulls his pistol but drops it as you finally get two rounds into his neck. He stops moving all around and just rocks in place, clutching his throat. The bastard on the left has managed to slug the black man with something shiny, then runs for the truck. You fire as he runs, missing several times. One bullet catches him in the leg and he stumbles to the ground. He is almost to the cover of the truck. You jump up and run through the brush, trying to get in for a better shot. You've lost count on the number of shots you've fired. He is standing in front of the truck, reaching for an AK. You fire two more shots, hitting him in his tactical vest. He falls to the ground and reaches for his pistol. You fire again. Click. The magazine is empty. There is no time to reload. You drop the carbine and pull your Glock, running in closer. You start shooting. You put several rounds into the guy in front of you before you can get two to his head. You change your aim to the bastard you shot in the throat and put two rounds into his head.

Running toward where the woman is, you can't hear Jill firing. It may be because the Glock is so loud. You see the bastard who was on top of the woman trying to get to his knees. You put three shots into his body, then one to his head. You turn to the last man. It's the giant. There is blood streaming from his face where Jill's bullets hit. The bastard is going for his AK. You are only a few feet away. You fire two shots into his chest when the Glock runs dry. The 9mm rounds hardly phase the man. He has the AK in his right hand and is swinging it around. There is no time to reload. You drop your pistol and step in quickly. As the barrel of the AK comes around, you grab it with your left hand and push it away to the left. The bastard pulls the trigger. A full automatic burst of fire spews thirty rounds of 7.62 124 grain projectiles out the barrel in less than three seconds. The hot barrel burns your hand, but you feel no pain. You step in and do a side chop kick to his right knee. His leg buckles, and he falls back, pulling the AK and you down with him. The impact of the ground causes you both to release the AK. You start pounding on the bastard. He is too big and too strong; you can't stay on the ground with him. You roll away and rise to your feet. You look for your Glock, but he is too fast. He is up and has a wicked looking knife in his left hand. He lunges straight for you. You step back and to the side with your left foot and turn your body to the side as the blade passes by, tearing the front of your shirt. As the blade moves in front of you, you grab his left wrist with your left hand and twist it over as hard as you can. The twist brings his elbow to the top and locks his arm straight out. You step in quickly, raising your right arm. Using all your strength, and twisting your body to add as much of your weight as you can, you smash down with the back of your forearm, directly onto the bastard's elbow. Pain radiates through your entire arm and shoulder from the impact as you feel the bastards elbow shatter and dislocate. He screams in pain and rage. The bastard recovers quickly and swings a massive right hand at your head. He is very fast. You block the punch, but not completely. Instead of landing on your jaw, his fist glances off the side of your head above your left ear. The force is staggering. Your knees start to buckle. You back away, trying to regain control of yourself. The bastard is relentless and he pounces on you sending you to the ground.

You land on your back; he is on you, hammering you with his massive right fist. You can't sustain many more of these blows. You've never felt anything like them before. You manage to grab his dangling left arm and bend it. The hammer blows stop as he screams in pain. Suddenly he picks the knife up from the ground. Despite the pain, he rears back and plunges the knife down toward your chest. You let go of his left arm and manage to catch his right wrist with both hands, stopping its downward path to your heart. The bastard is yelling a string of obscenities as he leans his massive weight onto his right arm. You feel your strength failing as the knife inches closer to your chest. It's only a matter of seconds, before your strength fails completely and the knife plunges into your heart. You say one last prayer before you meet your fate. "God, please protect Jill!"

Chapter 52 Jill - Day 10 - *Theo and Cassandra...*

John sits back down in the wash. He is looking into your eyes. You see something there you haven't seen before. He places his hand behind your neck and bends his head to yours. Despite all the turmoil around you, time seems to stop. He says softly "Jill, I . . . I . . ." He's going to say the three words you so want to hear! But the screaming brings time back to reality. John's mind has moved back to the conflict at hand. He says, "All right, Jill, rise up, but not all the way." You do. The scene before you is horrific. Inside you scream, "Oh, dear God!" The woman is being brutally assaulted. You want to throw up. You want to scream. You want to kill those evil men! You cover your mouth for fear the sound may actually come out. John squeezes your shoulder and looks into your eyes. He is willing you his strength. Yes, you will not let him down. You give him the thumbs up and settle in behind your Ruger, deciding which evil man you will kill first. Out of the corner of your eye, you see John head into the woods.

You want to close your eyes. You don't want to see what is happening before you. You're going to throw up. You drop back down in the wash and, bending over, you heave. You're trying to be silent, but you can't cover all the sound. After a few seconds, you return to your rifle. The scene is still before you. "John, please hurry!" How can such evil exist? You must stop crying. It's making your vision cloudy. You force calm into yourself as adrenaline pumps into your bloodstream. Finally, after what seems like an eternity, you hear the radio click three times. You start counting. One, two, three, four, fire! You send three small 22 caliber projectiles flying into the head of the man on top of the woman. You swing your aim to the other evil man. The giant has turned to look straight at you. You fire three more rapid shots. You see them impact the man's face. You swing back to the first guy. He is trying to sit up, and you put the remaining four shots into him. The small bullets impacting his neck and jaws.

You change magazines. You pull the bolt handle back to load a round from the new magazine, but it won't move forward. You try again. It still doesn't work! You turn the gun on its side and look into the chamber. There is a spent case still partially inside the chamber! You hear the sound of John's Glock barking loudly. "Oh, dear God! John needs my help!" You try to clear the jam, but the adrenaline has degraded your fine motor skills. Your fingers won't work properly. You look up in frustration and fear. John is in among them firing his Glock. The man trying to rise from the woman is quickly shot down. The giant is reaching for his AK. You watch the impacts of John's bullets, but they have no effect on him. It is all happening so fast! John's pistol is on the ground. You hear the sound and see the fire spit from the AK. The man and John are both falling to the ground!

John is in mortal combat with the giant; you must act now! You rise from the wash, bringing the shotgun with you. You run through the brush, limbs scratching your face. You hear the giant scream in pain, but you hear nothing from John. You see the giant on top of John, pounding him! You're almost there. A knife! He has a knife reared back to kill the only man who has ever cared for you! You raise the shotgun and pull the trigger, but it doesn't fire! You don't know how to work the gun! The knife plunges down and you scream, "No!" You race closer and pull your Glock. You start shooting the giant in his side. Once, twice, three times before he releases the knife. The knife falls the remaining few inches and sticks John in the chest! You continue firing. The giant either falls, or is pushed by John, to the side. You walk closer, continuing your steady rate of fire into the evil human being. Your Glock runs dry. You start changing your magazine. The giant is still moving! John now has the knife in his hand and he plunges it into the side of the evil man's head. John is on his hands and knees. He sees his Glock, and crawling to it, he changes magazines, then stands on unsure legs. His gun is at the ready as he looks around. You know he is dazed from such a fierce beating. You holster your Glock and raise your hands to the side. He turns toward you and you see recognition is in his eyes. You run to him. You wrap your arms around him and start to cry, "Oh, John!" They're the only words you can say, as the emotions pour out of your soul. You hold him tight never wanting to let go. From the corner of your eye you see the woman, naked, rising and running to the man on the ground. She bends over him. John says, "Jill, get your pack and help the woman. I'm okay." You look at him. The left side of his face is red and swollen from the massive blows of the giant. His shirt has an increasing red spot of blood from his chest. You look up into his eyes. He says, "Help her first, then you can help me."

You turn from John and run back for your packs. John's is too heavy. You open his pack and retrieve his first aid kit and his trauma kit. There will be more supplies in his kits than in yours. You run back, with your pack slung over one shoulder. John is not far from the man and woman, picking up his carbine and changing the magazine. The woman is still naked, trying to revive the man on the ground. You approach them and kneel down close. You open the pack and give her a bottle of water. She immediately opens it and starts rinsing her mouth. You hand her the soap and towel from your hygiene kit. She reaches for them and is looking you straight in the eyes. Her face is swollen. There are tears in her eyes, but she is not in shock. She says, "Thank you. Those . . . those . . . animals burnt my clothes." Understanding, you pull out the remaining clean clothes you have and hand them to her, along with another bottle of water. She stands and walks to the other side of the truck, passing John as she does.

Getting another cloth from your bag, you wet it with water from your last remaining plastic water bottle. You start wiping the man's face. It is bloody and swollen. He starts coming around. He starts struggling, not quite fully conscious. He calls out, "Cassandra!" You hear the woman, "I'm here, Theo. I'm coming." You see her come from around the truck. She has the pants on and is buttoning the shirt, as she runs to his side. She kneels down and cradles his head and says, "I'm here, baby. Everything is going to be okay." You hand her the wet cloth.

Rising, you look for John. He is sitting next to a tree, slumped over. His shirt is open and you can see the knife wound. It is still bleeding. You get John's first aid kit and run to him. He looks up and smiles. Even though the swelling in his face causes it to be crooked, you think it is beautiful. You kneel down beside him and open the first aid kit, retrieve some gauze and start cleaning the wound. It's not very large, as the knife did not enter very deep. You clean it and apply two steri-strips. After putting some antibiotic cream on it, you cover it with non-adhesive gauze and tape it in place. Your hand is on his chest. You look at him; he is looking in your eyes and says, "Jill, if we ever make it home. I have something I want to say to you." Looking intently into his eyes you say, "You can say it to me right now, if you want." Then the woman screams.

Chapter 53 John - Day 10 - *The Perry County Militia...*

With reluctance, you urge Jill to leave you and help the woman. You need her embrace; it gives you peace and comfort and strength. The beating you took from that giant bastard will be painful for days. Every part of your body hurts. Your head is throbbing. You haven't been in a physical altercation since ... since the incident with Clyde Baker, fifteen years ago. You unbutton your shirt and look at the knife wound. It doesn't look bad, yet it is still bleeding a little. The bastard was just too powerful. If Jill had not been there, you would be dead. "Thank God for Jill!" You walk over for your carbine, passing the woman and the man on the ground. She looks up at you, and watches you as you walk by. There is nothing you can personally do for her. The last thing she'll want right now is another man around her, especially a white man. She is still naked and her face is puffy from abuse, yet she is beside her man, trying to revive him. Women are so much stronger than men, they truly are. Not physically, but in nearly every other way they are. Jill is going for your med kits and should be back shortly. But the help that woman needs, you doubt Jill can provide.

Bending over and picking up your carbine up from the ground, you almost fall, as the sudden bending has made you light headed. The giant bastard landed too many blows to your head. It hurts, it hurts bad. A few more blows and you would have been gone. You would be dead now if Jill had not saved your life. The words she spoke come back to your mind, "Whatever you do, I will not leave you, nor will I forsake you . . . I will fight with you and I will fight for you." She didn't leave you and she did fight for you. You whisper a prayer, "Dear God, for your mighty hand of protection, I give thanks."

You pause, leaning on the truck. Jill is beside the woman now. You avoid looking in that direction, knowing the woman is still naked. A few moments later, she walks by you with a bundle in her arms. She doesn't say anything, nor does she shrink away. You move off to give her the privacy she deserves. Finding a tree with some shade, you sit down. This whole encounter, from the first shot fired to the last, lasted less than five minutes. Five minutes, yet you feel as though you've been through hell and back. You are not a soldier, yet you did what had to be done. You are thankful you took the time, through the years, to prepare yourself mentally and physically for hard times. The scene flashes through your mind. The knife descending, your death imminent, and then Jill fighting to keep you alive. You look over at her. She is helping the man now. You remember what her father told you just a few months ago. You had gone to see him about a traffic ticket he had given you more than twenty years before. He told Jill about it, but he didn't tell her all of your conversation. He said he had been watching you from an early age, and how sorry he was that Kathy had passed away. Then, he said these words, "Son, I know you are a good man. I knew you would be, because your father is a good man. Jill is a good woman. Son, she is one to ride the river with. You would be wise not to think of her as your little sister, anymore." The next day he called you over and made you promise to do him a favor sometime in the future. You thought it was odd at the time, but you are beginning to understand now. That promise is still in your dresser at home.

The adrenaline crash has made you weak and tired. You slump back against the tree. Just a little rest is all you need. You hear Jill running toward you. You sit up and smile. She smiles back as she sits beside you. You feel the gentle touch of her hands as she tends to your wound. You don't think of the pain as you watch her every move. Jill is a complete woman. Just the touch of her hand brings you comfort. Her mere presence gives you courage and strength. You should tell her how you feel, but something holds you back. You don't understand why. Her hand is still on your chest as she looks up at you. You cover her hand with yours and say, "Jill, if we ever make it home, I have something I want to say to you." She looks intently into your eyes and says, "You can say it to me right now, if you want." Her gaze is steady. It's as if she is looking into your soul. She has given you permission to say the words that will change both of your lives forever. You start to speak. Then the scream!

Your focus changes and you scan the surroundings. The emotions of the moment are gone. A new threat is at hand. You look at the woman. Rapidly approaching, are armed men. They are all wearing the same camouflage. They have the same insignia. They each have side arms and the same tactical combat vest. They each have a black rifle. Two are already upon the woman and man, with their rifles pointing directly at them. Two are rapidly approaching you and Jill. There is no time to reach for your carbine. Something inside tells you any effort to bring a gun to bear will result in your immediate death. Jill turns, her instinct is to fight. She reaches for her Glock, but you catch her hand, stopping her. She looks back questioningly as she loses her balance from your sudden intervention. She falls backwards into your arms. You simply shake your head, "Not now, Jill. Not now." You say a silent prayer, "Dear God, show me a way!"

You study these men. They have a serious, controlled and determined look about them. These guys are professionals, no doubt. They each have a camouflage pattern that reminds you of Vietnam War movies. Their sidearms are 1911s. The rifles are M1As, and their fingers are on the trigger guard and not on the trigger. Their insignia is some rendition of the Confederate Battle flag, but in green and black hues. The letters SF05 appear under the flag patch. You see eight men. No, not eight, but seven men and one woman. The woman and one of the men are black. The remaining six are white. The women is smaller, but similarly outfitted, except she is carrying a Mini-14 instead of an M1A. Two of the men are covering the woman and man on the ground. Two are covering you and Jill. Two are looking around outside the area, as if standing guard. An older man and the woman are in the middle. The older man says, "All right boys, let's gather them up over here. Make sure they are disarmed." One of the men facing you says, "Let's do this nice and slow. No sudden moves and you won't get hurt. Do not touch your weapon. If you do, you will be shot. Do you understand?" You and Jill both nod your heads, "yes." The man continues, "Ma'am, you first, stand up slowly." Jill rises to her feet. The man speaks again, "Joe, retrieve her weapon." Then, directing his attention to you, he says, "Sir, your turn. Stand up slowly." You start to stand. The man seems to notice your bloody shirt and bandage, and says, "Sir, do you need assistance?" You respond, "No. I'm okay," as you stand on your feet. The man says, "Joe, retrieve his pistol and the carbine on the ground. Do either of you have another weapon? If you lie to me, I promise it will not go well for you." You say, "Only our knives." He says, "Joe, get their knives. Pat the man down. We'll let Shondra pat the women down when we get over there." Joe secures your knives and pats you down, finding nothing. The soldier's words bring relief to you. Your guns may be stolen, you may be arrested and sent to some detention camp, but you feel certain this group of disciplined men will not harm Jill.

You walk over next to the truck, where the older man is. The woman, Shondra, is standing next to him. The older man says, nodding at Jill, "Shondra, if you don't mind." She walks over to Jill and pats her down, finding nothing else. The man and woman are already standing. The older man speaks, "Where is the rest of your group?" You are taken aback. You look at Jill. She seems to be surprised, as well. You answer, "Sir, we are not part of a group. What you see is all we are." The older man says in an irritated voice, "Bull sh . . . !" Then, with a somewhat softer tone, he says, "Pardon me, ladies . . . bull crap! Then who killed all these bastards on the ground? Anderson, check the ground." The guy who had been giving you and Jill orders walks off and starts surveying the area. He comes back in a few minutes and reports, "Sarge, I see 9mm brass scattered here and there and what looks like one magazine dump of 7.62x39 steel case. There are five AK47s, five Taurus 24/7 pistols and one Mossberg shotgun lying around. I also see a knife sticking out of that giant bastards head." Sarge looks over to where Anderson is pointing. He turns back and looks at you intently for a few moments, then turns and looks at the guns on the hood of the truck, your carbine and Glock 19 and Jill's Glock 19. Sarge looks back at you, "Where are your other guns?" You hesitate, not sure if you want to reveal where your ATV and other guns are. Jill speaks up, "My Ruger 10/22 is back at the wash through the trees right over there. It jammed on me and I had to leave it. The shotgun on the ground over there is ours too, but I couldn't figure out how to use it." She looks over at you, "I'm sorry, John." You think, "What is she sorry about?" She saved your life and deflected this man's question. She is definitely a quick thinker.

Sarge shakes his head. He ask the man and woman, "Where are your guns?" The man speaks, "My name is Theo Jones. This is my wife, Cassandra Jones. Our guns were confiscated by the Brent Police early this morning." Sarge presses his questions, "Then how did you four manage to kill these five bastards?" Theo says, "We didn't," and pointing at you he says, "He did." He continues, "Those animals attacked me and my wife." He gets choked up, yet continues, "They did some bad things to my wife." Cassandra buries her head into Theo's shoulder and weeps. "This man and his wife killed them."

Sarge looks over at you, then says, "Men, lower your weapons. Perimeter security. Martin, you and Shondra tend to Mr. and Mrs. Jones." Martin, appears to be a medic of some type. Martin and Shondra take the Joneses to the back of the truck. Two men remain with Sarge. Their weapons remain at the ready, but aren't pointed at anyone. Sarge looks at the weapons on the truck hood. Picking one up at a time he says, "A Kel-Tec Sub 2000 with suppressor. A nice combination. A Glock 19. A nice combination with the Kel-Tec. Can I assume, ma'am, the G19, with the pink outline belongs to you?" Jill says, "Yes, sir." Sarge starts again, "You mean to tell me you attacked these five heavily armed bastards with these?" Jill says, "I did use the Ruger for ten shots." He looks back at you, "Mister, are you some type of Rambo, or are you just plain lucky?" You really don't know how to answer. "I'm not a Rambo. I couldn't have done it without her and help from above." Sarge says, "I've never seen anything like this before. I want to shake your hands. My name is Sergeant John McCoy. I'm with the Perry County Militia, Swamp Fox Unit." He extends his hand and shakes yours, then Jill's. You say, "Sergeant, my name is John Carter. This is Jill Barnes. Are you going to take our guns?" The older man says, "No, son, we aren't thieves. We've been trailing these bastards for two days. They have been on a rape and murder spree through this area. We almost gave up hope of finding them when we heard the automatic weapons fire. That's probably the AK casings Anderson found on the ground back there. Just call me, Sarge."

You ask, pointing at the dead bastards on the ground, "Where are they from?" Sarge responds, "Don't know for sure. This is the first I've seen of them, but I think they are part of a larger group." You say, "I heard the oldest bastard say they needed to be above Montevallo before dark." Sarge smiles and says, "That's interesting. I suppose if they had made it up there, they would have met a similar fate from the militia there. I'm going to have my men pick up their weapons and gear up and put it on back of the truck. I assume you are going to want the truck, right?" You look over at Jill and reply, "I'm pretty sure Theo and Cassandra will want the truck, though I haven't even spoken with them yet." Jill says, "I haven't either, not really." He shakes his head again, "You and your wife fought these five bastards for people you don't even know? That's amazing! Let's gather back together and decide what should be done." He starts walking back to the truck.

At the truck, he tells Anderson, "Give these folks back their guns. Have all the weapons and gear of these bastards brought and placed on back of the truck." Anderson obeys, and your and Jill's guns are returned. Sarge says, "If you don't mind, please keep your sidearms holstered and either lean that carbine against the truck, or keep it slung over your shoulder. No handling of the guns." You say, "Sure, no problem." Jill says, "Yes, sir." Sarge says, "Don't call me, sir. I work for a living." He looks to the back of the truck, "Shondra, can we come to the back?" She responds, "Yes, Sergeant." The three of you walk to the back. Shondra says, "The man, Theo, he's going to be pretty sore for a few days, but he's going to mend up. Cassandra, really needs to see the doctor."

The woman has been looking at you intently since you walked up. Finally, she walks over. She places her hands on either side of your face, and looks into your eyes. She draws you down and embraces you tightly. Sobbing, she says, "Thank you. May God bless you." Theo walks over and embraces you as well, saying, "You and your wife have saved our lives. Your selfless act, and the valor by which it was carried out, will never be forgotten." Then they both embrace Jill. Jill walks over by your side and looks up. You place your arm around her and draw her close to your side. Sarge, with moist eyes, clears his throat and says, "All right, now let's decide what needs to happen next."

Chapter 54 John - Day 10 - *On to Marion…*

Sarge says, "Let's just start this discussion by introducing ourselves; as it seems, you folks don't seem to actually know each other." You say, "I'm John Carter. This is Jill Barnes. We are trying to get to Jackson, in Clarke County." Theo speaks up, "Jackson?" You say, "Yes. Jill lives in Jackson. I'm not far from there." Sarge says, "Y'all aren't married? How do y'all work as a team so well? I mean, that had to take some team work for you two to take down those five bastards." You look at Jill. She shrugs and you respond, "I don't know. We just do." Theo says, "My wife, Cassandra, and I are trying to get to Jackson. My dad was from there and my grandfather used to teach school there." Jill asks, "Your grandfather? Is his name Joe Jones?" Theo says excitedly, "Yes, that is his name." Jill smiles and says, "He was one of my favorite teachers." Sarge says, "Well, y'all have a truck now. Y'all can just ride together. How have you been traveling?" Theo says, "We have bikes around here somewhere, if those animals didn't destroy them. I see our two packs are in the back of the truck." Sarge looks over at you, "Well, John, how were you traveling?" You hesitate for just a moment, but then answer, "We had bikes for part of our journey, then a truck for a very short ways, now an ATV. We are traveling at night." Sarge cocks his head and looks at you harder, "You sure you don't have some tactical training? Night time traveling is probably your safest time, provided, of course, you can see. Do you have an NVD?" You respond simply, "Yes." "So," Sarge continues, "my guess is you have a camp somewhere close by." You answer, "Yes."

Sarge says, "Well, y'all have a truck, some full automatic AK47s, pistols and ammunition, and looks like a couple of cases of MREs in the back of the truck. You also have your ATV and an NVD. What are your plans?" You look at Jill, she nods her head, then you look at Theo and say, "Theo, you can have the truck if you want. If you want, we can travel as a group, but I'm only going to be traveling at night. After the beating I took a little while ago, I don't think I'm going to be able to travel with the NVD tonight. I'm going to have to rest until tomorrow night. If you want to travel alone, that's no problem with me. We can split the food and guns and part on good terms." Theo thinks for a moment, "I would like to travel together, but it seems to me driving at night will draw attention to the lights." You say, "If we travel together, we won't be using any lights. In fact, we'll have to black out the truck." Sarge says, "May I make a suggestion to you folks? My unit and I are going to be traveling back to our compound, south of Marion, in just a little bit. I can get you set up with a place to stay for the night. You'll have to provide your own security, unless you have something you want to trade for security services." Looking at Theo, Sarge continues, "Your wife really needs to see our doctor. I can't let you stay at our compound. Actually, the decision isn't mine to make, but I know what the answer will be. We can get you tucked away in the house, then take you and your wife, blindfolded, to our compound and she can see our doctor. I think that is the best option for all of you."

You say, "Whatever Theo decides; your suggestion works for me. I don't mind using the odd AK47 to pay for security for tonight, and our clothes washed and enough water for us each to have a bath." Sarge laughs, "Son, if you trade one of those AKs, the tactical vest and the pistol that goes with it, I promise you, you'll have all the things you asked for—and two hot meals! One this evening and another tomorrow before you leave." Theo says, "I'm good with it, but you'll have to explain that blackout idea for the truck to me later." You say, "Okay, I will, but first let's open one of those cases of MREs and eat. I'm starving!" That meets with everyone's approval.

It takes a full case of MREs to feed you, Jill, the Jones' and the Swamp Fox unit. But the good will gained was well worth the price. You ask Sarge, "Do you guys have a working HAM radio? I mean, do you have one that will transmit?" Sarge shakes his head, "We were using our good unit when the EMP hit, so we lost it. We've been having problems getting the backup unit to work properly. So I'm not sure if it's working now or not. Why do you ask?" "For two reasons. One, I'd like to know what is going on around the country. The last I heard the President had been arrested and the Chairman of the Joint Chiefs was claiming temporary authority. Second, back in my community we have a HAM setup that might have survived the EMP." Sarge says, "We'll see. I can't bring you in without the Unit Commander's permission. I'm sticking my neck out for the Jones', because I know Mrs. Jones needs medical treatment badly. In fact, we better get moving. How long will it take you to demobilize your camp?" You look at Jill and say, "I think we can be packed and ready in fifteen minutes. Keep in mind, I'm driving an ATV. It won't travel as fast as these trucks." Sarge says, "Be back here in fifteen minutes, and we'll leave. We have two trucks. I'll be in the lead. We'll put you and the Jones' in the middle, and Anderson can bring up the rear." You say, "Okay" reach down and help Jill up. Sarge is watching the both of you and says, "You sure you two aren't married?" Laughing, you and Jill walk back to your camp.

You pick up the shotgun as you walk back to the wash. At the wash, Jill picks up the Ruger and shows you what happened. You've seen it before on 22 semi-automatics. You pull your multi-tool out, remove the stuck casing, and work the action a few times to make sure it is working properly. You say, "It could have been caused by the ammo, or dirt, or a number of other things. We'll clean it tonight." Jill starts to re-shoulder her pack. You stop her. She looks up and you say, "Jill, thank you for saving my life. You are a brave woman and true to your word." She smiles and taps you on the arm, "Ah . . . don't worry about it. That's what little sisters are for."

You walk quickly back to the camp. Arriving, you work together to take it down and stow it. You say, "You have this set up pretty good. You must have had a good teacher." She smiles, "I have the best. Now let's go, John. I'm really tired." "I know you're tired. You should have woken me up earlier so you could sleep." She says, "John, that wasn't going to happen. By the way, your iPhone is almost dead." "Yeah, I almost forgot about that. The GPS needs charging, too. Maybe we can get some good sunshine tomorrow for the solar charger. Jill, if you want, I'm sure the Jones' won't mind if you ride with them. You might be able to rest better on the way to Marion." Jill says, with a small laugh, "And not have this shoulder to drool on? No, thank you." You drive out of the woods and back to the gravel pit. Sarge lines everyone up in a convoy. You are the second of the four vehicles.

You look at your watch; it's 1:30. Sarge pulls out on the highway and the rest of you follow. He gets up to 35 mph before you start losing ground. He slows back down. You wish you could travel all the way home like this. Ten days. Ten days! You have been trying to get home from the Birmingham area for ten days, and you aren't even half way there! You feel Jill lying against your back. She deserves to drool all she wants.

Chapter 55 Jill - Day 10 - *I don't want you to…*

You feel the rumblings of the ATV. It's different than the previous nights. The air is warmer, and the wind is stronger. The ATV seems to be vibrating more. You open your eyes. Of course, its daylight and you're following Sarge. You sit up and place your hands on John's shoulders. Darn it! There is a big wet spot on his shoulder, again. Oh well, at least John bartered for laundry services. And the bath! Yes, you so want a bath! You hope this house Sarge was talking about is clean. It will be good to sleep in a bed again, and you feel as if you could sleep for two days. You should be sleepy. Since you left last night, from below Montevallo, the only sleep you've had has been on back of the ATV. John's shoulder feels nice, but you really need a pillow! You are driving through Marion now. You must have slept for nearly an hour. The place looks different, really different. You don't see a lot people moving around, of course; you never saw a lot moving around, even before The Day. You pass by the apartment housing on your right. There is smoke and a large group of people in a gathering. Someone is using a tiller, tearing up the green grass. Maybe they are going to try to plant a garden, but they aren't near the road, so you can't tell. A few kids run toward the road, waving. You smile and wave back. It hits you. You've seen this before, on TV. You start tearing up. These children are malnourished. You start to weep. Here in America, kids are going hungry!

Approaching the overpass, there are several men standing on top. A few have rifles, but they aren't pointed at the convoy. You ask, "John, do you see them?" "Yes, I don't like it." The convoy passes without incident. Soon, you are leaving the town. You notice some old tractors at work and armed men in the gardens. They look up, but that's all. A few miles later you turn right down a county road, and then a couple miles later, you turn left onto a dirt road. The road ends about a half mile more, at an older wood frame house.

It looks nice. It has green stained wood of some type and has a nice front porch. Sarge parks his truck and John pulls beside him. Theo jerks the truck he is driving to a stop. The last truck stops further back and turns around facing the way you drove in. The militia men unload and Sarge calls out, "Perimeter security!" The men spread out and start observing all around. Theo gets out and so does Cassandra. John says, "I'm going to have to show Theo what good manners look like." You slap him lightly on the shoulder and say, "She isn't his little sister." John gets off the ATV. He says, "And you aren't mine, either," as he reaches back his hand to help you off. You take his hand and get down. It's one of those little things you like about John. You say, "That might be a good thing." Theo walks up and, pointing at the truck, says, "I don't like a manual transmission."

Sarge walks over, "Let's get you folks situated, then we need to get Cassandra to the doctor." He walks up on the porch, opens the door, and says, "There are two bedrooms and a bathroom attached to each bedroom. The water is not running, so unless you fetch some water from the creek behind the house, DON'T use the toilets. There are a couple of buckets on the back porch. There is this great room, the kitchen, which has a gas stove you can light with matches from the drawer next to the stove, and some other rooms which won't concern you." You say, "Sarge, who do we thank for the use of this house?" He says, "That would be me. You're welcome. I'm staying back at the camp. Anderson and Joe will be providing security. You'll have to feed them with some of the food that will be brought over later. Make yourselves at home. Theo, Cassandra, we should go." Cassandra says, "Yes, please let's do. I'm starting to run a fever." You walk over to Cassandra and give her a hug and say, "We'll see you shortly." She gives you a faint smile and says, "Yes, later." Then they walk out.

You and John are alone in the house. Sitting on the couch, he says, "Looks like you're the woman of the house for now. The room on the right or the room on the left?" You get up and open the door on the right. It looks like a room a woman would decorate. It definitely doesn't look like one Sarge would use. You surmise the one on the left is Sarge's room and probably sparsely decorated. You say, "This room will do. Let's go get our things."

John jumps to his feet. "No, I'll take care of our things. Go lie down and rest." You start for the door and say, "I will, but let me help you first." He is by your side, in a flash he scoops you up in his arms. You say in a light tone, "John?" He carries you to the bedroom and sits you on the bed. He spins you around and you lie back on the pillow. He takes your shoes off and sets them next to the wall. He walks back over and says, "Your Glock?" You wiggle it out of your waistband and he sets it on the side table. "Jill," he says as he bends over, "I know my shoulder is nice, but you need this pillow. Get some sleep." Then, he kisses you on your forehead and heads to the door. At the door he says, "Call me, if you need me. I'll be in here." You sit up, "John, please don't sleep in there." He says, "I won't, Jill. I've got a few things to do before I can lie down. I'll be back." He closes the door and you lie back down. You are so tired. You close your eyes, try to think . . . but darkness overtakes you.

You start to wake. It's dark outside. You reach over to touch John, but he isn't there. You panic for just a moment, but then remember you have security outside. But what if . . . you rise out of bed, but it's too dark to see. You pull your keychain light out of your pocket and turn it on. You retrieve your Glock and head for the door. You see a faint light coming from underneath the door. You open it slowly, with your Glock in your hand. There is a candle on the coffee table, but no one present. You hear some noise from the back. You softly walk in that direction. There is a dim light in there, too. You can see it's the kitchen. On the table is a big pot and John is getting bowls from the cabinet. He looks at you and sees the Glock in your hand. He says, "I surrender!" and raises his hands. You laugh and holster your Glock. "When have you ever surrendered?" He thinks for a moment, then responds, "This afternoon, when two militia men pointed their rifles at me, and just now when a beautiful woman pulled her Glock on me." "John, you are impossible," you say, "if I'm to believe what you say, don't tell me I'm beautiful when I look like this." He says, "Okay, you are kind of scruffy looking right now, your hair is a mess and you don't smell like apple blossoms, but allow me the liberty of thinking of you as beautiful." You say with a smile, "Okay, John, you are free to think what you want. Is that supper?" John says, "Yes, they just brought it over and it's still hot; Red Beans and Rice; looks like some meat in there, too. There is also some cornbread and milk. I've already given Anderson and Joe their portion. So . . . would you care to join me for a candle light dinner?" Smiling, you say, "Yes, I would like to. Where are Theo and Cassandra?" John says, "Sarge came by and brought this and the water we asked for. He's going to pick up our dirty clothes tomorrow morning. The doctor wants to keep Cassandra overnight, and Theo is staying with her."

The meal is pleasant. The small talk with John feels natural. You like his company. Taking the dishes to the sink, you both clean things up in the cold water. John sets a big pot on the stove and fills it with water and lights the gas. You look at him inquiringly. "Well," he says, "with a little warm water, you might be able to do something about that scruffy look, messy hair and rotten apple smell." You say, "John!" and then, "I don't have any clean clothes." John laughs, "If you don't mind them being a little baggy, I can let you use some of mine."

He carries the hot water to the bathroom and pours it in the tub, then he pours in some cold water. He says, "I'm sorry there isn't enough to make for a soaking bath." He turns to walk out, then says, "Get what you want from my bag and I'll make do with whatever is left." You walk back into the bedroom and open his pack. You can hear him in the kitchen, heating some more water. You dig around in his pack. All you can wear is the olive drab shirt he loaned you back at the barn and your choice of two pairs of boxers. One gray, the other black. You choose the black. As an afterthought, you get his razor from his hygiene kit. Thinking, "Just in case." In the bathroom, you slip into the tub. The water isn't hot, but it isn't cold, just slightly warm. Well, it beats nothing. You're glad John made it part of the deal. You reach for the body wash. Apple blossoms!

You put John's shirt and boxers on. You're going to have to be careful with those boxers because they are way too big. You dig around in the cabinets till you find some ribbons. Tying several together, you make a belt of sorts, and tie it around your waist to keep John's boxers from falling down. You hear John in the bedroom. Guess he is wanting his turn. You open the door and walk out. John is digging in his bag. Without looking up, he asks, "Do you know where my razor is? I took a bath in . . . ." He looks up at you and stops speaking. He's just staring with his mouth still open. You blush, though with only the candle light in the room, you are sure he can't tell. "I'm sorry, John. I used it on my legs. I can't find mine." He stutters, "Ah . . . yeah . . . no problem . . . I mean, I don't mind . . . ah . . . can I use it now?" His eyes haven't moved from you. You say, pointing into the bathroom, "Do you want me to get it for you or do you want to shave in here?" He doesn't say anything. "John?" He seems to come from whatever trance he was in and says, "I'll just shave in here." He walks by you, close by you. You catch your breath as he passes by. You walk over to the bed and pull the covers down and get in under the sheet. John returns and walks over and stands on the opposite side. "Jill," he says, "Maybe, I should sleep in the other room." You sit up, "John, please don't. I don't want you to." He gets into the bed and stays on his side. You turn toward each other. You reach out with your hand, and John takes it in his. You are both looking at each other in the dim candle light as your eyes close in sleep.

Chapter 56 Jill - Day 11 - *I have to...*

You're awake. Daybreak is at hand, and the light is dimly invading the bedroom. John is stirring, yet he continues to hold your hand. A little later you feel his hold on your hand lessen as he starts to rise. You squeeze his hand harder and open your eyes. You see John across from you, he eases back into his pillow. His shape is becoming more distinct as the morning light returns. You continue to hold his hand. The experiences of the past nine days have only drawn you closer to each other. A bond has been formed. Maybe it was formed out of necessity, but maybe necessity only accelerated what was meant to be. He is looking at you, not saying anything. You look back, eagerly awaiting enough light to see into his blue eyes. You told him you would not leave him, nor forsake him. You told him where he went, you would go. You said you would not part ways with him. Did you really mean it? You reflect on the events since The Day, really since the barn. You've known John most of your life. The things you have seen and experienced the past few days have revealed a depth to the man that you never knew before. How he has gone from extreme violence to tender caring in a matter of moments. You've seen rage growing inside him, only to be defeated by his inner man; and instead of vengeance, he granted forgiveness. You've seen him weep from having to do such violent things, yet he didn't shrink from such violence to save people he didn't even know. A man that can become so violent so fast, is he someone you can trust with your life? Is he someone you can trust with more than your life—your heart, your very being? Can you trust him to care for Lizzy, the daughter of a man you know he despises? He is still looking at you without speaking. You look into his eyes, searching for your answer. The answer is yes. He is a trustworthy man. You have known that all your life. He has not abandoned you. He has placed your comfort before his. He has placed your life before his own. Yes, you do trust him with more than your life. You trust him with Lizzy's life. You trust him with your heart. He is the man you want to spend the rest of your life with, whether that be long or short.

You've seen the look in his eyes and the attempts he made to tell you something deep from inside, only to have events foil his efforts. He has never once reached out during the night to draw you to him. Had he done so, you would not have resisted. The look in his eyes last night and the internal struggle you sensed inside him when he suggested sleeping in the other room tell you volumes about what this man feels. The truth is, you don't want to be parted from him. Still, looking into his eyes, as the morning light starts to tint them with blue, you say, "John, when we get home, I'm willing, if you want and if you love me. Sooner, if you can't wait." You hope he understands your words. You watch, as his eyes grow wider. You sense his breathing becoming deeper and stronger. After a few moments, he says, "Jill, I'm not sure how to express what I feel. Your presence gives me courage and strength. The touch of your hand gives me comfort and peace. The smile on your face brings joy to my heart. The sound of your breathing makes me want to protect you. The image of your beauty makes my heart race. Your gentle spirit fills me with a glow. Jill, I love you more than I love my own life. As long as I have breath, I will love you." Tears are flowing down your cheeks. He releases your hand and touches your cheek softly, saying, "Please, don't cry." You say, "I have to, John. I have to." He continues, "Jill, these past few days have shown me what I already knew. You are a woman full of strength and intelligence. You have been faithful by my side, even risking your life for me. I know things are moving so fast for us, yet they seem so slow. I wish the time was different, that I could court you and win your heart and your love. Your father was right; you are a woman to ride the river of life with. I don't want to be parted from you. I want to share all that I am and all that I have with you. I want you to be my wife." Your tears start flowing even more. "Wife? You want me to be your wife?" He says, "Yes. Jill, there is no greater expression of my love for you, than asking you to be my wife." "Oh, John," you say as you place your hand softly on his cheek, "You are the best man I have ever met. I have always loved you. I have always trusted you. Ever since the fifth grade, when you came to my rescue, I have loved you."

You continue to lie there in silence for a few more moments, then, having managed to stifle your tears, you say, "John, won't it be hard to get a marriage license now?" John smiles and says, "I'm not asking the State of Alabama if I can marry you. I'm asking you to be my wife. I don't need permission from the state. All I need is your consent and a witness before God." You say, "I gladly consent to being your wife. Where will we find the witness before God?" John says, still smiling, "I know where a preacher lives. I can wait a little longer." You move closer and kiss him softly on his lips. You feel the rapidity of his breathing increase as he kisses you more firmly. He stops and says, "Jill, we better get up or I won't be able to wait." You smile and say, "I love you, John Carter. I can wait a little longer, too. How about coffee on the front porch?" He says, "Yes, the first of many for years to come." You both rise and head to the kitchen.

Sitting on the front porch with John feels so right. The first cup of coffee of the day, sharing it with the man you love, brings a smile to your face. Despite all the turmoil, despite the constant peril, you are happy. Even though you have been traveling for more than ten days and haven't even made it half way home, you feel content. You hear a truck coming down the dirt road. You get a little nervous and look at John. He has his Glock on his hip and carbine at the door. You didn't have anywhere to tuck your Glock, as you're still in John's shirt and boxers, so you left it on the nightstand. John doesn't seem nervous or concerned. Your security should be around somewhere, though you don't see them. John looks at his watch and says, "Right on time. Jill, we are having a little company. You may want to put some pants on. Would you mind heating some more water?" "Company? What company?" He says, "You'll see. We may get some good news. I don't know for sure." "Yes, John, keep everything a mystery." You walk back inside and find your dirty pants. Maybe they are coming for your dirty clothes. If so, you're going to have to take them right back off. You walk to the kitchen and heat some more water. The coffee supply is dwindling; there is enough for maybe six more cups.

While in the kitchen, you hear men's voices on the front porch. You walk out and see John, Sarge and another man. John says, "Captain Kelly, this is my fiancé, Jill Barnes. Jill, this is Captain John Kelly, Commander of the Perry County Militia." You extend your hand and Captain Kelly takes it and says, "Pleased to meet you, ma'am. I've heard of your bravery in the recent action above Marion." "Thank you, Captain. It's a pleasure to meet you, but, I'm not a very brave person." John chimes in, "I beg to differ. I think you are very brave." Sarge says, "Did I hear you say fiancé?" John says smiling, "Yes. You said we worked well as a team. So we decided to team up permanently. This morning I asked Jill to marry me. She said yes." Sarge says, "Do you need a preacher? We have one back at camp." John says, "We'll see, depending on how our conversation goes in a few minutes." You say, "I have water ready for coffee. Would you gentlemen care for some?" Sarge and Captain Kelly both respond, "Yes, black please." You return to the kitchen and fix Sarge, Captain Kelly and John a cup and return with a tray.

After handing each a cup of coffee and receiving thanks from each, you hear Sarge say, "Everything is set. I've already talked with Theo. He is okay with everything. We'll have to spend the night, so you are going to have to put us up." John says, "That's not going to be a problem." Sarge says, "We'll be back at lunch with a meal, then we can leave." Both men rise, say goodbye and leave. You look over at John, "John, what is going on?" He says, "I didn't want to say anything until I knew for sure. I've just now received the answer." "Well, what is it?" John says, "Yesterday evening, while you were sleeping, Sarge came over with the food. We had a good conversation. Apparently, Captain Kelly wants all the weapons we captured to outfit another squad, and he wanted to trade for them. So, I made a deal with Sarge. He had to get it approved by Captain Kelly. It was a pretty hefty deal, but I think it was worth it." "Okay, John, now tell me what it is!" He says, "I have traded the truck, all the weapons, ammunition, three of the Gen 1 NVDs I found in the packs of those bastards, fifty-five gallons of gas and one hundred ounces of silver, for an armed escort of Perry County Militia to Jackson." "Really? An armed escort? Where are you going to get the gas? Do you have more silver on you than the ten coins you showed me?" John says, "The weapons and gear will be turned over to them immediately. We'll give them the truck when we arrive in Jackson. They are going to have to come to Repose for the gas and silver. The silver will go directly to the men escorting us, at ten ounces per man. They agreed to the arrangement just a few minutes ago on the front porch. Sarge is working on the details, but we will be leaving around noon. That's about five hours from now. They will spend the night with us back home, then return tomorrow. The only catch is, there won't be time to do our laundry."

You are speechless. You can hardly believe what you just heard. An armed escort home! Today! You walk over to John, kiss him full on the lips, look him in the eyes and say, "John, when we get home you better find that preacher!"

Chapter 57 John - Day 11 - *Just in case...*

The moistness of Jill's lips lingers on yours as she says, "John, when we get home you better find that preacher!" She turns and walks inside. You sit there, looking into the trees surrounding the house, but you really don't see them. Your mind is thinking of this morning and the professions of love and commitment you and Jill made to each other. You didn't know if you could ever feel this way again. You think of Kathy and a tinge of guilt enters your soul. Kathy was the love of your life, yet she is no longer here. Is it wrong to love again? Is loving Jill in the same way you loved Kathy being unfaithful? That's been part of your dilemma, ever since you showed Jill how to use your carbine back at the barn and those deep feelings began to stir. Is it right to love again and to love Jill as deeply as you do? You and Kathy were deeply in love. She helped make your life complete. She helped shape you into the man you are. No, it's not wrong; Kathy would not want you to live life alone. What would be wrong is to live a life alone, when you have so much love to give.

You've tried hard not to mix your emotions too closely with Jill while you traveled. You didn't want things to become confused and complicated and make your journey more difficult and perilous. Twice, you almost gave in and told her your feelings. The first time yesterday, before engaging those evil bastards. At the time you measured your remaining life in minutes. Then again, when she cared for you after saving your life. Last night, when you saw her at the bathroom door, you knew there was no turning back. It was only with the greatest effort that you could restrain from drawing her close to you during the night. But you must get her home. You must get her home safely. To do so, you must think clearly. You must not let the fog of emotions sweeping over you divide your thoughts. All your efforts and thoughts must be concentrated on getting her home. No matter the cost, you must get her home. When you get there, you will find the preacher!

The deal you made with Sarge was costly. In pre – The Day dollars, your deal would be worth nearly $20,000. Today the items you traded are near priceless. You would pay many times that value if it would get you and Jill safely home at this very moment. Based on the encounters you and Jill have had with evil men, you know the odds of continued survival are slim. If Sarge's militia had been evil bastards, you would all be dead now. The cost is high, but it is well worth it if it gets you and Jill home safe. Theo and Cassandra will be coming, too. According to Sarge, the doctor was able to get Cassandra's fever under control and has given her enough antibiotics for the next week to help stave off any infections from the brutal assault. That, too, has cost you. Ten of the hundred silver coins are for the medicines Cassandra will be using. You had to use the last ten silver coins you have with you to pay her medical charges.

You hear the screen door open. Jill is walking out. She has some MRE bread covered with peanut butter and jelly. She gives one to you and says, "Breakfast." You take one and bite into it. It's toasted. You look at her in surprise. She says, "I used a fork and held it over a burner. I hope it's not too dark." You smile and say, "No, it's just right." She says, "John, I don't mind wearing my dirty pants again, but, would you mind if I hang onto your shirt?""No, you are welcome to anything I have, even my razor." She says, "You will appreciate my use of your razor soon, I promise. I need to check your stitches. Betty said they would need to come out today." You think out loud, "Has it really only been a week since leaving the barn? It seems like a lifetime." Jill, says, "Yes, that was the first time I thought I lost you. I can't think about it. Let me check your stitches." She walks close and runs her fingers through your hair, finding the stitches. "It looks really good, John. I think I can take them out now. You're lucky that monster only hit you on the left side of your head. Otherwise, this may have come back open." Her touch is working on you again. "It wasn't luck. His left arm was broken." "Is that why he was screaming?" The image flashes back into your mind. The descending knife, your imminent death and Jill fighting to keep you alive. You say, "That was one of the reasons, but he was too big and too strong for me. You saved my life, Jill." "I told you not to worry about it. That's what little . . . ." Then she stops and kisses you and says, "I love you, John Carter! That is the last kiss before we get home. Think, John, stay focused. Keep us alive long enough to find that preacher."

You help Jill tidy up the place and make the bed. You retrieve your razor from the bathroom. Looking at your razor and the extra hairs in it, you think, "Guess I better get used to it." You say, "Jill, I filled both toilet tanks with water, if you need to use them." She says, "Yes, I know. Thanks."

"Come here, I want to show you something." She walks over. You say, "I told you I included three Gen 1 NVDs in the trade. There were actually five NVDs in the packs of those bastards. I didn't tell Sarge and the Captain about these two other NVDs, as I figure they would have insisted they be included in the deal. So, I don't want anybody to know we have these." She says, "Okay, my lips are sealed. Do they work like yours?" "Yes and no. They have similar controls, which are simple, but they really don't work as well as mine. It will be easier for me to show you. Let's find the darkest room." Jill says, "There is a large closet in the kitchen. It must have been a pantry, but it's empty now, except for a few non-food items." "That will work." Jill leads you to the empty pantry. Entering, you leave the door open for some light, though it is still dim in the room, and say, "All right, I'm going to turn this Gen 1 device on. Look through it. Now I'm going to close the door." Jill says, "To start with, it was pretty good, but now I can hardly see anything. I'd say it's broken or something." You say, "Well, not really. All NVDs have to have some light. Some require more than others. This Gen 1 requires more light than my Gen 3. In complete darkness, neither will work unless you use an infrared source. Both units have a built-in IR illuminator. I'm going to turn yours on." "Yes, I can see now." "Now," you say, "use my Gen 3." "Wow, John it is really bright. Did you turn the IR on?" You say, "No, it is using the light from underneath the door." Jill says, "I can see where the Gen 3 has a much greater advantage over the Gen 1 units." "Yes, it does, but this Gen 1 device will work, and work pretty good, outside under starlight. I just wanted you to see how it compared. Let's put these up. Hopefully, we won't need them anytime soon."

You find some note paper and envelopes in a desk drawer in the great room and start writing notes. The first is to your father, the second to Will, the third is to your brother, and the last has no name on it. Jill walks in from the porch, asking, "What time did Sarge say he was coming?" "Around lunch." Looking at your watch you add, "Probably in an hour or so." Jill walks over and asks, "What are these for?" You hand Jill the envelope with no name and say, "Jill, I want you to keep this envelope in your pocket, at all times, until we get home. It is not for you to open. If something happens to me, go to Repose and give this to my father, or Will, or my brother. Promise me you will keep it with you at all times." Jill says, "Okay, I will. Nothing is going to happen to you, John. We are going to be home today. Why can't I read it?" You say, "If you need to use it, then you'll see it. But unless you do, you don't need to know what it says. Just trust me. These other letters, please keep in your pack. They are important, but not as much as the other." Bending over she wraps her arms around you from behind the chair. Hugging you, and kissing you softly on the neck, she says, "I trust you John. I'll keep them like you asked."

Looking out the window, you ask, "Jill, weren't there some empty Walmart bags in the pantry?" "Yes. There was one of those bag holding things full of them. You want them?" "Yes, how about help me with a little project. Grab the bags and meet me on the porch." You go to your pack and get your duct tape. Jill is already on the front porch waiting. "Jill, I'm going to see if I can find a shovel. Will you take the duct tape and cover all the reflectors on the truck? All of them." She says, "Yes, I will. But why? We are going to be driving during the day." You say, "Just in case" and walk to the utility shed in search of a shovel. In the shed you find an assortment of yard tools, including a shovel. Retrieving the shovel, you walk over to the sand pile you saw earlier next to the porch. Looks like Sarge had a paver project planned out before The Day. You fill two dozen bags and carry them back to the truck. Jill walks up and says, "I've got everything covered. What are you doing here?" You say, "Just a little extra protection, just in case." She says, "What is it with you and 'just in case'?" You reply, "I don't know, Jill. Thinking about 'Just in case' through the years, has saved both our lives so far." She walks closer, puts her hand on your shoulder and asks, "What are we doing for 'Just in case'?" You say, "Improvising armor for the door." Using your multi-tool, you remove the window crank from the door and, with some difficulty, take the plastic inside panel off the door. Jill says, "That's hollow inside there." You say, "Not completely," as you reattach the crank handle and let the window down. The space is still mostly empty, but now the glass is inside the door panel. "How about start passing me some of those bags," you ask. She starts passing them to you. Once you have filled as much of the void with the sand bags as you can, you reinstall the side panel and crank handle. Jill observes, "You won't be able to let the window up and down." "Yes, we'll have to drive with them down. Let's do the other side." You have to get eighteen more sand bags before you get both doors complete. You lean the truck seat forward. There is a narrow storage space behind the seat. You say, "Jill, how about grab our gloves and let's fill this space with those pavers."

Once everything is complete you say, "Jill, if we get in a bind and come under fire, get as low in this truck as possible. The engine block will provide some protection up front." She says, "It's going to be tight in there with the four of us and that floor shift." You give a sly smile and say, "Yes, it is." She slaps you on the arm and says, "Behave." You pause in thought. Your interaction with Jill, the traveling together, the caring for each other and the word play, it just seems natural. Glancing at her, you say, "Jill, I can't explain it. I feel so comfortable with you." She smiles. "Yes, I feel the same way with you."

As you are washing up, you hear Jill call from the front, "John, they are here." You walk outside and see Sarge and eight other men. All are heavily armed. They have two trucks. Theo and Cassandra get out and walk over. Jill goes to Cassandra and hugs her. Sarge says, "I have sandwiches. Let's go over the plan while we eat, then hit the road." There are a variety of sandwiches. The bread is homemade. You see what looks like deer, pork, and chicken sandwiches, along with some peanut butter and jelly. Sarge says, "Bruno, how about fill the water jugs up on back of John's truck and let's get the ramps ready to load the ATV." Turning to you, Jill, Theo and Cassandra, he says, "I've already gone over the plan with my guys. I think, since we are as large a group as we are, we can travel during the day. We could travel at night using the NVDs you provided. If we were fewer in number I probably would, but in this case I think speed is our best friend." He hands Jill a GMRS radio and says, "John, I'm going to assume you are driving, since Theo has been complaining about that transmission all the way back here. Jill, you operate the radio. Your call signs are as follows, Cat 1 for John, Cat 2 for Jill, Cat 3 for Theo and Cat 4 for Cassandra. The radio is preset for the right channel and security code. Each of you look at it and memorize it, in case something causes the radio to go off channel. My call sign is Duck and the operator in the lead truck is Dog. You're not going to need the call signs of everyone else. If something happens, try not to get involved. Me and these boys have been training together for awhile. Most are ex-military. John, only get involved if you absolutely have to. I know you have skills, but we function better when we work as a team and you've had no time to train with us. You others don't get involved, period, except to protect your own lives." You say, "No problem, Sarge. Are y'all going to be using the AKs?" Sarge says, "No, I left them back at camp. We haven't tried them out yet and I won't take an untried weapon into combat. John, you will be driving in the middle. I'll be in the rear and Anderson will be up front. Any questions?" You say, "No." The others do likewise. Sarge looks over at his sand pile, then at the truck. Looking back up at you, he says, "Good idea, son. Good idea."

Sarge barks out, "All right, you ladies," and in a softer tone, "and you real ladies. Take your potty breaks now. They'll be no stopping for the powder room along the way. John, get your gear, weapons and ATV loaded up." After loading everything, you stand at the driver's truck door waiting for Jill. She and Cassandra walk down from the porch. Jill towards you, and Cassandra towards Theo. It is a tight fit with all four of you in the truck. You crank the truck and reach for the stick shift between Jill's knees. She says, "Watch those hands. We haven't found the preacher yet." You laugh as Sarge bellows, "Let's move out!"

Chapter 58 Jill - Day 11 - *Leaving Marion...*

John's hand moves close to the inside of your legs each time he shifts the transmission, but you don't mind, not really. They'll be closer once you're home and find the preacher. Once on the highway and getting up to speed, he won't be having to use the shifter as much, anyway. You hear John mumbling under his breath. "What's that, John? I can't understand you." He says, "I'm sorry, Jill, with all the talking, planning and getting things ready to leave, I forgot to pray with you. I was praying for us and our families." You say, "Thank you, John. We need God's continued protection." After a pause, you ask, "John, do you think we are in the end times of the Bible. I mean, do you think Jesus could return soon?" John doesn't say anything for a few moments; then says, "I haven't had time to think about it really hard, Jill. We've been so busy trying to stay alive. I believe Jesus could return at any time. Whether we are living in end time events, or are getting close to them, I don't know. What I do know is this— for such a time as this, God has brought us together. We are here now, and as long as God leaves us here, I'm going to do the best I can, with the best I have, to live and," he turns and looks at you, "to help those around me live." You smile and say, "You always have."

The air flowing through the window is warm. Theo and Cassandra are quiet. Cassandra has had such a traumatic experience. You thank God that John was able to save you from a similar fate. You hope she can recover mentally and physically from the event. Theo hasn't spoken much at all, but you've really only been around him for a short period of time. His face is still swollen. It's actually worse than John's. They seem like nice enough people. Especially considering what they have been through. They were certainly gracious in thanking you and John. John is driving the truck at almost normal speeds. It seems so different after riding on the ATV for several nights, just creeping along. You wonder if John made the right decision driving slower at night versus driving fast during the day. You shudder to think what would have happened if you had come across those evil men while traveling during the day. Yes, John probably made a wise choice. He seems to be pretty good at those things.

"Home today!" It sounds so good, so, so good. You're anxious to see Lizzy and your mom. Soon you are going to be a wife again, but this time you will have a real husband. You look over at John. He seems to be concentrating on the surroundings. He is always observant. He called it "situational awareness." It's worked well so far. "John, what is the first thing you're going to do when we get home?" He says, "Find the preacher." "Yes, that's good. Well, what about the second thing?" He smiles and looks down at you. You blush and say, "Don't answer that." You continue, "Besides that, what is in store for us? I mean, what do we do?" John answers, "First, we have to get up to speed on where things are. We need to see how well our community plans are being implemented and how well they are working. Then, we need to reach out to surrounding areas and see if there is anything we can help them with. Then, further out. It's going to take a lot of work and effort for us to survive. But Jill, no matter what we do, thousands of people are going to die in Clarke County. Did you notice those kids back in Marion? How malnourished they looked?" "Yes, it was horrible. It breaks my heart." "Jill, that is after less than two weeks since The Day. It's going to get much worse in six weeks." You say, "What can we do?" John says, "First, we stabilize our own community, then we reach out. Jill, no matter what we do, people, including children, are going to die. I'm sorry, but that's the truth. Very few people can take care of themselves anymore. Most have lost the skills required for self-reliance. Those skills can be relearned, but for many, it will be too late.

John continues, "You see the fields of crops along the road?" "Yes." He asks, "Do you know what they are?" "Not really, except I think some of it is corn." Johns says, "Yes, some of it is corn. Much of it is soybean and cotton. Soybean has been used as a food filler and for other things for many years, but have you ever seen canned soybeans on the grocery store shelf?" "No. I don't think so, but I've never looked for them." He says, "I haven't seen them, either. All those beans out there, how are people going to eat them?" You say, "I don't know, but what about the corn?" John says, "Corn is easily turned into edible food. The corn back there was less than six weeks old. It takes nearly one hundred days for it to become fully ripe." You say, "I see. People are going to be out of food before the corn is ready." "It's worse than that, Jill." "How can it be worse?" you ask, not knowing if you really want to know the answer. John says, "Did you notice the three large tractors in various locations in the middle of the fields? Did you notice how large those fields are?" You say, "Yes." John continues, "Those newer tractors must have had some type of computer or electronic controls. It looks to me as though they have been sitting out there since The Day, meaning they will likely never run again. Jill, the farmers won't have the equipment required to cultivate fields of that size, so the yields of the harvest are going to be lower. Sadly, without those tractors, much of the produce will never make it out of the fields. It's going to ripen and rot, right there in the fields, with thousands of people starving." The magnitude of what has happened is beginning to sink in. "John, please don't tell me anymore, at least not now." He says, as he reaches for your hand, "I'm sorry, Jill. I shouldn't have been so blunt about this. If we work together with our neighbors and can keep our community protected, Repose will be much different. I promise. You and Lizzy will be safe. If for some reason things were to go to crap there, I have another plan." You look up at John. How did he ever think of all these things? "John, you keep saying 'the plan.' What is 'the plan'? He answers, "It'll be easier if I show you, and more private too. Keeping our plans just amongst ourselves is a key to our success or failure." You smile, "John, I'm glad you love me." He smiles and says, "And I'm glad you love me too, Jill, but even if you didn't I would have protected you, Lizzy and your mother." You squeeze his hand and think, 'He probably would have.'

Further down the highway, you start seeing large fish ponds. These are commercial ponds. There are lots of people standing around them fishing. You wonder how far they came from. There aren't many houses between Marion and Safford. You also see smaller and older looking tractors at work.

Looks like people are going to start planting, if they haven't already. This whole area, with the large fields and ponds, is so beautiful. Some of the pastures run way back to the tree line, almost out of sight. A lot of food and livestock could be raised here. Maybe places like this can make a difference. The small tractor looks like a toy in the midst of the large fields. Things are certainly going to be more difficult. You hope whoever did this to the country has been turned into a pile of ashes.

Sarge speaks on the radio, "We are approaching the Safford intersection. Let's close the gaps. We will not be stopping at the hardware store." John speeds up and gets closer to Anderson. The radio crackle again. This time it's Anderson. "Lots of people ahead. Don't slow down any more than necessary to make the turn. No stopping. Looks like a massive crowd close to the hardware store, walking south." Highway 5 makes a sharp turn at the intersection with the highway to Selma. You see Anderson making the turn, maybe a little too fast, as he fish-tails his truck slightly. John slows a little as he makes his turn. The crowd is so large they must have come from Selma. John said people would be fleeing the cities moving to more rural areas. The road is covered with people, maybe hundreds, all walking south. Some are running toward the truck, trying to wave you down. John keeps moving. You look back. Sarge just makes it through before his way is blocked. John says, "This is going to be bad, real bad for everybody in the path of these people. They are going to be like locusts, devouring everything along their way. If they aren't diverted, or stopped, they will make it to Thomasville within a week." You think for a moment, then ask, "How are Sarge and his guys going to get back? They can't drive through a crowd like that." John says, "Jill, you are an observant woman. It's one of the things I love about you. You are correct. Sarge will have to make adjustments to his route back, but who knows. The crowd may dwindle in size or may head up to Linden or over to Camden. These poor folks along here are fixing to lose everything they have."

You've traveled another ten miles, seeing a few people walking along the road. None try to stop the trucks. They simply stand far away and watch as the trucks go by. You're starting to get excited. Theo and Cassandra still haven't spoken, except to answer direct questions. They are still processing a lot of pain right now. You pass the Catherine road sign. There used to be a school in Catherine. "John, it's less than thirty miles to Thomasville. Being in Thomasville is almost like being home! I'm getting excited. John, we are actually going to make it home!" John looks at his watch and says, "If we can keep this up we may get to Jackson before 4:00, but things will probably slow when we try to go through or around the towns." Then he slams on brakes as the truck in front of you explodes!

Chapter 59 Jill - Day 11 - *Keep moving...*

As John slams on brakes to avoid the damaged truck, your body flies forward. John's arm flashes out, trying to buffer your impact with the dash, and mostly succeeds. Theo and Cassandra are not as fortunate, as they both hit the dashboard hard. Then the pop, pop, pop of gunfire is heard as bullets impact the truck. In a booming voice over the radio Sarge is barking orders, forgetting call signs as he does, "John, an IED, damn it! Don't stop. Keep moving! Move through!" John starts working the gears and guns the truck with power as he maneuvers around the mangled truck. Bullets continue to impact the truck. The truck is being fired upon from both sides. Cassandra is screaming. John yells, "Get down, Jill, as low as you can!" as he pulls you down toward his lap. It is with difficulty you lower yourself, as John works the stick shift. The truck speeds around the wreck. John starts slowing. He says, "Sarge is pulling over. He must be helping the other guys." Sarge's booming voice can be heard, even over the screams of Cassandra, "John, get the hell out of here! Keep going! Don't stop!" John hesitates, as bullets continue to impact the truck. Sarge bellows out, "John, move now, damn it! We'll catch up later, if we can! Go! Go! Go!" John presses the accelerator and the truck surges forward.

On the east side is clear cut land, and on the west a small pasture. In just a few moments you are beyond the clear cut and pasture. Trees are again on both sides of the road. The bullet impacts stop. John slows down and you sit up and look back. One truck is on fire. Sarge's truck is in the ditch and the men are in the ditch seeking cover. You hear the voices over the radio, "Can anyone spot the shooters." "Yes, about 100 yards on either side. Can't tell how many." You hear the continuous pop, pop, pop of rapid gun fire. You look at John. He is looking into the rear view mirror and says, "They are pinned down. They are going to get cut to pieces." You say, "John, is there anything we can do?" He says, "If we don't do something, they will all likely be killed." "John, we must do something!" you say almost in a scream, trying to be heard over the screams of Cassandra.

John turns down a faint dirt road on the east side of the main road and heads into the trees. He drives in about twenty-five yards, then stops and jumps out, leaving the truck running. He yells, "Everybody, stay in the truck!" He scans the area and studies the road. After a few moments, he is back in the truck. "Doesn't look like anybody has been down this road. No truck tracks, for sure." He backs the truck into the woods off the road, turns the truck off, and gets out. Everyone is getting out. Cassandra is crying. Theo is screaming, "What are you doing? Get back in the truck, and let's go!" John says, "If we don't help them, they will all be dead soon." Theo says, "I don't care, we have got to go!" John reaches into the truck and pulls the keys and hands them to you. Theo and Cassandra are on your side of the truck now, next to you and John. John starts barking orders, "This is what we are going to do." He grabs his pack and yours off the truck and sets them on the ground. He gets his carbine and the hunting rifle. "I'm going to go down this road and see if I can flank the shooters. If I can do that, Sarge and the guys might have a chance." Theo is beginning to curse and plead to leave. John ignores him. All his attention is on his guns and you. "Jill, I will call you or click the radio three times every ten minutes or so to let you know I'm okay. I want you and the others to get your packs and head into the woods and hide. Take my pack, too. If you need me, call me. If you don't hear from me within thirty minutes, or if I call and tell you to leave, you must get in the truck and drive to Thomasville. Do you understand?" You protest, "John, I'm not going to leave you!" John bellows back in a loud voice, "Damn it, Jill! If you don't promise to do what I say, I'm getting back in the truck and we're leaving now!" You're startled by the sternness in his voice and start to tear up. In a more tender voice he says, "Jill, you have to promise me you will do what I say or I can't help these guys." You say, "I promise, John." Tears start falling down your cheek. "I promise to do as you say." He reaches out and draws you close. He kisses you deeply and says, "Jill, I love you. I will be back. If anybody comes down this road, just stay quiet and hide. Don't let your presence be known. If you have to leave without the truck, walk only at night using the NVDs." He reaches inside the truck and gets Sarge's radio. He pauses one more time, pulls you close, kisses you again and says, "I won't fail you." Then he starts at a trot down the road.

Your tears are flowing heavily. Theo is screaming after John, but you pay him no attention. Your man is going off into certain danger. Danger he must face to save his new friends. The sounds of gunfire are loud, your heart is hurting, not knowing the future. He is out of sight now. You turn back toward the truck to get the packs and comply with John's instructions. You look at the door. Sand is pouring out of five bullet holes. You fall down to your knees and start praying, "Dear God, oh, dear God, please bring John back to me! Please grant him strength and courage! Please save Sarge and his men! Help me to be strong! In Jesus' name, Amen!"

Theo is now screaming, "We have to go. We have to go now!" You reply, "You heard what John said. We're going to follow his instructions." You start reaching for your pack. Theo continues to scream, "Sarge said for us to keep going. That's what we have to do." You say, "We aren't leaving until John returns, or he tells us to leave, or we haven't heard from him in thirty minutes. Now get your gear and let's move into the woods." You sling your rifle over your shoulder and reach for John's pack. It's too heavy for you to carry. You're going to have to drag it. Theo is still bellowing, "John is not in charge and neither are you!" You turn to look at him. He has the shotgun pointing directly at your face. You freeze. Cassandra starts protesting, talking for the first time, "Theo, what are you doing!" Theo says, "Jill, either get in the truck and let's leave now or give me the keys to the truck!" You say, "If you hurt me, John will track you down and kill you." Theo says, "I'm not going to hurt you unless you don't give me those damn keys!" Cassandra pleads, "Theo, these people helped us. We can't do this!" Theo says, "I know what they did, but what use was it for them to save us if we are only going to get killed right here. I won't let anymore white bastards get their hands on you!" You see the fear and turmoil in his eyes. You realize you have no choice. You say, "Let me get the ATV and our gear, and I'll give you the keys." Theo says, "Okay, but hurry." He tracks you with the shotgun. You set the ramps up at the back of the truck. On the truck, you quickly load your supplies onto the ATV. You've never driven an ATV up or down ramps before. It looks scary, it is scary. You slowly maneuver down the ramps and drive the ATV into the woods. Theo has been tracking you the whole time with the shotgun. You walk over and give him the keys. He says, "I'm sorry, I truly am. Cassandra, get in." After she gets in, he cranks the truck and, jerkingly, drives back to the highway.

You hide the ATV as best you can, then, take your rifle and walk farther into the woods, hiding and waiting for John's call. "Just in case" saved your and John's life again. The gunfire is intense. You start in earnest prayer. It seems like forever before you hear the three radio clicks. You click back and continue in prayer.

Chapter 60 John - Day 11 - *End around...*

You retrieve Sarge's radio from the truck and turn it all the way down. You pause in front of Jill. There is so much you want to say. So much you feel, but there is no time. You kiss her and taste the salt of her tears on her lips. You say, "I won't fail you," then turn and trot down the road deeper into the woods. As you run, you pray, "Dear God, give Jill strength, keep her safe. Guide my path and steady my hand. Give me clarity of thought and fight my enemies before me. In Jesus' name, Amen." There is no more time to think of Jill, not now. But you lick your lips one more time, then turn your attention on what's ahead and on the task at hand. You heard on the radio, the bastards were about one hundred yards off the road. You're getting close to that now. You'll run a little farther, then cut through the woods to get behind them. You might be able to pick them off with the suppressed carbine, if you can get close enough, or at least injure them enough to take them out of the fight and give Sarge and the guys a chance to escape. Whatever you do, it must be done quickly.

You're trotting with your carbine in the ready position. The gunfire is getting louder. You round a bend and come to a sudden stop. Right in front of you are two men. Both are holding shotguns hanging down in one hand. Your surprise appearance freezes them into inaction, but their presence prompts an instant response from you. You raise the carbine and shoot the one on the right in the face. You are already swinging to the other before the first hits the ground. The second bastard drops his gun and raises his hand, pleading, "Don't shoot, don't shoot!" You hold your fire and rapidly cover the remaining fifteen yards. You place the muzzle of the suppressor under his chin and say forcefully, "You have just a few seconds to live, unless you tell me exactly what I want to know! How many shooters are on this side of the road and on the other side? If you lie to me, I will do worse than just kill you!" The bastard is little more than a boy, maybe seventeen or eighteen, but he's old enough to carry a gun and help these others attacking your friends. He starts in a shaking voice, "There are three guys behind cover in the clearing, two more guys in the woods on the other side. One guy sitting in a lawn chair behind the guys firing down. The other side is the same, except nobody in a lawn chair." You say, "All right, you little bastard, that sounds so stupid it must be true. If you've lied to me, you are going to beg to die." The boy is crying and wetting his pants, but you have no pity for him. You pat him down, checking for other weapons. You find a knife in his back pocket and toss it into the woods. There is a pack on the ground not far off. Putting the carbine on the boy's chest you push him toward the pack. "What's inside? Answer quickly!" The boy says, "Rope, duct tape, tie wraps. Stuff like that." These bastards must have done this before, but there is no more time to talk. Time for action. Keeping the gun on his chest, you open the pack and pull the duct tape out. You say, "I'm going to either duct tape you or kill you. I don't really care which. If you resist any at all, I will kill you. Now hold out your hands!" The boy holds his hands out. You lower the carbine and look him straight in the eyes. He's shaking as you tape his hands together. You command, "Get down." He obeys and you tape his legs. There is deep fear in his eyes as you tape his mouth. He starts squirming when you open your knife and move it toward his face. You command, "Be still you little bastard, before I cut your throat!" You cut a slit in the duct tape, for air. Pocketing your knife, you continue through the woods.

You click the radio three times to give Jill comfort, though you doubt it's been ten minutes since you left. Ahead is an opening through the woods. You crouch and approach. The noise of the gunfire is intense. They must have a lot of ammo. Looks like you're about twenty-five yards behind them, as you make it to the edge of the woods at the clearing. Taking cover behind a pine tree, you go prone and survey the scene. The little bastard didn't lie, at least about the ones firing. There are three of them, spaced about ten yards apart, behind pushed up logs. There is one guy wearing a Hawaiian shirt in a lawn chair, smoking a cigar and drinking a bottle of beer! He is the first bastard you are going to kill. All their attention is toward the road. You can't tell for sure what weapons they are using, but by the rates of fire they must have large capacity magazines.

You consider the angle of the shots to each bastard and estimate the distance. The beer bastard is about twenty yards away. The bastard on the left is about thirty yards; the one in the middle about forty, and the one on the right, sixty or more. The last bastard is beyond the optimal range for your carbine. You unsling the hunting rifle and set it on the ground in case you have to transition to it for the longer shot. You whisper a prayer: "Dear God, make my hand steady, my aim true and my speed greater than that of my enemies. Amen." You pull the trigger. A puff of red mist erupts from the front of beer bastard's head. The gunfire masks the metallic sound of the carbine's action chambering another round. You aim at the bastard on the left. You send two 9mm projectiles. One impacts the base of his head and the other behind his left ear. You swing around to the bastard in the middle. He is turning to look at the guy slumped over. He calls out to him as you send two more projectiles. One hits him in the cheek. A non-fatal shot, as it exits just below the right eye before it imbeds into an oak log. The second is two inches higher, entering through his left eye, before it exits above his right ear. The third guy is onto you. He spins around firing an AK47. Bullets are impacting the ground all around you, spraying you with dirt and debris. His barrage is relentless. You are unable to return fire. He stands and approaches, firing as he does. A bullet hits the tree right next to your head and sprays wood splinters into your face. Then, his head explodes. A shot from the road has taken him out. You get the radio and turning the volume up you say, "Ducky, this is Tiger Cat. The Tangos at the clear cut are down, except for two in the woods to the north. If you get somebody to flank them, I can move to cover and fire on those to your west." You hear Sarge on the radio, "Tucker, left flank up the tree line at the clear cut. Two tangos. Go get them. The shooters are down on the east side. I repeat the shooters are down on the east side. And who the hell is calling me Ducky! Is that you John? I told you to get the hell out of here!" You say, "Jill wanted me to check and see how you were doing." You replace the magazine in your carbine with a fresh one. Shortly, you hear gunfire off into the woods and then the radio squawks,

"Two tangos down, left side woods." Sarge barks out, "John, Tucker, take up firing positions and pour the lead into those bastards across the highway. Nobody fire into the clear cut."

Tucker emerges from the woods and you both approach the log cover. You click your radio three times, then prop the Remington 700 across a log. The scope is a high quality Leupold. You turn the magnification up to 6x and spot one of the bastards across the highway. He hasn't figured out yet that his buddies over here are dead. He must be about 250 yards away. If this was your rifle, you would have it sighted for 200 yards. You make your adjustments accordingly. You send a 7mm, 140 grain soft point boat tail projectile racing across the intervening space. You see the shooter jerk and slump to the side. The other two shooters rise and start running for the trees, but are quickly shot down by the deadly accuracy of the M1A rifles. Into the radio you say, "Sarge, a prisoner told me there were two more tangos in the woods on either side of the pasture." Sarge barks into the radio, "Bruno, Miller, flush the two on the left. Joe and Mitchell, the ones on the right." It isn't long before you see four men running into the open field. You hear on the radio, "This is Bruno, we are clear, the birds are in the open." Then, "Sarge, this is Joe, my birds are in the open. We are clear." Sarge yells so loud you don't need the radio to hear, "FIRE!" Shots rain upon the bastards. They all four go down under multiple shots, then silence. The silence is so intense, it is almost deafening after listening to the sustained rifle shots for so long.

Sarge speaks on the radio, "Everybody rally to the truck. We leave for Marion in five minutes. John, son, we are shot the hell up. We have one KIA and three wounded, one serious. Your little end-around came at just the right time. Thanks, son. I'm glad you stayed back. I've got to get these guys to medical care ASAP. Take your truck and complete your journey. We aren't going to be able to go any further." You say, "I'm sorry, Sarge. I'm sorry for your men. I can't pay you here." Sarge replies, "Son, you already have, with our lives. You take care of that little woman and get her home safe. We're leaving now. Sarge out." You say, "Take care, Sarge. Thanks for everything."

You pick up your radio and call Jill, "Barney, this is Pumper. Everything is okay. I'm on my way back." You hear, "Barney here, 10-4, come to me,

Pumper." You walk over to one of the dead bastards. This guy has a Ruger mini-14 rifle and a Springfield XD9 pistol. You sling the hunting rifle and mini-14 over your shoulder. The XD9 you tuck in your waist. You stuff all the magazines in your pockets. You consider checking the other bastards for weapons, but you need to get out of here and you can't carry much more anyway. You turn and head back to the woods. You walk up to the young bastard taped up on the ground and say, "All your bastard buddies are dead. Maybe you should join them." The kid's face grows pale as you open your knife. He shakes his head rapidly, as if begging for his life. You slash down with your knife and cut the tape at his legs. "You've got another chance to do right. Don't waste it." Then, you get up and head back to Jill.

You approach where the truck should be, but there is no truck. You call frantically, "Jill, Jill where are you?" You see her running from the woods, "I'm here, John!" She wraps her arms around you. Her frantic embrace and the extra weight of the guns send you to your knees. She looks down, "John, you're hurt. You are bleeding!" With all the action, you had not noticed. You say, "Let's grab our packs and you can take care of it for me. Then, we have to get out of here. Where did you put the truck? Where are Theo and Cassandra?" Jill frowns and says, "John, I'm sorry. Theo took the truck. He pulled a gun on me. I didn't have a choice, but I was able to get the ATV. It's over here." You say, "Oh Jill, I'm sorry. I didn't think of something like that. You okay? Did he hurt you?" "No, he didn't hurt me, and yes, I'm okay. John he was scared something would happen to Cassandra." You say, "Come on; let's clean my face up so you can give me a proper kiss." You walk to the ATV and set the extra guns against the back rack. Jill says, "Come help me with your pack. It's too heavy for me." You follow her another twenty yards or so into the woods and get your packs. Back at the ATV, Jill pulls your first aid kit and starts working on your face. "Looks like some large wood splinters. There are only a few." Using the tweezers, she pulls them out. It stings a little, but not as bad as the alcohol wipes she uses next. She puts two band aids on, then looking into your eyes, she kisses you. "Jill, at the rate we are going, there may not be anything left of me by the time we find a preacher. I've been shot, beat, and stabbed. I've got to look pretty rough."

She kisses you again, "John, I think you are a handsome man. If you do have any scars from this journey, every time I see them it will only remind me of how much you love me." Then she asks, "What about Sarge?" You answer, "Sarge's guys are pretty shot up. One is dead and three injured. They can't go any farther with us and are returning to Marion." Jill gasps, "Oh no!"

She says, "You aren't mad about the truck?" You reply, "At you? No. At Theo? Not about the truck, I don't think it was going to be of much use anymore, but he is sure going to pay for pulling a gun on you. I promise you that." "John, we probably won't ever see them again." You say, "Oh, yes we will." Jill touches your arm and looks up at you, "For my sake, please don't hurt him." You stop and look down. Those beautiful green eyes. You say, "Trust me, Jill," as you mount the ATV, "he actually kept me from having to make a really hard decision. Let's go. I want to get away from here and find a place to hole up until dark. Plus, we have to keep some distance between us and that mob heading this way." Jill asks, "What do you mean by hard decision?" You smile over your shoulder as you pull the ATV out of the woods, "You'll see." She just rolls her eyes as you give the ATV more fuel.

Chapter 61 Jill - Day 11 - *Hello Theo…*

You roll your eyes as John powers the ATV forward. "You'll see" is what John said. Good grief. Can't the man give you a straight answer? You're surprised he isn't furious about the truck. You covered more ground in an hour with that truck than what you've covered on any of the nights since you left Betty's home, but if you push him, he's going to give you one of those disarming smiles and give another cryptic response. Guess you'll just have to wait and see. You are just thankful the only injury he suffered was from wood splinters. There were so many gunshots, you were almost certain he would be badly hurt. You love this man and don't want anything bad to happen to him. You thank God for keeping him safe.

"John, how is Sarge going to get through that mob?" He says, "I'm not sure. There were several roads off the highway between us and the mob, maybe he took one of those." You say, "I hope so. I liked him. He was so nice to let us use his house." John reaches up and pats your hand on his shoulder and says, "Yes, he was. I'll never forget him. I'll never forget what this day has meant for us both. Jill, I love you. I'm going to get you home. I'm going to get you back to Lizzy and your mother." He continues, "I never would have thought we would see IEDs on the side of roads, here in America. Never thought it." "Do you know which of the guys was killed?" John says, "No, Sarge didn't say, but I think we should honor him in our thoughts. Those men fought for us and one died for us." You say, "Yes, we should, and we will."

You wrap your arms around John and squeeze tight. He flinches. "John, you okay?" He says, "Jill, that giant bastard did a number on me yesterday. I'm going to be hurting for days. You were true to your word and didn't forsake me. Thank you for keeping me alive. You are a very brave person." You say, "John, I would give my life for you." He says, "I know you would.

I missed too many shots and ran out of bullets. Things were happening so fast; I didn't have enough time to reload. But my mistake wasn't yesterday. It was two weeks ago, when, trying to save weight in my pack, I replaced the one 33 round magazine I had in my pack with a 15 round magazine. If I had not done that, I would not have gotten beaten so bad." "John, you are a brave man. I don't think I could make it home without you. Did you know your sandbag 'just in case' trick worked? There were bullet holes in both doors. The sandbags stopped them." John says, "I should have used more and protected more of the truck. I just didn't think about it at the time." You say, "What? Where else?" He says, "I just should have used more. You'll see." You say, "John, I don't like that." You see that darn smile spreading across his face as he says, "I know, but it'll be clear soon. You'll see." You grit your teeth. You knew not to push it.

"How far are we going?" you ask. He says, "We've gone about five miles. It's about ten more miles to Pine Hill. I want to check it out after dark. It shouldn't be long." It starts to register on your mind that the truck you have been approaching is your truck! John says, "Be alert, Jill. It's going to get tense real quick. Trust me." You say, "I will and I do." You can see Cassandra toward the front of the truck, with the hood open. You see legs sticking out from underneath the truck. You think, "Oh no! Cassandra has run over Theo!" You are quickly approaching. Cassandra sees you and runs towards Theo. Theo scrambles out from underneath the truck.

The ATV is at the truck. Before it can stop, John is off with his Glock in his hand. Theo is reaching for the shotgun, as John points the pistol directly in his face. Theo freezes. John says, with a little sarcasm, "Hello, Theo. Having a little truck trouble? Maybe, low on fuel?" Theo says nothing. Cassandra is crying and pleading for John not to kill Theo. You stop the ATV and draw your Glock, not sure what to do. John grabs the shotgun by the barrel with his left hand and says, "Jill, put this by the ATV, please." You get off the ATV, walk over and take the gun from John. You walk back and put it on the opposite side of the ATV. John backs up just a little, then gives Theo a fast and hard shove into the side of the truck. Theo still has not said anything, but his eyes tell you everything you need to know. Given the opportunity, he would hurt John. You keep your Glock ready. John backs to the ATV, while keeping his gun pointed at Theo's face. Cassandra is on her knees, pleading. John seems to be ignoring her. He says, "Theo, twice this woman standing beside me has interceded on your behalf. Twice she has saved your life. I stopped here for three reasons and three reasons alone. First, I want to give you a chance to explain yourself." Theo stares hard at John; then his glance leaves John for the first time. He looks at you, then lowers his head and in a contrite voice says, "I was afraid for my wife. I'm sorry. I truly am." He looks back up and says, "You deserved better." You say, "I forgive you, Theo. I hope only God's blessings on you both." Cassandra looks relieved. John's gun is still pointed at Theo. He says, "That's real touching, Theo. I think you just might mean it. So, my second reason is to give you some advice." Theo over at John as John continues, "Theo, it's about twenty or so miles to Thomasville and another thirty to Jackson. If you do things right, you and Cassandra should be able to walk that in three to four days." Theo says, "Can't we ride with you on the ATV?" John says, "No, that's not going to happen. You're going to need water. You have any water?" Theo shakes his head, "No." John asks, "Do you have any food?" Theo says, "Only what Jill left us." John says, "Jill, please set two gallons of the water on the ground behind the ATV and four of our six MREs next to the water." You are slightly confused, wondering what he is doing, but you say, "Yes," then proceed to do so. Theo looks up. His eyes are moist. Cassandra has gone silent. John continues, "Jill, would you mind leaving your bottle of chlorine with the water?" You say, "No, I don't mind." You know what he's doing now. He's saving their lives again. You open your pack and get the small squeeze bottle of chlorine, and also two coffee filters, and set them next to the water. John says, "You can use the chlorine to treat water, if you need to. The instructions are on the side of the bottle. Don't drink anything you haven't boiled or treated." Theo is still silent. John continues, "I suggest you travel only at night and sleep in shifts during the day. Someone should be awake and watching at all times. Don't sleep where you can see the highway. You need to camp well out of sight. Remember, fires create smoke and can be smelled. Don't guide somebody directly to your camp."

"Jill, will you cover Theo? Shoot him, if he does anything stupid." You draw your Glock and have it ready. John walks over to his pack. He is getting something out. Then, he opens a side pouch and gets something else. He walks back over to Theo and says, "Theo, this is an NVD. It's one of the units I took off those bastards from yesterday. It mounts to the headgear like this." John shows him how. He demonstrates how to put the headgear on, then hands it to Theo, saying, "Here, put it on. The top button turns the unit on. Don't turn it on now, wait till dark. The bottom button will turn the IR source on. Don't turn it on for any reason. It shouldn't be dark enough to need it, and it will only be a beacon for anybody else who has an NVD. You adjust the focus by twisting the eyepiece and the front lens. Here is one set of spare batteries; it's all I can give you. If you let yourselves get caught up in that mob coming this way, you will never see Jackson."

John walks over to the ATV and gets on. You climb on behind him. Theo speaks to John, "Why are you doing this?" John looks at Cassandra and then back at Theo and says, "Theo, that's a good woman you have there, and I think maybe there is a good man inside you. Wish I could do more." John cranks the ATV. Theo asks, "What was the third reason?" You look at John, he says, "A promise." His expression turns hard; his eyes are boring into Theo. It scares you. It scares Theo and Cassandra. In a voice of steel John says, "If you ever draw a gun on my wife again, I will kill you." After a moment of intense silence, he says in a more normal tone, "I'll drop this shotgun and a pistol off for you right up the road. Don't pick them up till I'm out of sight." John drives off. He stops about a hundred yards later and sets the shotgun, the XD9 and two pistol magazines on the pavement. Then, getting back on the ATV, you both drive off.

"John, you knew they were going to be stopped, didn't you? How?" He answers, "I thought they probably would be. I smelled gas where I parked at the woods. I figured the fuel tank got hit. I should have put sandbags around it. I'm sorry I didn't think about it before we left Sarge's." Sorry? This man is sorry? This man has kept you alive for nearly two weeks. He's helped save the lives of how many people? A lot. He just helped two more survive. Two, who left him for dead. He's sorry? "John, you have nothing to be sorry for."

He says, "Jill, I could have had you home safe tonight, if I had thought more thoroughly." "No, John, you might have gotten Theo and Cassandra home tonight, but you and I would be right here. John, you may have just saved their lives a second time." He says, "Jill, we did, not me. Don't think for a minute I don't know how much courage it took for you to wait for me. How much courage it took for you to consent to follow my instructions. How much courage it took for you to want to help Sarge. You kept your wits and were able to keep the ATV for us. You have saved us more than I have." "John, making that promise was the hardest thing I've ever had to do." He says, "I know, but by doing so, you helped save Sarge and his men. I love and respect you all the more because of it. Let's check this wood trail."

John steers the ATV into the woods on the left side of the road. After going past the tree line, he stops and says, "Wait here." He walks up the road a little and studies the ground. He walks back and says, "Don't see any tracks. I'm going to check the road to make sure no one was following. Be ready to go, just in case." He comes back after about ten minutes. You continue along the trail for a ways, further in. Then, John turns into the woods to the left and drives until he finds a spot for camp.

He gets off the ATV, then reaches his hand back to help you off. He looks at his watch and says, "It's only a few hours till dark. Let's skip the tarp this time. I'll set the tent up for you, if you want." You say, "No, I don't think I could sleep right now. Let's just sit under the trees." John sits down and leans his back on a huge beech tree. It is shady and cool. You sit in front of him and lean back onto his chest. His knees are up on either side of you and his arms are wrapped around you. You feel safe. "John, you called me your wife when you talked to Theo. I don't mind, but why did you?" He says, "I'm sorry, if I've jumped the gun. 'I will not leave you, nor will I forsake you. Where you go, I will go. I will not part ways from you.' Those were your words. Your actions speak of their truth. I can't think of any greater vows." "No, John, you haven't jumped the gun. Whether we find a preacher or not, I'm yours, and I always will be. I will give myself to you fully when we get home, but I would like to find a preacher first, if we can." He says, "We will. I promise, when we get home we will find one. Can you stay awake? I need to close my eyes for just a few minutes." You say, "Yes, I can, John. Get some rest." Soon, as you keep watch, you hear the soothing sound of John's steady breathing.

Chapter 62 John - Day 11 - *We aren't stupid...*

You open your eyes. It's dark outside. You feel Jill lying in your arms. She is on her side, curled up. You look around through the darkness. You can see very little under the trees. You see the outlines of the ATV, just ten feet away. You listen intently, as your vision is limited at the moment. You hear crickets and other nighttime woods sounds, but nothing to cause alarm. You and Jill both being asleep was not a good idea. In fact, it was really dangerous, but you can't fuss at her. The past several days have left you both with little chance to rest and have assaulted you with many moments of stress. You wish you had your NVD on, but you don't want to wake Jill at the moment. If someone had seen or heard you, they probably would have already attacked, if that was their intention. You don't know what time it is, but it's late. You look at your watch. It's one of those automatic, self-winding types with luminous dial. It winds itself as you move around. The dial is too faint to read. You'll have to use your keychain light, but not right now. You're going to let Jill rest. Her body has been through a lot over the past two weeks. She's been stressed, assaulted and in a major accident. Most of her sleep, the past few days, has been while riding on the ATV. She is exhausted, no doubt. You know her body is bruised. It must be, as there are still faint signs of bruising in her face, along with the scratches from tree limbs. But, you sense strength in her; strength, despite the constant struggle.

It seems as though a lifetime has played out on this day. Professions of love. Commitments of a lifetime. Hope of returning home. Disaster. Conflict. Death. Betrayal. Forgiveness. Contentment. Uncertainty. All this in one single day! Your body is still racked in pain. Pain lingers from the ambush a week ago, from the limbs scratching your face, the physical beating you took yesterday, and the constant ups and downs of conflict. The physical pain, though intense, does not measure up to the toll of the constant mental and emotional stress. You thought you were prepared for hard times, but the constant stress and conflict is taking its toll. Jill—Jill is the only thing that has kept you stable. She is your anchor to stability. You thank God for putting her back in your life. The gentle touch of her hand has brought you back from the brink more than once. You stroke her hair. You can't see the detail of her features in the dim forest night, but you sense her beauty through the darkness. You wish you could find a hole in the ground and hide with Jill; hide and shelter until this apocalyptic time has passed. But, you know the struggles for survival have only begun. It is going to take all your preparations, skills, determination and strength to survive these next few years. All you can do, as long as God leaves you on this earth, is to do the best you can, with the best you have, to live and help those around you live. This woman, lying in your arms, is the best you have.

You have about two days of water left and four days of food. You should be home within two days, but you should have been home nearly seven days ago. Nothing can be taken for granted. You are entering more familiar territory, an area where you know more people, but you can't let that lull you into being any less cautious. You have to go through, or around, the towns of Pine Hill, Thomasville and Grove Hill before getting to Jackson. You have no idea how the authorities have reacted to this monumental crisis. That's why you want to scout Pine Hill in the dark, just to see if road blocks and check points are set up. You are not going to give up your ATV or guns to any despotic police force or city government. Doing so would likely mean death for you, and rape for Jill. That was going to happen to Lisa and did happen to Cassandra, all because the Brent Police confiscated their weapons. You will fight anyone who tries to take yours. Two weeks ago that would have been a strange thought for you. But there is no more law and court system to depend on, at least not for now. Right now, the only justice, the only protection you have is what you provide for yourself.

You didn't get a chance to recharge the batteries for the NVD or GPS. You'll hook up one of the rechargeable power packs and transfer its power to the NVD batteries. There won't be enough power for the GPS too. Its battery will be weak, but you should have enough non-rechargeable batteries to make it home. You gave Theo one set, but you should still have enough, and Jill has some in her pack. You shouldn't need the GPS once you enter Clarke County anyway. You have about seven gallons of fuel left, plus what's in the ATV fuel tank. That should be more than enough to cover the fifty miles to Jackson, then another fifteen to Repose. Unless something unexpected happens you shouldn't have to stop for supplies before arriving home. But the unexpected has happened nearly every day since The Day.

When you get home, somehow you have got to find a day to rest and recover. You are almost spent and not sure how much longer you can hold up to the mental strain. Perhaps with Jill by your side, she can give you enough strength to make it home. And . . . you have to find a preacher!

Jill starts to stir. She snuggles into your chest; then with a start she sits up. She says, "Oh, no!" You ask, "What is it?" She says, "John, I'm so sorry. I fell asleep!" You say, "Everything is okay. We were both just too tired. We do have to be careful, though. Let's stay on the alert till we actually walk in our door." She settles back against you and says, "Our door. I like the sound of that, but John, I've never even been to your place. Are you really going to let me walk in and take charge of your house?" You say, "Our house. And yes, I need someone to cook, wash dishes, mop floors, and wash clothes." Jill says, "Hmmm . . . my fee for those types of services is going to be pretty high. You may want to find a housekeeper instead of a wife." You say, "I'm willing to pay whatever fee is required, but I'm only kidding about the other. Will and I have been alone for a long time. We know how to clean up after ourselves." She says with a grin, "Good, because that would be my first rule." You say, "Okay. What's the second rule?" Jill is silent for a moment, then says, "My second rule is: I don't like rules, but John, we are going to have to come up with some for Lizzy and Will." You say, "Yeah, you're right. I hadn't thought of that. We'll work it out, Jill. Let's get home first." "John, are we really going to make it home?" You say, "Yes, Jill, I promise I will bring you home."

You say, "I think we should get moving. I want to get closer to Pine Hill, then proceed on foot to see if there are any road blocks or check points. We may be able to go right through. If not, we can find a way around, but it'll add a lot of miles." Jill stands up and reaches down to help you up. You both walk over to the ATV. You get your NVD out and put it on. It hurts your bruised head! You turn it on, get spare batteries, and put them in your pocket. You then get the other Gen 1 NVD out for Jill and some more spare batteries. She puts the head gear on with your help. You say, "You'll probably want to adjust the focus." She does, then says, "John, through these things you look weird with that headgear on." You reply, "Yeah, you do too, except in a pretty kind of way. You hungry? I have a couple of sandwiches left from lunch. They are peanut butter and jelly." She takes one from your hand. You eat in silence, occasionally drinking from your stainless water bottles.

Jill says, "I'm ready to go. I'm ready to get home." You say, "Let's go. But remember, even though we are close to home, we still have to be vigilant." You get on the ATV and Jill gets on behind you. You start back for the road, stop close to the highway, walk the rest of the way, and scan both ways. Seeing nothing moving or unusual, you return to Jill. You mount the ATV and pray together, then continue south on AL5. You are about five miles north of Pine Hill. Considering you're having to drive slowly again, it should take about half an hour. "Jill, it's 9:35 right now. We should get to Pine Hill around 10:00." She says, "Sounds good. You think it would be all right if I just take this NVD off until I need it? It's tight on my head and I keep bumping you with it." You say, "Yes, I think that's a good idea." You pass a few cars on the side of the road, and several log trucks. You wonder how many log trucks actually delivered to the mill each day. There was always a steady stream flowing in when you were there. At a few of the houses, you see a faint light emanating from the inside; must be candles.

With the NVD you start seeing a faint light up ahead. You can't see it with your bare eye. It's either an IR source or is too dim to be seen unaided. You hope the latter. As you get closer, it grows much brighter in the NVD and you start picking it up in your bare eye. You approach slowly. About a half mile away, you slow and pull into the woods. "Jill, I think I should approach on foot and see what's up. How about put your NVD back on and find a place along the tree line where you can watch the road, yet remain unseen. Make sure you don't turn the IR source on. Let me know if you see anything." You give her a quick kiss, then start for the pavement, walking quickly, but quietly, south toward the fire. You approach the intersection with AL10 highway. There is a dump truck abandoned in one lane. To the west is one log truck and to the east, towards the mill, you see several. South of the intersection, about a quarter mile, there are cars pushed across the travel lanes. In the middle is a gap about the size of one car. The fire is on the west shoulder. You approach as quietly as you can, trying to keep the dump truck between you and the fire. Once you get to the intersection, there is no cover. The road block appears to be poorly set up. It only covers the pavement and doesn't extend to the cleared right-of-way on either side of the pavement. The fire is really a bad idea. It's a beacon for all to see, shouting "I'm here!" It will also degrade whatever natural night vision these men have. You move to the opposite side of the road from the fire and proceed, crouching, up to the cars on the east side. You can hear the talk clearly now. Seems like they're talking about trying to set up a community fishing crew. That's probably a real good idea. You bend low and approach along the north side of the car barrier until you reach the last car. You stop at the hood of that car, trying to keep the engine between you and the men. The men are not being very alert at all. They are clustered around the fire, looking into it.

You can hear their voices distinctly now. Then you hear one you think you recognize. You hear him speaking again. You flip your NVD and raise your head above the hood of the car. The man speaking has got to be Bill Sanderson, and he is looking directly at you. He rises from his chair with a start, causing the other men to do likewise. You duck down as you see his rifle start to rise. You call out, "Bill Sanderson, don't shoot. Don't shoot, Bill. This is John Carter." Bill calls back, "John who?" "Come on Bill, you know me. We worked on the controls upgrade for the paper machine a little while back." Bill says, "John? John Carter? What the heck are you doing out here?" You say, "Lower your weapons and we can talk." Bill says, "Yeah, sure. Come on over here by the fire. It helps keep the insects away." You stand and see all the rifles are now down, but still in each man's hands. You really don't want to be around that fire. It will make you vulnerable, but you don't have much choice. You need to talk to these men. But before you do you call out, "Bill, are y'all confiscating firearms and vehicles?" Bill says, "Hell no. We aren't stupid. The first day, the Chief thought he was going to confiscate some vehicles. Well, he tried the wrong one. When he woke up the next day, he decided maybe the town didn't need one after all!" You click your radio mic three times, then walk around to the fire. Bill says, "Geez, John, you look like a borg or something out of Star Trek." You chuckle, "Yeah, maybe I do, with this night vision device on my head. How are things here?" Bill says, "Like crap. Everybody is low on food. No running water. No sewers. The worst is no beer. What are you doing here John? Don't you live close to Jackson, in Repose?" You say, "I was up around Birmingham on The Day. I've been trying to get home ever since." One of the other guys says, "Birmingham? That's a long ways. You walk all the way?" You respond, "No, I had a bike for a ways and I had a truck. It broke down about ten miles up the road. I've been walking for a little while." Then you change the subject: "Bill, what about getting through town?" He says, "There is a curfew from dusk till dawn, but during the day you can ride straight through. I'd tell you to go ahead on through now, but the Chief might wake up and shoot you." You continue to press for information, "How about south, going into Thomasville, how are the roads?" Bill says, "We have a few people come and go each day between here and Thomasville and haven't gotten any reports of bad trouble. In Thomasville, the National Guard is working with the city and handling the check points. You can pass through Thomasville, but not with your guns. If you have guns, you have to go around. At least, that's what I heard second or third hand." "What about further south to Jackson?" Bill says, "I haven't talked to anybody coming from down there. Heck, I was at the mill when it happened, and I haven't been outside Pine Hill since I left work." You press again, "So, I can't go through tonight?" He says, "John, I don't care, but the Chief might do something stupid. I wouldn't do it if I was you." You say, "Okay, I'll be back at daybreak." You turn and start back up the highway. Bill asks, "Where you going?" You say, "I left some things up the road. I'll be back at daybreak. See ya, Bill."

Once you are out of ear shot, you call Jill. "Barney, this is Pumper. On my way back." Jill acknowledges. You find her waiting at the tree line, explain your conversation to her, then say, "Let's move in a little deeper. We'll set up camp for the night and be in Pine Hill at daybreak. We still might make it home tomorrow." She says, "Yes, that will be wonderful. I'm so anxious to see our families." You set the tent up and roll your ground pad and Jill's sleeping bag inside. You roll yours on the outside, next to the tent. Jill asks, "You aren't joining me?" "Not tonight, Jill. We still have to stay on our guard. You get some rest. I'll take first watch. I'll wake you up in a few hours. You watch Jill enter her tent. Even with the NVD, you can see how beautiful she is. You'll just have to wait a little longer.

Chapter 63 Jill - Day 12 - *In Clarke County...*

You reach down with your hand and touch John's shoulder. His eyes open as you look directly into them. The dim light of the break of day prevents you from seeing the blue hue of his eyes, nonetheless you see deep inside. He is looking back into your eyes. You bend a few more inches down and kiss him lightly on the lips. You pull back and say, "It's the break of day, sleeping beauty, time to rise and shine." He smiles and says, "I think I'm going to enjoy getting waked up by an angel every morning." He sniffs the air. You say, "It's the last we have. So you better get us home today." He sits up and you hand him a cup of coffee, then sit next to him. He takes a sip of the coffee and says, "The first cup of coffee, at the break of day, sitting next to a beautiful woman, this is the life for me." "Well, if you like this kind of life, you better get us home, because I'm serious, that's all of our coffee." He smiles and says, "Jill, I think we might make it today. If we don't, we should be close, but I'll settle for the beautiful woman any day." You reach over and run your fingers lightly through his hair, feeling the scar from the gunshot wound. "I think your hair will cover this scar nicely in a few more days. How does your head feel?" John twists and bends his neck around and says, "It's still sore, but not as bad as yesterday. Yesterday was tough, really tough." You study his face a little more; the light is still a little too dim to see all his features, but you know it's there; and it was there yesterday. "John, you have a shiner. A big shiner." You bend over and kiss his cheek softly, then you rise and reach down and say, "Come on, cowboy, take your woman home." John reaches up with a smile and takes your hand.

You've already packed the camp up. The only thing remaining is John's sleeping bag and the cups. John pulls the Mini-14 off the ATV and starts going over it. He unloads it, cycles the action several times and dry fires it. He then puts a magazine in and cycles all thirty rounds through the action.

After reloading the magazine, he says, "Jill, let me show you how to use this. I made the mistake of not showing you how to use the shotgun and it almost cost us our lives." You walk over and he shows you how to hold the rifle, operate the safety, work the action and turn on the red dot. He is standing close, real close. He is standing behind you, with one arm reaching over you alongside your own arm. You feel the warmth of his chest upon your back. The warm air of his breath is on your shoulders. The feeling is electric. You lower the rifle and say, "John, are you trying to seduce me, because if you are, it's working." He smiles and backs up just a little, and says, "Later." You hand him the rifle. He reloads it and places it in the holder where he carried the shotgun before Theo got his hands on it. He has three spare full magazines and one partial magazine. He puts them in a pouch on the side of his pack. You pray together, then mount the ATV and head out of the woods.

At the highway, John stops and scans both directions for a few minutes, then pulls out and heads south. "John, what time is it?" He looks at his watch and says "6:15." You arrive at the intersection of AL10 and AL5. John slows down as he drives across to the makeshift road block. Some men walk over and John starts to speak, "Bill, this is Jill . . ." But Bill interrupts him, "Jill Barnes! How are you doing? Did you spend the night alongside the road?" You say, "Hello, Bill. Actually we were in the woods." Bill says, "John, why didn't you tell me Jill was with you. I would have put y'all up in my home. Couldn't have offered you much more than a safe place to sleep, but I would have been glad to have done so. I know Sue would have been glad to see you again, Jill." You say, "If John had told me it was you up here, I would have insisted he bring me down, but all is good." Bill says, "Jill, how did you get together with John? Were you in Birmingham, too?" You look at John's amused face, as he is left out of the conversation, and say, "Yes I was, we actually got together a few days later on our way home. I'm so anxious to see my mom and Lizzy. Can we drive through town now?" Bill says with a smile, "Of course. To make sure you don't have any problems, I'm going to ride through with you. My shift is almost up, anyway." He walks over and gives you a hug then says to John, "Come on, John, follow me. Get Jill home safe." John follows Bill's ATV through town. John says, "Okay, that was interesting. I think you should do the talking from now on and I'll just do the shooting." You laugh a little, "I helped Sue with her physical therapy after she had knee surgery. They are nice people."

As you drive through town you see lots of stalled cars and several stalled log trucks. Some with logs, some empty. You also notice several busted windows, but nothing bad. The worst is the little quick-stop. It looks like it has been looted. Just past the church is the other road block. John says, "This one is set up better. It's at a bridge over the creek; a good control point." Bill stops where the other men are and talks to them as John eases the ATV toward the opening in the bridge. When he gets even with the men, he stops and says, "I almost forgot to mention something very important. When we came through Safford yesterday, there was a large cluster of people heading this way. I'd say more than a hundred. You better get ready." Bill says, "Thanks, we will. Take care." John eases through the opening and powers the ATV forward.

While driving toward Thomasville, another ten miles further south, you see cars, trucks and log trucks along the highway, and a few people walking. Most are armed, but they don't raise their weapon. That's a really good thing. Considering what you and John have been through, he would probably shoot them if they did, whether they intended to shoot us or not. It's going to take about thirty minutes to get to Thomasville. Your speed is pretty good, but at a few places the stalled cars are so close together that John has to be very cautious. He usually just leaves the highway and goes around. He says, "Jill, Bill told me they wouldn't let people with guns into town. We will likely have to drive around. Depending on what we see when we get there, I may just try to go around, or talk to them at their checkpoint." "Okay, John, whatever you think. I'm good either way." John says, "Maybe I ought to let you do the talking." You smile, "It worked with Bill, but no. If I know somebody there, okay, but otherwise, you do the talking and I'll just sit here looking pretty." He laughs.

At Thomasville, the check point is set across the highway just south of where US43 and AL5 intersect. It runs from the Burger King parking lot to the Chevron gas station. John says, "If we have to go around, we'll go north on US43, then cutover toward Chilton, but I'm going up to the barricade first. I hope Bill is right. I don't think I can fight these guys if they try to take our weapons." This road block looks much different than the one in Pine Hill. There are National Guard Troops in digital BDUs armed with, what John says are M4 rifles. As you approach, a soldier steps out and raises his hand, indicating to stop. His rifle is not raised, but his hand is on the grip, ready for action if needed. He says, "Good morning, sir, ma'am. What can we do for you?" John says, "We are trying to get to Jackson." The soldier inquires, "Where are you coming from, and why do you want to get to Jackson?" John says, "We were in the Birmingham area on The Day and have been trying to get home ever since. Jill is from Jackson. I live in Repose." The soldier says, "Birmingham! Y'all came from Birmingham! That's hard to believe." John says, "Nonetheless, that's where we were. We are both very tired and just want to see our families." The soldier says, "I'm sorry, only residents of Thomasville are allowed to bring guns into town. You're going to have to go around. Do you know how to go through Chilton?" John says, with a sigh, "Yes. Can you tell me anything about travel conditions south of Thomasville?" The soldier says, "We've heard there has been sporadic violence." John says, "Okay. We'll be moving on." The soldier says, "Wait, did you say you're from Repose?" John says, "Yes, I am." Pointing at you he says, "She's from Jackson." He says, "Do you know a Robert Carter?" John says, "Yeah, I recognize you now. The helmet threw me off. I'm John Carter, Robert's brother. You were up hunting last season. That was my camp you stayed in." He says, "Yeah, those were some good times. How is Robert?" John says, "I haven't seen him in about three weeks. I don't know where he is. Before The Day, he was supposed to be in Dallas, but I have no idea now." The solider seems to be considering something, then he speaks, "My relief will be here at 07:30, that's in about ten minutes. If you want, I'll give you an escort to the south side of Thomasville." John says, "Yeah, that will be great. It will save us nearly an hour." The soldier says, "Pull on in and wait over there. Don't say anything to anyone. We'll just keep this between us." John says, "Okay," then parks at the indicated location.

You ask, "What was that all about?" John says, "That soldier is one of

Robert's buddies. I met him back in December, when he came hunting with Robert. His name is Rick Taylor. If he can get us through Thomasville, it will be great." You say, "Yes, it will John. I'm feeling almost at home now." You both dismount the ATV and stretch. John gets a protein bar out of his pack and gives you half. It's blueberry, one of your favorites. It's not long before a Humvee pulls up. Rick walks over and says, "Follow me. Don't stop. Only people who live in Thomasville are allowed off of HY43." John says, "No problem. Our top speed is around 30 mph." Rick says, "Okay, let's go." You look at the buildings as John stays close to Rick's Humvee. The Walmart has barb wire stretched all around. There are lots of people there. You see more barb wire around the other grocery store. In this parking lot, it looks like a cook tent has been set up. You wonder what time they feed people. There didn't look like much cook activity going on, but the line is at least a half mile long. About half the cars you see have been vandalized, and half of those burned. Broken glass and trash is scattered everywhere. It brings a tear to your eye as you remember how clean Thomasville always looked. It takes about twenty minutes to make it to the south check point. It's located at the bridge, just south of the community college. Rick stops and walks over to the ATV. He says, "Good luck to you both. I checked with the guards here and they said they haven't heard of any major trouble on HY43, but there were reports of a biker gang being in the more rural areas." John says, "Thanks, Rick. Listen, if you find yourself in need of a place to stay and work, look me up. Take care, Rick." With a wave you are gone.

"John," you say, "we only have about twenty-five more miles to go. I'm getting excited." "Yeah, I am too, but we need to stay vigilant. "The morning air is pleasant, flowing across your face. You snuggle up to John's back and close your eyes.

John squeezes your leg and says, "Jill, we're coming up on the Grove Hill bypass." You sit up. Things look pretty much the same, with stalled cars and trucks scattered along the way. You watch two 4-wheelers pull out just ahead as you approach the road that leads to the Sheriff's office. John says, "Looks like they just pulled out from the Sheriff's office and they have badges. Maybe we can follow them all the way to Jackson." John follows about 200 yards behind them. They don't seem to mind the shadow.

About twenty minutes later you crest a hill and see an old church on the west side of the road. "John, isn't this the road in to Repose?" John says, "Yes, that's the Toddtown Road. It's one of the ways. It's the way we'll travel when we go home." Home, yes, home! It'll be new to you, but for some reason it just seems that when you get there, it really will feel like home. Your thoughts are interrupted as you are slammed into John's back from his rapid braking of the ATV. You hear John utter a curse and look forward. You can see and hear the swarm coming out of Echo Ridge Road.

Chapter 64 John - Day 12 - *The swarm...*

You feel Jill's chest as it slams against your back. You curse as you see what is ahead. The two deputies are swarmed by at least a dozen bikers pouring out from Echo Ridge Drive. You have stopped, trying to decide your course of action, but the decision is already made for you. You hear gunshots, as four of the bikers turn in your direction. They will be upon you in seconds. There is no time to flee, and nowhere to get the ATV into the woods. You have only one choice. Fight, right here, right now. You tell Jill, "I love you, Jill. Stay behind me and keep your head down. Be prepared with your Glock."

You shoulder the Mini-14 and begin firing. The bikers are about 75 yards away and closing fast. Your third shot brings down the lead biker in a crash. The second biker drives into the wreck and flips his bike. The remaining two separate and zig zag on their route to you. They start firing pistols. You track the one to your right and continue to fire. He goes down ten yards in front of you. The fourth biker drives past you fast as he continues to fire. None of the rounds fired by the bikers have hit you or Jill. When the bike passes by, you quickly dismount the ATV. "Jill, get my carbine and drop to the road on the woods side of the ATV! Do it now!" From the corner of your eye you see Jill complying. The red dot is continuing to track the last biker as he turns around about a hundred yards away. You start firing. The biker finally falls about twenty five yards in front of you. You put six more rounds into him to make sure he doesn't get back up. The metallic sound of the carbine in action reaches your ears. You turn to find Jill engaging two of the bastards from the front. Your earlier shots had not killed them. You raise the Mini-14 and empty the remaining magazine into their bodies. "Jill, head to the tree line for cover. Watch our back. Turn on your radio. Be ready to retreat into the woods." You remove the empty magazine and quickly grab the spares from your pack. You turn and head toward the two deputies.

In front you can see the two ATVs stopped. The deputies are between them trying to use them for cover. The bikers are weaving wildly and firing. You trot within one hundred yards, then go to your knee and commence firing. It's hard to get a good target on the moving bikers at this distance, but you start firing, taking the best shots you can. Two of the bikers are already down from the fire of the deputies. You take one down, then you hear the loud boom of a very large caliber rifle behind you. The arm of one biker is separated from his body. You hear the boom a second time and a biker is lifted off his seat. The remaining bikers streak off to the north on HY43 towards Grove Hill. You fire as they pass by, but see no impacts. As you change magazines, you turn back toward Jill. A man is kneeling beside the tree Jill has used for cover. You call on the radio, "Barney, are you okay?" You get no response. You call again. "Jill, are you okay?" You see her running toward the ATV. She gets on and drives to you. She says, "I couldn't hear you." You check your radio. The battery is dead. You jump on behind Jill, saying, "Take us to the deputies." Jill gives it fuel and you speed forward. At the scene, you dismount and quickly dispatch any biker moving. Both deputies are injured. One is bleeding badly. You ask, "Do you have an IFAK or trauma kit?" They both say, "No." You grab your trauma kit and IFAK from your pack and say, "Help me, Jill," as you run to the men. The less injured of the two is trying to stop the bleeding from the other's arm, but he is having little success. You quickly remove your CAT tourniquet and place it up high on the bleeder's left arm, cinch it down and twist the windlass. The officer screams in pain. You say, "I'm sorry, man. It's the only way to stop the bleeding." You twist the windless until the bleeding stops, then set the windlass in its retaining clip and strap it in place with the Velcro. Speaking to Jill, you say, "I need the sharpie, gloves and Celox gauze, then I'll need the trauma pad in the green package." Taking the shears, you cut the shirt off the man's arm. After putting the gloves on you probe the wound with your fingers. Looks like a through and through shot that maybe nicked the artery. You start packing the wound channel with the Celox gauze. The man passes out from the pain. You say to Jill, "Get the ace bandage and a roll of gauze ready, instead of the trauma pad." Once the wound is packed, you cut two pieces of gauze about twelve inches long. Making them into a pad, you place one on the entry wound and the other over the exit; then you wrap the ace bandage tightly and secure it.

The guy with the big rifle shows up breathing hard. He says, "My name is Randy Chason. Is there anything I can do?" You say, "Randy, what kind of gun are you shooting?" You check the deputy for anymore wounds, finding none you remove the gloves and use the sharpie to write the time on the tourniquet tag. You move over to the other guy, saying, "Jill, another pair of gloves, please." She hands you a new pair, and you put them on before checking the next guy. Randy says, "300 Winchester Magnum." You say, "I thought it was something big. Check to see if these ATVs will crank and run." You ask the second deputy what his name is. He says, "Jerry Hunt." "Okay, Jerry, let's check you out." You hear both ATVs crank. Randy comes back over and says, "They'll both crank, but they have several bullet impacts. Don't know how long they will run." You say, "Randy, keep a look out for any of those bastards that might return." Jerry has a skin wound where a bullet ran down the length of his arm, just cutting the skin. Jill has the gauze wrap and ace bandage ready before you ask. You look at her, she smiles and says, "I'm a fast learner." "Jerry," you ask, "do you know if the ER is still functioning?" He says, "Yes, I think so. I can drive one of the ATVs, but somebody is going to have to drive Mike." Jill says, "John, get Randy to drive Mike. My boss lives down Echo Ridge Drive. I want to go check on her, if we can." You say, "All right, Jill, I suppose if any of these bastards were still down there they would have already come out here after us. We can go." You call out to Randy, "Randy, can you drive Mike to the ER? It's going to be awkward, I know, with him being unconscious. Jill and I are going to check on the folks on Echo Ridge." Randy says, "Yes, but I need somebody to give me a ride back here."

You help the guys get loaded up and they head for Jackson. One of the ATVs is smoking pretty bad. You hope it makes it. Jill asks, "What do we do about all these bodies?" You say, "There is nothing I can do about them. We'll let the police know in Jackson when we get there, but I don't know what can be done." Jill gasps, "John, you don't think they will just be left here do you?" You answer, "I don't know. I just don't know, but at the moment there isn't anything I can do about it. Let's go check on your boss." You turn the ATV around and head for the small road. There are several houses on either side of the road. There are no obvious signs of damage or struggle—until you get to the last house. Jill starts crying. Lying in the yard is the naked body of her boss, Julia Sanders. She gets off the ATV and runs over. She kneels down beside the body. You kneel down beside Jill. The angle of the woman's neck and the glassy open eyes tell you she is dead, yet you check for a pulse. You wrap Jill in your arms as she sobs.

You and Jill have had to fight for yourselves, nearly every day, in order to reach safety at home. Now you are in an area you call home, yet you find no safety. You say, "I'm going to see if I can find a shovel." Jill says between sobs, "Thank you, John. I can't leave her like this. She was always so good to me and everyone. John, it's not supposed to be like this here. This is where we live." You say, "I understand. When we get to Repose, it will be different. I promise." She looks up, "John, how can you know?" You say, "Trust me, Jill. Just trust me." You leave her by her friend and walk toward the back where you saw a utility shed. Inside, you find a shovel. Two hours later, you and Jill lower Julia's sheet covered body into the grave.

It's now 11:30. You're hungry from all the exertion, but you know this is not the time nor place to eat. Jill is still whimpering as she climbs on back of the ATV, and you continue toward Jackson.

Chapter 65 Jill - Day 12 - *Jackson…*

Before John gets to US43, he pulls under a shade tree on Echo Ridge Drive. He dismounts, reaches his hand back and helps you off. You look at him, still sniffling, and say, "What is it, John?" He says, "We are going to be in Jackson very soon." He reaches in his pack and retrieves a towel and wets it with water from his stainless water bottle. "You don't want your mom and Lizzy to see you like this, do you?" He hands you the towel. "No. I don't. Thank you." You wipe your face. The water is not cool, but it's not hot either. It feels good as you wipe your face. You look over at John. He is looking at you with obvious concern. The man needs a break. You don't know how he keeps going. The constant conflict and stress have got to be taking their toll on him. You hope he is right about Repose. You both need a sanctuary for a few days. You say, "I'm okay, now. Let's go. I want to see Lizzy." You both mount up, and John continues south on US43.

It isn't long before you come up to the road block on US43. John says, "The road block is just north of Walmart. If I know who's there, I want to talk to them to see how things are." "Okay, I may know them, too." John approaches the entrance to the road block. There are two police officers and one National Guardsman. Each has an M4 rifle and a pistol. They flag John down, then walk over. "Hey John, man I haven't seen you since before the EMP. Geez, looks like you've been in a fight with a cross between a bear and a wildcat." John says, "Yeah, Mark, it was something like that. We were in Birmingham and are just getting back. How about the deputies? Do you know anything about them?" The other officer says, "Birmingham? I don't believe it." The officer speaking is Eric Wilson, the one bad apple on the city police force. A few months back, you were performing physical therapy on his knee—until he kept coming on to you and didn't want to take no for an answer. Julia was gracious and assigned someone else to work with him. John gets off the ATV and shakes Mark's hand and the hand of the soldier, Corporal Sims. He doesn't shake Eric's hand. You dismount and stand close to John. Eric moves toward you and asks, "Jill, you with this guy or just with this guy?" You say, "This is John Carter, my husband." Hoping that would make him leave you alone. Eric says, "I know who he is. My offer still stands. Move in with me. Things are tough. You're going to need a man to take care of you." You say again, "Eric, this is my husband." Eric says, "I heard you, but it doesn't change anything. Looks like he's had his ass whipped already." You're wondering how long it will take . . . then you see a flash and hear the smack, then you watch Eric crumple to the ground. Mark says, as he looks at Eric on the ground, "John, I've been wanting to do that all week. Thanks. You know the Mayor is not going to like it. That's his wife's nephew." John says, "It makes no difference to me." Mark says, "I didn't figure it did. Sims, would you mind disarming Eric. We don't need to let this get worse when he wakes up."

Mark continues, "The deputies went to the ER. They are only taking trauma cases, nothing else. I haven't heard from them. Did you do the patch work?" John says, "Yeah, Jill and I did." Sims says, "Nice job, John. Looks like you've had some training. You an EMT or ex-military?" John says, "Neither, but I've had some training." Mark says, "We didn't talk long, but it sounds like it was part of the biker gang we've heard about that came into the county. We've heard rumors of them harassing the rural areas. What we've heard is about fifty bikers came in through Coffeeville, but it's all second hand information. We don't have the resources to patrol outside of town." John asks, "How are things here?" Mark says, "Like crap and getting worse." He looks at you and says, "Do you want to hear this, Jill?" You say, "No, but I need to." Mark says, "We've had over a hundred killings here in town. Two dozen arsons. Most of the elderly in the nursing home who don't have local families have died. People have been rioting and looting. Our orders are to shoot looters on sight. Food is almost gone. Running water completely stopped yesterday. Two officers killed. It's only going to get worse." John says, "Mark, I have to check on Jill's family and then on mine, but I'll come back into town as soon as I can and see if there is anything I can do to help." Mark says to John, "I saw your dad yesterday, coming into town. I didn't see him leave, though that means nothing. Jill, I haven't seen your mom or Lizzy, but that doesn't mean anything either." You ask Mark, "Did John's dad say how things were in Repose?" Mark responds, "He said they were getting by, whatever that means."

John says, "Mark, we're going to check on Jill's place." Mark says, "There is a dusk till dawn curfew. Here is a pass. It may help, if you have any problems." John says, "Thanks." You both mount the ATV. Waving bye, you drive on toward town. Passing Walmart, there are more National Guardsmen and some military vehicles. John says they are probably a reactionary force for the road block on US43 and the other one on Walker Springs Road. You wonder if there is anything left in Walmart. The gift card you got last Christmas, that you never used, will never be used now for sure. The liquor store is gutted. All the windows are broken and smashed bottles are everywhere. You are approaching your street. It's before you get into Jackson proper. Cars are stalled all over US43 and more of the stores have been damaged. The tobacco shop looks like it's been gutted, too. John turns onto Parker Street. You live just a few blocks down. You're getting so excited. You hope to see your mom and Lizzy. John thinks they are with Will, and if they are, that will be okay, too.

John turns into your yard. "Oh no! No! No! No!" you exclaim. You are off the ATV, running for the door before John can kill the motor. The door is shattered and glass is covering the front porch. As you reach the steps, John grabs you and wraps his arms around you. You scream, "Let me go! John, let me go!" But he holds you firmly. You struggle to get free, but it's no use, he is too strong. You turn and bury your head into John's chest and start to cry. "Oh John! Oh John . . . ."

Chapter 66 John - Day 12 - *Jill's house...*

You pull in to Jill's front yard on Parker Street. Before you can brace Jill for what you are looking at, she is reacting. In an increasingly fearful tone, she says, "Oh no! No! No! No!" She is off the ATV before you can kill the engine. You have to stop her. She can't go in there until you've checked it out. You switch the key off and catch her at the bottom steps. Wrapping your arms around her from behind, you try to calm her raging soul. She screams, "Let me go! John, Let me go!" But you can't. You just can't do it. She is struggling to free herself, but you hold her firmly, yet tenderly. When her struggles cease she turns, lays her head on your chest, and cries, "Oh John! Oh John . . . ." Your eyes start to mist, as you feel the agony seeping out from Jill. You want to cry. You want to tell her everything is okay, but you can't. Mrs. Barnes and Lizzy are probably with Will in Repose, but you don't know that for certain. You must check the house out before Jill goes in. You have to. With Jill's face buried in your chest, you say, "Jill, I don't think they are in there, but let me check the house first. It's probably looters who came after your mom and Lizzy left with Will." Her crying has slowed. You lift her face toward yours and say, "Wait for me here. I need you to keep a watch on our gear. We are going to need it to get to Repose. I'll scan and clear the house of any threats, and talk to you on the radio as I do. Okay?" She nods her head and says, "Of course, John, you're right. I'll watch our gear. But John, don't talk to me on the radio. Just let me know what you find when you get out." You admire this woman's courage and resiliency. You say, "Okay, I'll have my radio, just in case you need to call me. I'll be using my pistol to clear the house. You use the carbine. If you have trouble, call me because I may not be able to hear the carbine from inside the house." Jill says, "Yes. Go ahead, John, please don't take long."

You replace the dead battery in the radio and perform a radio check with

Jill, then proceed up the steps. Up on the porch, you see blood on the floor trailing into the house. You pray, "Dear God, please let this not be from Mrs. Barnes or Lizzy." You walk through the front door, scanning all around. The blood trail continues further into the house. You clear what looks like the master bedroom. Drawers have been pulled out and some dumped either on the floor or on the bed. You proceed to check the closets, under the bed and the bathroom. You walk back out and continue clearing rooms in a counterclockwise direction. It takes some time to clear each room, cutting the corners as your friends taught you. Each room you come to, you utter a little prayer, hoping to find the room empty. You finally come to the kitchen. The blood trail leads inside. You cautiously enter the room, using the same technique as used for the previous rooms. The blood trail leads to the sink and you see bloody dish cloths on the floor and counter. Foot prints have smeared the blood on the floor. It takes about fifteen minutes to clear the house. Mrs. Barnes and Lizzy are not there.

Back on the front porch, Jill looks over at you. You walk down the steps with a smile. "Jill, the house is clear. No one is inside. There is blood on the floor, but I'm pretty sure it's from whoever kicked the door in. Let me secure the ATV in your garage and we can go in together." She says, "Yes, please, let's do." You go back in, enter the garage from the kitchen, and clear it, as you did the house. Then, using the manual bypass to the electric garage door, you open the door. Jill drives the ATV in. You say, "Put the keys in your pocket. I'm going to close the door; then we can go in."

After closing and securing the door, you walk into the kitchen together. Jill gasps as she sees the blood on the floor. Her hand covers her mouth. Before you can speak, she moves to the bar and moves the bar stools. You watch her, wondering what she is doing. She looks under the top, then she pulls a piece of paper out. A big smile crosses her face. She hands you the paper. It says, "At Johnathan Carter's place. Bev." Jill says, "Under the counter top is where we put our secret messages." You smile, "Geez, that's a great idea. I never would have thought of that." She says, "I wouldn't have either, if my dad had not told me about it." She continues, smiling, "I feel better. You were right. They are in Repose, but at your dad's instead of your place." You say, "Yeah. Good. Let's pack as many of your things as we can take with us. We can come back for the rest later, if we can." Jill says, "I'll get some garbage bags from the kitchen, if they weren't stolen. I'll do my own packing. You can carry them to the ATV." You say, "Okay," and sit on the couch. You think about that note. Something just seems a little odd, but you can't place your finger on it. Well, you'll know soon enough when you take Jill to Repose.

Jill is packing everything! Or so it seems. One bag is mostly cosmetics and soaps and perfumes. It's kind of heavy. You take it out and set it by the ATV. The next bag is full of clothes. You start to open the bag and Jill snatches it and ties it closed, saying, "You don't need to see what's in this bag. You will soon enough." She packs three more bags and says, "Looks like mom already packed a lot of our stuff and took it with her, either that or it was stolen." You carry the bags to the ATV, and with Jill's help, get them secured. You have to be careful, as you don't want anything interfering with your access to your weapons. Jill says, "Oh, one more thing. Come with me. You are going to like this." You follow Jill into the living room. She says, "This was one of my Dad's pride and joys." She runs her hand along underneath the large coffee table. You hear a slight click and the top separates to reveal a secret storage area for guns, but there aren't any guns there. Jill says, "I guess mom and your dad already packed them." You return to the garage, open the door, drive the ATV out, and stop under a large shade tree. "Jill, you mind if we have a picnic in your front yard. I'm starving." She says, "I don't mind, John, but do you think we should, with food being so scarce in town?" You say, "You are right. I didn't think of that. Protein bar again?" She says, "Yes." You reach inside your pack for the last of the blueberry bars. Breaking it in half, you hand Jill a piece. You mount the ATV and Jill climbs on behind you. She says, "Let's go home, John. Let's go home." You crank the ATV and ease back to the highway.

Chapter 67 John - Day 12 - *The Jackson PD...*

Before pulling back out onto US43, you park the ATV in the shade on Parker Street. You ask, "Jill, is there anyone specifically you want to check on before we leave Jackson? It could be a while before we can get back." She seems to be thinking, then says, "Yes, there are a lot I would very much like to check on, but I know we can't, and I want to see my mom and Lizzy. But if you think it's all right, I'd like to check on Rachael. She lives behind the football field." "Doesn't she work with you?" Jill says, "No, actually she's an RN. She works at the ER. We just do a lot of things together. You know, us girls getting older, with few prospects of male companionship. I knew all along there was somebody special out there for me. Well, here you are." She turns your face around and kisses you softly on the lips. A big smile spreads across your face.

You pull back out onto US43, heading into town. A few people are moving about, most on foot, a few on bikes, even a couple of golf carts and 4-wheelers. "Jill, you think Rachael might be at the ER?" Jill says, "She could be. Probably is. It's on our way to her house, let's stop and check, if you don't mind." You say, "I'm going to take College Avenue, instead of staying on US43. I know it'll take a little longer, but I want to see more of what the town looks like." "Yes, I do, too." Turning up College Avenue, you see the gas station, Hardee's, Walgreen's and the auto parts store have all been looted. That's too bad those were valuable resources; if used properly, they could have been a big help to the town. There must still be fuel, as you see an armed guard at the gas station. The parking lot at the shopping center is full of stalled cars. Trash and busted bags of various food items are scattered around. The glass door at the food store entrance is smashed. You see no guards; it must have been completely looted. There are more scenes, just like this, as you head further into town. Jill says, "I had no idea people in our town could do this. They're doing it to themselves. John, I don't know what I would do if you hadn't found me. This doesn't look like a community anymore." You say, "Jill, they better get a handle on things PDQ, or it's all going to fall apart, but I think they will. The mayor is slow to act, at least he was, but Ben Hunt is a pretty solid police chief. I need to talk to him, soon."

You make it around to the back of the hospital, where the ER is located. There is a considerable crowd. Police in uniform are walking about, keeping watch. There is a nurse at the door talking to the crowd. Some are walking away, some are angry. The police are on guard. Jill says, "That's Rachael, right there. I'm going to go over and talk with her." "Okay, be careful. Keep your radio on. I'll be here with our gear." Jill dismounts and walks up to the ER door. One of the police officers stops her. You can't hear what they are saying, but Jill returns. She says, "They say, I can't go in with my gun. I'm going to leave it here." You say, "I'm not so sure it's a good idea to go in there unarmed." She says, "I'll be all right. The police are right at the door." One of the police officers walks over to you and says, "Are you John Carter?" You become alert. You're not going to let him take you into custody. You say, "Yes, I'm John Carter." A big grin spreads across his face. He says, "My name is Pat Ryan. I've been wanting to punch that smart ass in the face for a long time. They are in there wiring his mouth shut. Apparently, you broke his jaw." You ask, "Do you know where Ben is?" Officer Ryan says, "He's at the AL69 road block. It's at the top of Stave Creek Hill, but he'll be here shortly."

It's not long before Ben shows up. Ben is Jackson's first black Chief of Police, but that doesn't mean as much to you as it does to some. What does mean a lot to you is that Ben is a good guy and your friend. He sees you and walks over. He says, "The Mayor wants me to arrest you, and I should arrest you for assaulting one of my officers." You become alert and your demeanor and posture change. Ben is your friend, but friend or not, you are not going to allow yourself to be taken into custody. You observe where the other officers are and make your plan for defense. Ben observes the change and says, "Relax, John, I'm not going to arrest you. Probably couldn't without a fight, and if I did, what would I do with you? We hardly have enough resources to feed ourselves, much less prisoners." You relax a little and say, "That's good, Ben. You have no idea what I've been through getting here from up around Birmingham. I've seen what happens to disarmed people. It's not going to happen to me. Eric got what he had coming. It might have saved his life. Somebody less restrained than myself would have shot him. I haven't even been able to get home yet." Ben says, "Actually, I've wanted to fire his ass for months, but he's been a pet of the Mayor's. I was afraid he would get one of our good guys killed. We've lost two during the looting and riots; Paul Anderson and Vic Beckham. That's when we decided to shoot looters on sight." You say, "I'm sorry about Paul and Vic. They were good guys. Tell me, how are things around here?" Ben says, "John, I'm not going to pussy foot around. It's worse than what you and I talked about awhile back. The worst is yet to come. The two key things are food and water. Food is low, way low. Running water has stopped. Randy, at the Water Department, got a handle on things real quick and was able to ration water, but it has run out. Might've lasted longer, but the fire department hooked to a fire hydrant to fight a losing battle on a house fire before Randy could shut the water supply back off. John, we are on the verge of losing it here." "Ben, I've got a couple of ideas that might help things. If you want, I'll meet with you and the mayor and talk about them. It might make a big difference. But first, I've got to get home and check on Will and my dad. I haven't spoken to either of them since The Day." Ben says, "Sure, if you have any ideas. The mayor is pretty pissed at you right now, so it may be a day or so before he would meet with you." You say, "I'm pretty sure I can help get the water back on, but it will take a team to do it. Ben, you need to broaden your horizon. Jackson, Grove Hill, and Thomasville are only going to survive if this county survives. Leaving the outlying rural areas at the mercy of roving gangs is only going to make things worse here." Ben says, "You think you have some magic answer? We have been busting our asses trying to figure out what to do." You say, "No magic, Ben, but I have some ideas I've been thinking of for years, but it's up to you. I'm not going to the Mayor directly, or to any of these other folks. If any of this works, it'll be because of you. If you don't want my help, that's okay, too. I have a place I can go and hunker down until the dust settles around here, then return." Ben says, "I'm sorry, John. I know you are trying to help. If you think you can actually get the water back on, I'll get the meeting set up. It'll probably take me a day or two to get things set up. I'll let you know." "Ben, make sure the Mayor knows I'm not going to allow myself to be disarmed. If disarming is a condition to anything, count me out." Ben says, "That's not going to be a problem. Here is a pass. This will get you through any of our checkpoints, unhindered. I've got to go check on Eric. At least we won't have to listen to him running his mouth for a few weeks."

"Wait, Ben, tell me more about this biker gang." Ben says, "All we know is what we've heard from the few folks coming into town. So everything is second, maybe third hand. This is the scoop we are getting. A few days ago, a large group of bikers came in through Coffeeville on US84. Depending on who you talk to, there are as few as twenty or as many as seventy-five. They have been harassing the rural areas and haven't tried anything in the cities or on US43. Today's attack is the first on US43, or against any law enforcement officers, at least as far as I know. By the way, thanks for patching my nephew, Jerry. I think Deputy Miller is also going to pull through." Ben turns and walks to the ER.

You consider your conversation with Ben. You had hoped getting closer to home would offer more safety, but with this biker gang, it may be just as dangerous as the rest of your travels. If the guys back in Repose have worked the plan, things should be okay there, but you have to get there. The biker gang was right at the Toddtown Road, your planned route home. If that whole group had swarmed you, you and Jill would be dead now. You have to consider, carefully, how you're going to make this last leg of your journey. Getting complacent because you're so close to home, and letting your guard down, could get you and Jill killed.

You see Jill approaching. With tears in her eyes. She says, "I wish there was some way to get Rachael to safety, but she won't leave. She is living in the hospital." You say, "Jill, I know we both want to get home as soon as we can, but considering the biker gang we encountered this morning, I think we need to be cautious. If that gang had swarmed us like they did the deputies, we would be dead. I want to stay here in town until dark, then travel to Repose during the night." She says, "I am anxious to get home and see my mom and Lizzy, but you are right, we are still in a dangerous situation. I trust your judgment. You haven't led us astray. Like I said before, where you go, I will go." You smile, "All right then, this is what we are going to do. We know the gang was operating close to the Toddtown Road, maybe even on the road itself. I want to take AL69, then the cutoff road back toward Repose. Then we'll hit the paved road into Repose. It'll add about ten miles to our trip, but I think the likelihood of the gang on the dirt road is pretty slim. If we leave around 9:00 tonight, we should get there around midnight." Jill says, "Okay. You want to try to stay at one of my friends' homes until dark—or one of yours?" You say, "If you have a friend close to Stave Creek, let's see if they will let us stay." Jill says, "Yes, I have a friend, Melissa Chance, who lives on Club Riley Road." "Is that Jack Chance's wife?" Jill responds, "Yes she is. They are super nice people." You say, "Okay, we'll go check, but first I want to go to the check point at AL69 and let the guards know to expect us during the night. Don't want to surprise them and get shot." Jill says, "Okay, let's do it."

Chapter 68 Jill - Day 12 - *Jack's wife...*

It is good to see your friend Melissa. You are thankful to have a place to stay for a few hours. Melissa is waiting for her husband to return from Atlanta. Seeing you and John has given her hope that Jack, too, might make it home soon. Jack is a loan officer at the bank. He really is a good guy. He worked with you each step of the way when you bought your home on Parker Street, a few years back. He even gave you a complimentary membership in AAA. Too bad it didn't work during the apocalypse. Looking back, though, you're not so sure how prepared he was for unusual events. You once had a conversation with Jack about emergency supplies, but you can't remember exactly how it started; it was during a cookout at their house. It was after the ice-over in Birmingham. He was kind of miffed when you commented about the general unpreparedness of many folks facing that mini-disaster. You remember him saying, "You don't need a lot of supplies in your vehicle. All you need is a few snack items for the trip, and a good coat and shoes and, of course, a cell phone and a membership in AAA. With the cell phone I can summon all the help that might be needed. Besides, people should to be able to find help by just walking to the nearest business or house, then call 911." Not wanting to argue, you just dropped the conversation. You feel bad now, though. If Jack was no more prepared than that, he will not ever see Jackson and his family again.

Melissa presses for details of your trip. You don't want to scare or depress your friend, so you say, "The trip has been incredibly difficult. I'm really glad John and I were able to travel together. Actually, we are getting married as soon as we find a preacher." She says, "Married? How long have you known this guy? Is he forcing himself on you?" You say, "Of course not! I've known John forever. There is no doubt in my mind we love each other. John is a perfect gentleman. The bonds that bind us together are greater than anything

I have ever known." Melissa says, "Okay, just wanted to make sure. A lot of men are going to be taking advantage of vulnerable women. I've already had a few offers to take care of us, for a fee."

Melissa asks, "Why is John staying in the garage? I know he set up the lawn recliner, but why doesn't he come in?" You say, "He is allowing us to visit together. Someone has to watch our equipment and supplies at all times. If we had lost our supplies along the way, I'm not sure if we could have made it." Melissa looks far into the distance, right through the living room wall, then says, "I wonder if Jack had any supplies?" You don't know how to answer, so you don't. "Melissa, do you have a gun?" She says, "Yes, it's in a lock box on the top shelf in our closet—though, I think Jack has the key." You ask, "Would you mind if John tries to open the box for you and shows you how to use it?" She says, "Yes I would mind! Those things are dangerous. I don't want to touch it. The neighbor's watch dogs keep people away. Besides, we really don't have to leave home. Jack bought a few cases of MREs from a guy in the National Guard after the last hurricane. We should be okay till Jack gets here. We can use our swimming pool water if we need to. I know we have to boil it, but there is plenty of gas for the grill." You ask again, "Are you sure? I know John wouldn't mind helping you. You know, just in case." You're starting to think like John: "just in case." Melissa says in an agitated tone, "What do you mean, 'just in case'?" You pick your words carefully, as you don't want to frighten or anger your friend. "You know, just in case the dogs are asleep or gone for a walk. Just in case it takes Jack longer to get here than you expect." Melissa says flatly, "Jack is going to be back real soon. Y'all are here, so that tells me he should be here soon. Jill, I don't want to be rude, but I'm very tired. If you will excuse me, I'm going to take a nap. If you need to leave before I get up, please just lock the door on the way out." You can't believe what is happening, but before you can respond, Melissa is in her room and the door is closed.

You step outside to where John is. He smiles as you approach. He asks, "Have a nice visit?" "Yes, it was nice. It was good to visit my old friend, but no it really wasn't nice, as my friend refuses to comprehend the new reality. I'm afraid for her. I wish there was something we could do for her." John says, "Maybe she'll adjust to this new reality. Jill, you can only advise people; you can't make them do what they need to do—even if the doing is in their best interest."

John says, "Come sit in the lawn recliner. I'll sit against the wall." You say, "No. I'll sit against the wall. You need to get some rest." John gets up from the lawn recliner and sits with his back to the wall. You look at the lawn recliner, then at John. You crawl up to him and sit with your back to his chest. He kisses you softly and says, "Get some sleep. I'll wake you shortly, when it's time for us to leave. I want you to be sharp for our trip home." You say, "I am tired, but you are, too. You try to sleep. I promise I won't fall asleep this time." John says, "It's not that, Jill. Too many people saw us come in here. I felt safer camping in the woods. I will not sleep until we get home. Please, lie back and rest. It'll help me later." You close your eyes and fall asleep, safe in John's strong arms.

Chapter 69 John - Day 12 - *On the Reservation...*

Jill is asleep against your chest. Your arms hold her close. You want to keep her safe. You're almost home. Almost, but almost isn't the same as being there. You've got to be careful and stay vigilant. There are still potential threats along the remaining few miles. When you are within three miles of Repose, you should be within range to contact the base radio at the command post in Repose. But until then, you are still on your own. Well, that's not really true. You and Jill are on your own, not just you. You reflect on the events of the past two weeks. Your plans for being home within five days only lasted for two days. Practically every plan you have made since, has changed the very next day. The constant conflict has changed you and you're not sure it's for the better. You are tired, physically and mentally. The struggle has been intense; far beyond anything you anticipated. You shudder to think of what you might have become had not Jill been able to rescue you from your dark thoughts. You have worked hard to be a good man, and you know you are, but there were moments you felt yourself slipping into something else; only Jill's calming touch and soft words were able to save you. You thank God for placing her into your life again. The warmth and softness of her body feels good against you. The glow stick emanates a soft green light. Looking at her, you marvel at her beauty. Then you see deeper. You see her strength, her ability to adjust and think quickly. This woman who refused to leave you and fought for you and stayed waiting for you even when uncertain of your return. She has showed you a love that is impossible to describe.

It's time to go. You give her a gentle squeeze, then squeeze a little tighter until she starts to squirm, then you say, "Time to go." She opens her eyes, then sits up and stretches. Watching her is, well . . . you have definitely got to get her home. No more time for those thoughts. Getting her home is your primary focus. You must set everything else aside for the moment. She turns, gives you a soft kiss, and says, "I'm ready, but before we go I need to go in for a few moments. It'll be all right if I use my flashlight, won't it?" You say, "Yes, I'm sure. I'll be out here." In a few minutes, Jill returns and says with a grin, "Melissa was up. She said to tell you congratulations for being the luckiest guy in Clarke County!" You say, "I am a fortunate man indeed. We'll see how lucky I am when we get home." She says, "Yes, you will. I promise. Now, let's go home."

Wanting to be as invisible as possible during the night, you put on your NVD and give Jill hers, saying, "Jill, go ahead and put this on for now. When we get out past the checkpoint, you can take it off." She puts it on and tells you, "Okay, I'm good." You open the garage and Jill drives the ATV out. After closing the door you mount the ATV. You pull out of the subdivision onto AL69 and stop about a quarter mile back from the check point. Using your LED flashlight, you flash the code you prearranged with the guards earlier. After receiving the proper response, you drive to the checkpoint. Ronnie Wilson is one of the guys; you don't recognize the others. He says, "You sure you want to be riding out of here during the night?" You say, "If you've seen what I have seen, you'd want to be as invisible and silent as possible while traveling. Ronnie, I'll see you later sometime, if I can. Take care." Ronnie says, "Yeah, take care, John, and you too, Jill." You give the ATV fuel and head down Stave Creek Hill. It takes about thirty minutes, at your slow rate of speed, to make it to the cutoff road. The cutoff is a narrow dirt road, not heavily traveled. There are several, lesser known ways to travel close to Repose and actually inside the community. You considered going over the "mountain road" in Salitpa, but opted not to because of the extra time required. Besides you may encounter another road block there, as you know there are some likeminded individuals living in that community as well. You are tired and you don't want to start making foolish mistakes. The cutoff road is called Bethlehem Road and sometimes has a sign, when the kids don't steal it. The condition of the unpaved cutoff road requires you to drive even slower. Nearly an hour later, you hit the paved section of the cutoff. You stop the ATV, dismount and help Jill off. The dirt road was tough on your back. You stretch and walk around. Jill hands you a bottle of water. She asks, "What time is it?" You look at your watch and say, "10:35. We might still make it by midnight."

Your speed on the paved road increases. Up ahead are a few houses on either side of the road. You see some lights, most likely from candles. Then you see a glow in an odd place. You slow down, but continue to approach. It is a man, standing in the road, smoking a cigarette. You say, "Jill, I see someone standing up ahead. Put your NVD on." As you slow the ATV to a stop, you can't tell if he is aware of your presence. If he has an NVD, he will likely see you. If not, it's possible you could get within twenty-five yards before he knows you are there. Jill says, "I'm set. Yes, I think I see him. I see his cigarette for sure and the glow of it on his face." Picking up your carbine, you turn the IR laser on and sweep in front of the man several times. He makes no response. You say, "All right, be ready. I'm going to ease forward." When you are about fifty yards from the man, you stop. You ask, "Would a panther scare you?" Jill says, "What?" You start making a noise, using your best imitation of a panther. The reaction of the guy is immediate. He stiffens. You see him pull a gun and look around. He obviously sees nothing. You continue making the sound grow louder. The guy is scanning around quickly; then suddenly he runs for a house, about fifty yards off the road. That's when you decide to make your run. You power the ATV and scoot by before he can reach the house. Jill is giggling so hard she almost chokes. She says, "I've never heard a panther, but I think that would scare me too!" You can't help but chuckle, too.

Continuing on the cutoff road, you think about what just happened and realize the needless risk you took. You scold yourself for being so stupid. If the guy had been carrying a shotgun, he could have pelted you with pellets easily. No farther away than you were, he could have spotted you with a flashlight and maybe hit you with his pistol. It's careless mistakes like this that gets people killed. You say, "Jill, I made a big mistake back there. I shouldn't have done what I did. It exposed us to needless risk. I'm sorry." She says, "What are you talking about?" You say, "We can talk about it later. I want to refocus my attention to what we are doing. Just believe me when I say I'm sorry. It won't happen again." The area doesn't look exactly the same seeing it through the NVD, but you can tell almost exactly where you are. The road into Repose is just ahead.

You continue a couple more miles, then stop. Jill asks, "What's up?" "Let's see if anybody is at home. We are less than three miles from Repose." You turn your radio to the prearranged frequency and call, "Tin Man calling Texas. Tin Man calling Texas." Jill asks, "What?" You say, "You'll see shortly. It's all part of the plan." You hear over the radio, "Tin Man, this is Texas. Authenticate Blue Delta." You respond, "Texas, this is Tin Man. Authenticate Red Charlie. We are outside Nevada about three clicks." "Tin Man, it is good to hear your voice—damn good to hear your voice! Hold your position. We have Tangos one half click from Nevada and Utah. Standby." Jill says, "What's going on John? Don't keep me in the dark." You say, "I don't mean to. Texas is our command post—actually it's Charlie Dixon's garage. Nevada and Utah are our main checkpoints on the county road. They are set up at bridges. There are people with possible hostile intent camped near each entrance. The one we are approaching is Nevada. Let's just wait to hear back." Jill says, "We are three miles from home, and we still have trouble?" "Maybe, maybe not. Let's wait and hear back from the watch commander. There are other ways into Repose, and I know how to find them. They should be watched, too. Since Texas didn't mention anything about them, there probably aren't any problems at the other entries."

The radio crackles, "Tin Man, this Ice Man, WC for the night. We have four tangos near Nevada and four more near Utah." You reply, "Do you know their intentions?" Ice Man replies, "Yes, hostile. Definitely hostile. They are behind cover. Two on either side of the road. Appears they have AK47s." You ask, "How do you want to handle this?" Ice Man says, "I want you to approach through New York. Authenticate X-ray 1." You answer, "Roger. Approach New York. Authenticate X-ray 1." Ice Man replies, "WC, out." You reply, "Tin Man, out."

Jill asks, "Please explain this to me. Are we in danger?" You say, "I don't think so, not immediate danger, anyway. The Watch Commander wants us to approach through New York. I know where that is. It's an old hunting trail that spurs off an old logging road. We'll have to back track about half a mile to access it. The logging road hasn't been used in recent times and is mostly grown over, so it's going to be rough driving. I've got to pull my notepad for the authentication code for X-ray 1." You open one of your side pouches, retrieve your notebook and turn to the back. Next to X1 is Willie Nelson. Next to Willie Nelson is Michael Jackson.

You turn back along the county road, then turn left onto the old logging road. "Jill, this is probably going to take at least half an hour. I've never driven this during the night." Heck, you think to yourself, you've only driven it once, about a year ago, when this part of the plan was set up. The longitude and latitude are stored in your GPS and iPhone, so you shouldn't have to worry about getting lost. You just hope the briars aren't too thick. Once you are down the old road for about twenty five yards, you stop and get off, telling Jill, "I want to obscure our entry, if I can. I'll be right back." You walk to the paved road and start back, scattering leaves here and there, trying to give it a natural look. It's hard to tell how natural it looks with the NVD. The few small trees you bent over, you attempt to straighten. Those that won't straighten, you forcefully bend them to the front, away from your direction of travel. You make it back to Jill and proceed further. A little further you see a briar patch in the road. Great. "Jill," you say, "There is a briar patch up ahead. Let's keep those nice legs of yours unscarred. Pick your feet up and wrap them around me if you can. It might help keep you from getting scratched up." Jill wraps her legs around you then you proceed forward. You feel the briars tug at your pants and a few stick your legs. Fortunately, this is a small patch and you are soon through. You stop and pick the thorns out of your pants legs. A few stuck your legs and still sting. Jill says, "Thanks, John."

You approach New York and call on the radio, "Tin Man calling New York." You hear, "New York to Tin Man. Approach slowly." You reply, "Tin Man approaching." A few moments later, you receive the verbal command, "Stop. Authenticate Willie Nelson." You reply, "Authenticate Michael Jackson." The man approaches. It's Ray Tucker, one of your group of twelve. Actually, he is one of your inner group of five—five friends you have specially trained with through the years. He gives you a big hug and says, "John, it's so good to see you. It really is. Who is this behind you?" You turn, and looking at Jill through the NVD, say, "Ray, this is Jill Barnes, my soon to be wife." In a surprised voice Ray says, "What? Who?" You say, "Jill Barnes. You know Jill." Ray says, "Yes I do. Hey, Jill! This is a very pleasant surprise. Go up to your dad's right now. There are some people who are going to be surprised and happy to see you both. Go. We can talk later." You say, "Thanks, Ray. Yes, let's catch up later. Is everything under control?" Ray says, "If you are referring to our visitors, yes; they'll be taken care of before dawn. Mike already has a plan put together. We aren't going to need your help on this, so go to your dad's. We have this." You smile and say, "Thanks, I really need a break." Jill says, "I'll talk to you later, Ray." You can hear Ray muttering to himself, "Jill Barnes, unbelievable." On the radio you hear, "New York to Texas. Tin Man is on the Reservation. I repeat: Tin Man is on the Reservation. He's heading to the Wizard. New York out."

You make it across the creek. Ray has already removed the obstacles from your path. You continue on the path until you turn onto another, more heavily traveled, woods road. Then shortly you are back on the county road. You can't help but be excited. You feel Jill trembling behind you as you turn down the dirt drive to your dad's. "Jill, this is the drive to my dad's. My place is about a half mile further down the county road. You hear her starting to sniffle. You stop and look at her. Fighting back tears, she says, "John, you did it. You got us home. I love you, John. Thank you." You reply, "I love you, too. Let's go see our families so we both can cry."

You look at your watch. It's 1:15 a.m. You drive up to the porch and dismount. Helping Jill off, you see the door to the front porch open and the LED lights are turned on. Your dad is stepping out the door. You have your arm around Jill as you walk up the steps. She is trembling so bad you are afraid she might fall. At the top of the steps, you release her as she steadies herself against a post. You turn and look at your dad. You embrace each other. You both start crying, "Dad, it is so good to see you. It truly is!" He says, "I love you, son. I knew if anyone could make it home, it would be you. I never gave up hope. It does my soul good to see you." He separates from you and looks at Jill, in obvious surprise. His mouth is open, as if to say something, but words don't come out. You hear a woman's voice from inside,

"Johnathan, is that John?" Then you see Beverly Barnes walk through the door. Her eyes lock onto Jill. The shock is so evident, and is more than she can bear. She starts to fall, but your dad is quick and catches her in his arms. Jill is at her side in a flash, sobbing. In a few moments, Mrs. Barnes regains herself and starts crying, "Oh, my baby! Oh, my sweet baby! I thought I would never see you again! Praise be to God for answering a mother's cry! Oh, my baby girl!" Jill and Mrs. Barnes are locked arm in arm as they walk into the house.

Your dad is still on the porch. You ask, "Dad, where are Will and Lizzy?" Your dad says, with a grave expression, "Son, we need to talk."

Glossary of Acronyms

4X4 – Four-wheel drive vehicle

1911 – A type of 45 caliber semi-automatic pistol. Formerly used by the US military.

AAA – American Automotive Association.

AK47 – A civilian variant of the original AK47 rifle as developed for the Russian military.

ASAP – As soon as possible.

ATV – All-terrain vehicle. A common term referring to 4-wheelers and utility vehicles.

Cal – Calories

CAT – Combat Application Tourniquet.

CIA – Central Intelligence Agency.

CRKT – Columbia River Knife and Tool Company, maker of knives and other useful small tools.

ER – Emergency Room.

EMP – Electro-magnetic pulse.

EMT – Emergency Medical Technician

FBI – Federal Bureau of Investigation.

FEMA – Federal Emergency Management Agency.

FMJ – Full Metal Jacket ammunition, commonly used by the military and for target practice.

GHB – Get home bag. Sometimes called different things. Contains useful supplies to help you make it home in the event of an emergency situation.

Glock – Manufacturer of pistols of various types. Common pistol used by law enforcement agencies. The Glock 19 (G19) is the most popular pistol sold in America.

GPS – Global Positioning System, used by many navigational devices.

HAM radio – Home amateur radio. Sometimes referred to as short-wave radios.

ID – Identification.

IED – Improvised Explosive Device.

IFAK – Individual First Aid Kit.

IR – Infra-red.

ITK – Individual Trauma Kit.

IWB – Inside the waist band holster—as distinguished from a holster worn on the outside of clothing.

LED – Light emitting diode.

M1A – A civilian variant of the M14 rifle formerly used by the US military.

M4 – Current US issued military rifle. Similar to the civilian AR15 version except with a shorter barrel and capable of full automatic fire.

MACE – Non-lethal eye irritant contained in small spray cans for personal defense. Trade brand.

MRE – Meal Ready to Eat. Common pre-prepared long shelf life food. Used by the military and others.

NAPA – National Automotive Parts Association. Auto parts store.

NSA – National Security Agency.

NVD – Night Vision Device.

PD – Police Department.

PDQ – Pretty damn quick.

RPM – Revolutions per minute.

QD – Quick detach.

SKS – A civilian variant of the Chinese military rifle.

Sub2K – A slim, folding, semi-automatic pistol caliber rifle manufactured by Kel-Tec CNC Industries, Inc.

SWAT – Special Weapons and Tactics. Refers to law enforcement units used in high threat situations.

SWOT – Strengths, Weaknesses, Opportunities, Threats. Common term used in business for strategic planning.

Tangos – Bad guys.

TP – Toilet Paper.

UN – United Nations.

USB – Universal Serial Bus. Common cable port/outlet found on computers and many handheld devices.

WC – Watch Commander.

Made in the USA
Lexington, KY
31 December 2016